KAY BLAKE

The Dark Between Stars

THORN &
THREAD
PUBLISHING

*For those who survived the dark
before they ever found a light.*

Contents

Prologue	1
Chapter 1	7
Chapter 2	14
Chapter 3	22
Chapter 4	29
Chapter 5	38
Chapter 6	45
Chapter 7	51
Chapter 8	59
Chapter 9	67
Chapter 10	76
Chapter 11	84
Chapter 12	93
Chapter 13	103
Chapter 14	111
Chapter 15	122
Chapter 16	128
Chapter 17	134
Chapter 18	147
Chapter 19	154
Chapter 20	161
Chapter 21	169
Chapter 22	177
Chapter 23	185

Chapter 24   196
Chapter 25   205
Chapter 26   214
Chapter 27   223
Chapter 28   230
Chapter 29   241
Chapter 30   247
Chapter 31   257
Chapter 32   264
Chapter 33   277
Chapter 34   284
Chapter 35   293
Chapter 36   302
Chapter 37   306
Chapter 38   313
Chapter 39   326
Chapter 40   335
Chapter 41   343
Epilogue   349
About the Author   356

Prologue

The First War

The path to the Light Well has not changed in millennia, and as we walk it now, the ancient stones still glimmer faintly beneath my feet, pale veins of light threading through black rock, breath moving beneath living skin. This place has always carried a presence, a constant and eternal hum that pressed gently against the senses and reminded all who approached that something vast and alive waited ahead.

The steady vibration I've felt beneath my skin since entering the Well vanishes.

I take another step and falter. The silence isn't true silence. Footsteps still echo. Fabric still rustles. But something underneath it all is missing, leaving the world feeling strangely off-balance. Empty.

Another step.

The air loses its weight. My ears pop. A chill skates across the back of my neck.

I stop listening and realize that's the problem. For the first time since we arrived, I'm listening at all. I should be feeling. The invisible current that had been pulling us forward is gone.

My pulse quickens. I slow without meaning to. One step. Then another. Every instinct I possess begins to scream that something is wrong.

I stop.

The chamber opens before us, vast and circular, its ceiling swallowed by a dim wash of starlight that fails to reach the ground. At its center lies the Light Well. It's empty. There is no spill of brilliance rising from its depths, no living glow breathing warmth into the stone. What remains is only a hollow basin carved with ancient sigils, their once radiant lines dulled and lifeless, resembling scars long abandoned by blood and memory alike.

"There should be light," someone says behind me, their voice quiet but edged with disbelief.

I step forward, my hand hovering just above the rim, and for a brief moment I expect resistance or heat or the answering surge of power that has always been there. Instead, my fingers brush the stone and find nothing waiting for them. No warmth answers my touch, no energy stirs, and the silence that follows feels profoundly wrong, as though something vital has been torn from the world and left unreplaced. The hum that once filled this chamber is gone entirely, leaving only a pressure behind my eyes and a growing sense of unease that settles deep in my chest.

"This place was sealed," another voice says sharply, the words cutting through the stillness.

"It was protected," someone else replies. "Guarded by law older than any of us."

I straighten slowly, drawing my hand back from the lifeless stone as the truth becomes impossible to ignore.

"Then something stronger than law came here," I say. "Summon the elders."

No one argues. We remain where we are far longer than reason demands, standing at the edge of what should not exist, staring into the empty heart of the Well. We listen for any sign of returning light, any echo of the power that once defined this place, and we wait for the world to correct itself.

The High Court convenes in darkness as I take my place among them and figures emerge from shadow and smoke to fill the obsidian tiers that ring the chamber, while a restrained and dangerous fury coils through the air and settles heavy against my skin. At the center of the court, an image forms and holds steady, revealing the Light Well as it now exists, hollowed and drained of the brilliance that once defined it.

"This is not dimming," a councilor says coldly, their voice echoing through the chamber. "It is absence, and absence is not an accident."

"The seals remain intact," another replies, their tone sharpened by certainty. "Which means the power was not stolen through force or breach."

A murmur spreads through the assembled court as the implication takes shape.

"Then it was drawn," someone says, "and only those bound to the Light itself could have done so."

Silence follows, thick and deliberate, as the accusation settles. I feel again the echo I sensed at the Well, a resonance that stretches beyond this chamber and presses against the edges of the Void like a memory refusing to fade.

"A pulse crossed the veil," I say, and the attention of the Court turns fully toward me. "It was faint, but it carried intention, and it bore the signature of Celestial power."

Several figures shift, shadows tightening around their forms.

"A pulse crossed the veil," I say, and the attention of the

Court turns fully toward me. "It was faint, but it carried intention, and it bore the signature of Celestial power."

Several figures shift, shadows tightening around their forms.

"That pulse has not been felt since the Celestials first claimed dominion over the Light," one of the elders says. "Since before the realms were divided by treaty and restraint."

"The balance has been broken," I continue, my voice steady as the truth takes shape. "The Light has not vanished, nor has it been lost to chaos. It has been gathered, shaped, and moved by Celestial design."

The realization settles across the chamber like falling ash. The shadows deepen, attentive to the judgment unfolding.

"If the Celestials have drained the Well without consent," the leader of the Court says at last, their voice carrying the weight of law older than any of us, "then they have broken the covenant that kept the realms intact."

A pause follows, heavy with consequence.

"This is not imbalance," the leader continues. "It is provocation, and it is the first strike in a war they believe we will not answer."

The chamber doors explode inward.

Every head turns.

A watcher staggers through the opening, cloak torn, shadows unraveling from his shoulders. He falls to one knee before the Court, breathless.

"My Court—"

"What is it?" the leader demands.

The watcher lifts his head, and for the first time since entering, I see genuine fear in his eyes.

"It is the mortal realm."

A murmur ripples through the chamber.

"The sky is breaking."

Silence.

"What are you talking about?" an elder snaps.

"Light," the watcher says. "It is falling from the heavens. Not sunlight. Not stars. Raw power."

The chamber stills.

"Impossible," someone whispers.

"We have seen it across multiple regions. Streams of it. Fragments. Entire rivers of radiance tearing through the veil and striking the world below." His voice shakes. "Where it lands, people are changing."

A dozen conversations erupt at once.

"Changing how?"

"Who unleashed it?"

"Is this a Celestial attack?"

"No," the watcher says. "Or if it is, it is unlike anything we have seen before."

He swallows hard. The Court falls silent once more.

I feel it then. The connection between the pulse I sensed and the disaster unfolding beyond the veil. Eyes turn toward the rifted window at the edge of the chamber, where the Void stretches endless and awake, no longer content to remain separate.

"Prepare the watchers," the leader orders.

The shadows throughout the chamber shudder in anticipation.

"Unseal the old paths and summon what was bound. The Celestials have reminded us why the realms were fractured in the first place."

The leader rises.

"And find out what is happening in the mortal realm before the world drowns in Light."

Chapter 1

Present Day

The gravel path crunches beneath our feet, a quiet rhythm against the soft hum of the park. Spring sunlight filters through the trees, the first real warmth the city has offered in weeks, and it loosens the knot between my shoulder blades. The air smells like damp earth, cut grass, and something sweet I can't place. A bus exhales at the street beyond the gates; somewhere closer, a kid shrieks from the playground and then laughs.

After too many twelve-hour shifts beneath fluorescent lights and the steady hiss of the steamer wand, the sun feels warm at my back. I tilt my face into it. My skin drinks it in, greedy for anything that isn't stale coffee and recycled air.

I've worked at Harbor Street Coffee for almost four years, long enough to know exactly which customers tip, which ones ask for extra foam after you've already handed them their drink, and which ones treat baristas like background noise. Every year the place gets busier—new apartments, new offices, new people who need caffeine to survive, but somehow we get less staff. My boss, technically runs the place, but he's more myth than man at this point. He pops in once every few weeks, mumbles something about numbers, and disappears again like he's allergic to his own business.

I didn't plan for this to be my life. I actually went to school for something practical, or at least I convinced myself it was. Four years earning a degree in Literature Studies, fully expecting to become some kind of cardigan-wearing editor in a charming publishing house. Instead, I landed an internship where the lights flickered and I spent my days reading manuscripts that made me question whether humanity deserved books at all. After slogging through one too many epic fantasies with twelve maps and no plot, I realized the only part I truly liked was imagining myself liking it. So I bailed.

And now I live in the city with my best friend, Marin, working a job that pays the rent and nothing more. I use to spend more time with dad. Lately, those days feel fewer and further between, he's been slipping into the cracks of my schedule.

But now, there's sunlight on my face, my dad is beside me and it's the closest thing to peace I've felt all week. Dad passes me a coffee, steam curling into the cool air.

"See?" he says with a grin. "A little fresh air never hurt anyone."

I smile into the rim of the cup. "You said that last time — right before I broke my arm on the monkey bars." He chuckles, eyes crinkling. "You were fearless back then."

"I was six."

"Exactly." He nudges me with his elbow. "You could use a little of that again."

"Fearless doesn't pay the rent," I say, but it comes out softer than I intend. The guilt's been sitting on my tongue since I texted him this morning: *Today? Finally?* Trying to buy back something I let slip for far too long.

He glances sideways at me now. "Still at the coffee shop?"

"Yeah. It's been... a lot lately." I tuck a strand of hair behind my ear. "We're short-staffed again. New manager loves scheduling doubles like he's punishing the espresso machine. By the time I get home, I can't even stand the smell on my clothes "You always did take on too much."

"Someone's got to keep the lights on." I shrug, the gesture small. "Besides, busy keeps me out of my own head."

He doesn't argue. He just watches the pond as we pass it, sunlight shattering into small gold coins across the surface. For a second, the reflection is so bright it almost looks wrong, too sharp, the light is cutting rather than shining. I blink and it's just water again.

"You haven't been by in a while," he says.

"I know." The words feel heavier than they should. "I meant to. Things got away from me. Work. Bills. Marin's schedule..."

"How's Marin?"

"Good. Stubborn. You know her." I can't help the faint smile. "She sent me a photo of her breakfast this morning because she thinks I forget to eat when I'm stressed."

"She's probably right." Dad's mouth twitches. "You were always terrible at taking care of yourself."

"Not true," I protest lightly. "I'm here, aren't I?"

"Yeah." His voice gentles. "You're here."

Something in the way he says it tugs at my chest, there's more sitting behind the words but I push the feelings away. I always do when something starts to ache. Because he's all I've really had. After Mom died, it was just the two of us, him working long shifts at the station, me waiting up on the couch because the house felt too big without her.

People always said I looked like him. *Spitting image of your dad*, they'd insist, even when I was a kid and had no idea why adults thought telling a girl she resembled a grown man was a compliment. But I never minded. I have his dark brown hair, his green eyes, even that same little crease above the eyebrow when we're thinking too hard. I'm a little taller than he is now, which he pretends to be offended by, but he still says I'm the best thing he ever made. If I had to look like anyone, I'm glad it's him.

He tried so hard to be everything at once: the steady one, the soft one, the one who packed lunches and remembered picture day and learned how to braid hair badly, but proudly. And even now, even with the distance I let creep in, he still shows up for me in every way that matters.

We fall into an easy rhythm. The park is busy in that city way, people everywhere but no one really colliding. A guy strums a guitar by the fountain. A woman walks briskly, heels ticking against the path. Two teenagers skate past us and leave a smear of laughter behind. The trees are on the edge of leafing out, green just teasing the tips.

It's been months since we had time like this. No to-do lists, no half-finished conversations across a sink of dishes, no checking the time to make sure I'm on time for the night shift. Just us. Just this narrow strip of path between one obligation and the next, pretending it's its own little world.

"Remember when you used to drag me here every weekend?" he asks. "You'd feed the ducks and give them all names."

I laugh under my breath. "I was convinced they were the same ones every time."

"They were, to you." He takes a thoughtful sip of coffee.

"What did you call that round one?"

"Greg." I lift a shoulder. "Greg had personality."

"Greg had no sense of moderation." He smiles, and it lands lightly in my chest, settling in with all the other stupid, ordinary memories I didn't realize I was hoarding. We walk a few more paces. "You seem different lately. Quieter."

"I guess I've just been thinking a lot."

"About what?"

"Everything. How fast it's all moving. How... loud it gets, even when it's quiet." I wince at myself; it sounds like something I'd write down and then delete.

He nods, like he understands anyway. "You don't have to outrun the quiet," he says. "You can let it catch you."

"You and your fortune cookie wisdom."

"Some of the cookies are right."

We share a small smile. The path curves, and for a moment the trees open to a wide green that makes the city feel generous. Sunlight pours over the grass in long, bright rectangles, striping the ground.

My smart watch buzzes against my wrist. The spell breaks, snapping the quiet open. I reach into the pocket to grab my phone, pat around, fingers brushing lining, loose receipts, nothing useful. After a bit of rummaging, my stomach dips as the realization hits.

"Oh, crap," I mutter, checking the other pocket just in case. "I left my phone in the car in my bag."

I picture it exactly where I left it, front pocket of my bag, which is on the passenger seat, strap tangled, half-zipped, my whole life stuffed inside: wallet, keys, the book I keep meaning to finish, the coffee shop schedule I'm pretending not to dread. Of course I'd forget it. My brain's been a messy drawer lately, everything jammed in the wrong place.

Dad smirks. "You and that thing are inseparable."

"Five minutes," I promise, stepping backward. "Don't move."

He lifts his coffee in salute. "I'll be right here."

I jog toward the street, the sun turns the edges of things bright, the rim of a bicycle wheel, the chrome of a bench, the fine hairs on my forearm lit. My breath fogs once in the cooler air of the shade and then disappears when I break back into light.

By the time I reach the curb, something tightens in my chest. Not the run. Something else. A thread pulling taut in a room I can't see. It's the same wrong-note feeling I get sometimes waking up, like I've stepped out of a dream too fast and left the door open behind me.

The car waits beneath a plane tree, its windshield throwing the sun back at me. I open the back door and duck in for my bag, crack my head on the roof, and hiss through my teeth. "Damn it." I rub the spot and then laugh once at myself for being so tired and clumsy. I'm always in a hurry. The bag strap catches on the seat buckle; I tug it free.

When I straighten and turn toward the park, the sound goes thin. The bus on the street is a picture moving, but without presence. Even the wind seems to forget how to touch my skin. The hairs on my arms rise. I take a step forward, then another, my bag suddenly heavy against my shoulder. "Dad?" I call, louder than I mean to, because the air swallows my voice.

There's a figure on the path where he stood. Wearing all black. Their hood is up and their face is masked. The figure isn't bulky, it's more like a shadow gathered itself and decided on a human shape. My brain takes a beat too long to understand what I'm seeing. A flick of metal, a sharp, precise motion. My father folding at the middle as if his body forgot which way to hold itself.

"Dad?" The word tears out of me. My feet are already moving.

Chapter 2

The figure turns, only a pivot, nothing dramatic, and the blank face glances past me as though calculating. For one heartbeat, it feels like its attention brushes over me in a cold, measuring way and my skin crawls. Then the shadow figure runs. Across the grass. Between the trees. It's fast, but practiced. In seconds it's a smear of dark where the shadows deepen, and then there's only the dapple of leaves and my breath punching in my throat.

I drop my bag. The gravel burns under my shoes as I sprint. By the time I reach him, he's on his knees. His coffee cup lies crushed beside him, the liquid spreading and catching the light. "Dad!" I drop hard, rocks biting into my knees, and press both hands to his abdomen. Heat and wet touch my hands. The slide of blood between my fingers. "Dad, please— look at me."

His eyes find mine. Glassy and fading, but still present, and for a second it's like he is holding himself open for me. His fingers flutter, searching for my wrist, and land. His mouth shapes words he doesn't have breath for, then pulls them up anyway.

"Tell them…" The whisper is thin, carried more by will than air. "When the moon drowns in daylight… you'll find the door."

The words slither under my skin, strange and heavy. I think I've heard them before in a dream I can't pull into focus.

"What?" I bend closer, my hands shaking against him. "Dad, what door? What are you talking about?"

His lashes tremble. His grip loosens. The weight in my hands shifts, too light, and the breath that was barely there a moment ago is gone. His chest stills.

"Dad?" My voice snaps, brittle. "Dad!"

The cry rips out of me and seems to travel further than sound should. I press harder, counting without counting, willing anything, any twitch, any startle of air, to prove that the world hasn't just split along a line I can't see.

Light gathers under my palms. It gathers sharply, unnaturally, condensed into a single point. For a heartbeat the world feels double-exposed, grass and brightness and something red overlapping in the wrong places, and then everything beneath my hands is simply... gone.

I slam forward onto my palms. Cold grass meeting my hands. The earth feeling damp. No body. No blood. No warmth slicking my fingers. The imprint of my knees remains in the flattened green, but the weight I was holding is gone. I scramble backward on hands and heels, my gaze scanning for anything that makes sense. "What the—" The word dies, too small for the hole it's trying to fill.

The world resumes. A golden retriever barrels past with a tennis ball, tail high. The guitarist at the fountain tests a chord. A woman scrolls her phone, one earbud out. A boy skims by on a scooter, humming to himself. The city hum comes back.

"Did you—did anyone see that?" My voice cracks on the

new air. "He was just—he was right here!"

People look. A man frowns, confused. The woman with the phone pulls out her other earbud, stares, puts it back in. A teenager glances from me to the empty space and then away. Their faces settle into the expression strangers wear for other people's problems, blank, polite, at a distance.

"No." I push to my feet and sway. The crushed coffee cup glints at my toes. "Please, listen—my dad—he—" I point at the grass, "He was here. He was attacked."

The words sound thin, ridiculous, even to me. My heartbeat is too loud. My hands won't stop shaking. The air smells like grass and sunscreen and fresh-cut oranges from a cart near the gate, and all of it is suddenly unbearable.

A jogger slows. "Miss? Are you okay?"

"I'm not—no—I'm not okay." I swallow hard and try to breathe through it. "My dad was stabbed. He was right here."

The jogger scans the empty grass. "I... don't see anyone."

"Because he's gone!" The pitch of my voice is louder this time more frantic. "He was here and then he—he just disappeared." I hear how that sounds. I can't make it sound different. "Please."

Two parents by the swings stop pushing. An older couple on a bench turns their heads together. A man with a dog pauses, his hand tightening on the leash. Whispering scrapes at the edge of my hearing.

"Someone call the police," a woman says, not unkindly but worried. The words land like a box closing.

"Wait—don't—please." I take a step toward her, then stop when she flinches. "He needs help. I need—" I look down. My palms are clean. They shouldn't be. "He said something— about a door." My voice drops. "I don't understand."

Sirens bloom at the edge of the city's noise and grow closer, twisting through the streets until they bleed into the park. I stand still because I don't know what else to do. I stand with my hands open and my knees aching and the sun too bright on the water where ducks drift like nothing has rearranged itself.

Two officers step out of the cruiser, one older, with the steady, measured movements and one younger, eyes wide and unsure, his badge still shining like it's brand new. Relief slams into me, sharp and dizzying, and my knees nearly give. For a second, just seeing the uniform feels like a lifeline.

"Ma'am?" the older one says, careful, palm resting near his belt. "You the one who called this in?"

"No, but—thank God—listen." Words tumble. I point to the grass, to the cup, to the air itself. "My dad was right here. Someone in black—a hood and mask—came up behind him. I saw it. There was blood and then there wasn't. He said something before he—before he vanished."

They exchange a skeptical look.

"You said he was attacked?" the older one asks.

"Yes!" My breath hitches. "There was blood on my hands and my shirt and now there's..." Nothing. There is nothing. I look down again as if the evidence might just choose to reappear out of pity.

The younger officer scans the ground. "There's no blood here, ma'am. No sign of a struggle."

"Because it's gone." The words sound wild. "I don't know how—it just—" My throat closes. I try again. "Please. Help me find him."

The older officer steps closer, voice low and even, "Alright. Let's sit you down. We'll get you some water."

"I don't need water, I need my dad." I flinch when his hand lifts toward my arm. "Why aren't you listening?"

The radio on his shoulder crackles, a voice I can't parse. He sighs into it. "Dispatch, this is going to be a psych eval. Will transport."

"No." Panic spikes, a clean white stab. "No, I'm not—I'm not crazy. He was here. He's gone."

They move fast after that, too fast for the part of me that can't catch up. One takes my wrist and I pull back; the other lifts a palm and tells me to breathe, and I can't. Someone nearby raises a phone to record because that's what people do now, collect moments like they're souvenirs.

"Let me go," I gasp, twisting. "You don't understand—he's out there—you're wasting time—"

"Ma'am, calm down," the younger one says, voice firming. "We're taking you to the hospital to get checked out."

"I don't—please—" The world blurs at the edges. The cruiser door opens and I'm pushed in, the door slamming shut behind me. The city shrinks to the rectangle of the window and my reflection, wide-eyed, mascara running down my cheeks, wrecked, not someone I recognize.

The ride is short and too long. The siren is off. The officer in the front talks into his radio about nothing that matters to me. I try to slow my breathing and fail. Every time I close my eyes I see that impossible light underneath my hands.

I'm escorted into the emergency room, flanked by both officers. Like they're afraid I'll run for it if they leave my side. They hand me to an ER nurse like I'm a problem to solve. "Found in the park," the older officer says quietly. "Hysterical. Reports a murder. No evidence at the scene. Possible hallucinations."

The nurse nods, professional sympathy settling on her face. "We'll take it from here."

They lead me down a bright corridor into a small room with four white walls and a bed bolted to the floor. A security guard leans against the door frame, neither in nor out. The room smells like antiseptic and air-conditioning.

"Can I call someone?" My voice scrapes. "Please. My dad—he needs help."

"Let's get you settled first," the nurse says gently. She takes my bag and sets it on a chair I'm not sure I'm allowed to sit in. "We just want to make sure you're safe."

The word makes my skin crawl. Safe from what?

When she leaves, the silence in the room feels colder than the park's. I pace. I try the door. It opens two inches before the guard's hand appears to close it with soft finality. "Best to wait for the doctor," he says, gently.

Time loosens and then gathers in strange clumps. My hands shake and then go still. My throat burns from crying and makes me realize I've finally stopped. A cart squeaks past in the hall. A woman somewhere down the hall cries in hiccups. Footsteps. The distant, constant beeping of machines measuring things that don't help me. Eventually a doctor comes in with a clipboard and an expression well-practiced into calm. He introduces himself. His name slides off my mind.

"Rachel," he says, "we think you may have experienced an episode of acute psychosis. Possibly stress-induced. We'd like to keep you for observation tonight and start something that can help you rest."

"I'm not psychotic," I say, too fast. "My dad was murdered. He was there. I held him."

I almost say, *I watched him disappear*, but even in this room, the words feel too sharp to put in the air.

He nods in a way that means I hear the words if not the reality of them. "We'll talk more in the morning."

When he leaves, I sit on the bed and stare at my hands. The lines in my palms mean nothing. My knuckles are clean. The scrubbed smell of the room creeps into my throat. A phantom slickness lingers on my skin, memory of warmth that isn't there.

I stand. I can't not move. The phone on the wall looks like a lifeline and then like a prop. I lift it anyway and dial my dad's number. It goes straight to voicemail. I call again. Voicemail.

I swallow and dial another number. Marin picks up on the third ring, groggy. "Rach? It's late. Are you—why are you calling from a hospital?"

"Marin." Relief hits so hard my knees nearly give. "Listen, I need—I need you to come. My dad—he's missing. He was stabbed in the park. I saw it."

Silence. Then, cautious, gentle: "Rachel… your dad's been gone for years."

I freeze. "What?"

"You know that," she says softly. "We've talked about it." A breath. "Stay put, okay? I'm coming. Just—stay."

My grip tightens on the receiver. The hallway hums. The room tilts a fraction. "No," I whisper, the word tearing at my throat. "No, that's not—he was just with me. Yesterday. He was there."

"Rach." Her voice is a hand I can't feel. "I'm on my way."

I hang up. The phone lands in the cradle harder than I mean it to. The sound seems too loud for such a small room.

"Dammit," I breathe, fingers in my hair. The world is too

bright and too distant at the same time.

I slide down the wall until I'm sitting on the cold floor, knees to my chest. The fluorescent light hums. I press my palms over my eyes until colors pulse behind them. My breath skitters.

For the first time since the park, a thought I've been refusing edges in and sits down across from me. Maybe they're right. Maybe I am losing my mind.

Chapter 3

The air outside the hospital smells like rain and car exhaust;
after three days of recycled air and fluorescent lights. Three
days of pretending. Three days of nodding when they said
hallucination. Three days of swallowing the little white pills
that made my mind hum. I smiled when they said I was doing
better. Told them the meds were working. Told them the
"visions" were gone. They smiled back, like I was a good little
patient, and handed me my discharge papers. Now I'm free.
Free, but not okay.

I need answers. I need to know what really happened to
him… and why the truth feels like it's hiding just beyond the
edge of my vision. Because I know I'm not crazy. Whatever
happened in that park, whatever I saw, it felt more real than
anything in that hospital ever did.

I head toward Dad's apartment on foot. The city is louder
than it should be, car horns and rain-soaked pavement, the
echo of my boots on the sidewalk. Every passing bus gusts
wet air into my face. A siren wails somewhere distant, rising
and falling. By the time I reach his building, my legs burn,
and my chest feels tight. The hallway smells faintly of mildew
and someone's overcooked dinner. Peeling paint, humming
lights, the same ugly carpet pattern I've known since I was

a kid. Dad's apartment feels different before I even open the door. The key sticks in the lock. Once I hear the flick of the lock, I push open the door.

Inside, the air is still and smells of dust and old coffee. The silence feels heavy. His mug sits on the counter, a ring of dried coffee at the bottom. His jacket is still draped over the chair. Everything is exactly how he left it. Exactly how he left it the last time I saw him. Exactly how he left it years ago, if Marin is right. Both things sit in my head at once, clashing.

"Hey, Dad," I whisper, even though I know no one will answer.

The air tastes like a memory. For a second, I can almost hear him humming to himself in the kitchen, that off-key sound he used to make when he was deep in thought. It hits me harder than I expect. In my head the sound is coming from the next room and not from the past.

His office is worse than I remembered; everything is cluttered and chaotic. Every surface buried under papers, folders, and books that are worn and centuries old. Maps of constellations spill across the walls, corners curling from age; equations snake through the margins of notebooks; envelopes sit abandoned in small, chaotic piles.

I stand in the doorway for a moment, palms sweating. The last time I was in here, I was a teenager, told not to touch anything because *"the math will get offended."* Now it feels less like an office and more like a shrine to something I don't understand.

I start going through the papers, carefully at first, then faster. I'm not sure what I'm looking for. Stacks shift as I pull from the pile. Notes slide to the floor. Hours pass, or maybe just minutes; time feels slippery here, stretching and snapping back. His handwriting shifts from frantic to precise, as if he was racing to capture something just out of reach and then suddenly caught it by the throat.

The symbols don't make sense, but they almost do. Numbers mixed with markings, alive beneath my fingertips. Curves and lines that stir something deep in my chest, a language I shouldn't know but almost remember. Each page hums with meaning just beyond comprehension, a song I once knew the words to but can't quite recall. Every note or book I pick up seems to have the same theme.

The deeper I dig, the stranger it gets. Notes about lunar alignments, eclipses, and something he's labeled *The Light.* The words veil, doorway, threshold repeat in different places, underlined hard enough to dig grooves into the page.

One line is circled three times: *when boundaries thin, the Light remembers the way home.*

My stomach twists.

There's dust everywhere, it coats my lungs when I breathe too deep. I wipe my hands on my jeans, leaving gray smudges. The air feels heavy and charged. The hairs at the back of my neck lift, the same way it did in the park right before everything went wrong.

A stack of old journals leans precariously on the desk, one sliding off and thudding to the floor. I jump, pulse quickening. "Get it together," I mutter, crouching to pick it up. As I lift the journal, something catches my eye, a faint glint beneath the desk. At first, I think it's just a bit of metal or light reflecting off a paperclip. But when I push aside the fallen books, I see it: a small metal case wedged behind a pile of dusty notebooks.

It looks out of place. The rest of the room feels lived-in, chaotic; this thing feels hidden on purpose. I hesitate, a faint hum crawling through the air. The silence feels thicker now and I realize I'm holding my breath.

I drag the case out, wiping a layer of dust off the top with my sleeve. The metal is cold, heavier than it should be, etched with patterns that look almost familiar, only older, deeper, carved rather than drawn. Circles intersecting with three straight lines, over and over, the same shape repeating.

My heartbeat quickens, curiosity and dread threading together. Whatever this is, Dad didn't want it found easily. I sit cross-legged on the floor, breathe once, and flip the latch. A puff of dust bursts out when it opens, straight into my face, shimmering gold and silver flecks. It swirls in the light, glittering starlight shaken loose from a sky, and before I can move, I breathe it in.

I cough, stumble back, eyes burning. "Dammit—" I knock into the desk, sending more papers flying. My vision goes white for a second. When it clears, everything shimmers. The edges of things flicker with a rainbow haze.

I stumble into the bathroom, splash water on my face, blink until my eyes sting. But when I look up, the light is still there, faint, iridescent almost, a film over my vision. I squeeze my eyes shut. "It's just the meds wearing off. You're fine," I whisper to myself. "They said this might happen. Side effects. That's all."

But the air hums, low and electric, the same wrong-frequency hum I felt in the park right before everything went silent. The walls, once plain and yellowed, are covered in writing; not ink, but light. Sentences curl and twist in looping script I can't understand, glowing gold, each word breathing in rhythm.

When I move, the light shifts with me, aware. Books tremble

on the shelves, their spines flickering. Titles blur, reform, rearranging into names I've never seen before, names that hum in my bones when I read them. A few symbols match the ones in his notes, the same circle and three lines, repeated until it burns into my vision.

One of the books exhales. The pages lift and fall. A soft gust of warmth brushes my face, carrying a scent like ozone, smoke, and burnt honey.

My stomach drops. "No," I whisper. "No, no, no."

The air thickens, alive with whispers too quiet to hear but too loud to ignore. The dust I breathed in glows faintly now, hanging in the air around me. Shapes form in the glow, lines, constellations, symbols twisting into patterns I almost recognize. Moons nested inside circles. Lines crossing in threes. My pulse hammers. "Stop it," I whisper to the room. "Please, just stop."

The light pulses once, faintly, as if it heard me. For a heartbeat, everything sharpens, the words, the symbols, the feeling that I'm standing inside the answer to a question I haven't asked yet.

That's enough. I grab my bag and run. The hum follows me into the hall, vibrating in my ribs, chasing me down the stairs until I burst outside. Sound slams back into the world all at once; cars, voices, brakes hissing. The street looks normal and too bright, every color is turned up a notch. Light fractures on everything, breaking into rainbows that hover in the air before dissolving.

I rub at my eyes. "Please just stop," I mutter, stumbling forward, half-blind, half-panicked. The sidewalk tilts, steadies. Every window reflects back a version of me I don't quite recognize. I don't see him until it's too late. Strong hands catch my arms before I can hit the pavement.

"Whoa, easy," a voice says, low, calm, threaded with warmth. Warm hands on my shoulder meant to steady me.

I blink up, breathless. Sunlight behind his head flares, turning him into a dark shape rimmed in gold. For a second, the shimmer around him looks just like the light in Dad's office, that same fractured colors, that same too-bright edge. Then it settles, and I see him clearly: dark hair, stubble, eyes that catch the light in an impossible shimmer.

For a heartbeat, the shimmer stays. Then it's gone.

"Great," I mutter. "First glowing walls, now glowing men. Totally fine. Definitely fine."

"What was that?" he asks, voice low but faintly amused.

Heat rushes to my face. "Nothing," I say quickly, pulling my sleeve down to hide the trembling in my hands. "Just... talking to myself. Occupational hazard of losing it in public."

He huffs a quiet laugh, "Well, maybe pick a safer place next time. You almost ran into traffic."

"Yeah, guess I'm going for 'most chaotic pedestrian of the year.'" I try to smile, but my hands won't stop shaking. The spot where he's holding my arms feels strangely warm, like my skin is buzzing under his fingers.

He studies me, not in a creepy way, in a curious way. Like he's trying to decide if I'm about to faint or disappear.

"You sure you're okay?" he asks finally.

"I don't know," I admit. The truth slips out before I can catch it. "Probably just a migraine."

"That bad, huh?"

"Let's just say it's been a day."

He nods, the hint of a smile returning. "Fair enough. Take care of yourself, alright?"

"Yeah," I say, though I don't mean it. "You too."

His hands leave my arms reluctantly. He gives a small nod before turning away, slipping easily into the crowd. For a moment, I watch him go, trying to steady my breathing. The sunlight flashes off a car window, and the shimmer dances across my vision again, tracing faint lines in the air, circle, three lines, gone. I blink hard. "Nope," I whisper. "Not doing this. I just need sleep."

I start walking fast putting my head down to avoid the shimmer, the city is too loud and bright around me. Every reflection I pass feels like it's watching. A bus window. A shop door. My own eyes are doubled and distant. I press a hand to my temple.

"It's fine," I tell myself. "Just stress. Just exhaustion. Just... everything."

Marin will know what to do. She always knows what to do. She'll tell me to eat something, take my meds, stop spiraling. She'll ask questions until the pieces line up. She'll make it make sense, or at least make it bearable. I just need to get home. Get answers. And maybe, finally, sleep.

Chapter 4

By the time I reach the flat, my pulse is still hammering. My key barely fits in the lock because my hands won't stop shaking. I push the door open hard enough that it bangs against the wall.

"Marin!"

Her voice floats from the kitchen, completely unbothered. "You know, most people knock before entering a dramatic episode!"

I drop my bag, still half out of breath. "You won't believe what just—"

She appears in the doorway wearing an oversize tie-dye hoodie, hair piled on top of her head in a lopsided bun, a face mask smeared unevenly across her cheeks like green war paint. She's holding a mug that says *Mercury Made Me Do It.*

"Jesus, Rach," she says, eyeing me up and down. "You look like you just outran your trauma."

"Something happened," I start, pacing. The words are already trying to spill out of me faster than my lungs can keep up. "At my dad's place. I—I don't even know how to explain it. The walls—there was writing, glowing writing—and then this dust, and—"

"Okay, pause." She holds up a finger and takes a slow sip

of her tea. "Are we talking, like, mold spores kind of dust or cocaine kind of dust?"

"Marin."

"Because those have very different outcomes, babe."

"It wasn't that kind of dust!" My voice cracks. "It was—it shimmered. It got in my eyes and then I saw things. Things that aren't there. The walls had words on them. The books—" I rake a hand through my hair, trying to find air. "And then in the street, I ran into someone. I swear I saw it again—in his eyes—this shimmer. And no one else sees it. No one."

Marin just blinks at me, then shrugs. "Well, either you've opened your third eye or you need sleep. Honestly, could be both."

"Marin, I'm serious!"

"So am I." She sets her mug down and crosses the room, puts her hands on my shoulders. Her palms are warm, grounding, her thumbs rubbing little circles. "Hey. You've been through hell. You were in the hospital for three days. You probably haven't eaten a real meal since, what, the Obama administration? Your brain's just... doing fireworks."

I pull away, rubbing my temples. "It didn't feel like fireworks."

"Fine. Cosmic migraines, then." She tilts her head, studying me with a little too much delight. "Although, if you did unlock some ancient magic power, I want credit when you get a Netflix deal."

I shoot her a look. "I'm losing my mind and you're pitching my documentary?"

"I cope with humor," she says simply, grinning. "It's that or cry. Humor's cheaper."

Despite myself, a laugh sputters out. She always does this,

talks me down with chaos, makes the world feel a little less like it's spinning out of control.

"Okay," she says, waving her hands like she's settling a courtroom argument. "Here's what we're gonna do. You shower. I'll make something that vaguely resembles food. Then you tell me everything from the beginning, and we'll see if this is a paranormal awakening or just a mental breakdown. Sound good?"

I exhale, the first real breath I've managed since the park. "Yeah," I say softly. "Okay."

She pats my cheek and says with more enthusiasm than I can handle right now, "Atta girl. Now go scrub the existential crisis off your face."

Steam fogs the mirror, softening everything into shapes that could almost belong to someone else. I wipe a hand across the glass, leaving a streaked oval of clarity and my own face staring back. For a second, I almost don't recognize it.

My hair, still brown, but deeper and richer. My skin looks brighter and slightly glowy too. My green eyes, usually muted, mossy, catch the light differently now. They're somehow greener and sharper. Almost reflective. Even my nose looks straighter, my cheekbones a little more defined. I lean closer, studying the reflection. "Weird," I whisper.

The rainbow haze still floats faintly around my vision, but it's softer now, diluted. I blink, once, twice. It's still there, a faint halo over everything. Maybe it's just the steam. Or exhaustion. Or the meds. Or whatever the hell that dust was.

Marin would say something like, *You're finally seeing yourself clearly, babe. The universe just upgraded your camera settings.* I almost laugh at the thought. Almost. I tug the towel tighter around me, pressing my palms to the counter. My reflection does the same, obviously, but for some reason, I check anyway. Just in case it doesn't.

People have always said I look "kind." I never knew what to do with that. Like my face should apologize for things before I even open my mouth. I've been told I have "gentle eyes," which I think is code for please don't cause a scene. Now, staring at myself, I can't tell if I look more like me or less.

The shimmer around the edges of my vision pulses faintly when I breathe slow, steady, rhythmic. My pulse, in color. When I hold my breath, it tightens, sharpens. When I exhale, it loosens again.

"Get some sleep," I mutter. "You're fine."

But when I turn to leave, my reflection lags just half a heartbeat too long before it moves. I freeze.

Then I blink, and it's back to normal. Perfectly mirrored. Perfectly wrong. I force a shaky laugh. "Great. Add haunted mirrors to the list." Still, I don't look back as I leave the bathroom.

The smell of sweet floral chamomile hits me before I even step out. Marin's sitting cross-legged on the couch in one of her galaxy print robes, a mug in each hand and an incense stick burning crookedly in a potted plant like it's perfectly normal. Her hair has always been white blonde that somehow is natural and glows in the lamplight like spun moonlight. She's got her over-sized glasses on again, the round ones she doesn't actually need but insists make her "look wise and approachable." They do. Of course they do. Marin's the kind of pretty people either envy or instantly trust.

"There she is," she says, grinning. "The freshly steamed phoenix, risen from the depths of shower hell. Tea?"

I take the mug she offers, the heat seeping into my hands. "You really have a tea for every crisis, don't you?"

"It's a gift," Marin says solemnly. "Some people can speak to ghosts. I can identify emotional breakdowns by beverage."

A laugh escapes me before I can stop it. Marin squints at me over the rim of her mug.

A knot tightens in my stomach. "Do I look different?"

She blinks.

"Different how?"

"I don't know." I shrug, suddenly feeling ridiculous. "Just... different."

Marin sets her mug down and studies me with exaggerated seriousness, tilting her head first one way, then the other.

"Hm."

"Marin."

"Hm."

"Stop being weird."

"I'm conducting science."

"Science requires qualifications."

"I watched three documentaries this week."

I roll my eyes.

She leans forward, examining my face. "Your skin does look annoyingly good."

"What?"

"Seriously. It's glowing. Like you drank eight gallons of water, got twelve hours of sleep, and achieved inner peace."

"I definitely did none of those things."

"Then congratulations. You've accidentally become one of those people in skincare commercials."

I snort into my tea.

Marin points at me. "That's it, though. You still look like

Rachel. Same face. Same grumpy little wrinkle right there when you overthink things."

"I do not have a wrinkle."

"You absolutely do."

"Rude." Despite myself, some of the tension loosens in my chest.

Marin gives me one last look and shrugs. "Maybe your skin's clearer. Maybe your hair's shinier. Maybe showering finally paid off. But no, you don't look dramatically different."

I nod slowly.

"Why?"

I stare into my tea. "No reason."

But the image from the mirror refuses to leave my mind. The sharper eyes. The strange brightness under my skin. The feeling that something had shifted while I wasn't looking. She pats the cushion beside her. "Now sit, breathe, and tell me about your little hospital vacation. I've been dying for the gossip."

"Vacation," I echo, sitting down. "Yeah. That's one word for it."

Marin leans forward, eyes sparkling. "Start from the top, babe. Give me the drama. Did you at least get one of those cute hospital bracelets? Oh—wait." She spots it on my wrist and gasps. "Collector's edition!"

"Marin," I warn, but she just grins wider.

"Okay, okay." She waves a hand. "Serious face. I'm listening. Tell me what happened."

So I do.

I tell her everything, the park, the man in black, my dad collapsing, his words, *when the moon drowns in daylight, you'll find the door*, the light, the blood. How he vanished right out of my hands. How no one saw. How they locked me in that sterile room and called it psychosis.

The words spill out faster the longer I talk, my throat tight, my hands gripping the mug too hard. Marin doesn't interrupt, doesn't joke, not until I get to the part about the shimmer, the light, the dust, the impossible glow that turned his office into something alive.

When I finally stop, the room is quiet except for the soft hiss of the incense. The tea in my mug has gone lukewarm. My pulse is still racing.

Marin blinks. "Okay. Wild theory time."

I groan. "Here we go."

She raises a finger. "Option one: you are the chosen one, and this is your cosmic awakening. Option two: your meds and your brain are having a toxic relationship. Option three—hear me out—you're actually in a simulation, and I'm the comic relief."

Despite myself, a laugh escapes. "That's your takeaway?"

"Babe, that's my coping mechanism." She nudges my shoulder. "You tell me about glowing dust and vanishing dads, and my brain goes full *X-Files*."

"Marin—"

She softens a little, her grin fading. "Hey. I believe you believe what you saw."

"That's not—" I start, but she holds up a hand.

"No, listen. I know you wouldn't make this up. But, Rachel…" She hesitates, eyes flicking to mine. "Your dad's been gone for years."

The words hit harder than they should.

"What?" I whisper, even though I already heard it in the hospital.

She watches me carefully, voice gentle now. "You know that, right? He died in that car accident."

I shake my head, the room spinning. "No, he... Marin, I saw him three days ago. We had coffee. He said something to me, and then—" My throat closes around the memory of his weight in my hands, the light, the way the world snapped back.

Marin reaches for my hand. Her fingers are warm, familiar. "Rach..."

I pull back, heart pounding. "No. Don't. He was real. I'm not crazy."

"I didn't say you were."

"You don't believe me."

"I—" She swallows, choosing her words carefully. "I think maybe your mind's trying to make sense of something it can't yet. You've been through a lot. Sometimes memories... shift."

I stare at her, my voice barely a whisper. "You think I imagined him?"

Marin doesn't answer. Her silence answers for her. The incense burns low, smoke curling between us in thin, ghostly ribbons. The hum at the edge of my hearing flares for a heartbeat. The silence between us feels heavy and fragile. Marin's still watching me like I might break, her lips pressed together like she wants to say something.

I stand up fast enough that my tea sloshes over the rim. "You know what? Forget it."

"Rach—"

"No." My voice shakes, but I keep going. "You think I made it up. You think I imagined all of it. My dad. The park. The dust. Everything."

Marin sighs softly. "I didn't say that."

"You didn't have to."

I storm down the hall, my heartbeat thudding in my ears. The flat feels smaller than it did a minute ago, the walls closer, the air thicker. I shove open my bedroom door and slam it behind me, hard enough to rattle the frame. The sound echoes through the flat, followed by Marin's voice calling something muffled and apologetic that I don't bother catching.

I kick off my shoes, drop my bag to the floor, and flop face-first onto the bed. The mattress creaks in protest. I don't care. For a while, I just lie there, breathing hard, staring at the dim blur of city light bleeding through the curtains. My pulse won't slow down. There's a faint shimmer around the window, the rainbow haze clinging to the glass.

She doesn't believe me. Of course she doesn't. How could she? If someone told me this story, I'd think they were crazy too. Still, it hurts, the way she looked at me, careful and kind. I press my face into the pillow, my voice muffled against the fabric. "He was real," I whisper. "I saw him." The words sound small in the dark. And for a second, I swear I can still smell the coffee on his jacket, faint and familiar. The air hums once, soft and familiar, a breath drawn in beside me. Then it's gone, and I'm alone with the silence and the fading shimmer at the edges of my sight.

Chapter 5

I'm small again. Bare feet on cool tile. The smell of coffee and something sweet. Morning light spilling through the kitchen window, catching the dust in gold ribbons. Dad's at the counter, humming under his breath. I remember that, the sound, low and steady, a song that didn't need words. The world had its own background music and he was the only one who knew it.

He looks over his shoulder and smiles when he sees me. "Couldn't sleep?"

I shake my head. My hair's a tangled mess. I'm clutching my worn blanket like a shield, the edge frayed and silky from being rubbed between my fingers a thousand times.

He crouches down to my level, eyes bright in the half-light. "You know what that means?"

I grin sleepily. "What?"

"It means the stars are still keeping you awake." He brushes a strand of hair behind my ear.

The light through the window shifts slightly. Brighter. Too bright. I squint against it. The dust floating in the air starts to shimmer, gold and silver specks swirling together until the kitchen looks suspended in some quiet galaxy.

Dad's still smiling, but now his eyes look wrong. Not unkind. Just... glowing. Light gathers in them like it's leaking through from somewhere else.

I take a step back. "Dad?"

The hum in the air deepens, vibrating through my ribs. The light catches the edge of his face, breaking it into fragments. The dust ribbons twist, forming faint shapes—circles, lines, something like a symbol trying to be born.

"When the moon drowns in daylight," he says softly, "you'll find the door."

I shake my head. "Stop. Please."

But he's already fading.

Light spills from him in thin, unraveling strands, as if he's coming apart at the seams. It pours from his eyes and mouth, impossibly bright, swallowing the shape of him.

His voice rises, urgent now.

"When the moon drowns in daylight," he says, the words carrying above the growing roar of light, "you'll find the door."

"Dad!"

My own voice snaps me awake. I'm sitting upright in bed, heart racing, the room still half full of his light. The curtains flutter in a breeze that shouldn't be there. For a moment, I swear I can still smell the dark roast coffee, exactly the way he used to drink it. And then it's gone. My heart won't slow down. The dream still clings to me, my dad's voice echoing. I glance toward the window. It's still dark outside. The clock on my nightstand blinks 2:47 a.m.

I swing my legs over the edge of the bed and press my bare feet to the floor. It feels cold, real, solid, and grounds me, a small anchor in a world that keeps shifting. The flat is silent except for the soft hum of the refrigerator. Marin's door is shut, a sliver of pale moonlight spilling from the gap beneath it. I pad down the hall to the kitchen, half expecting something to move in the shadows. Nothing does. It's just me and the faint smell of burnt incense from earlier, clinging to the walls.

I open the fridge, the light spilling across the tiles. My reflection wavers faintly in the glass door. My face reflects back worn with tired eyes. Hair still damp from the shower. I grab the first thing I see: a slice of leftover cold pizza, congealed cheese and all.

As I eat, I lean against the counter and stare out the small kitchen window. The city outside looks muted, washed in blue-gray light. The streetlamps hum softly, their glow bending just slightly.

The shimmer is still there. It dances faintly at the edge of my vision, tracing halos around the window frame, the sink faucet, the silverware glinting in the drying rack. When I blink, it fades. Not gone, just waiting.

I take another bite and force a laugh under my breath. "You're losing it, Rachel." But even as I say it, the reflection in the window flickers. Not enough to be sure, just enough to make my skin prickle. I set the plate down carefully and step closer to the glass.

Outside, the street is still and empty. But in the reflection, there's movement, a faint ripple, the unmistakable sensation of someone brushing past me sends a chill down my spine. For the barest second, I think I see a tall shape over my shoulder, a smudge of shadow where there shouldn't be one. I turn fast.

Nothing.

The refrigerator buzzes in the corner. Somewhere inside the walls, a pipe knocks once and settles. The incense holder on the counter is nothing more than a chipped ceramic tray with ash scattered across it. Just as it's always been.

I press my palms against the edge of the counter until the cool laminate grounds me in something solid. The mug in my hands is warm. The floor beneath my bare feet is real. Everything is normal.

"I'm losing it," I murmur.

The words disappear into the quiet.

But as I turn toward the hallway, I hesitate.

The refrigerator's hum seems to rise and fall.

Once.

Twice.

In time with the faint thud beneath my ribs. I stand perfectly still, holding my breath. The sound continues. A slow, steady vibration threading through the walls, the floor, the air itself. By the time I force myself back toward my bedroom, the hairs on my arms have lifted, and I can't shake the feeling that something in the darkness has become aware of me.

Sunlight drags me awake. Not gently, either. It slams straight through the curtains. For one blissful second, I forget everything. The park. The hospital. The dust. My dad. Then the memories return, one by one.

The way his body folded. The way his eyes went distant. The way my hands shook trying to keep him here. I felt him die. Right there, right in my arms. That's not something you misunderstand. That's not something you hallucinate. And yet... that's exactly what everyone keeps telling me. Doctors. Nurses. Even Marin.

Marin, who's believed every impossible story I've ever told her. Marin, who's defended me in situations way more ridiculous than this. If anyone was going to say, "I believe you," it should've been her. But she looked me in the eyes and said he died years ago. Years. As if everything I saw, the blood, the light, was some kind of fantasy my brain stitched together.

I groan, pull the blanket over my head, and pretend the world doesn't exist. But the thoughts don't stop just because I'm hiding from the sun. Why doesn't anyone believe me?How can an entire world insist someone's been dead for years when I watched him collapse yesterday? How can an apartment that smelled like him just... not be his?

None of it makes sense, and the more I try to untangle it, the more knotted everything becomes. But one thing cuts through the mess, sharp and clear: Someone killed my dad. Someone took him from me. And if the world refuses to admit he was ever alive... that means whoever did this doesn't want me finding answers. They picked the wrong person.

I shove the blanket down and stare at the ceiling, my pulse pounding in my throat. I don't know what happened in that park, or why no one else saw it. I don't know why the world has rewritten itself around me. But I know what I saw. I know what I felt. And I'm not dropping this, not until I find whoever killed him and figure out what really happened to him. Even if I have to tear reality apart to do it.

From the other room, Marin's voice carries through the apartment, singing off-key to some 70's rock song that doesn't deserve what she's doing to it. The smell of coffee drifts in, along with the faint scent of burning toast. Of course she's making breakfast. Of course she's burning it. I drag myself out of bed, run a hand through my hair, and shuffle to the kitchen.

Marin's already there, barefoot, hair a wild halo of near-white waves around her face, robe hanging half-off one shoulder. Her over-sized glasses are perched crookedly on her nose as she squints at a pan.

"You're up," she says cheerfully. "Miracles do happen before noon."

"Barely," I mutter, reaching for the mug she's already set out for me. "Do I even want to know what you're cooking?"

She looks at me like I've insulted her ancestors. "Excuse me, this is artisanal avocado toast. It's just... extra artisanal right now."

"You mean burnt."

"Charred," she corrects, flipping a slice. "It's rustic."

I take a sip of coffee. It's strong enough to wake the dead. Perfect. The warmth hits my chest and spreads outward, smoothing some of the jagged edges inside me.

Marin glances over her shoulder. "You were talking in your sleep, by the way."

That gets my attention. "What?"

She shrugs. "Couldn't really hear what you said. Something about stars. Or doors? Maybe both? You're weirdly poetic when you're unconscious."

I freeze, mug halfway to my lips. "Stars?"

Marin's grin softens when she sees my face. "Hey, I'm kidding. It was probably nothing. You okay?"

I nod, too fast. "Yeah. Just a rough night."

"You want to talk about it?"

"No." I stare into my coffee for a second, then add quietly, "And I'm still pissed at you."

Marin doesn't miss a beat. "Good. You look hotter when you're mad."

I glare at her. "I hate you."

She smirks. "That's just your anger chakra talking. Give it

coffee."

I roll my eyes, but the edge softens. That's the thing about Marin. She never apologizes the normal way. She just makes me laugh until the hurt can't stand being in the same room.

Chapter 6

Later that morning, I'm on the floor of my bedroom, surrounded by chaos. A half-empty mug of coffee sweats on the carpet beside me. The other half of Marin's "rustic" toast sits abandoned on a napkin, blackened around the edges. Crumbs everywhere.

The pile of papers I grabbed from my dad's apartment is spread across the floor in a lopsided circle, star charts, crumpled receipts, pages of notes that look like gibberish to anyone without a PhD in cryptic handwriting. Most of it doesn't make sense. Numbers in the margins. Doodles of constellations that don't exist. Circles intersected by three straight lines, over and over. A few lines of poetry that don't sound like him at all.

Light caught in gravity's throat.

Where the stars fall, the door remembers.

I sip my coffee and squint. "Yeah," I mutter. "Totally normal dad stuff." One of the papers catches my eye, not because of what's on it, but because it seems to breathe. I blink. The page looks ordinary, yellowed, creased, but as sunlight hits it, the ink shimmers faintly. I lean closer, brow furrowed. "Okay, maybe less coffee next time." Still, I pick it up carefully.

The glow dims as soon as my fingers touch it. Across the top, my dad's handwriting curls in bold, looping strokes:

The Lyrid Event — 1134 A.D.

The rest of the text is dense, more historical report than notes. I skim through it, half expecting to find burn marks or spilled coffee stains instead of actual information.

An unprecedented meteor storm recorded across multiple continents... Witnesses described not fire, but ribbons of light that sang as they fell. The storm lasted three nights. Afterward, astronomers noted unusual magnetic interference, compasses reversed polarity, timepieces stopped entirely.

The writing trails into more personal notes. My dad's voice between the lines.

Some believe it wasn't a storm at all. They called it The Falling. Light given form. Carrier of something the earth wasn't meant to hold.

My skin prickles. The same hum from his office crawls up my spine, familiar and wrong at the same time. The rest of the page blurs where the ink fades into indecipherable sketches, circular symbols that look like orbits, or maybe eyes. Or doors. Tiny arcs of ink forming half-familiar shapes I've seen in other pages, and if I'm honest, in the edges of my dreams.

I trace a finger over one of the faded drawings, and for a heartbeat, the ink warms under my touch. I recoil, and the page tumbles from my hand. The glow disappears. I laugh under my breath, shaky and forced. "Jesus. Too much caffeine. Definitely too much." But when I glance down again, one faint line remains visible, glowing softly where my hand had touched.

When the stars fall, they do not die. They hide.

The words pulse once and fade. I sit there, frozen, coffee

cooling beside me, heart pounding in my throat. Outside, a car horn blares, startling me back in the real world, in my too small bedroom with its crooked posters and chipped furniture. I stare at the paper until the glow fades completely, until it's just ink and dust again. My pulse finally starts to slow, but my brain refuses to stop.

The Lyrid Event. 1134 A.D. Ribbons of light that sang as they fell. It sounds ridiculous, something you'd find on the History Channel at three in the morning between UFO sightings and Bigfoot documentaries. But my dad wrote it. And I've never seen him write like that before. Not for work. Not even for his conspiracy forums.

I grab my notebook from the nightstand and scrawl the words down before I lose them.

The Falling — Lyrid Event — 1134 — light that sang.

The words look insane in my own handwriting. I run both hands through my hair and laugh softly.

"Yeah, okay, sure. Glowing dust, ancient meteor storms, singing light. Maybe I really am losing it." Still, I can't stop staring at the page.

There's a date, a name, a pattern. Something to chase. And then it hits me, Lyrid Event. I've heard that before. A meteor shower. A real one. Documented. Predictable. And if he wrote it down, if he circled it like it mattered...

A slow, cold thread winds down my spine. What if this isn't just cosmic nonsense? What if this is the first breadcrumb? What if looking up *Lyrid Event* leads me to someone or something connected to what happened in the park? My dad didn't scribble random clues for fun. He followed trails. He mapped patterns. He warned people. And he died right after trying to warn me. If I'm imagining things, fine. Then I'll prove it.

But if I'm not…

I glance toward the window. Afternoon sunlight spills across the floor, washing over the stacks of my dad's papers. For a heartbeat, the sunlight lingers on that page while the rest of the journal remains in shadow. I grab my bag and shove the glowing page inside before I can second-guess it. Marin's advice drifts faintly from the kitchen, something about manifesting positive vibes and doing a "cleansing dance" for the toast she burned again. I smile despite myself, slip on my jacket, and head for the door. If I want answers, I'll have to find them myself and I'll have to find them where my dad always did. The library's only a few blocks away. And if nothing else, at least libraries don't talk back.

I make it to the library by mid-afternoon, the heavy doors groaning as I push inside. The scent of aging paper and lemon cleaner hangs in the air. A few people glance up from their laptops, but no one cares enough to linger. I head straight for the front desk, where a librarian with silver hair and half-moon glasses looks up at me over a mountain of returns.

"Hi," I say, trying to sound casual. "I'm hoping to get into the archives."

Her eyebrows lift a fraction. "The restricted archives?"

"Uh… yeah. If that's okay."

She studies me in silence, as though weighing the odds of me making a terrible decision and deciding they're uncomfortably high. Then she sighs and slides a clipboard across the counter.

"Sign in. Full name and time. And no food or drinks beyond the first door."

I scribble my name, *Rachel Calloway* and the time, resisting the urge to add *Please let this help* in the notes section. When

I hand the clipboard back, she softens, just barely. "You researching something specific?"

I hesitate. Saying it out loud feels ridiculous.

"Meteor events," I finally say. "Historic ones."

Her eyes brighten with the unmistakable spark of a librarian who secretly loves a rabbit hole. "Astronomy. Good." She reaches under the desk and produces an old fashioned brass key hooked to a leather strap. "Archives are downstairs. Door on the left. Lock it behind you."

I thank her, sling the key over my wrist, and follow the creaking steps down to the basement. The archive door is heavy oak banded with black iron hinges, worn smooth by decades of hands. As though generations of stories have pressed themselves into its grain. I unlock it, step inside, and flip on the overhead lights. The room hums to life, rows of filing cabinets and glass cases stretching into a quiet maze.

Hours slip by, measured in coffee sips and dust motes. Every lead I chase ends the same way: nothing. A few mentions of meteor storms. Old newspaper clippings full of grainy black-and-white photos. Scientific articles that might as well be written in another language.

Nothing about *The Falling.* Nothing about *light that sang.* Nothing that feels like the thing I'm actually looking for. But the more dead ends I hit, the more convinced I become that I'm close. Because my dad wasn't the type to leave nonsense trails. And if he wrote it down, he meant it. I rub my temples, exhaling hard. "Come on, Dad. What were you chasing?"

Most of the books are old enough that their pages crackle when touched, carrying the scents of aged paper, dried glue, and faint woodsmoke. I pull another from the shelf, a journal bound in cracked brown leather. The label reads *Observations,*

1832.

Halfway through, something catches my eye: a small hand-written entry near the back.

April 24th. The sky erupted tonight. A storm of light so brilliant it seemed the heavens themselves were aflame. The villagers called it a divine warning. I called it beautiful.

The words pull me in. My pulse slows. It's not much, but it's something. I lean closer, tracing the ink with my eyes, trying to decipher the rest of the scrawl.

They say those who stood beneath it could hear it sing.

My breath catches.

I felt it in my chest. Like a heartbeat.

I mouth the words silently, pulse slowing to match the rhythm on the page. There's a stillness in the air, a kind of reverent quiet that feels heavier than silence. "Jesus," I whisper.

A soft sound breaks the quiet. The scrape of a shoe on tile, the faintest throat-clear.

I jump so hard I nearly drop the journal. "Holy—"

I spin around. For a second, my brain refuses to process it. "You've got to be kidding me."

He raises his hands slightly, a hint of amusement in his voice. "Didn't mean to startle you." The air hums again, soft and familiar. And for one impossible second, the light around him bends the way it did on the street.

Chapter 7

Standing in the aisle behind me is the guy from the street. Same dark hair, same calm expression, same impossibly steady gaze. Somehow he seems taller in the soft library light, his presence filling the space between the shelves.

I press a hand to my chest, glaring. "You did. Congratulations."

"You know," I say, "there are less creepy ways to say hello."

"Noted. I did knock." He gestures lightly toward the shelves. "You were... focused."

"I'm in a library. That's kind of the point."

"Touché." He smiles faintly, the corners of his mouth barely moving. "Didn't think I'd run into you again."

"Yeah, well, I don't usually haunt archives."

"Haunt?" His tone lifts, amused. "Fitting."

He's teasing me, but it's too subtle to call him out on. The air around him feels strangely still.

I narrow my eyes. "What are you doing here?"

"Research," he says easily. "Family history."

That lands too close to home. "That's convenient. Same."

He leans a shoulder against the nearest shelf, looking so comfortable you'd think he belonged here more than the books did. "Really? What kind of family history?"

I hesitate. The truth feels too messy, too raw, too *you sound unwell, Miss* waiting to happen. So I lie.

"Old genealogy stuff," I say instead, forcing a shrug. "You know, charts, names, boring dead people."

"Thrilling," he murmurs.

He steps closer, trying—and failing—to be subtle about peeking at what I'm reading. He's near enough now that I catch the faint scent of rain and old paper. Sunlight filters through the narrow windows overhead, catching on his skin in a way that makes me blink. I deadpan, closing the journal a little too hard. He looks down at it, still half in my hands. "You looked like you found something interesting."

"Just an old diary," I say. "Some farmer losing his mind over the weather."

"Maybe the weather deserved it."

I blink. "You always this philosophical before lunch?"

"Only when provoked."

"Great. We should get you a podcast." He laughs softly. Something in my chest tightens before I can stop it.

"Do you visit libraries often?" he asks.

"Only when I'm trying to avoid real life."

"How's that going for you?"

"About as well as you'd expect."

He glances toward the small windows where dust drifts in the light. "Seems like a good place to hide from things."

"Or find them," I counter, and immediately wish I hadn't.

His gaze flicks back to me, sharper now. "What exactly are you trying to find?"

The way he says *what* sends a strange hitch through my chest, quiet and unsettling, as if he's not asking a question but stating something he already knows.

I look back down at the journal.

"Nothing," I say. "Just family stuff. I told you."

He tilts his head, a faint smile tugging at one corner of his mouth. He doesn't call me out, but the look in his eyes says he isn't buying a word of it.

"Right. Family."

The word settles between us. The silence that follows feels strangely alive. I look away first.

"Yeah."

The lie tastes like metal.

He doesn't challenge it, but he also doesn't rescue me from the quiet blooming between us. Instead, he moves a fraction, slow and intentional , as he reaches for one of the books stacked beside him. He flips through the pages with easy concentration, pausing now and then to scan a line of text. I should feel relieved. Instead, I find myself shifting under the weight of his silence. His eyes never leave the journal, but somehow that makes it worse.

The storm returns in cycles. Those who carry its light will not age as others do. They burn.

My skin prickles, a low tremor crawling up my arms. I can almost feel the dust from Dad's office in my lungs again. But it's the next line, half-faded and barely legible, that makes my stomach twist.

The cycle begins again where the vessel is kept.

I blink. *The vessel.*

In my dad's notes, he'd written something similar, messy scrawl, half unreadable, in the margin beside a diagram.

The vessel erupts when...

The ink had dragged off there, the pen clearly running ahead of his hand. My pulse spikes. I flip back a page, searching for context, but the ink blurs into a tangle of symbols and dates—1134, 1832—and then a familiar shape. A circle divided by three lines, identical to the one carved into the latch of the metal case I found in his office. The case.

My throat goes dry. For a heartbeat, I feel like I'm back on the floor of his study, dust glowing, books breathing, the world humming too loud. I could close the book. Pretend I hadn't seen it. But the thought of not knowing felt worse than whatever comes next.

I feel him before I hear him. A quiet shift of air. The faint scent of rain. "Everything okay?"

I snap the journal shut, the sound slicing through the silence. "Fine."

His brows pull together just slightly. "You sure? You went a little pale."

"Just... forgot I have somewhere to be." I sling my bag over my shoulder, forcing my heartbeat to slow. "Family emergency."

He frowns slightly. "Did I say something?"

"No. It's not you."

His gaze drifts to the journal in my hand, lingering there. "You sure?"

"I'm sure." My voice comes out thinner than I want it to. "I have to go."

He watches me for a moment longer, weighing whether to call me on it, then nods once. I push past him, heart racing for reasons I refuse to examine.

"Wait."

I pause, hand on the door handle.

"What's your name?" he says.

I glance over my shoulder. "Why?"

"So I know what to call you next time you sneak into my archive."

"*Your* archive?" I snort. "You really need to work on your ego."

He grins, slow and deliberate, and it hits me that he actually means it. "I don't want to have to make one up," he says, eyes glinting. "I'm terrible at guessing. Don't want to accidentally call you, I don't know… Gertrude."

I fight the smile threatening to creep in. "You wouldn't dare."

"Try me."

"Fine," I say, crossing my arms. "It's—" I stop. Why am I even considering it? This guy's a stranger. A stranger who's way too comfortable in the back corners of libraries and shows up exactly where I am. "Actually, no. I forgot it."

His grin widens just a little. "You forgot your name? Okay, suit yourself." He straightens, the air shifting slightly between us. "I'm Riven."

"Good for you."

He tilts his head, unfazed. "Well, it's nice to meet you too, mystery girl."

The words shouldn't land the way they do. Light, teasing, but there's something underneath them. A note I can't quite name. I open the door. "Let's not make this a regular thing, Riven."

"Can't make promises I don't intend to keep," he says easily. I don't look back, but I feel his gaze follow me all the way to the elevator. The hum in the air doesn't ease until the doors close.

The chill hits me the moment I step onto the sidewalk. People stream past in both directions, heads down, coffees in hand, conversations half-lost beneath the noise of traffic. No one looks up. No one seems to notice the way my pulse won't settle.

I tighten my grip on my bag.

The journal rides against my hip.

The storm returns in cycles. Those who carry its light will not age as others do. They burn.

And the way the ink shimmered under the library lights like the paper was breathing. By the time I reach my dad's building, my chest is tight again. I climb the stairs two at a time and fumble with my key. It doesn't fit.

"What the hell…" I try again. Same thing. The key scrapes against the lock, accomplishing absolutely nothing. I knock before I even think about it, because for a second, I forget this isn't just a door. It's his.

Footsteps shuffle on the other side. The latch clicks. A young woman answers, holding a toddler on her hip. The smell of cereal and fabric softener drifts into the hall.

Behind her, a television chatters softly. A child bursts into laughter somewhere deeper in the apartment.

Toys litter the carpet.

Bright plastic blocks.

A stuffed dinosaur missing one eye.

The spot where my dad's old couch used to sit is empty now, filled with things that belong to another life. I stare past her into the apartment. Nothing is where I remember it. Nothing looks like him.

For a second, I just stand there. My brain can't seem to translate what my eyes are seeing. The faded rug is gone.

The bookshelf, the coffee rings on the table, the half-broken lamp... gone. The pale walls I remember are gone, replaced by a warm honey-colored paint that catches the afternoon light. Framed family photos crowd the shelves. A knitted blanket is draped over the arm of a chair. The apartment feels tighter somehow, every corner claimed and filled.

I take a step toward the doorway before I can stop myself. The apartment is right there. Close enough to touch. Close enough that, for a ridiculous second, I think if I just get a little nearer, the years will peel away and everything will be where it's supposed to be. The woman's posture stiffens. She draws the door in tighter.

"Can I help you?"

Her voice pulls me out of the trance.

"I—uh—sorry." My own voice wobbles. "I must have the wrong apartment."

"This is 3B," she says, adjusting the toddler on her hip. "We've lived here a few years now. Maybe I can help you find who you're looking for?"

A few years.

My stomach drops, the words echoing in my head like they're falling down a well.

"That's... impossible."

The woman frowns, glancing down the hallway like she's considering whether to call someone. "You okay, miss?"

"I'm fine," I lie automatically. "I just—sorry. Wrong place."

She gives me a polite, uncertain smile and closes the door. The latch clicks. The sound echoes like a gunshot. I flinch in response.

I stare at the door. Then the number. Then my own

trembling hands. The hallway suddenly feels too narrow, too bright. My breathing goes shallow, the edges of my vision flickering like an old film reel. No, no, no. The hallway isn't right. The paint color looks different. The air smells cleaner. Even the light fixtures aren't the same. The world feels like it's been... edited. Rearranged.

"This isn't real," I whisper.

The light overhead hums, faint at first, then louder, vibrating through the air. I press a hand to the wall for balance, but the wall moves under my palm, the paint shimmering. The shimmer pulses up my arm, racing under my skin, spreading in thin, glowing threads that crackle. The same hum from the library crawls up my spine, sharp and familiar.

"No," I choke out. "Not here. Not again."

The light builds, too bright, too alive. The air thickens, pressing against me, suffocating me. I stumble back, bumping into the opposite wall as the hallway ripples. The hum deepens into something almost alive, a low thrum that syncs with my heartbeat.

The shimmer bursts from me before I can stop it, color exploding across the walls, bending the fluorescent light into ribbons that twist and pulse around me, those same circles and lines I've seen in Dad's notes, now drawn in light instead of ink. And for one breathless second, everything pauses.

I reach for anything, the railing, the wall, the air, but my fingers close on nothing. My vision tunnels, collapsing into a narrow circle of light. The hum becomes a roar again, deep and familiar. The last thing I see is the sunlight splitting into gold and white and impossible blue.

Then everything goes black.

Chapter 8

The world comes back in fragments. There's Beeping and white lights. The sharp antiseptic tang of disinfectant mixed with something floral and fake lavender, maybe. My throat is dry. My tongue feels like sandpaper. My skin feels too tight.

For a second, I think I'm still in the hallway, that the light hasn't stopped, that I'm pinned in that shimmering, humming not-space. Then a voice cuts through the haze. "Finally," Marin says. "I was starting to think I'd have to smuggle you out of here *Weekend-at-Bernie's* style."

My eyes snap open.

She's perched in a plastic chair beside the bed, legs crossed, glittery slippers on her feet, hoodie declaring *Mercury Is Always in Retrograde, Don't Talk to Me.* Her hair is pulled into a messy knot on top of her head, strands escaping wildly.

"You've gotta stop scaring the locals," she adds, sipping from a travel mug that's definitely not hospital-approved. "Someone found you passed out on the pavement, mumbling to yourself. Real main-character energy, by the way."

I blink. The ceiling lights have halos. The monitor beside me flickers once, its rhythm spiking in time with my heartbeat. "What?"

"They called an ambulance. You've been out for hours."

She sets the mug down next to a half-eaten granola bar. "You really don't remember?"

"No," I croak. My voice doesn't sound like mine. "I was—at my dad's apartment, and—"

Marin's expression softens. "Rach..."

"No, listen." I push myself upright, wincing as my muscles protest and the leads tug against my skin. The monitor beeps faster for a second, then steadies. "There was a woman there. A family. She said they'd lived there for years."

Marin tilts her head, pale hair catching the fluorescent light. "Maybe you had the wrong building?"

"I didn't." My voice tightens. "It was the same place. Same hall, same number. 3B. But everything was different, the furniture, the walls, even the air."

"Okay, whoa." She stands, palms raised, as if calming an unruly crowd. "Let's dial it down from conspiracy-theory radio hour. You've had a rough few days. Hospital lights do weird things to your brain."

"I wasn't hallucinating."

She gives me that skeptical half-smile. "You were found unconscious on the street, muttering about doors and stars. If that's not hallucinating, it's at least poetic."

I glare, but she just grins, brushing invisible lint from her sleeve.

"How did you even know I was here?" I ask.

"Emergency contact, remember? Which, by the way, I am nailing." She points to her **VISITOR** badge, scrawled in Sharpie. "You're welcome."

Despite myself, I laugh, a rough sound, but real. "Of course you are."

Marin's grin softens. "You really scared me, you know."

The room quiets. Machines beep steadily. There's a faint hum beneath it all. It's the same frequency I felt in the hallway, in Dad's office, in the library, like the world humming under its breath.

"What were you even doing out there?" she asks gently.

"I was looking for answers."

"Answers to what?"

I open my mouth, then close it again. How do I explain any of it? My dad. The family in his apartment. The shimmer under my skin. The way time feels like it's folding in on itself. "Never mind," I say finally. "It doesn't matter."

Marin sighs and pulls her chair closer, the plastic legs squeaking on the tile. "You always say that right before it clearly matters a lot."

"Marin—"

"Fine, fine." She leans back again, stretching her legs out. "But you're not leaving this bed until they clear you. You need rest, hydration, and maybe less caffeine."

"I'm fine."

She arches a brow. "You fainted in public. That's Victorian heroine levels of not fine."

I groan and flop back against the pillow. The monitor complains for a beat and then settles. "You're impossible."

"That's why you love me." She smiles, and for a moment the room feels normal again, just two friends trading sarcasm in a too bright hospital. But when I glance down, the illusion fractures. Beneath the thin blanket, faint light traces the veins in my hands, pulsing softly. For a second, it syncs with the beep of the monitor, then drifts into its own rhythm. My own private constellation. I curl my fingers into fists until the glow dims.

Marin drives us home later, her voice filling the silence with small talk and half-baked astrology theories. I nod in the right places, forehead against the cool glass, watching streetlights smear into lines. My reflection flickers in the window, familiar, but not. My eyes catch the passing lights and hold them a fraction too long. The shimmer is still there, faint but constant, breathing with me. By the time we reach the apartment, my chest feels tight again and I realize I've been holding my breath since the hallway.

Inside, the air smells like incense, always too strong, always comforting. Smoke and sandalwood and something floral. It wraps around me like a blanket. I drop onto the couch, the one place that still feels solid, and sink into the cushion until my bones stop buzzing. Marin plops down beside me, tucking one leg under herself and handing me a mug of tea she must've made the second we walked in. "Okay," she says. "Let's do this."

"Do what?"

"The part where you tell me what's actually going on before I stage an intervention involving tarot cards and your therapist's voicemail." I stare at the steam curling off the mug. It shimmers faintly, tiny rainbow threads weaving through the vapor. "You wouldn't believe me."

"Try me."

"Marin—"

She raises a hand. "Hypothetically."

I blink. "What?"

"Hypothetically," she repeats, tone patient and maddeningly calm. "Let's say I'm your incredibly open-minded, non-judgmental best friend, and I'm going to believe everything you say purely for the sake of science and drama. Okay?"

Despite everything, I laugh. "Hypothetically."

"Good. Now talk."

It comes out in fragments: the park, my dad, the blood that wasn't there, the hospital, the glowing pages, the *Lyrid Event- The Falling*, the word *vessel*. The case in his office. The family in his apartment that shouldn't be there. The way the hallway bent like heat, the way the light came from me this time, not just at me. Marin doesn't interrupt, just listens, eyes thoughtful behind her glasses. When I reach the part about the apartment, my voice cracks.

"And then everything went dark," I finish quietly. "Like someone turned the world inside out. Next thing I know, I'm in the hospital, and everyone's acting like I just collapsed in the street."

Silence settles between us, heavy but not hostile. Marin's thinking; I can see it. Her gaze flicks to my hands, like she's remembering the weird glow in my veins from the hospital too.

Finally, she exhales. "Okay," she says slowly. "Hypothetically speaking, if all this were happening—"

"Yeah?"

"I'd say maybe the universe is trying to get your attention."

I stare at her. "That's your takeaway?"

"Well, that and you should probably sage yourself."

I groan. "You're impossible."

"Hypothetically impossible."

I laugh despite the ache in my chest. "You're ridiculous."

"Thanks. It's part of my charm."

The tension loosens for a breath. The room feels warm again, safe, almost. The hum in my bones quiets. Then I say it, the thing I've been avoiding.

"There's… also this guy. And the worst part is, when he looks at me, it doesn't feel like curiosity. It feels like recognition. Marin's eyebrows shoot up. "A guy?"

"It's not like that."

"It's always like that."

"No, seriously. He just keeps showing up. In weird places. First the street, then the library. And he's—"

"Hot?"

I pause with my tea halfway to my mouth and look at her over the rim through narrowed eyes.

"…Suspicious."

"Uh-huh. And hot."

I glare. "You're not helping."

"I'm always helping," she says. "Especially when it comes to mysterious men with bad timing."

I sink back into the couch, half-smiling. "You're incorrigible."

"Thank you. So, hypothetically, if he shows up again, do I get to meet him?"

"Marin…"

"What? Hypothetically." She lifts her hands and makes a theatrical come-here motion toward the universe. Her grin softens. "Okay, seriously. Mystery men and glowing dust aside, like I said—maybe the universe is giving you a really inconvenient metaphor about closure."

"Closure?"

"Yeah. Maybe it's time to face it. Really face it."

"Face what?"

She hesitates, then sets her mug down gently, the ceramic clink sounding louder than it should. "Rach… maybe seeing your dad's grave would help."

My chest tightens. "I've already—"

"Not for him," she says quietly. "For you."

The words hang there, heavy but kind. "You've been holding your breath since it happened," she says softly. "Maybe it's time to let some of it out."

I stare down at my hands. For a second, the faintest glow gathers along my knuckles, then fades when I curl my fingers in. The steam from my tea has thinned into almost nothing. "I don't know if I can."

"Then I'll come with you," she says simply. "We'll go together. Tomorrow."

A lump forms in my throat. "Marin…"

She waves a hand. "Don't get all sentimental. I already bought new sage sticks, and you know I'll burn them whether you're there or not. Might as well get a free cleansing out of it."

I laugh, a small, shaky laugh but real. She leans back, satisfied.

"Now here's what's going to happen: you're going to rest tonight, eat something that isn't coffee-flavored, and tomorrow, we'll go. After that, you'll pretend to be a functional adult again and let me handle the weird spiritual maintenance."

I roll my eyes. "You're bossy when you think you're right."

"I'm always right," she says, utterly serious. "But at least I'm pretty about it."

I smile despite the ache in my chest. "You promise you'll come?"

"Cross my heart, burn some sage," she says, miming a solemn oath. "We'll go together. No more collapsing in public, no more glowing, no more haunted apartment adventures. Just you, me, and some good old-fashioned emotional avoidance at the cemetery."

I laugh again, and it feels a little less hollow this time. I know if I don't go now, I'd keep running, not from ghosts or light, but from the truth I've been circling since the park. The hum under my skin settles to a low, steady thrum. Marin grins, pleased. "That's the spirit."

If the universe really is trying to get my attention, I think, staring into the dark tea in my hands, then tomorrow it's going to have to share me, with Marin, with grief, and with whatever's waking up under my skin.

Chapter 9

Daniel Everett Calloway
Born: August 12, 1974
Died: March 3, 2022

The letters blur before my eyes. For a second, I think it's sunlight on polished granite, but when I blink, I know it's not the light. It's me. My pulse stutters, each beat louder than the last. He died three years ago. 2022. Three years, on paper. Five days, in my blood. He died five days ago, right in front of me. I saw the blood on my hands. I felt it. I heard his voice, his last words.

When the moon drowns in daylight...

My throat tightens. Wind slips through the cemetery grass, whispering between the rows of stones. Somewhere, a crow calls, low and distant. The sky is too blue for this place. I kneel before I realize I've moved. My knees press into damp earth. Cold seeps through my jeans. I trace the carved letters with shaking fingers, the name, the dates, the cold permanence of it.

"This can't be real," I whisper.

Marin stands a few paces behind me, paper cup in one hand and a half-burned sage stick in the other. Her voice is softer than usual. "It's real, babe. I know it hurts."

"I don't remember this," I say.

Marin glances up from her crouch, tucking a wild strand of white-blonde hair behind her ear. The breeze lifts the rest, making her look even more unreal in this place of stone and dates. "What?"

"The funeral. Any of it. I don't remember him dying."

Her expression softens around the edges. "That's kind of the point, babe. You were in shock. Everything was a blur for weeks."

I shake my head, the air catching in my throat. "No, I mean I don't remember it at all. No hospital calls, no casket, nothing. Just... blank space. Like someone cut it out of my head."

She studies me for a long moment, all teasing gone. "I remember," she says quietly.

I look at her. "You do?"

"Yeah." She exhales, sitting back on her heels, sage stick resting forgotten across her knees. "Your dad's service was small. Close friends, a few from his old station, some people from your work. You were... you were barely there. Just standing by the casket, staring. I think you spoke once, said he'd hate all the flowers."

A small, humorless sound escapes me. "He hated flowers."

"I know." She smiles faintly, then looks down, twisting the cup in her hands. "You know, he was kind of my dad too."

I blink. "What?"

"You forget, I didn't have parents growing up. Foster homes, group placements, all of it." She shrugs one shoulder. "When I met you in uni, he called me his 'extra kid.' Always asked if I'd eaten. Always slipped me gas money when I was broke." She lets out a shaky laugh. "You weren't the only one he took care of, Rach."

Something in my chest cracks open. All this time I've been hoarding him like he was only mine. "I didn't know you felt that way."

"Of course I did. We both lost him. We just... did it differently."

I stare at the headstone, at his name carved in stone. "You think this is me finally losing it, don't you?"

She doesn't answer right away. When she does, her voice is gentle. "I think you've been pretending to be fine since the day he died. You worked nonstop. You never cried, not once. You organized his things, paid his bills, held everyone else together. Someone had to."

"I hate falling apart."

"I know." She squeezes my hand, her fingers warm around my cold ones. "Maybe now you can. Maybe that's what this is. A delayed collapse. Your brain making you stop running."

Silence stretches. The wind shifts, rustling the trees above, making the leaves whisper. My gaze drifts back to the dates.

Born. Died. Full stop.

"Maybe you're right," I say softly. "Maybe that's all it is."

Maybe it's grief. Maybe it's trauma. Maybe it's my mind making stories because it can't handle the truth straight on. Or maybe there really was blood and light in that park and someone rewrote my life around it. I wanted Marin to be right, because grief I could survive. Magic would change everything.

Marin squeezes my hand once more, then stands, brushing grass from her knees. "Good. Here's the plan. You rest. You eat something. Tomorrow you go back to work. Routine. You've earned a little normal."

I nod, though normal feels like a language I've forgotten

how to speak.

"Come on," she says, offering her arm. "Let's get you home. I'll sage the car before we go, in case the ghosts are clingy."

Despite everything, I smile. "You never quit, do you?"

"Not on you." She loops her arm through mine as we walk toward the gate. "Besides, hypothetically, I'm the best friend you've got."

Three weeks pass. Three perfectly normal, blessedly uneventful weeks.

No glowing walls. No whispers in the air. No mysterious men in libraries or doorways. No collapsing hallways or humming veins. Just work, coffee, and the steady rhythm of pretending everything is fine.

And for a while, it almost feels true.

The morning rush hums around me. Milk steams. Espresso hisses. The bell over the door chimes every few minutes. The smell of roasted beans clings to my hair, my skin, my clothes. I've been back at the shop for two weeks and I am getting good at this again, the routine, the small talk, the pretending.

"Order for Alex," I call out, sliding a cup across the counter. The college kid grabs it with a distracted thanks, earbuds already back in. The lull between customers stretches just long enough for me to breathe.

Maybe Marin was right. Maybe I just... cracked. Trauma resurfaces in strange ways. Hallucinations. Dissociation. The brain grasping for meaning where there isn't any. A delayed collapse, just like she said. Maybe that is all it was.

I take another customer, then another. By noon, my hands move on autopilot, grind, tamp, pull, pour. I eat actual food. I take breaks. I sleep, mostly. The shimmer at the edge of my vision has faded to almost nothing. Almost. If I stare too long at the coffee machine's chrome, sometimes the light bends just a little. I blink and it's gone. Normal. I am almost normal again.

A guy steps up.

"Large drip," he says, dropping a few coins on the counter.

"Sure thing."

I reach for the change and stop. One of the coins isn't right. It looks too heavy. Too old. The metal catches the fluorescent light differently than the others, warm where it should be dull. Its edges are uneven, worn by something more than time. And stamped into its surface is a circle divided by three straight lines.

My breath catches. The symbol from my dad's notes. The symbol etched into the latch of the case. For a second, all I can do is stare. The customer clears his throat. I barely hear him.

Slowly, I reach out. My fingertip brushes the metal. Cold. Then—

Heat explodes up my arm. The coin flashes white. The fluorescent lights smear into streaks. The smell of coffee vanishes beneath smoke and rain and something older. The floor drops away. My pulse slams once against my ribs.

And the world folds in on itself.

I'm small again, maybe six. The air tastes like dust and metal. We're not in an apartment; we're in a house I half-recognize from old photos. Dad shouts my name, "Rachel, stay behind me!" as shadows move in the doorway. Glass shatters. Three figures force their way inside, cloaked in black. My father's voice turns low and fierce, in a language I don't know. There's a symbol on the back of one cloak—a circle, three lines. Something flashes, gold light, quick and blinding, erupting from his hands—

The shop hums back into focus. The hiss of the machine. Voices. The sharp, burnt-sugar smell of espresso. My hands are still on the counter. The coin is still in my palm warm enough to sting. Even though the symbol is gone, the heat stays. The man who handed me the coin is gone.

A woman in line sighs. "Come on, some of us have to get back to work."

I blink, disoriented. My heart is in my throat. I drop the coin. It hits the counter and spins, ordinary and small. What just happened?

I look up and see the last person I expect. Riven stands a few feet away in the line, too composed in the middle of noise and chaos. The coffee shop buzzes around him, but he looks like he's been dropped in from somewhere quieter. Of course. He's allergic to normal entrances.

I manage a tight smile. "You've got to be kidding me."

"Nice to see you too," he says. "You okay? You looked like you were about to pass out."

"I'm fine."

"You sure? Because that didn't look fine."

"Do you just... show up places?" I ask. "Is that your thing?"

"Coincidence," he says, though it sounds like anything but.

"The universe has a twisted sense of humor," I mutter, and slip into the back. "I need a break."

"Five minutes," I call to my boss. He waves without looking up. I lean against the counter in the tiny back room, trying to breathe. My pulse is still sprinting. My fingers tingle. How is he always here?

A few seconds later, the door creaks open.

"Great," I say. "You again."

Riven closes it behind him, voice low. "What happened out there?"

"Nothing."

He gives me a look that says he doesn't believe me for a second. "You spaced out for at least two minutes. The light seemed to shift around you. It was weird. People noticed." My pulse stutters. "What are you talking about?"

He steps closer. "What did you see?"

"I didn't see anything," I snap. "I lost focus. It's called stress. Humans get it."

"Right," he says, eyes flickering with concern or recognition. "But what did you see?"

"You don't get to keep showing up and asking questions."

"And you don't get to pretend you're fine when you're not."

"Watch me." We stare at each other. The silence thickens, charged.

He exhales, then steps closer. "You should get some air."

"Don't tell me what to do." The words are sharper than I intend.

He hesitates, eyes searching my face. "Hey," he says quietly. "I'm not your enemy."

Something in the way he says it makes my pulse stumble. He reaches out, slow enough to be careful. His fingers graze my arm. It's enough. Heat and static spark through me. For half a second, the air ripples. Faint light threads the space where his hand meets my skin.

I jerk back. "Don't—" My voice cracks. "Don't touch me."

He lifts both hands in surrender, but doesn't retreat. "I wasn't trying to—"

"I don't care." Words spill faster than I can stop them.

"Everything was fine. Three weeks of normal, no weirdness, no voices. I thought I was done. I thought I was better."

"Better from what?" he asks.

"From being crazy." I sigh.

"I didn't say you were." He weighs something, then says, "After you left the library, I looked at what you were reading. I shouldn't have. But you looked like you were walking into something dangerous."

"You what?"

"The journal," he says. "And the notes you left."

"You went through my stuff?"

"I was curious," he says, almost unapologetic. "And I found something."

"Found what?"

He pulls a folded scrap from his jacket, paper older than both of us. A faint circle is drawn on it, divided by three clean lines.

The symbol.

My breath catches. "Where did you get that?"

"Hidden in the binding," he says. "Same mark you were tracing."

My head spins. "Why show me this?" His eyes soften, resolve settling in them. "Because whatever you saw today..." He steps closer, voice low, words careful but sure. "It isn't over. And you're not crazy."

For a heartbeat, neither of us moves. The world seems to hold its breath around us. I should tell him to leave. I should walk away. But the words catch. Even if I don't trust him, I want to believe him. I need to.

Riven watches me, searching my face, just... waiting. He slips the scrap of paper back into his jacket. "When does your shift end?"

I blink. "Why?"

"Because I found something. Something I think connects all of this." He hesitates, just for a second. "I'll show you." The café noise hums behind us, milk frothing, cups clinking, but all of it feels strangely far away.

"You want to meet after my shift?" I ask, trying to steady my voice. He gives a small, almost tired smile. "It's safer than pretending this isn't happening." My pulse stutters. This is reckless. Stupid. Exactly how people end up in missing-person documentaries.

"Fine," I whisper. "Six-thirty." Riven nods once, slow. "Ok, see you then." He turns toward the exit, pausing just long enough to look back at me. The door chimes softly as he leaves, and I swear the sound echoes long after he's gone.

Chapter 10

I almost talk myself out of going. Twice. But if I didn't go, I'd spend the night staring at my ceiling, waiting for the world to fold again. By six, the shop is empty. My manager is locking up when I see him through the window, leaning against a lamppost across the street. Of course he's early. I grab my bag and step into the evening air. "You know, most people text."

"You never gave me your number," he says.

"Right. My mistake." He gestures down the street. "Come on. I'll show you what I found."

"Where?"

"The library."

I raise a brow. "Pretty sure it's closed."

"Not to me." There's something in his tone, not arrogance, exactly, but certainty. I should press. Instead, I follow.

After dark, the library looks different. The front doors are locked. Streetlamps throw long shadows across the marble steps, turning the stone lions into something watchful.

"How—" I begin, but he's already unlocking a side entrance with a key.

"You break into libraries often?" I ask.

"Only when they hide things worth finding."

"That's comforting." He pushes the door open. "Ladies

first."

Inside, the air is cooler, still smelling of paper and dust. Emergency lights flicker on, washing the corridor in pale gold. We move quietly. Our footsteps sound too loud in the hush. He leads me down the stairs, past the archive room I used before, and stops at a heavy metal door I swear I didn't notice last time. No label. A keypad beside the handle.

Riven presses his palm to the pad. His hand tremors slightly near the keypad. There's a faint hum, a tiny flicker of light. The lock clicks open.

I blink. "How—?"

He smiles. "Trade secret."

The room beyond is smaller and colder. Rows of steel shelves. Old boxes. Crumbling ledgers. Loose sheets sealed in plastic. It smells less like a library and more like a vault. He goes to a central table and spreads out the papers he's gathered.

"This," he says, tapping one page, "is from an astronomical journal, 1834. Mentions a 'falling starstorm' over northern Europe. Says it wasn't meteorites. Described the lights as living."

"The Falling," I say.

He glances up, impressed.

He slides another paper over. "Seventeenth century. An order that recorded the symbols—the circle and lines. Used it to track the 'vessels.'"

"Vessels," I repeat. The word feels too heavy for the room.

He nods. "Objects. Or people. The writing isn't clear."

"That's not helpful."

"History rarely is."

My pulse quickens. "So the symbol has been around for

centuries?"

"I'm saying it isn't random." He pauses. "And it isn't the first time it's been tied to disappearances."

A chill slides down my spine. "Disappearances like…?"

"People who saw things they shouldn't," he says. "And then vanished."

"You're terrible at reassurance."

"I'm not trying to reassure you."

We dig.

Files, maps, clippings. Every scrap adds confusion. Symbols, patterns, dates that echo each other. 1134. 1832. 1893. Notes about lights that sang, stars that fell but didn't burn out, orders formed to "guard the threshold." The air in the archive has that stale, dry weight only libraries and tombs share.

Time unspools. At some point, Riven reads from an 1893 paper about a "lightfall witnessed in multiple provinces." His voice is steady. The words blur.

"My brain stopped absorbing things an hour ago," I say.

"That's when the good things start," he says. I laugh, and it sounds like a sigh. The quiet stretches. Only the hum of the lights and the faint scratch of turning pages. Then, footsteps. Slow. From the corridor beyond the metal door.

I frown. "Did you hear that?"

"Old building," he says without looking up from the book he's reading. "Probably the pipes."

"That is not pipes." My voice jumps. "That's someone walking."

He checks his phone. Blue light lifts his features. His brows rise. "It's six."

"In the evening?"

"In the morning."

"Oh my God." I shove back from the table, chair screeching. "We've been here all night."

"Guess we lost track of time."

"People come in at six. Opening prep."

Right on cue, the footsteps stop outside the door. A key rattles in the lock.

"Shit."

Riven calmly stacks the papers. "Relax. We'll leave through the side exit."

"The side exit is locked."

"Not to me."

The latch begins to turn. My pulse leaps. "You can't be serious—"

The door creaks open. A sliver of yellow light cuts through the room.

A woman's voice yawns in. "Huh. Must've forgotten the lights again."

She flips a switch near the door. Riven is already tugging me toward the back corner.

"There," he murmurs, nodding to something I somehow missed before. A door. Narrow, half hidden behind a shelf stacked with cracked boxes. Same color as the wall. Invisible unless you knew exactly where to look. My pulse jumps. How had I missed it?

He doesn't hesitate. He grips the handle and eases it open like he's done it a hundred times. The dark beyond swallows us whole. I follow because there is no time to argue. My breath is shallow. My heart hammers. The air changes. Cooler. Still. Dust and metal. A stairwell drops into dimness, steps narrow and steep. I glance back at the archive, at the faint glow of overhead lights, at the quiet hum of a building waking, then at him.

Who is this man? How does he know this place? What happens if we're caught? He's already descending, unhurried. I grip the railing and move. Each step creaks too loud. A thought hits, sharp and cold. We could be arrested for this. Riven doesn't seem to care. He doesn't look back. I keep close anyway. What else am I supposed to do?

Halfway down, he stops and gestures to a door set into the concrete wall. "Here," he says. The stairs continue downward, swallowed by complete darkness. A shiver runs through me. "What's down there?" I whisper.

He doesn't meet my eyes. "Just empty storage," he says at last. "I never go down there" He pushes the door open before I can ask more. Cold morning air hits my face. We step outside. For a second, I can't tell if my hands shake from the cold or from the thought of that black stairwell waiting below us. We slip into the alley, the city gray and half-asleep.

"I can't believe we almost got caught by a librarian," I say.

"Worse ways to go," he answers. I laugh, half nerves. At the bottom of the steps, he glances sideways. "You never did tell me your name."

I hesitate. "Rachel."

He repeats it, quiet. "Rachel." Something in his tone makes my ribs tighten. I shove my hands deep into my pockets and start to turn away. "Well. I should—"

"Get home?" he finishes.

"Yeah." It comes out thinner than I intend.

We walk a few steps together before the sidewalk splits. A quiet settles, not uncomfortable, just... heavy with everything neither of us is ready to ask. I pause. "Oh, and Riven?"

He stops, looks back over his shoulder. The early light hits him at a slant, turning the edges of him gold.

"Thank you," I say. For the archives. For believing me. For not running when I panicked. For all of it. Something flickers across his face, surprise first, then something softer, something unreadable. The smallest smile pulls at his mouth, there and gone. "Anytime, Rachel." We part at the corner. Early sun spills over the city like a secret.

By the time I make it back to the flat, the sky has gone from gray to gold, and my body feels like it's been running on fumes. Marin is already up, perched on the couch with coffee and her eyebrows halfway up her forehead.

"Where have you been?" she asks. "It's six thirty in the morning. You don't even stay out past ten."

"I was at the library."

She pauses mid-sip. "While it's closed?" Her tone turns mischievous immediately.

"Riven had a key."

"Oh, *Riven*, huh? First-name basis?" She leans forward. "So what happened? Spill."

"Nothing," I say, too tired for curiosity. "I just want to sleep."

She starts to protest, but I'm already down the hall, pulling my door shut. The latch clicks and I let out a breath I didn't realize I was holding. The memory of that dark stairwell flickers. Whatever is down there, it is better left in the dark. For now.

The shower fogs the mirror, softening the edges of everything, as if the world itself has blurred. Towel, pajamas, brush teeth, brush hair. The rhythm feels like safety. Sunlight bleeds through the curtains, too bright and loud. I pull them shut tightly until the room falls into a cool hush. The bed looks impossibly inviting. I crawl under the blanket and sink into the quiet.

For a moment, I only breathe. The rainbow shimmer is still there, faint but present. It halos the room in soft color, bending light around the edges of things. I should be alarmed. Maybe I was, at first. Now it just feels... normal. That's the part that scares me.

My mind drifts back to the library, the smell of dust and paper, the pages that shouldn't exist, the symbols that shouldn't have glowed. The circle with the three lines flashes behind my eyelids. It was carved into stone and drawn on coins and burned into memories. Three lines. A door. A key. *A vessel.*

Riven knew more than he said. I saw it in the way he looked at it, recognition, maybe even fear. I didn't push. I wanted out. Now I wish I had asked. He edges into my thoughts anyway. The way he moved, too calm for someone breaking into a locked building. The way his eyes caught the light. The way his hair seems tossled just right. He is handsome, though I would never admit it out loud. I don't have time for distractions, especially ones that look like him and ones that walk through locked rooms like they're merely suggestions.

I roll onto my side. My body is heavy, but my mind refuses to stop. It circles back to Dad, his voice, his laugh, the way he tapped the steering wheel to the radio. I miss him. More than I let myself say. Marin says grief needs a door, that pretending I'm fine makes it worse. Maybe she's right. Maybe mourning him is the only way to stop feeling like I'm unraveling.

I close my eyes and hold a good memory in place, Dad reading to me at night, pages turning, his voice low and steady.

I focus on that until the colors at the edge of my vision soften, melt together, and fade. Somewhere beneath the quiet, under skin and bone, something hums in time with my heartbeat. Sleep finds me before I can decide whether it's comforting or not.

Chapter 11

The world erupts before I can catch my breath. Smoke claws at the air, thick and choking, curling through the narrow lanes of a village I have never seen. Small houses, thatched roofs already catching fire as people run with buckets sloshing water over their hands. The ground trembles under bare feet and frantic shouts.

"Move. Get water."

Another voice, deeper and desperate, cries, "We're under attack!"

I turn, but everything is motion. Men, women, children, faces streaked with soot and fear. A woman stumbles past me, clutching a baby to her chest. The child's wails tangle with the roar of flames. Somewhere, a bell rings wildly, the sound cracked and frantic.

Overhead, the sky is alive with light. Bright streaks fall like stars, but when they hit, roofs burst into fire. It's raining fire. Not meteorites. Not debris. Ribbons of light, like the descriptions in my dad's notes, curling, twisting, singing as they fall. The sound is high and sharp, almost musical, and it makes my teeth ache.

I spin, trying to make sense of it, panic pressing against my ribs. Then I see her.

A small child stands alone in the middle of the street, hair tangled, cheeks streaked with tears and ash. Bare feet in the dirt. Everyone rushes past her, too consumed by the flames to notice, bodies splitting around her.

She's crying for someone, words lost in the noise. "Papa! Papa!"

"Hey!" I shout, pushing through the smoke toward her. My voice echoes strangely. "Hey, it's okay, don't stand there—"

A burning beam crashes nearby, sparks leaping across the dirt. Heat licks at my face. I flinch, shield my eyes, and when I look again, the child is gone.

"Wait—"

The world tilts. The air hums. Another flare rips the sky. For a split second I see it, the circle with three lines, burning in the clouds like a brand. The streaks of light curve toward it, drawn in.

Everything dissolves into white.

I jolt awake, heart pounding so hard it hurts. For a second, I don't know where I am. Fire, screaming, falling light still burn behind my eyes. The shadows of my room come into focus, familiar and somehow wrong. My lungs drag in air that tastes like sleep instead of smoke. A dream. At least, I think it was.

I roll onto my back and stare at the ceiling. My skin is damp with sweat. My pulse refuses to settle. The village felt too real, the smell, the heat, the sound of the singing light. And that circle again. It has to mean something. It's everywhere now, bleeding into memories and dreams and walls.

A loud metallic rattle sounds outside my door. I freeze. "Marin?" My voice sounds small. No answer. Another sound follows, the distinct scrape of a drawer slamming. Not the fridge. A drawer. Sharp, irritated, like someone rifling through our stuff. Every hair on my arms lifts.

I slip out of bed, heartbeat in my throat. My phone on the nightstand is dead, of course. I thumb the button uselessly, then set it down with shaking fingers. I open the door just enough to peer into the hall. Everything is still. Evening light leaks through the blinds in the living room, cutting the space into pale stripes. The sky outside is dimming into blue-gray; I must have slept through sunset.

Another noise, closer. A clatter. Something metal hitting tile. I yank down the nearest thing from the wall, a framed photo of me and Marin at the coast, cheeks windburned, laughing. Ridiculous weapon, but it's something to hold. The glass bites into my palm.

Step by step, I move down the hall as carefully as I can so I don't make any noise. The living room is empty. Marin's blanket is still thrown over the couch.

"Marin?" I try again, quieter. Silence answers.

I take another careful step. The floor creaks. Then I see it.

Something in the kitchen moves. At first, it looks like a shadow cast by the window, but it is too dense, too dark, shifting in a way shadows shouldn't. It clings to the air like smoke and yet doesn't rise. It has a human outline without a body. Smoke forced into shape, restless and seething. Edges blur and reform as if the light can't decide where it begins or ends. It yanks open the drawer where Marin keeps her sage and lighters, scattering them like it's hunting by instinct.

"Marin," I whisper, even though I know it is not her.

The shape stills. It turns. Or its head does. It's impossible to tell. Where a face should be is only deeper shadow. Cold races down my spine. My scream rips out before I can stop it. I hurl the picture frame. It shatters mid-air, glass exploding across the tile in a spray of glittering shards.

The shadow jerks back as if it was struck. For a heartbeat, the air around it ripples, and then it unravels, pulling itself apart. Threads of darkness twist, stretch thin, and vanish into the corners of the room. Within seconds, it's gone.

I stand shaking, staring at the mess and the glitter of broken glass. The air is thick, not recovered from whatever that was. The room smells faintly scorched. For a second I just stand there trembling. Afraid it might come back. Whatever "it" was. I finally let out a shaky breath, my knees nearly buckle. I crouch to start cleaning up the broken glass. The glass glitters like a hundred small mirrors, each catching the light. My hands won't steady, but doing anything is better than standing still with the memory.

A shadow that was not a shadow. Smoke that moved on its own. Looking for something.

I tell myself I imagined it. Overtired. Losing it. But the drawers hang open and the contents spill like a crime scene no one will believe. I grab the dustpan and sweep. The scrape of the broom is almost calming, grounding me to the sound of bristles on tile instead of my own pulse roaring in my ears. My thoughts drift to the dream, the fire, the circle, the way it is bleeding into real life. Maybe this is what losing your mind feels like. Slow, quiet, logical in the wrong places.

A hand lands on my shoulder.

I scream. The dustpan flies as I spin, nearly clocking Marin in the face. "Jesus, Rach," she yelps, stumbling back with her hands up. "It's me. Put the broom down, you psychopath."

I clutch my chest, breathing hard. "Don't sneak up on me." She takes in the disaster. "You're the one armed with cleaning supplies at eleven in the evening. Is this *Final Destination: Domestic Edition?*"

A half laugh, half sob escapes. "There was..." I stop. It will sound insane. "Someone was here."

Marin's expression softens, humor dimming. "Unless they are hiding under the fork pile, I think your someone left." She nudges an open drawer with her toe. "You sure you're not seeing things again, babe?" I want to say no. I know what I saw. The words die in my throat.

"Yeah," I say instead, sweeping the last shards. "Maybe I am."

She watches me, grin not quite reaching her eyes. "You sure you're okay?"

"I'm fine," I lie, tipping glass into the bin. My pulse has not slowed once. The flat feels off, like something is still here, watching from the edges of the room. I kneel to grab one last piece by the door. That's when I see it.

A small black mark above the baseboard near the front door. At first, I think it's soot from the frame. I lean closer. My stomach drops. The circle. Three lines. Burned into the paint.

"Marin," I whisper. She crouches beside me. "What the hell is that?"

"I don't know." I hover my fingers above it. The edges are singed, as if seared with heat. Tiny cracks spider out from the lines. "It was in my dream. And at the library."

She shivers, rubbing her arms. "Okay. You're officially creeping me out."

"I'm serious. Riven showed me old books. Symbols like this. One glowed when we touched it."

"Glowed? Like, glowed glowed?"

"Yes." I catch myself, breath shuddering. "Sorry. It's just... this isn't random. It's connected. To my dad. To what he was researching. Maybe even to why he—" I stop, the word died snagging on the tip of my tongue. Marin's teasing drops away completely. She looks at the mark again, jaw tight. "I hate that thing."

"Same," I say, pushing hair out of my face. "But I need to know what it means. I think Riven knows more than he told me."

"So call him."

"I can't. We didn't swap numbers."

Marin groans. "Of course you didn't. Mystery hot library guy who breaks into buildings and knows ancient symbols, and you didn't think, 'Hey, let's trade info in case a shadow demon breaks in later'?"

"Marin."

"Right. Humor. Coping." She rubs her arms again. "So what now?"

I look at the mark. The edges faintly smoke, as if still alive, as if the wall itself is exhaling. "Now," I say, "I find Riven."

By morning, I am running on three hours of sleep and too much caffeine. The air outside still smells like smoke, even though Marin swears it's my imagination. She spent half the night waving sage like an exorcist while I sanded the burned mark until my hands cramped. The paint is uneven. The flat reeks of sage and fresh paint. I have no answers.

I pull my jacket tight and start walking. The city feels different. Too bright. Too loud. The bus brakes hiss louder than usual, and every car horn feels aimed at me. People rush past with coffee and phones, living normal lives while I chase a ghost. I start at the library. Nothing.

The doors are open, but no staff recognize his name. Tall, dark hair, too calm, weird eyes. Heads shake. No one by that description works here. No one remembers seeing him in the archives. My skin crawls.

Next, I check the coffee shop where I ran into him before. I sit by the window for nearly an hour, pretending to read, eyes flicking up at every dark-haired stranger. Waiting for him to stroll in with that casual *fancy seeing you here*. He does not.

By noon, my patience is gone. "Of course," I mutter, stepping back into the sun. "The one time I want him to appear, he's allergic to being found." I keep walking, looping through streets I barely remember choosing. My thoughts circle the same things. The dream. The fire. The mark on my wall. My father's words.

When the moon drowns in daylight, you'll find the door.

The door. The symbol. The lights. It has to connect. Maybe I'm looking in the wrong place. Maybe this isn't just history. Maybe it's stranger. If it's tied to the sky, maybe I need someone who reads the sky. An astrologer. Or one of the crystal-shop mystics Marin mocks.

Ridiculous. But then, so is everything else. I look. A crystal store. A psychic sign. Anything. I find three on the main stretch. One closed. One boarded up. One that looks like it hasn't been dusted since the seventies. I stand outside the last one, staring at shelves of stones and pendulums and incense, and wonder if I have officially lost my mind.

The day slips away, one lead dissolving into nothing after another. Every corner I turn, I half expect Riven to appear, smirking. He never does. By dusk, my feet ache. I walk home with the faint hope he'll be leaning on the stairwell with that smug half grin. Inside, the flat is empty. Marin is out. A note on the counter reads, *Don't burn the place down. xo.*

I drop the note and lean against the counter. The same image loops in my head: the circle and three lines, my father's voice carried forward by time, by dreams, by symbols burned into paint.

The next morning, I am done waiting. If Riven won't find me, I'll find answers another way. An hour of digging through university directories turns up a name that makes me stop.

Professor Elias Harland, *Astronomy and Folklore Studies,* Publications are sparse, but one title jumps out: *Celestial Phenomena in Folklore and Preternatural Accounts.* Close enough.

Campus is a blur of movement. Students crisscross the quad with coffee and backpacks. The air hums with conversation and car horns. The smell of espresso and wet leave fills the air. Once upon a time, that would have been comforting. Not today. Today I feel too tired, and aware that the wrong question could sound unhinged.

I have a building and a room number scrawled on paper. Aldridge Hall, Room 8H. The university seems designed by someone who hated logic. Every hallway leads to three more, each less labeled than the last. Two students near a vending machine point me down a tree-lined path. "Old brick building past the fountain."

Aldridge Hall looks like it has stood since the dawn of time. Ivy climbs its walls. Stained glass catches pale light, fragments of color scattered across the stone floor inside. The steps creak with history.

Inside, it's quieter, the kind of quiet that hums with fluorescent and the faint whisper of turning pages behind closed doors. Dust hangs in the beams of light appearing suspended by galaxies. Room 8H hides in the far corner of the third floor. The plaque reads *E. Harland, PhD*, half the letters peeled away. I hesitate with my hand on the knob. If this man laughs at me, I'll deserve it.

I push the door open.

The room smells of old paper and stale coffee. It's barely big enough for a desk, two chairs, and the explosion of clutter across every surface. Stacks of books lean toward collapse. Charts of constellations and planetary alignments are taped to the walls, layered with pages of symbols and scribbles. A string of fairy lights droops from the ceiling, half burned out, giving the place a strange, cozy apocalyptic vibe.

"Hello," I call, stepping carefully between piles. "Professor Harland?" No answer.

I move closer to the desk. Notes cover every inch. Looping script, numbers, diagrams, fragments of something larger. Most of it makes no sense, references to meteor showers, myth cycles, something about "recurring celestial thresholds." Then I see it.

A sketch pinned under a stack. Faint pencil lines form a familiar shape. A circle. Three straight lines. My pulse jumps. I reach for it, easing it free without disturbing the rest, but the papers snag under a heavy book. I tug.

The entire stack avalanches. Books slam to the floor. Papers whirl like startled birds, fluttering around me in a storm of ink and edges.

"Oh no, no, no," I whisper, scrambling to gather them, heart pounding. "Shit—"

I'm halfway through stacking when a deep voice behind me, calm and amused, says, "Can I help you?"

Chapter 12

I freeze mid-reach, a handful of papers still clutched to my chest. Slowly I turn. A man stands in the doorway, older, maybe late fifties or early sixties, with a wild kind of energy about him. His shirt is untucked, one sleeve rolled higher than the other, and there are dark ink smudges on his fingers... and a few on his shirt too. His graying hair looks as if it's been through a wind tunnel or a very long night, and the thick glasses perched on his nose magnify eyes that are sharp, curious, and just a little unhinged.

He doesn't look like someone who's slept in the last day or three. Or someone who even believes in the concept of "bedtime." For a second, I seriously consider putting the papers down and backing slowly out of the room. Every university has that professor, the one the students whisper about, the one who lectures on conspiracy theories during faculty meetings and spends office hours arguing with ghosts.

And I've clearly found him.

I open my mouth, fumbling for some kind of apology, when he tilts his head slightly, studying me like I'm an equation he hasn't seen before.

"Interesting," he murmurs. "You've got a refractive edge to you."

I blink. "My—what?"

He steps further into the room, setting down the mug in his hand. "Your light," he repeats, squinting at me through those enormous lenses. "It hums differently. Most people's energy is muddy, predictable. Yours is... refracting."

Refracting. Like the rainbow haze that's been hovering at the edge of my vision. Like the shimmer around other people's edges that no one else seems to notice. Okay, so definitely that professor.

I hesitate, torn between bolting for the door and staying long enough to ask the questions that have been clawing at my brain since last night. Because if anyone might have answers about the symbol, the lights, any of it, it's probably the eccentric man with ink stains and a coffee mug that's older than the moon.

I straighten, clutching the stack of papers a little tighter. "You're Professor Harland, right?"

He glances up, distracted, as if remembering who he's supposed to be. "That's what they call me, yes." His mouth quirks. "Depends who you ask."

Something about the way he says it is half joke, half truth, which makes me think maybe I can ask. I take a breath, trying to figure out where to start. "Okay, this is going to sound insane," I warn, "but I'm looking for information on a symbol."

Professor Harland perks up immediately, sliding behind his cluttered desk like a crow drawn to something shiny. "Insanity and information are my two favorite things," he says, waving a hand. "Go on."

I move closer, setting down the handful of papers I'm still clutching. "It's a circle. With three straight lines cutting through it. I've seen it twice now, one a picture of it carved into stone in a book I found at the city library and again..." I hesitate, "...burned into my wall this morning."

That gets his attention.

He stills, eyes narrowing slightly behind his huge lenses. The playful edge drains from his face, leaving something keen and alert. "Burned, you say?"

"Yeah. Like scorched into the paint." My voice sounds small even to me.

He nods slowly, muttering something under his breath I can't quite catch, something that sounds a lot like "too soon." Then he rummages through a nearby stack of books, pulling out one that looks crumbled. The cover is cracked leather, the spine patched with tape.

He flips through it with surprising precision, ink-stained fingers leaving faint smudges on the yellowed pages. "That symbol," he murmurs, "appears in several celestial manuscripts. Mostly European, some older. It's been called a trinity sigil, though the name changes depending on the source." He taps the edge of the page. "It's often linked to reports of... the Falling." My skin prickles.

"The Falling." The word sounds too familiar. "My dad mentioned that. In his notes."

He looks up sharply. "Did he, now?"

I swallow. "I found some of his research. Star charts. Weird notes about a meteor storm that wasn't a meteor storm. He called it 'The Falling.'"

Harland's gaze sharpens even more, "The Falling," he says, more carefully now. "A recorded event, though 'recorded' might be generous. Most historians dismiss it as myth. Accounts date back centuries, describing lights descending from the heavens. Some call them stars, some call them fire, others... divine punishment."

A faint chill crawls up my arms. "I had a dream about that, I think. People running, screaming, houses burning. There were lights falling from the sky." He studies me with that same unnervingly focused gaze, the kind that makes you feel someone is peeling back layers you didn't know you had. "Dreams often carry echoes," he says. "Sometimes echoes of memory, sometimes of lineage."

I frown. "What's that supposed to mean?"

He doesn't answer directly. Of course he doesn't. Instead, he flips another page, tapping a finger against an old illustration, villagers standing under a sky streaked with light. The drawing looks too close to what I saw for comfort. "Descriptions vary. Some say the Falling was a storm with lightning, perhaps a meteor shower. Others claim it was something darker: spirits cast out, their descent burning the homes of the wicked. A few texts say that those who stood beneath the Falling either perished instantly... or were forever changed by it."

"Changed how?"

He shrugs one shoulder, but his expression stays intent. "Depends which story you believe. Some say they became vessels—half in this world, half in another. Others say they were marked. Touched by whatever force fell from the sky."

He pauses, eyes flicking up to me. "And those marks sometimes manifest as light. Or as sight."

My stomach knots. "Sight?"

"Seeing what others cannot." He gestures vaguely at the space around my head. "Light where others see air. Echoes where others see absence. Threads where others see nothing at all."

I exhale shakily. "You think that's what's happening to me? That I'm seeing... echoes?"

He smiles faintly, but it's not comforting. "I think," he says carefully, "that whatever you saw—whatever you are seeing—is older than you realize. And I think that symbol is a door you've already started to open."

I stare at him, my heart beating unevenly. "A door to what?"

But he just leans back in his chair, the faintest spark of curiosity lighting his tired eyes. "That," he says, "is the question, isn't it?"

I grip the edge of the desk, knuckles whitening. "If this is real—if the Falling, the symbol, all of it is real—why don't people talk about it? Why isn't it in, I don't know, documentaries or textbooks or something?"

"Oh, some have tried," he says lightly. "They're usually labeled zealots. Or madmen. Or they vanish, and the archives list their work as 'misplaced.' History is written by the survivors, Ms...?"

"Rachel," I say automatically.

"Rachel," he repeats, "History is written by the survivors," he goes on, "but it's edited by the frightened. People prefer their stars inert and their light obedient. The Falling was neither."

My brain snags on something else. "You keep saying *vessels.* Vessels of what?"

He tilts his head, studying me again. "Tell me," he says softly. "When did you first notice it? The light?"

I think of my dad in the park. The glow under my hands. The way it swallowed him and left nothing behind. The dust in his office, shimmering like captured stars. The glow in the library. The veins in my wrists lit from beneath like filaments.

"I... I don't know," I lie.

He smiles like he knows better. "Of course you don't." He reaches under a stack and pulls out another page, a careful ink drawing of the circle and lines, surrounded by smaller symbols. "The oldest sources call it a threshold sign. A warning. Or an invitation. The language is... ambiguous."

"Great," I mutter.

Harland lets out a short, dry laugh. "Ambiguity is the universe's favorite joke." He hesitates, then adds, "Do you have any family with a history of... unusual perception? Unexplained events? Stories that were never quite explained but always politely ignored?"

My dad's face flashes behind my eyes. The dream of him standing between me and the three figures in black. The way his voice in the dream had sounded.

"Mm." He sips his coffee, grimaces, and sets it down again. "Then I would suggest you read. Carefully. And pay attention to what pulls at you. The Falling is not just an event, Rachel. For some people, it is a cycle."

"A cycle," I repeat.

"Yes. It returns in different forms, in different skies." His gaze doesn't leave my face. "Sometimes it returns through bloodlines." A cold thread winds down my spine.

He looks away, rummaging through the chaos on his desk until he finds a leather-bound volume. It's small, thick, the edges of the pages darkened with age. He holds it out to me.

"This," he says, "was given to me by someone who claimed their ancestor stood beneath the Falling and lived to write about it. I doubt the claim, but the account is... interesting."

I take it carefully. The leather is warm. It smells like dust and candle wax, like old churches and older secrets.

"I can borrow this?" I ask, surprised.

He waves a hand. "Bring it back tomorrow. Same time. If it reacts, I need to know exactly how." I stare. "I'm sorry—if the what starts to what?"

Harland smiles, just a little. "You'll see. Or you won't. Don't read it all at once. If you start hearing a hum or seeing the margins shift, stop." Before I can ask what that's supposed to mean, he's already turned back to his notes, muttering about "refracted signatures" and "lineage echoes".

By the time I leave the professor's office, my head's spinning. I have more questions than when I walked in. The sun's sinking low as I make my way back through the city, the light turning everything gold and soft. Late-afternoon warmth clings to the buildings, but a chill is threaded through it.

I walk without really watching where I'm going, the book pressed against my chest. I flip it open as I go, careful with the fragile pages. The handwriting is cramped and slanted, the ink faded to brown. Strange diagrams fill the margins, circles, stars, constellations that don't exist on any chart I've seen. Lines that cross each other in patterns that make my eyes ache.

One section catches my eye, a heading written in Latin and half-faded: *De Caelo Cadentium—Of Those Who Fell from the Sky.* My brain's buzzing with it all, the professor's words, the dream, my dad's message. Every piece feels connected, but the lines don't make sense yet. It's like holding a puzzle where half the pieces are invisible.

I turn a corner—

—and slam straight into someone. Hard.

The book nearly flies out of my hands.

"Sorry, I—" I start, then look up and feel my stomach drop.

Of course. Riven.

He stands there like the universe is in on some private joke, dark hair a little messy, that same unreadable half-smile tugging at his mouth. His eyes flick once to the book, then back to my face. "Oh," I say flatly. "You again."

He raises an eyebrow. "You sound thrilled."

I huff, tucking the book protectively against my chest. "You know, you're one hard person to track down."

His smile widens, lazy and infuriating. "Most people would take the hint."

"Well, lucky for you, I'm not most people."

"I'm starting to notice that." His gaze drops briefly to the book in my hands. His gaze flicks past me, toward the building I just left."You were in Aldridge Hall," he says. Not a question. "Harland's handwriting. He's still giving that one out to anyone who asks questions he shouldn't answer?"

I blink. "Wait—you *know* him?"

"He wrote a paper once that nearly got him erased from the archives." Something flickers across his face, too quick to catch. He takes a step closer, eyes flicking up to meet mine. "Though if you're reading that, I'm guessing you've already crossed something else."

The way he says it makes my skin prickle.

I tighten my grip on the book. "You know what the Falling really is, don't you?"

He doesn't reply, just gives that same half-smile again, softer this time, like he knows exactly how deep I'm in and how much deeper it goes. There's no surprise in his eyes. Only recognition.

"How do you—" I start, then stop myself. "You knew about the symbol. You knew about the archives. You knew about the back stairwell. And now you know Harland and his doomsday scrapbook. How long have you been… watching this?"

"Watching this?" he asks lightly. "Not as long as you're imagining."

"That's not comforting."

"Wasn't meant to be." But his tone is gentle, somehow. Riven watches me for a moment, as if deciding whether I'm ready for whatever he's about to say. Then he nods toward the street. "Come on. There's something I want to show you."

I hesitate. "That's not creepy at all."

He smirks. "If I wanted to hurt you, you wouldn't still be holding that book."

"Awesome," I mutter, but the words lose some of their bite.

Because the truth is, for all the ways he unnerves me, I don't feel unsafe with him. Confused, irritated, pulled toward him like a moth toward a questionable porch light, but not unsafe.

"You keep showing up," I say. "Every time something… happens. Why?" He studies me like Harland did, but softer. "Because doors don't open quietly, Rachel. And when one finally starts to move, it tends to shake more than one world." My throat goes dry. "You really are allergic to straightforward answers, aren't you?"

"You'd be bored if I were straightforward."

"Try me."

He just smiles, turns, and starts walking. I stand there for half a second, city noise pressing in around me, book heavy in my hands and Harland's words echoing in my head.

The symbol is a door you've already started to open. My dad's voice layers over it. *When the moon drowns in daylight, you'll find the door.* The circle and lines burn behind my eyes.

"Fine," I say under my breath, and fall into step beside him.

I follow anyway.

Chapter 13

We walk through the city in silence for a while, weaving down side streets and quieter roads until the traffic thins and the buildings turn to stone instead of glass, ivy climbing their faces like a second skin. Shopfronts give way to older façades with tall, narrow windows and soot-streaked cornices. The light is fading, and the chill evening air smells of rain and exhaust.

After a few blocks, Riven finally speaks. "You have read about the Falling by now, right?"

"Enough to know no one agrees on what it actually was," I say.

He nods. "That's because most accounts are fragments. Myths, oral stories, scraps of half-burned journals." His voice is even, like he's told this story before, but his eyes stay alert, scanning the street. "Everyone described the same event differently. Fire from the sky, spirits cast down, stars breaking apart. But the common thread is this: wherever those lights touched, something changed."

"Changed how?"

"That's where it gets vague," he admits. "Some records say the light killed everything it hit. Others claim it powered people, like the energy didn't destroy, it rewired. The ancient texts call them the Falling Ones. People who survived what should've been impossible."

I glance at him. "And you think this happened here? In this city?"

"Here and somewhere else." He gestures ahead. "Three locations line up with the earliest reports. One is hundreds of miles away. The other two are right here in the city."

We turn down a narrow lane between two warehouses, the kind of place that looks forgotten by time and city planning. The air feels heavier here, quieter. A bike clatters past at the far end and the echo dies faster than it should. He stops at a small iron gate half hidden behind an overgrown hedge, the metal flaking with rust. From the sidewalk, it looks like nothing, just another sealed-off courtyard the city hasn't bothered to develop.

"This used to be part of the old observatory," he says, pushing the gate open. The hinges groan in protest. "Back when the city still had clear skies." The gate creaks shut behind us with a soft thud.

Inside, the path winds through crumbling stone arches and the remnants of a courtyard. Empty plinths squat where instruments must have been bolted once. The bones of a rusted mount reach for the sky like a skeletal arm. Moss crawls over everything. The air smells old. The thought jars me. We're outside, open to the wind. How can open air smell old? It's a scent I know from basements and sealed boxes. Centuries pressed into the breeze.

I slow without meaning to. The quiet is strange here, as if the city forgot this place exists. A gull cries somewhere beyond the dome of trees and even that arrives dull, as if cushioned.

Riven walks a few paces ahead and the hairs on my arms

rise. I have the sudden, foolish impression that the space recognizes him. He is careful with where he steps, not tentative, he knows the pattern and is fitting himself to it.

"Been here a lot?" I ask.

"Once or twice," he says. But the way he says it sounds like more. Near the far wall, shallow grooves mark the stone. At first I assume they're cracks, but then I see the shape repeating, softened by time. Circles scored into the face of the rock, each with three straight lines cut through. Most are no bigger than a coin. One, near the ground, is the size of a plate. My chest tightens.

"They're easier to notice once you know what you're looking for," he says. He does not touch the carvings. He looks at them the way you look at a grave or a warning sign.

We step into the center of the courtyard. The air shifts. A faint tang of ozone rides the breeze and coats my tongue.

Riven stops. There, near the middle, a ring of dark scorch marks stains the stone in a perfect circle, almost black against the pale slabs. It's not just a random burn; it's too precise, edges too clean in some places.

My heart stutters. "What is this?"

"This," he says quietly, "is where it supposedly happened. The first Falling recorded in this region." I crouch and trace a finger near the edge. The stone is colder here. Under my skin there is a slow pulse, a moth-wing flutter I can't name. The smell is the air from my dream. Burnt thatch. Lightning. A thin metallic taste at the back of my tongue.

Riven watches me carefully. "No one knows exactly what it was. Maybe lightning. Maybe divine punishment. Maybe something not meant for this world. But it left traces."

"Traces?" I look up at him.

"Energy. Residual fields. People feel it when they stand here. Some say it wakes something up."

I snort before I can stop myself. "That sounds like the kind of thing they print on tourist brochures."

One corner of his mouth twitches.

"Seriously," I continue, standing. "People love haunted places. You put an old ruin in front of them and suddenly every cold breeze is a ghost and every weird feeling is destiny."

"You don't believe any of it."

"I believe people convince themselves of things all the time."

The words come easily, but the confidence behind them doesn't. The air feels heavier than it should. Every breath tastes faintly metallic. My pulse keeps stumbling for reasons I can't explain.

Riven's gaze drifts to the blackened circle. "And what do you believe is causing that?"

"Causing what?"

"The way you're staring at the ground like it's talking to you."

Heat crawls up my neck.

"I'm not staring."

"You haven't looked away since we walked in."

I force my eyes from the scorch marks. Immediately I wish I hadn't. The pressure in my chest sharpens, as if something inside me notices the movement and strains against it.

I swallow hard.

"Coincidence," I mutter.

"Of course."

Before he can warn me, I step into the ring. The wind stirs, cold and soft, bringing the ozone smell again. A strand of hair lifts from my cheek and settles. Beneath my feet, the stone hums so gently I could pretend I imagined it. The scorch ring briefly beads with frost. Almost like it's remembering something. Or recognizing someone.

My skin prickles. "Normal people come here and what, get a headache?" I ask, trying for flippant. "Some get dizzy," he says. "Some feel nothing. Some have visions. Once in a while, someone like you steps inside the ring and the place... pays attention."

The longer I stand inside the circle, the stranger the air feels. It's thick, almost humming under my skin.

My chest tightens. The pressure gathers behind my eyes and for a beat the courtyard blurs at the edges. In the slip of vision, the scorched ring brightens, with attention as if the space itself is leaning in.

A whisper rides the hum. Not words. A cadence I know anyway. My father's last breath. *When the moon drowns in daylight...*

"No," I tell myself, out loud, quiet and shaky. "Not here." Something about this place is wrong.I feel like I'm being watched by something that does not blink. Riven has not moved in several seconds. His hands are open at his sides, fingers loose. He's waiting for me to bold or for something that might wake inside me.

"You feel it, don't you?" he asks softly.

"I feel like I'm about to vibrate out of my skin," I say. It comes out thinner than I'd like. "And like if I stay here one minute longer, something's going to... notice."

"Something already has," he says, and the honesty in it makes the back of my neck go cold. I straighten and rub my arms, trying to shake off the sensation crawling over my skin.

"Okay," I say, a little too brisk. "That is fascinating. And creepy. And I think I've hit my quota for supernatural history tours today."

His mouth twitches, almost a smile, as if he's been waiting for me to ask to leave. "Fair enough." He nods toward the gate and turns away from the circle. I don't need to be told twice. I step out of the ring a little too quickly, tension humming in my calves like they're ready to run. The moment my foot hits the stone beyond the scorch marks, the pressure eases a fraction. Not Gone. Riven looks briefly relieved when I step out of the ring.

I follow him back through the arches, trying not to look over my shoulder even though every instinct says someone or something is watching us from inside those ruins.

The observatory falls behind us. With every step the city returns. A bus sighs at a stop. A siren yawns awake a few streets over. A dog barks. I tell myself the pressure in my chest loosens because of the distance. Not because something is letting me go.

Once we're back on the main road, I finally exhale. The tension doesn't leave my shoulders, but it drops enough that I can think again.

"So," I say, breaking the quiet, "you mentioned another location?" He glances at me sidelong. "Another one like this, North, near the coast. Most of the original records trace back there."

"Then that's where I want to go next."

"You don't waste time, do you?"

"Not when people are breaking into my flat and burning hieroglyphs into the wall."

That earns a faint grin. "Fair enough." He considers.

"Tomorrow then. I'll pick you up early."

"I can swap my shift," I say, even though I don't know how yet. "But define early," I say, suspicion creeping back.

"Before sunrise."

I groan. "Perfect. My favorite hour to chase ancient death energy."

"I'll bring coffee."

"Make it strong."

"Noted."

We part at the corner. He goes one way, I go the other, but the feeling of being watched doesn't peel off with him. Every shadow feels a little too sharp, every sound stretched thin. I try to tell myself it is nerves. Exhaustion. Adrenaline that has nowhere to land.

By the time I reach my building, the back of my neck is prickling like static. Streetlights buzz overhead. One flickers as I pass, then steadies, then brightens again, too white for a breath.

I fumble for my keys and pause because the air around me shifts the way it did in the courtyard, pressure moving sideways, like a tide change. The rainbow haze edges into my vision, not an after image anymore, but something present now, brighter and closer than before. It gathers at the corner of my eye and curls, slow and curious, learning the shape of me.

Across the street, a window light flares and dims as if in answer. Another follows, farther down. A thin scent of ozone threads the air again. For a heartbeat I think I hear the quiet cadence from the circle again, the almost words settling at the edge of hearing.

My key hovers inches from the lock. "It's nothing," I

whisper. "It's just me. It's just stress." The haze does not fade. It holds its place, patient and sure, as if it has decided it will be there whether I see it or not.

Chapter 14

I wake up before my alarm, which feels like some sort of cosmic joke. The sky outside is still gray, heavy with the kind of silence that only exists before sunrise. For a minute, I just lie there staring at the ceiling, wondering what kind of person actually agrees to meet a mysterious, maybe criminal man at an hour when even the birds are still asleep.

Apparently, me.

I push the blanket off and pad to the bathroom, the tile cold under my feet. The light flickers when I flip the switch, and for one horrifying second I think the rainbow haze is back, but it's just the bad wiring. Great. Add "haunted electricity" to the growing list of my problems.

I turn on the tap, splash my face, and try to convince myself I'm fine. Just another day. Just another weird adventure involving ancient cosmic symbols and a man who smells like danger and arrogance. I brush my teeth, then start brushing my hair, and that's when it happens, the slow, creeping realization that I'm actually trying to look nice.

I freeze mid-stroke, staring at myself in the mirror.

No. Absolutely not.

This isn't a date. This is an investigation. A fact-finding mission. A "please explain why supernatural graffiti is appearing in my flat" situation. Still... my reflection doesn't look half bad.

My hair's behaving for once, falling in something that almost resembles intentional waves. My skin looks a little brighter, like the faint light under it has decided to work with me instead of against me. My eyes are still ringed with tiredness, but they also look... sharper. Awake in a way that has nothing to do with sleep.

I sigh, rummaging through my drawer until I find a bit of concealer. Just enough to cover the sleep deprivation. And maybe a touch of mascara. Not for him, obviously. Just so I don't look like I crawled out of the abyss.

Ten minutes later, I'm standing there debating over which shirt looks more like "competent adult researcher" and less like "please kidnap me, mysterious stranger." Why am I even doing this?

Riven is a smart-ass. A walking contradiction with a smirk that could probably cause property damage. He's cryptic, moody, perpetually half in shadow. But then there's the other thing. Those piercing blue eyes. The dark, disheveled hair. That quiet way he studies me, like he's cataloging every reaction, every flinch, filing them away for later.

Get it together, Rachel.

He's bad news. He radiates bad news energy. Like one of those "do not touch, will explode" warning labels, but in human form. I tug my jacket on, ignoring the flutter of nerves twisting in my stomach. "It's not a date," I mutter to my reflection. "It's field research. In possibly cursed ruins. With someone who probably has a secret lair."

The mirror offers no argument. Once I'm finished getting ready, I make my way into the kitchen. Marin's door is closed, no surprise there. She could sleep through the apocalypse, and honestly, after the week we've had, I wouldn't blame her for trying.

I flick on the coffee maker, the low hum filling the silence. It's barely five a.m., but sleep wasn't happening. Every time I closed my eyes, I saw flashes of that scorched stone circle, the faint shimmer of light that seemed to move beneath it. I can still feel it, humming just below awareness, waiting for the right signal.

The smell of coffee starts to fill the air, rich and grounding. I wrap my hands around the mug when it's done, letting the warmth soak into my fingers. For a few quiet minutes, I just stand there, staring out the kitchen window.

The city's still half-asleep, streetlights blinking out one by one as the horizon blushes pale gold. A lone bus hisses at the corner. A cyclist glides past with their hood up, a ghost in neon. But even in the stillness, I can't shake the feeling of being watched.

It's faint, eyes on the back of my neck, there and gone in the same breath. Maybe it's paranoia. Maybe it's whatever residue that place left behind. Either way, it has me jumpy enough that I keep glancing over my shoulder, half expecting to see the shadow-thing from the kitchen standing behind me.

I take a long sip of coffee, trying to steady myself. What if today brings answers? What if Riven's right, and that second site really is connected to the Falling, to the symbol, to my father's riddle?

When the moon drowns in daylight, you'll find the door.

The words loop through my head again, every syllable heavier now that I've seen what's out there. Maybe this next place holds the key. Maybe it'll finally make sense of everything, the dreams, the mark, the strange pull I keep feeling toward all of it, a tide I can't see but can't fight. Or maybe it'll just open more doors I can't close.

I drain the rest of my coffee and set the mug in the sink, glancing once more toward Marin's door before heading to grab my jacket. The sky outside is just starting to lighten when my phone buzzes with a message from Riven:

Outside. Don't keep me waiting, sunshine.

I roll my eyes, muttering under my breath, "You're lucky I've already had caffeine." I grab my bag and head for the door. For a second I just stand there, keys in hand, the flat still and familiar behind me.

I lock the door and tell myself it's just another day. The air outside is crisp, the kind that nips at your skin and wakes you up faster than caffeine. I tug my jacket tighter as I step out, blinking against the early light, and then stop short.

Parked at the curb is a car that looks like it drove straight out of a spy movie: sleek, black, and expensive enough that I'm afraid to breathe near it. The kind of car that definitely doesn't belong to someone who breaks into libraries for fun. And leaning against it, looking infuriatingly relaxed, is Riven.

Of course.

He's in a dark coat, dark jeans that fit just right on him, hair still that perfectly disheveled mess. He straightens when he sees me, that familiar, smug little smile tugging at his mouth, eyes flicking over me in a way that feels like a scan rather than a flirt.

I blink between him and the car. "Okay," I say slowly. "This is... not what I expected."

He cocks an eyebrow. "You thought I took the bus?"

"Honestly? Yeah, kinda."

He grins, unapologetic. "I like to keep people guessing."

I circle the front of the car, muttering, "Guessing's one word for it," before sliding into the passenger seat. The leather is buttery soft, the door closes with a low, expensive thud.

When I glance over, he's still smiling, clearly enjoying my discomfort.

"What?" I ask.

"Nothing," he says, flicking the ignition. The car hums to life, dashboard lighting up. A faint, modern purr at odds with how old everything about him feels.

I arch an eyebrow. "Didn't want to open the door for me? Chivalry really is dead."

He glances sideways, amusement flickering in his eyes. "You got in just fine on your own. I'd hate to insult your independence."

"Wow," I say dryly. "You're a real gentleman."

"Never claimed to be one."

Before I can fire back, he throws the car into gear. The tires grip the road and we lurch forward, hard. My seatbelt's still in my hand.

"Riven!" I shout, fumbling to click it in as the city blurs past. "A little warning would be nice!" He just smirks, eyes fixed on the road. "Where's the fun in that?" He notices I haven't clicked my seatbelt and says nothing, but slows until I click it into place. I sink back against the seat, gripping the handle on the door. "You're an ass," I mutter.

"Probably," he says easily. "But I'm the ass who's about to show you something worth waking up early for." I roll my eyes, pretending not to notice the way my pulse jumps anyway.

We drive for what feels like hours. The city fades fast behind us, gray buildings giving way to empty stretches of road that twist through open fields and low hills. Mist pools low in the ditches, pale ribbons the headlights cut through. The kind of morning that feels half-real, half-dream. The air smells of dew and wet earth, faintly metallic, the promise of the sea somewhere ahead.

Riven barely says a word. He drives, one hand loose on the wheel, eyes fixed ahead, expression unreadable. I sip the last of my coffee and glance sideways at him. "So," I say, breaking the silence, "since we're apparently driving into the middle of nowhere together, maybe we should talk about something normal."

He hums, not looking away from the road. "Normal's overrated."

"Humor me."

That earns a faint smirk. "You want small talk."

"I want to make sure you're not an escaped convict," I say.

He chuckles under his breath, low and warm. "Fair point."

"Do you ever tell anyone anything about yourself," I press, "or do you just collect other people's secrets for fun?"

He finally glances my way, eyes bright against the shifting light. "I don't collect secrets. They just tend to find me."

"That's not an answer." He exhales through his nose, fingers tapping the steering wheel. "Family's... complicated."

"Whose isn't?" I ask. "Parents? Siblings? Some mysterious backstory that explains your brooding?"

He shoots me a look, "You're persistent."

"I'm a woman with trust issues being driven into the countryside by a man who talks like a riddle," I say sweetly. "You can't blame me for asking."

A hint of amusement flickers at the corner of his mouth. "My family's old," he says finally. "The kind of old that doesn't show up in public records."

"That's... not unsettling at all."

"It's not meant to be." His tone softens, distant. "They were scholars once. People who studied what others tried to forget. Some still do."

I tilt my head. "And you? You follow in the family business?"

He shrugs, eyes back on the road. "Sort of. I help people find things that were never really lost."

"That's cryptic," I say, crossing my arms.

"You asked."

I roll my eyes. "And here I was hoping for something normal, like 'I work in IT' or 'I make artisanal candles.'"

He huffs a quiet laugh. "Do I look like someone who makes candles?"

"You look like someone who sets them on fire."

That earns a real laugh this time, low, rough, and too easy on the ears. For a moment, the tension between us softens, replaced by comfort, almost.

The road stretches on, winding between cliffs and sparse forest. Neither of us speaks for a while, and the silence feels heavier now. Questions sit on the tip of my tongue but fade as soon as my lips form the words.

The hum of the tires fills the space between us. The landscape shifts, rolling fields giving way to winding coastal roads, the sea occasionally flashing silver through the trees. Sunlight filters through the windshield, and for a heartbeat I think I see a flicker of color in the glass, a shimmer, faint and fleeting. But when I blink, it's gone.

Riven glances at me. "You asked about my family," he says quietly. "What about yours?"

I blink, caught off guard. "Mine?"

He nods, still watching the road. "Seems fair."

I hesitate, fingers tightening around my empty coffee cup. "My dad," I start, then stop. The truth splits in two, cemetery stone and blood in my hands, both wrong, both right. "He—he died recently. In my arms."

The words come out too easily, muscle memory. But the moment they're in the air, something twists in my chest, a flicker of wrongness. "Wait," I say quickly, frowning. "That's not... that's not what happened."

Riven's head tilts slightly, though he doesn't interrupt. His gaze stays on the road.

"He died a few years ago," I correct, forcing a small laugh. "Sorry. I've been having weird dreams lately, feels like I can't tell what's memory and what's... something else."

The cemetery date slams into my mind. He doesn't press. Just gives a slow nod, the kind that somehow says *I heard you* without asking for more.

"My mom died when I was born," I continue, my voice softening. "So it was just Dad and me. No siblings. He was... everything, really."

Riven glances over briefly, expression unreadable.

"I have a best friend, though," I add quickly, trying to fill the air. "Marin. She's basically my sister. We've lived together for years. She's the loud one, the realist, the one who thinks I attract every kind of chaos like a magnet."

A small smile tugs at his mouth. "Sounds like she's not wrong."

"Yeah, well." I shrug. "She's earned the right to say it."

For a moment, it's just quiet again, the rhythmic hum of the car, the faint rush of wind outside. The conversation feels fragile.

Riven's voice breaks the silence, low and steady. "I'm sorry about your father."

I nod, swallowing the sudden lump in my throat. "Thank you."

He doesn't say anything else, and somehow, that's better. No hollow comfort, no awkward sympathy. Just presence. I turn to look out the window, the horizon stretching wide and endless ahead of us. The world feels strange, something's shifting beneath the surface, quiet but inevitable.

For the first time since this all began, I catch myself thinking that maybe Riven is safe. That maybe, under all that mystery and sharp wit, there's something solid I can lean against. The thought surprises me. And scares me, just a little.

"We're here," Riven says, easing the car to a stop at the edge of a narrow gravel path.

I blink at the view beyond the windshield, trees, cliffs, and not a single sign of civilization. "Here" apparently translates to the middle of nowhere.

"This is it?" I ask.

He nods toward the hills ahead. "Not quite. It's a short hike from here. The site should be just beyond the ridge."

I groan. "You dragged me out of bed before sunrise for a hike?"

He smirks, unbothered. "Don't be a baby. Come on."

"I'm not a baby," I mutter, shoving open the car door. "I just prefer my supernatural field trips to involve coffee and chairs."

He's already heading up the path, not waiting for me, which

of course only makes me walk faster. The ground is soft and uneven, the air sharp with the smell of salt and wildflowers. Seagulls cry somewhere in the distance, and far below, I can hear the dull crash of waves.

My brain, meanwhile, is running through a hundred different thoughts. The dream. The circle. The way that strange hum still clings to my skin. I realize suddenly that I forgot to leave Marin a note before I left and knowing her, she'll assume I've been kidnapped.

I pull out my phone as we walk, typing a quick message:

Me: **Hey, forgot to tell you I'm out of town for the day. Doing research with Riven. Will explain later.**

It only takes her a minute to reply.

Marin: **Riven?? Like mysterious-library-break-in Riven?? Tell him if he hurts you, I'm haunting him.**

I snort and type back, **I'll let him know.**

Riven glances back at me. "Everything okay?"

"Yeah. Just my best friend threatening your afterlife. Nothing major."

He raises a brow, clearly amused. "Good to know I'm already so popular."

We keep walking. The sun's higher now, turning the air warm and heavy. I peel off my jacket, tying it around my waist. "Is it just me, or did it go from brisk morning to 'we're walking on the surface of the sun' in about ten minutes?"

He glances over, completely unfazed, still in his usual all-black attire.

"Don't tell me you're not hot in that," I say.

He smirks. "I'm comfortable."

"Comfortable? You're basically wearing the color of heat stroke."

He gives me a sideways look. "Maybe I just run cold."

"Maybe you're insane," I mutter.

"Same thing," he says, without missing a step.

I roll my eyes but can't help the small smile tugging at my mouth.

The path narrows, the trees thinning as the sound of the ocean grows louder. The air tastes like salt now, sharp and clean. Wind tugs at my hair, cooler here, carrying the cry of gulls, a low, almost musical vibration I can't quite place under my feet gets my attention.

Riven moves ahead, his stride steady and confident. I shove my phone back in my pocket, fingers brushing the worn edges of Harland's book in my bag. The symbol flashes behind my eyes. The circle. The three lines. The way the stone at the observatory seemed to notice me. Somewhere ahead, the wind drops for a heartbeat, and the silence that follows doesn't feel empty.

Chapter 15

The trail finally opens onto a cliff-side clearing, the ocean stretching wide and endless below. Sunlight spills over the water, catching the waves in flashes of gold and silver. For a second, I just stand there, breathing it in, the salt in the air, the wind tugging at my hair, the sound of gulls echoing somewhere above. It's beautiful in a wild, almost dangerous way.

Riven, of course, doesn't stop to admire the view. He's pacing the length of the clearing, scanning the ground, searching for something invisible. "It should be about here," he mutters, half to himself. "But I don't see it. Maybe I have the coordinates wrong."

I tear my eyes away from the horizon. "You dragged me halfway across the state and you're not even sure?"

He glances up at me, one eyebrow lifting. "Would you have come if I'd said maybe?"

"Absolutely not."

"Exactly."

I sigh, turning back to the sea. The sunlight glitters on the water, too bright to look at for long. "Well, maybe whatever you're looking for doesn't want to be found."

He crouches, brushing his fingers across the ground, brow

furrowed. "No. It's here. I can feel it."

I roll my eyes and start walking toward him. "You *feel* it? What does that even—"

My boot catches on something solid buried just beneath the surface, and before I can catch myself, I stumble forward with an embarrassingly loud yelp.

Riven's head jerks up. "Rachel—"

"I'm fine!" I snap, trying to recover as gracefully as anyone can after tripping over thin air. My cheeks burn. "I just— tripped. On nothing." Except it's not nothing.

Where my foot hit, the dirt's shifted into a mound of dirt. I take a step back, brushing my hands off. A faint shape is starting to show through the soil: curved lines etched into stone, forming a pattern that makes my stomach twist in recognition.

Riven moves beside me, dropping into a low crouch. "Well," he says, his voice low, almost reverent. "You've got good instincts."

"I have terrible instincts," I mutter, staring as more of the design emerges. "I just fall a lot."

He brushes away another handful of dirt, revealing more of the symbol: a circle with three clean lines cutting through it. The same one. The same mark carved into the observatory stone. The same mark burned into my wall. The same mark in my father's notes.

I stare at it, my pulse pounding in my ears. "Riven... that's it."

He nods, expression unreadable. "Yeah. That's it."

The wind picks up, carrying the scent of salt and something else, ozone, sharp and electric, like a storm holding its breath. The ground beneath us seems to hum faintly, the same vibration I felt before while we were hiking up here, low and deep enough to feel in my bones.

I crouch beside the mark, the symbol half-buried in dirt and stone. It shouldn't feel alive, but it does, there's a faint vibration beneath my fingertips, like the earth itself is breathing, a slow inhale drawn around a single point.

Something in the air seems to lean toward me. "Careful," Riven says quietly, watching me from a few feet away. His tone isn't teasing now. It's warning.

"I just want to see something," I murmur. I don't even know what I mean by that. I just know I need to touch it.

The closer I get, the more the air seems to shift to something heavier, denser, humming with a low energy that raises the hairs on my arms. My hand trembles slightly as I reach out, drawn to it like a magnet to the curve of the circle.

The moment my fingers brush the carved line, the rainbow shimmer in my vision explodes. Light floods my sight, violent, blinding, pulsing through every nerve. The world around me drops away. There's only color, swirling and burning, so bright it hurts. Gold, violet, blue, all bleeding into each other until there's no sky, no ground, no sea, just light.

I gasp and jerk backward, the force knocking me off balance. I crash straight into Riven.

"Rachel!" His hands close around my arms, steady and solid. "What happened? Are you okay?"

I blink hard, but the colors are still there, flaring and fading, smearing the world into shifting light. The cliff, the waves, even Riven's face look like they've been outlined in iridescent ink.

"I—I don't know," I stammer. "My vision just... went crazy. It's like everything's glowing."

He shifts to crouch beside me, voice lower now. "Did you touch it?"

"I barely brushed it." I squeeze my eyes shut, trying to clear the haze. The rainbow aura dances behind my eyelids, alive and spinning. "It's like it hit me."

"Okay," he says, calm but tight. "Breathe. In and out."

He reaches out a hand to help me up. I take it automatically.

The instant our skin touches, the air around us *cracks*.

A soundless pressure builds and before I can even breathe, the world falls away again. The light shifts, sharper, colder, dragging me under. The ground, the sea, Riven, everything vanishes.

I'm falling.

Falling through color, through sound, through something that isn't time or space. There's pressure in my ears, the taste of salt and iron, as if the sea itself has followed me down. Wind roars past but there's no air, no up, no down, just movement and light tearing past me in ribbons.

In the distance, I can hear voices, a thousand whispers overlapping. Some sound like they're right against my skin, some like they're miles away. They tangle into something that feels like my name, and something that absolutely isn't.

And just before everything turns white, I see it.

The same circle, burning in the sky.

Only it's not etched in stone this time. It's huge, spanning the void above me, lines of light cutting through it, spinning slowly like an impossible, glowing wheel. In its center, a figure stands, black against the blaze, watching me.

The light sharpens until it's all I can see—pure white, burning at the edges of everything. I throw my hands up to shield my eyes, but it doesn't help. The glow cuts straight through my skin, through me, like I'm made of glass.

"Hello?" My voice sounds small, swallowed by the brightness. "What is this?"

There's movement ahead.

A shape begins to form inside the light. A person or something close to one. Tall, slender, wrapped in shifting color. The outline ripples, hard to pin down. I can't see a face, can't tell if it's man or woman, just a blinding silhouette that seems to pulse with the same rhythm as my heartbeat. Then it speaks.

Not loud. Not even like sound. It lands inside my skull, inside my ribs, vibrating through bone and blood.

"Astrid."

The name reverberates through me. The word vibrates under my skin, familiar in a way that terrifies me. A song I should remember but don't.

I flinch, looking over my shoulder, half expecting someone else to be there. "Who—who's Astrid?"

No answer.

The figure takes a step closer, the light around it tightening, focusing. The brightness intensifies until it sears the air between us.

"Stop," I whisper, stumbling backward. "Don't—"

But there's nowhere to go. The ground beneath me feels soft and the harder I try to move, the less the world obeys. The less my body obeys and suddenly I'm trying to run in a dream and my body won't move.

"Please," I say, panic rising fast. "I don't know what this is, I don't belong here—"

"Astrid", the voice calls again, louder this time. The word stretches through me until it's inside my bones, like it's been there

a long time and is only now waking up.

"I'm not—!" I shout, but the light surges forward, swallowing the space between us in a single, blinding pulse.

I spin, desperate for an exit, for anything that isn't this endless burning white. My pulse is pounding so loud it drowns out thought. The light flickers into a white, gold, violet then fractures, fine cracks spider-webbing through it.

I fall again.

Down through the cracks, through shards of color, through a long, shuddering silence. The last thing I hear before the world goes dark is the voice whispering one more word, soft and fractured and almost... relieved.

Found.

For a heartbeat, everything goes still.

Then it's gone.

Chapter 16

When I wake, everything is light and sound and disorientation. The world spins before it settles into shapes, sky, trees, the rush of waves below and Riven's face hovering above mine.

"Rachel." His voice is low, urgent, threaded with something that edges on fear. "Hey. Stay with me."

Something cold splashes across my cheek. Then another.

I blink hard. Water drips down my neck and onto my shirt. "What—what are you doing?" I croak, coughing as another splash hits my chin.

"Trying to get you to drink," he says, though it sounds more like an excuse than anything resembling medical technique.

I sputter, half choking, half laughing. "Riven, this isn't a wet T-shirt contest—stop!"

He freezes, the bottle still tipped in his hand. "You fainted," he says finally, voice rougher now. "Your eyes rolled back, and you started yelling. I didn't know what was happening."

He sounds genuinely shaken. That throws me harder than the water does. I push myself up only to realize I can't, because his arm is still around me. My head is resting against his shoulder. His other hand is braced behind my back.

I'm sitting in his lap.

Oh. Fantastic.

"Well," I manage, my voice wobbling, "guess first aid and fainting girls aren't your area of expertise." A ghost of a smile flickers across his mouth but it doesn't reach his eyes. "No," he admits quietly. "You're the first."

Something in the way he says it sends a flutter through my chest. He brushes a strand of hair from my face, his touch lingering just long enough to make my pulse stumble. "You scared me," he murmurs. "You were out for almost a minute."

"I—" My throat tightens. "I saw something."

He leans closer. "What did you see?" I swallow, the image still burned behind my eyelids. "Someone. Standing in the light. They called to me—but not by my name. They said *Astrid*."

Riven's brow furrows. "Astrid?"

"Yeah. I don't know who that is." My voice cracks, the fear I've been holding back spilling through. "I don't know what's happening to me, Riven. Ever since my dad died or I thought he did—everything's been off. The dreams, the colors, the symbols... it's like I'm losing my grip."

He shifts, tightening his hold on me just slightly. Grounding me.

"You're not losing anything," he says softly. "You're waking up to something most people never see."

When I look up, his face is closer than I thought. His eyes catch mine impossibly sharp and blue, too bright in the sunlight and for a second, the world goes absolutely still. There's a quiet hum between us, a live wire pulled tight.

His thumb grazes my cheekbone. My breath stutters. My hand ends up on his chest, feeling the solid warmth of him, the steady beat beneath my palm.

Neither of us moves—

—or maybe we both do.

The space between us narrows until his breath brushes my mouth. His eyes flick to my lips, then lift again and with a quiet exhale, he pulls away. Awareness slams back into me like a bucket of cold water.

I jerk away and scramble upright. "Oh—uh—I'm fine now. Definitely fine."

Riven blinks, equal parts amused and confused, as I brush imaginary dirt from my jeans with frantic, useless pats. He stands more slowly, too composed and calm while my heartbeat thrashes in my chest. "You sure you're okay?" he asks.

"Perfect," I lie, voice high and unconvincing. "Totally perfect."

He nods once. "Let's walk back to the car."

"Yep," I squeak. "Good plan."

We head down the trail in silence, the waves roaring below. I can feel him glancing my way sometimes, checking on me, and every time he does, my stomach somersaults.

By the time we reach the car, the sun has dipped low, setting the cliffs on fire with gold. The drive back is quiet and the air feels charged. Every few miles, he checks on me again with that flick of his eyes. I pretend not to notice, and pretend even harder not to care.

When he drops me off, the world feels dimmer without him in it.

I mumble a thank you, trip over my keys because of course I do, and once I'm inside, the quiet of the flat wraps around me too tightly.

I shower, hoping the hot water will rinse away the fear, the sand, the memory of his touch. It doesn't. My reflection in the fogged mirror looks both exactly like me and nothing like me.

By the time I crawl into bed, exhaustion drags at every limb. I replay it all the light, the voice, the name, the way Riven said I scared him. The way his hand lingered.

"Get a grip," I whisper to the ceiling. "You almost died, and you're thinking about a guy."

Sleep finally wins. I drift in slow waves, the ocean still echoing in my head. Then something shifts. A weight sinks onto the foot of the bed. My eyes snap open.

And before I can breathe, a hand clamps over my mouth. My body goes rigid.

The world narrows to the weight pinning me down, the heat of a palm across my lips, fingers digging into my jaw. I can't scream. I can't move. Panic slams through me so hard I see spots.

I smell something familiar, the sharp, metallic. Burnt ozone. Damp earth. Hot breath whispers against my ear, "Found"

Terror galvanizes me. I thrash hard, twisting beneath him, fighting with everything I have. My knee catches something hard. A shin, maybe. He grunts, grip slipping for the smallest fraction of a second.

It's enough. I wrench my head sideways, dragging a shredded breath past his palm. "M—" The sound dies in my throat.

I buck against him, legs kicking wildly, heel connecting with the edge of the nightstand. Pain shoots up my ankle. His weight shifts, pressing harder, trying to smother my movement. His hand drags across my cheek as he adjusts his grip.

I dig my nails into his wrist. Hard. Skin, if it is skin, gives under my nails like cool clay. My nails leave bloody crescent moon shapes behind. He jerks, surprised, and I suck in a ragged breath, I thrash, desperate, the grip loosens just enough for me to suck in a ragged breath—

"Marin!" I scream, muffled. "MARIN!"

The door bursts open, slamming into the wall. Marin stands there, hair wild, drowning in an over-sized T-shirt, pure horror on her face.

"What the hell—Rachel?!" Her scream changes everything.

The figure freezes. It lifts its head in a slow, unnervingly way and for the first time I see it clearly in the sliver of hallway light spilling across the bed.

A human outline.

But not human at all.

Shadow appear to cling to it. Smoke coils off its limbs in thin, writhing ribbons. Its edges flicker as though its shape is undecided, warping with each breath it doesn't take. Two hollows where eyes should be glow faintly, like embers cooling a shade too slow.

And then—

It tilts its head, studying Marin.

Something shifts in the room. The air buckles. Cold floods across my skin.

It unravels. It dissolves into black mist, the temperature in the room dropping so fast I feel the bite of cold on my skin. The cloud streaks toward the window, shattering it outward with a sharp crack and disappears into the night.

Silence roars in behind it.

I hit the floor, gasping, my entire body shaking. Sobs raking out of me.

Marin is at my side in an instant. "Oh my god, Rach—hey, hey, you're okay." She pulls me into her arms. I cling to her, sobbing, the terror still clawing at my throat.

"There was—there was someone—" I choke out. "It wasn't—Marin, that wasn't human."

"I know. I know, baby." Her voice wavers but she holds me tighter, anchoring me to the world. "I saw. I saw it."

I can feel her shaking, too. We sit like that, tangled on the floor, until the sobs turn into sharp, shuddery breaths. Neither of us says what we're both thinking. That thing wasn't human. It knew where I lived. And it called me exactly what the light did:

Found.

Chapter 17

Steam curls lazily from the mug in my hands, but my fingers won't stop shaking long enough to keep it steady. The tea Marin made is going cold, untouched honey and chamomile, her cure for every disaster but nothing about tonight feels like it can be fixed with tea.

The apartment feels smaller and thinner now. Every creak of the pipes, every hum of the refrigerator makes me flinch. A draft snakes in from the living room window we taped over, the one still fractured from where the glass blew outward. Marin hung an old quilt over it, bright patchwork squares meant to be comforting. It moves whenever the wind breathes, a slow, restless shiver that keeps reminding me that something came in.

And then left.

We're curled on the couch under mismatched blankets, shoulders pressed together. The TV is off. The lamps are low. The air smells like sage, tea, and dust. Neither of us has said much since I stopped shaking. My throat still aches from screaming.

Marin takes a sip of her tea, both hands wrapped around the mug. "Okay," she says finally, voice rough-edged but steady enough. "I believe you now."

I huff a small, humorless laugh. "Kind of hard not to when a shadow demon crashes your best friend's bedroom window." She doesn't smile. Just nods once. "I don't even know what I saw, Rach. It didn't have... edges. It wasn't like a person. It was like—"

"Smoke," I finish quietly. "But alive."

The word hangs there, wrong in the air.

My eyes wander down the hall to my bedroom—I can see the glitter of missed glass in the corner, the lamp still tipped on its side, Marin's abandoned sage stick balanced in a mug. Everything feels slightly wrong, the feeling of my safe living space being violated by the intrusion. I keep waiting for the world to click back into place, but it doesn't.

The cliff. The mark in the stone. The way it thrummed when I touched it. The vision. The voice.

Astrid. Found you.

I set the mug down before I drop it and press my fingers to my temples. "This started today," I say. "Right after I touched that symbol." Marin glances over, brow furrowed. "You think that... thing came from there?"

"I don't know." My voice drops. "But it feels connected. Like whatever I woke up followed me home." I can still feel it, not the thing, but the echo deep under my skin.

Marin exhales shakily and sinks deeper into the cushions. "You know what's wild? A week ago, I thought your weird dreams and rainbow-vision thing were stress. Like your brain finally decided to short-circuit."

"Thanks," I say dryly.

"I'm serious." She drags a hand through her hair. "I thought this was trauma and bad sleep. A very dramatic breakdown. Classic you."

"Wow. Love the support." I roll my eyes.

"But now…" She stares at the quilt over the broken window, fabric shivering. "Now I don't know what to think. That thing moved your whole room, Rach. It broke the window. I saw it. I felt it."

A chill crawls up my spine. "What if it's not gone?" I whisper. "What if it can get back in?"

Marin looks at me then, all the sarcasm stripped away. "Then we'll deal with it," she says. "Together."

The word lands like a hand on my back, steadying. My chest loosens by a fraction. But my mind won't quiet. Every time I blink, I see flashes of that sky in my vision, the circle burning in the light, the figure stepping toward me. The way the name *Astrid* settled into my bones.

"I just need to know what this is," I murmur. "What's happening to me. Why it's happening to me." Marin nods, hiding her own fear under a thin layer of bravado. "You said Riven might know something, right?" she asks. "You trust him?"

Do I?

I think about him standing in the circle, watching me like he was waiting for something to happen. The way his hand wrapped around mine on the cliff. The way he looked when I told him what I saw. He's helped me. He's also definitely not telling me everything.

Still, when I called and stammered out that something attacked me, he didn't ask if I was sure. He didn't suggest hospitals or meds or rest.

He just said, *I'm coming.*

"He said he'd be right over," I say.

"Of course he did," Marin mutters, tugging the blanket up

to her chin. "Of course the brooding, mysterious guy with the jawline shows up in the middle of the night to save the day."

"Marin—"

"I'm just saying. If he turns out to be evil, I'm haunting both of you." Despite everything, a broken laugh bubbles out of me. "Get in line." The laugh dies when someone knocks on the door.

Three sharp, deliberate knocks. We both freeze.

My heart rockets into my throat. I stand slowly, every nerve on high alert. "It's fine," I whisper, more to myself than to her. "It's just Riven."

Marin doesn't move, but her eyes track me, ready to launch herself at whoever comes through.

The floor creaks under my feet. The hallway light hums faintly on the other side. I unlatch the deadbolt and open the door just enough—

Riven stands there.

He's framed in the dim corridor light, hair windblown, dressed in black again. His coat hangs open, jaw tense, eyes sharp and scanning, checking the hallway for threats before he checks on me.

Marin peeks around my shoulder, takes one look at him, and mutters under her breath, "Well... damn."

"Marin," I hiss, quietly so Riven won't hear.

"What?" she stage-whispers. "You didn't tell me he looked like *that*."

Riven arches a brow. "I'll take that as a compliment."

So he definitely heard her...

"Oh, it was," Marin says. "You're welcome."

I groan. "Can we not flirt while I'm possibly cursed?"

Riven's mouth curves into a faint smile as he steps inside.

"Nice to meet you too," he says to Marin. Marin smirks and retreats to the couch, wrapping the blanket tighter around herself. I close the door and lock it again, as if that will help. Riven sits beside me too close, as always. His thigh is a warm line against mine through the blanket. Marin clocking the distance and arching an eyebrow like *we are absolutely circling back to this later.*

Riven leans forward, forearms on his knees, eyes on me. "Tell me everything," he says, calm but edged.

I tell him about waking up, about the weight on my chest, the hand over my mouth, the smell of burnt ozone and damp earth. How it looked like smoke that remembered how to be a person and decided not to bother. How Marin burst in, how it dissolved through the window like it was made of sky.

He listens without interrupting, gaze fixed on my face, intent on catching every little detail I can remember. When I mention touching the circle earlier that day, something in his expression tightens, just for a second.

"I think it's connected," I finish quietly. "Nothing like this happened before I touched it."

He sits back, thoughtful. "If that site still holds residual energy, you might've triggered it," he says. "Opened something that wasn't meant to be opened."

"Opened what?" Marin demands, voice sharper than mine has been all night.

He shakes his head once. "I don't know yet."

Marin throws up her hands. "That's comforting."

I stare down at my hands, knuckles white around the mug I'm no longer drinking from. "I need to go back," I say suddenly. Both their heads snap up toward me.

"What?" Marin blurts. "Absolutely not. We're not doing

round two of demon hide-and-seek."

"I need answers," I insist. "If that place is connected to whatever this is, maybe there's something there that explains why it's… attached to me. Why it keeps finding me."

"You're not going alone," Marin says immediately.

"Agreed," Riven says. "If you go back, we go together."

Marin narrows her eyes at him. "I still don't trust you, fancy-car boy."

His mouth twitches. "You don't have to. Just stay close to Rachel."

"I already do," she snaps.

I exhale. "Okay. So we go back. Tomorrow. All three of us."

Marin groans into her blanket. "Tomorrow. Fine. But if I get haunted and die, I'll rattle chains and ruin your sleep for eternity."

"Noted," Riven says dryly.

The three of us lapse into uneasy silence. The tea has gone stone cold. The wind presses at the quilt over the broken window, making it billow, sending a chill through the room.

I glance at Riven. "You really think it'll have answers?" His eyes meet mine. There's something dark and certain in them. "I think it'll have something," he says. He doesn't add that something might hurt. He doesn't have to.

Marin decides Riven isn't leaving.

She's in full crisis-host mode, bulldozing through the linen closet, muttering about "shadow goblins" and "emergency slumber parties." The couch creaks as she yanks a fitted sheet over it with the kind of aggression usually reserved for exes and tax forms.

"You don't have to—" he starts.

"You do," Marin says. "House rule. No mysterious men

leaving after demon incidents." "There," she declares, fluffing a pillow a little more agressively than necessary, "Not exactly five-star, but it's clean. Probably."

Riven stands awkwardly by the doorway, hands shoved in his coat pockets, expression halfway between grateful and out of place. "I appreciate it," he says.

"You should," Marin fires back. "I don't let strange men stay the night unless they're exceptionally handsome or involved in supernatural nonsense."

His mouth curves into that familiar half-smile. "Then I'm twice as lucky."

Marin waves him off. "Yeah, yeah. Don't get cocky, Bond. You snore, and you're out."

She tosses him a blanket. He catches it before it hits him directly in the face. "Try not to summon anything in your sleep, okay?" she adds. "Rachel's fear quota is maxed."

"I'll do my best," he says, amused.

Marin turns to me. "You're with me tonight. I'm not letting you sleep next to a broken window and ghost confetti."

"Yeah," I say, the word coming out smaller than I intend. "Okay."

When she disappears down the hall, the apartment shrinks to just me and Riven again, the lamplight low, the edges of everything soft and strange. He lays his coat over the arm of the couch. I pick up a pillow and fuss with the case because I need my hands to be doing something that isn't shaking.

"So," I say, keeping my voice low, "tomorrow. What exactly is the plan?"

He looks over at me. "We'll go back to the site at first light," he says. "Before anyone's around. I'll bring a few things to test the area, see if the energy's still active. See if it's anchored to anything."

"Energy," I echo. "Like... whatever that thing was made of?"

"Something like that."

"And if it comes back?" I ask.

He doesn't hesitate. "Then I won't let it touch you."

The way he says it, quiet and certain hits somewhere under my ribs. I stare down at the pillow, fingers twisting fabric.

"I just—" My voice cracks. I try again. "I don't know how to keep doing this. Every time I think it can't get worse, it does. I'm scared, Riven." He watches me for a long moment, all the sharp edges in him smoothing out. Then he steps closer.

As I lean to set the pillow down, his hand reaches out gentle, slow and catches mine. I freeze. His palm is warm and solid, fingers wrapping around mine as if he's done it a hundred times in some other life.

"Look at me," he says softly. It isn't a command. It feels like an invitation.

I take a breath and lift my eyes. He's closer than I realized, just inches away. The lamplight paints gold along his jaw, across the fine lines at the corners of his eyes. His gaze is steady, anchored on me.

"You're not alone in this," he says quietly. "Whatever's happening—whatever you've woken up—it's not just your burden to carry. We'll face it together. You are not losing your mind, Rachel. You're stronger than you think."

The words slip under my defenses. My eyes sting, and I hate it, but I turn my hand in his and squeeze back anyway. For a moment, we just stand there in that small pool of lamplight, his thumb tracing a slow circle over my skin. My heart pounds loud enough that I'm pretty sure he can feel it through my fingertips.

He takes a half-step closer. The space between us shrinks to almost nothing. His gaze drops, just for a second, to my mouth—

"Okay!" Marin's voice slices through the room like a fire alarm. "Everyone has sheets? Blankets? Emotional boundaries intact?"

I jump so hard I nearly headbutt Riven and yank my hand away suddenly. Riven clears his throat and steps back, composure snapping back into place, though there's a betraying quirk at the corner of his mouth.

"Marin," I groan, face burning.

She leans against the doorway, smirking. "Thought so. Carry on, demon hunters. Keep it PG-13, please." She disappears again, muttering something about "sexual tension and supernatural bullshit."

Riven huffs out a breath, somewhere between a laugh and a sigh. "She's... blunt."

"She's Marin," I say, hugging the pillow to my chest hoping it can shield how embarrassed I feel.

He nods once. "Get some sleep," he says. "I'll keep watch."

"Good," I reply, backing toward the hall. "Because if another shadow thing breaks in tonight, I'm not saving you."

That earns me a real smile, crooked and unguarded. "Noted."

I duck into the bedroom before he can see the answering smile tugging at my own mouth.

Marin's already under the blankets, hair an absolute disaster, grin sharp enough to cut glass. "So," she says as I climb in, "you two kissed yet or what?"

I throw a pillow at her. Cheeks turning red, "Go to sleep."

She catches it, still grinning. "I'm just saying, if the end of the world is coming, I'd like you to at least get laid first."

"Marin," I groan, burying my face in the blanket.

She laughs, but the sound softens as she settles. A few minutes later, her breathing evens out, ridiculous girl able to sleep mere hours after watching a smoke being burst through a window. I stare at the ceiling for a long time. I can still feel the ghost of Riven's hand against mine. Still hear that rasped voice by my ear: *Found you.*

Sunlight spills across the ceiling, pale gold, far too bright for how little sleep I managed. For a few seconds, I just listen to the quiet whoosh of cars in the street below, a gull calling somewhere distant, the refrigerator humming in the next room. The normal sounds of a soft murmur of a morning threading back into the world.

Marin is star-fished beside me, one arm over her forehead, the other dangling off the bed. She snores softly, because apparently near-death experiences don't interrupt her REM cycle. I slip out of bed as quietly as the floorboards will allow and tug on a sweatshirt. The floorboards creak anyways. Traitors.

The apartment looks different in daylight, gentler than it has any right to be. Sunlight reaches down the hall to where the quilt hangs over my bedroom window, glowing through the fabric in patchwork colors. If I don't look directly at it, I can almost pretend the glass under it isn't cracked. Almost.

Riven is still here. He's on the couch, elbows on his knees, staring out of the window, deep in thought. The blanket Marin gave him is folded neatly beside him. His hair's a little messier, but his eyes are clear, too awake for this hour.

"Morning," I say, voice rough.

He glances over his shoulder. A faint smile touches his lips. "Morning."

"You didn't sleep, did you?"

He shrugs, "Didn't feel like it."

I cross my arms, leaning against the door-frame. "You could have. The world didn't end while we were out."

"That's good to know," he says.

My mouth curves despite everything. "Thanks for staying," I add. "You didn't have to."

His gaze lingers on me for a second longer than necessary. "I told you," he says quietly. "I'm not going anywhere." The words land heavier than they should. Something in my chest loosens and tightens at the same time.

A loud yawn explodes from the hallway. Marin stumbles in, hair defying gravity, T-shirt twisted, one sock on. "If either of you made coffee and didn't save me a cup, I swear I'll—oh." She blinks at Riven. "You're still here."

"Good morning to you too," he says.

She squints at him, then at the still-folded blanket. "You didn't sleep?"

"He meditated mysteriously," I say, narrowing my eyes in mock suspicion.

"Of course he did," she mutters. "Men like him don't sleep. They loom broodingly until sunrise. It's in their contract."

Riven's lips twitch. "You make it sound like a full-time job."

"It must be exhausting," she says, shuffling toward the kitchen. "Anyway, whoever's possessed makes breakfast. House rule."

"That's you," I call after her.

"Exactly!" she shouts back. She disappears, banging

cupboards.

The quiet that settles between me and Riven is... different now. Not empty. Just full.

"How are you feeling?" he asks. "Like I fought a smoke monster in my pajamas," I say.

His mouth edges into a smile. "That's... accurate."

I glance toward the window. Sunlight glows through casting the room in bright light. Somewhere down the hall, the glass of my window still bears the spiderweb pattern of impact from last night.

"We're going back there today," I say. Not a question.

He nods slowly. "If you're sure you're ready."

"I don't think I'll ever be ready," I whisper. "But I can't keep pretending this is meaningless. I need to know why the symbol reacted, why the Falling happened, why Astrid and why it's me at the center of it."

He straightens, the easy softness in him folding back into focus. "Then we'll go after breakfast," he says. "I'll drive."

From the kitchen, Marin's voice drifts out: "You're damn right you'll drive. I'm not taking public transport to a haunted rock circle." Riven chuckles under his breath. "I'm starting to like her."

"She's the best," I say, watching her silhouette move behind the half-wall. "She's the reason I'm not in a psychiatric ward right now."

"She's your anchor," he says quietly. The word sits between us. Maybe he's right. Maybe Marin is the thing that keeps me from drifting too far out. Maybe the light, the voice, the shadows, they're all trying to pull me somewhere I'm not ready to go.

But as late morning light spills across the floor and catches on the tiny glittering shard of glass Marin missed last night, I can't shake the feeling that by tonight, nothing about this will feel normal ever again.

Chapter 18

The drive feels longer this time. The sky hangs low and heavy, clouds swollen with rain that hasn't decided if it'll fall. The hum of the car fills the quiet with a steady, low vibration that matches the unease sitting in my stomach.

Marin's in the back seat, one leg tucked under her, flipping through my playlists. Every so often she lands on a song and hums a few bars.

"This one's very 'brooding man with secrets,'" she says. "It suits you."

Riven huffs a quiet laugh, eyes on the road, fingers steady on the wheel. "I'll take that under advisement."

It's strange watching them interact. Marin so open, every thought broadcast in real time. Riven so contained, his reactions are tiny and measured. Two different worlds squeezed into one car, trading commentary over my music.

The road threads ahead, a thin gray ribbon cutting through the dark blur of trees. Branches lean over the asphalt, heavy from last nights rain. The farther we drive, the heavier the air gets thicker and is humming with something I can't name. It feels like the world itself is holding its breath, quietly trying to warn us not to keep moving forward. But my mind won't let go of the circle. The burst of light. The low vibration under the stone, sighing once I touched it. And the voice calling me *Astrid* as if it had been waiting years for me to hear it.

The memory squeezes tight around my lungs. I can still feel the echo of the impact buried somewhere under my ribs, a second heartbeat that isn't mine, beating out a rhythm I don't recognize. Too deep. Too steady. Too alive. It thrums underneath everything, a second pulse it forgot to hide.

What if touching it again makes everything worse? What if it wasn't calling to me but was calling for me? Like I'm not the witness. I'm the target. A chill walks up my spine, slow and deliberate.

The trees grow taller the farther we go, trunks stretching skyward like spines of ancient things. The road narrows until it feels like we're slipping through the ribs of something that swallowed the sun whole. The washed out light outside the windows shifts colder, fading into a muted steel blue that makes the world look waterlogged and haunted.

I catch my reflection in the glass, pale skin washed even paler by the dim light, shadows under my eyes, bruises of exhaustion, and that faint iridescent rim still ghosting the edges of my vision. It clings there stubbornly, as if it's not a symptom or a trick of light but a mark. A reminder.

The closer we get, the more it feels like something is waiting for us up ahead, in a patient, intentional kind of way, and it's far too familiar with my name. Maybe Riven's right. Maybe I didn't cause this. But the way the air hums now, faint and alive, I can't shake the feeling whatever's out there knows I'm coming back.

The coastline appears all at once, cliffs cutting sharp against the dull sky, the sea below restless and gray. We're almost there. No one says a word. We all know we're driving toward something we can't undo.

When we pull off the road and start down the trail, the ground feels steeper than before, lungs catching the cold, salted air. Gravel crunches under our boots, the sound swallowed by wind threading the cliffs. Marin mutters about blisters and haunted landscapes under her breath, but even her sarcasm is quieter now.

At the ridge, the world opens up to the ocean, where the horizon meets the sky in an endless way. And there it is. The circle. Not subtle. Not half-buried. Not something you'd miss if you weren't looking. It's there, carved into the stone at the center of the clearing, glowing softly in the gray light. The markings pulse with a low, barely there color that matches the haze at the edge of my sight.

I stop dead.

The air feels charged, the hum settling deep in my chest, syncing up with that not-quite-mine heartbeat. Every hair on my arms lifts. Marin edges closer to my side. "It looks... old," she says.

She's right. The etching is weathered and dull, just another mark on stone. But now it looks awake. Faint shimmer moves beneath the surface, something is breathing under the rock. Riven steps forward, scanning the perimeter, alert in that quiet way he has. He crouches at the edge of the symbol, the wind tugging at his coat. "It's active," he murmurs. "Almost like it's alive."

I swallow. "So what do I do?"

He glances up. "What do you mean?"

"I mean..." I wet my lips. "Do I just... touch it?" The question lands heavier than it should.

Riven rises slowly, flicking a look at Marin before his gaze returns to me. "You don't have to," he says carefully. "Not until we understand more. Not after last time."

"But what if that's the only way to understand?" My voice feels small against the wind and the sea. "It reacted to me before. Maybe it'll show us something again."

"Or maybe it'll knock you out and summon another smoke demon," Marin says, shrugging. It's not totally the worst case scenario here, "Just saying." Marin adds.

Riven's jaw tightens. He doesn't disagree.

We stand there, the three of us, listening to the ocean and the low, steady pulse of the circle. The glow flickers softly and in rhythm, like a heartbeat that never belonged to the earth. I take a step forward. "If it wanted to hurt me," I say quietly, "it would've already."

Marin snorts. "That is not the reassuring angle you think it is."

I give her a quick look, then glance at Riven. "You'll stop me if something happens, right?"

He hesitates for a fraction of a second, then nods once. "Always."

The word lands in my chest and stays there, heavy and warm. I step closer. The air thickens around me, pressure building in my ears. The shimmer reflects in my eyes as I lean down, colors ghosting over my skin. My fingers tingle, the pull now undeniable, magnetic and inevitable. Behind me, Marin whispers a prayer and a swear words fused together.

The wind rises. I reach out. My fingertips brush the carved circle, just a touch and the world drops out from under me. A surge floods me, not heat, not pain, but power. It crawls up my arms in a rush, spills into my chest, compresses my lungs until breath is a memory. The stone hums like a living thing, like a heart beating against my palms. Before I can jerk back, the ground, the cliff, the sky all tear away.

Light. Blinding and devouring.

The cliffs, the gray, the air, all gone.

I'm standing in a wide open field instead.

The air smells of smoke and rain and metal. Thatched roofs burn in the distance; hundreds of small shapes scatter beneath them, people fleeing, tiny figures against a horizon ripping open.

Above them, the sky is breaking. Shards of liquid fire the color of gold, silver, and electric blue is screaming toward the earth in streaks that vibrate the air. Each impact sounds like thunder hitting glass.

Screams everywhere. Bodies running. Bodies falling.

The light hits them mid-flight, slamming into shoulders, chests, hands raised too late. It bursts across the soil, skidding into pits and stones and water. Some collapse instantly, pale and still. And others.....others seem to ignite. The light doesn't kill them. It fills them.

They flare as veins of color race beneath their skin, branching like lightning through their bodies until they glow from the inside out. Eyes washed white. Hair lifting in wind that isn't there. The air around them warps, bending. It's beautiful and terrible in the same breath. Heat rolls off the ground; raw force hums through the air, thick and alive. Some people scream, the light, it's ripping them apart. Others gasp like they've been drowning their whole lives and just hit air.

It's happening everywhere I look. Across the hills, through the villages, along the riverbanks. Hundreds of lights falling. Hundreds struck. Some burn out instantly. Some stand, changed. A woman throws her arms around a child as a streak explodes nearby. The earth splits. For a heartbeat their faces shine brighter than the fires around them, too bright to look at and then they are gone. Dust. Ash. Light scattering.

Noise swallows me whole: thunder, screams, the bone-deep hum that vibrates my ribs until I'm sure they'll crack. I want to run. I want to scream. I can't move. Then, through the chaos, I see them. A small group standing in the middle of the storm.

The light hits them too, in thick, concentrated bolts, but they don't fall. They absorb it. Each impact sinks into them, ribs and hands and eyes blazing. The glow around them deepens until the world bends around their silhouettes. Their eyes find mine across distance and centuries. Their eyes appear luminous, unnatural, and endless.

Light rains harder, rivers of fire carving the sky, ribbons of energy twisting and burning through cloud. The ground heaves. Heat licks my skin. The air vibrates so violently its shaking me apart. People run. People drop. People rise burning. Each burst lands with the sound of a thousand hearts breaking. Some stand, blazing like new stars. Others don't rise at all.

One of them turns fully toward me, a man with silver eyes, hands lifted, holding the sky itself. Light pours into him, through him, cycling out again in steady, controlled waves. He opens his mouth, trying to speak. The sky above me suddenly splits open.

A streak falls faster than the rest, thick and alive and screaming. It feels aware. Aimed. I can only watch as it barrels down, so bright it erases color, so loud it silences sound. It's coming straight for me. When it hits, it is like being struck by the sun. I'm hurled backwards through field, through fire, through time. Flame erupts in my veins. My lungs seize. The scream rips out of me and it's not just pain, it's everything at once. Terror. Power. Loss. Recognition. The overwhelming sense that the light knows me, has been searching for me, and has finally found what it was sent to find.

My body arches, every nerve lit up. Thought shatters into brightness. Something ancient and vast pours into me not to destroy, but to wake. And when the scream finally tears free, it doesn't echo across the field anymore. It's here.

Chapter 19

Hands.

That feel real and warm clamp down on my shoulders. I suddenly feel cold air and wind. Riven's voice punching through the echo.

"Rachel! Rachel—look at me!"

I blink, dragging in air like I've been underwater. The cliffs snap back into place. Gray sky overhead. The circle under my knees, dimming. I'm shaking. Drenched in sweat. My throat feels shredded. Marin is crouched beside me, face pale, mascara smudged, eyes too wide. "Jesus, Rach, you were—" Her voice warps, muffled. The air feels too bright, too sharp, humming inside me now.

I look up into Riven's face. He's close, breathing hard, hands still braced on my shoulders to hold me in this world. There's shock there, and recognition, and something that looks a lot like fear.

"Riven..." I rasp. The sound of my own voice surprises me. His gaze searches mine, fast he's checking what's still here and what's not. In the quiet between us, I know he understands. He knows exactly what just happened. The world feels a degree off, like reality hasn't fully settled back into place yet. The wind has dropped to a whisper. The circle at our feet is fading to simple etched stone, the faint glow bleeding away.

Marin moves first. She brushes damp hair from my face, fingers shaking. "You were screaming," she says, voice soft and urgent. "Like, full horror movie screaming. Then you went dead quiet. I thought—" She stops, biting the word off.

I nod, though I only caught half of it. My ears still ring with a hum that doesn't belong to sound. Riven slowly lets his hands fall away from my shoulders and takes a small step back, away from me. His face shutters over, expression going careful and distant, in a calculated kind of way. He doesn't come closer again.

He just looks at me. Marin slips an arm under mine and helps me stand. My knees wobble, but the world eventually steadies. The metallic taste of the vision lingers on my tongue. My skin is buzzing, as if the light didn't just touch me, it moved in. No one talks on the walk back down.

The only sound is gravel under our boots and the muted crash of waves far below. Even Marin, who can narrate the end of the world and make it funny, is quiet. She glances at me every few seconds, worry etched into every line of her face, but she doesn't ask. Maybe she's afraid I'll actually answer. Riven walks ahead, hands shoved deep in his pockets, shoulders tight. He doesn't look back once.

By the time we reach the car, the sun has disappeared fully behind the clouds. The sky is flat and dull.. I slide into the passenger seat without a word. Marin climbs into the back, her door slamming harder than she probably meant it to. Riven starts the engine. Still no one speaks.

The drive stretches, long and silent, the road unspooling under us. My reflection in the window looks wrong, a version of me I no longer recognize, who's already seen too much. The vision loops behind my eyes in broken fragments. The light. The burning. The people who rose. The people who didn't. It didn't feel like watching history. It felt like remembering it.

Every nerve in my body still buzzes. The colors at the edges of my vision are sharper now, shimmering faintly whenever the light hits them.

Why me?

What did it mean, the ones who stood in the storm and didn't fall? The ones who took the light in and didn't break?

The chosen will rise from the Falling.

Why did it sound like it was meant for me?

I glance sideways at Riven. His jaw is tight. His knuckles are white where they grip the wheel. He hasn't looked at me once since we left the cliffs. The silence thickens until breathing feels like work. Marin shifts in the back. Her reflection flickers in the rear-view, eyes moving between us. Finally she exhales, loud and pointed.

"So," she says, dry as sandpaper, "are we going to stay dramatically silent until the end credits roll, or does someone want to say literally anything?" No one answers.

She mutters something under her breath and turns to stare out her window while crossing her arms. The car's tires hum, the only sound in the car while we drive. I watch the sky darken and try to slow my breathing, but the quiet just makes the noise in my head louder. The light is still inside me. I can feel it. Faint, pulsing, a secret heartbeat learning the rhythm of my own.

And Riven's silence sits between us too, sharp and deliberate. Not the silence of not knowing. The silence of choosing not to say. He pulls into our lot and kills the engine. Marin grabs her, impatiently and hurried, "Well," she says quietly, "that was the most fun I've ever had not talking." No one laughs.

"I'm going in," she adds. "Hot shower. Strong tea. Forty-five minutes of pretending that did not just happen." Her gaze flicks from him to me. "You two coming?" I shake my head, "In a minute." Riven says nothing.

She narrows her eyes at us suspiciously, then just sighs. "Don't stay long," she says. "And don't murder each other. Or make out. I honestly cannot tell which way this is going."

"Go, Marin," I say, almost smiling. She huffs and disappears inside, door thudding shut behind her.

The silence that follows settles over the car like a weight. Riven doesn't start the engine. His hands stay locked around the steering wheel, knuckles pale against the leather. The dashboard throws a cold blue glow across his face, carving sharp shadows beneath his eyes.

"Are you okay?" I ask, voice low. A breath escapes him. Too sharp to be a laugh. Too broken to be anything else. "Am I okay?" he repeats. "You're the one who scared the hell out of me."

"I didn't mean to—"

"I know." The words come out immediately, cutting across mine before I can finish.

He finally turns toward me.

For a second, neither of us says anything. When he finally does speak, his voice is low, frayed around the edges. He turns toward me. In the dim light I can see how tight his jaw is, how raw his eyes look. "You screamed," His voice catches. He looks away, toward the dark windshield. "..like you were being torn apart," he finally says. "I've heard fear. I've seen pain. But that..." He trails off, swallow visible in his throat.

"That was something else."

My throat tightens. The memory doesn't come.

"I don't remember screaming," I admit. "I remember the field. The light. And then… nothing."

He looks away, jaw flexing. "You were still," he says, the words are quiet enough that I almost miss them, "Too still. I thought you were gone."

The words knock the air right out of me. "I wasn't—"

He cuts in before I can finish. "You weren't breathing," he says, and now the control in his voice is hanging on by a thread. "Not until I touched you." I stare at him, pulse thundering in my ears. He keeps going, eyes fixed on the windshield. "You were cold. Completely cold," he swallows, "no pulse. Then all at once it came back. I thought you were gone." A muscle jumps in his jaw. The hum in my chest spikes along with my heart beat.

After a moment, he drags a hand down his face and exhales. "From what I've studied—what little anyone knows—I think you didn't just see the Falling," he says. "You experienced it. The first one. Like you were there." The hum of the engine cooling fills the quiet between us.

"You said I scared you," I manage, trying to make light of it, but my voice cracks halfway. "But you look… angry."

"I am," he says, just as quietly.

"Why?" His fingers tighten around the steering wheel. "Because I don't know what I'd do if I lost you."

The car might as well fall off the cliff for how hard my stomach drops. He drags a hand over his face again, like he's annoyed with himself for saying it out loud. His gaze finally lifts to mine, "You've become important to me," he says, voice barely above a whisper. "Faster than I meant to let happen.

And I knew that could be dangerous." Heat blooms behind my ribs, warm and terrifying. "Dangerous how?"

"Because I'm not supposed to get involved." His gaze flicks to mine, and for once there's nothing guarded there. Just honesty, raw and unpolished. "My role is to protect... not to care."

"Who makes those rules?" I ask.

"For people like me, it isn't a rule," he says. "It's a warning."

"People like you," I repeat. "Why the riddles, Riven? What aren't you telling me?"

His jaw clenches. His hands stay glued to the wheel. Silence stretches, thick and buzzing, until I can hear my own pulse in it. For a moment, I think he's going to say it, all of it, whatever it is but he just swallows it back down. Whatever he's hiding, he's guarding it with everything he has.

I turn back to the window. Streetlights flicker to life one by one, washing the lot in dull gold. "You said I saw the Falling," I say. "People burning. Others changing. The ones who absorbed the light. What happens next?"

He leans back, exhausted. "I don't know," he admits. "The records cut off. All we have are fragments. Warnings. Ruins."

"Then we find someone who does," I say, voice steadying. "Professor Harland. He's been researching this his entire life. He'll know more. Or at least more than we do." Riven looks uncertain, but he doesn't argue. "It's late," he says. "We should wait."

"I don't care," I say. "Waiting hasn't helped so far." A tired, real smile tugs at his mouth. His eyes hold mine, "Of course you don't." He turns the key. The engine hums back to life; the headlights sweep across the pavement. As we pull away, my reflection catches in the window.

For a second, just a second, the outline of me glows faintly, like someone traced me. My heart hammers, not just from fear now, but from something I don't have language for yet. When I look back at Riven, I see it there too. Not the glow, but the pull. The tether that wasn't there before and is somehow now the only thing that feels solid. Whatever's happening to me, to us, to the world, I have the horrible, exhilarating feeling that the circle was only the beginning.

Chapter 20

I've been on campus after dark before. During finals, half the student body practically lived here. It never looked like this. Tonight the quad feels abandoned. Inside the faculty wing, fluorescent lights hum overhead. The corridor glows an unnatural white, washing the color from everything it touches.

Professor Harland's office waits at the far end. The brass nameplate hangs crooked. One screw has nearly worked itself free. Light spills from beneath the door. A knot of relief loosens in my chest.

Good.

He's here.

I stop in the doorway. "Professor?" My voice disappears into stacks of books and leaning towers of paper. "It's Rachel. Are you here?"

Silence answers, I glance deeper into the office. Behind me, Riven's presence is a steady pressure at my shoulder. "We should come back in the morning," he murmurs. "This isn't a good idea." I glance back at him. "Are you scared?"

His mouth flattens. The look he gives me lasts exactly one second before his attention flicks back to the dark office. "I'm cautious."

"Same thing," I whisper, and before he can argue, I step inside.

I step just inside the doorway. Paper covers nearly every visible surface. Maps droop from shelves and tabletops, their edges curled with age. Journals lie open in uneven stacks, their cracked spines splayed wide. Photocopies overlap across the walls in crooked layers, pinned and taped wherever there was space until the paint disappears beneath them.

Red thread stretches from pushpin to pushpin over the largest map, crisscrossing the room in a tangled web. Some lines sag under their own weight. Others pull taut between distant points like tripwires.

A manuscript near the desk bears the ghostly rings of a dozen forgotten coffee cups. More papers spill from beneath it. Above them, a chipped ceramic mug balances precariously atop a tower of books that looks one vibration away from collapse.

The room smells like dust, old paper, and stale coffee.

Somehow, Professor Harland has managed to make it worse than the last time I was here.

I move carefully between piles. "Professor?" Louder this time. "It's Rachel."

The room answers with the radiator ticking and the fluorescent light buzzing overhead. Somewhere in the stacks, a page slips and settles. I jump anyway. I edge toward the desk.

Don't touch anything,

I tell myself, then immediately have to steady a listing stack of atlases with one hand. The smell in here is faintly metallic, ink, maybe. Obsession, definitely. My eyes keep snagging on the same symbol. It's everywhere. Scrawled in the margins of a notebook. Chalked faintly on the corner of the blackboard.

Penciled along the edge of a map in tight, repeated rows.

A circle. Three straight lines cutting down through it at slightly different angles. I've seen it so many times now it feels like it's watching me back. *What are you?* I think. *Warning, or invitation? Map, or threshold? Is everything connected somehow?*

Riven stays near the threshold, and I can feel his reluctance and hesitation as we walk further into the room.

"Rachel," he says softly, "if he's not here—"

"The light's on." I keep my voice even. "He's either here or he left in a hurry."

"You don't know what else is here."

He's not wrong. But the same pull that dragged me to the circle is humming under my skin now the sense of a line running from that stone to this room, to these maps and notes and strings. There's a pattern. I can feel it. I just need to grab one end. I move along the wall, reading fragments he's taped up. Phrases jump out in a collage:

> *—first accounts call it the Splitting Sky...*
> *—survivors exhibited phonic resonance ("pulse")...*
> *—sites occur in mirrored pairs: coast/inland, stone/river...*
> *—beware the watchers; they gather where the light thins...*
> *—Cycle markers appear in pre-Falling texts; humans misdate the fracture...*

"Professor?" I call again, aiming my voice toward the back of the room where a narrow canyon of boxes leads deeper in. "It's urgent. Something happened at one of the sites."

Still nothing. I edge around the desk, careful not to disturb more than I already have. I remember how he moved in here, weaving through chaos, a system only he could read. It is a system, I can feel the pattern now, the way the notes talk to each other across the room. Maps to journals, journals to photographs, photographs back to that symbol. Over and over. Circle. Three lines. Falling. Always the falling.

Riven's voice comes lower now, closer. He's stepped inside despite himself. "You shouldn't be in front of the windows," he says, almost absently. I feel him shift behind me, angling between me and the glass. "If he's studying what you think he is, others will be interested in it too."

"'Others,'" I repeat, questioning, eyes still scanning a line of cramped handwriting that snakes between clippings. "Very comforting, thanks."

A spiral bound notebook lies open on the desk, Harland's tight script marching across the page. I hover my fingers above it and force myself not to touch. I bend closer instead.

> *—accounts conflict on whether the Falling was random or deliberate. Patterns of impact suggest intention, but intention by whom? Not god(s) as popularly framed; more akin to—*

The sentence breaks off, narrowed toward a diagram of the symbol. Beneath, in darker pencil:

> *Three paths. Descent, divide, remainder.*
> *Circle = field, threshold, site.*
> *Lines = entries — NOT pillars — NOT spears — NOT rain.*

I whisper it back without thinking. "Three paths. Descent, divide, remainder." The words feel right in my mouth, like keys that already fit the lock. A shiver moves through the room that I tell myself is just the heating kicking on. I look up and catch my reflection in the dark glass, pale, eyes rimmed with that faint shimmer I've been pretending isn't there. It halos the edges of the papers, crawls along the red string, turns the chalk a shade too bright. Wherever my gaze lands, the symbol seems to glow a fraction stronger, like my attention is heat.

It responded to you, Riven said.

"Rachel." His voice is closer now. "If we're staying, we should at least make sure we're not alone." "I've been calling," I say, even as I admit to myself he's right. The professor isn't answering, and the silence in here feels like the wrong shape. "One minute." I crouch beside a crate near the bookshelf where old photographs spill from a manila envelope in black-and-white images of carved stones, riverbeds, coastal ridges. Two photos lie side by side. My breath catches. The cliff ring we found. And its twin, inland, etched into a river bend like a scar. Mirrored pairs. Coast, river. Stone, water. Harland has circled both in hard pencil and written a single word between them:

Confluence.

Above, the red string crosses in almost the same shape, an X over a map I don't recognize. My heart taps harder. "He knew," I murmur. "He was tracking both sites at once."

"And?" Riven asks, tone careful.

"And he connected them for a reason." I straighten slowly. "Whatever I touched today—whatever touched me—it doesn't end at one circle." The room feels tighter now. My chest tightening with every breath I try to take in.

"Professor?" I try one last time, voice steady. "We need your help. Please." Silence.

I blow out a breath of relief and turn to Riven. "He's not here."

He studies me, then the door, then the window again, always counting exits. "We should leave something. A note. Your number." I nod, then hesitate. My gaze snags on the blackboard. The symbol is drawn there again the same circle and three lines but tonight there's something else I didn't notice before. A fourth mark, faint, half-erased. Not another line. A curve. A crescent, nested inside the circle like a small moon drowning in daylight.

My skin prickles.

Dad's last words thread through my mind, cold and clear: *When the moon drowns in daylight, you'll find the door.*

I swallow hard. "Riven..." I hesitate then point to the board, "look."

He joins me at the board, keeping that half-step of distance like even chalk could be dangerous. His eyes track the lines, then the almost-curve. His brow furrows.

"What does it mean?" I ask, hating the way my voice thins.

He doesn't answer right away. Finally: "It means the professor saw something you haven't yet." I nod slowly, trying not to show how much that scares me. Then find it, I order myself. Whatever he saw, find it before something else finds you.

"I'll write the note," I say, and snatch a scrap of paper already scarred with coffee rings and someone else's half-finished thought. As I scribble my name and number with a pen that skips, I can feel Riven's unease tightening the air. He hasn't said it, but I know what he's thinking: we're not the only ones following these threads. The symbol is a map, for more than just us. When I set the note in the middle of the desk where it can't be missed, my hand moves on its own, adding one more line:

I saw the Falling.

The words look too stark against the mess.

"Okay," I breathe, stepping back. "We did what we could. If he's in the building, he'll see it. If he's not, he'll find it." Riven nods, eyes still flicking between window, door, hallway, like he expects the room itself to move. "We should go."

I take one last look around. The papers. The red string. The chalk. The crescent like a drowned moon. Answers exist, I tell myself. They're here somewhere. I just have to survive long enough to read them.

"Yeah," I say, turning toward the door. "Let's go."

I circle another table stacked in unstable towers of books and loose pages, my fingers brushing a line through the dust along the edge. A few sheets slide to the floor, fanning out like wilted feathers.

That's when I see him.

Chapter 21

The papers hit the floor with a soft flutter. I glance down automatically, then up. Something shifts in the darkness beyond the desk. My breath catches. For a second, I think it's a coat draped over the chair. A trick of shadow and clutter. The office is full of shapes pretending to be other shapes.

Then the desk lamp flickers. Light spills across a hand. A real hand.

I freeze.

Behind the desk, someone is sitting perfectly still. The chair faces slightly toward the window. One arm rests on the armrest. The other lies across a stack of papers that have slipped unnoticed to the floor. A cold knot forms in my stomach.

"Riven."

The word barely leaves my mouth. He's beside me immediately.

"What is it?"

I point. His gaze follows mine. Professor Harland sits motionless in the chair. The lamp throws uneven bands of light across his face. One side is hidden in shadow. The other is washed pale beneath the yellow glow.

His eyes are open.Not just open. Fixed. They stare past the

desk, past the wall, past me. For one horrible second, I think he's dead. Then his chest rises. The breath is so shallow I almost miss it. Relief crashes through me so hard my knees threaten to give way.

"He's breathing," I whisper.

I don't realize I've spoken until I hear my own voice.

"Look. His chest."

Neither of us moves. The radiator ticks again. Professor Harland doesn't blink. I take a careful step forward. Then another. The air feels different near the desk. Colder somehow. Thin enough that every breath seems to scrape my lungs on the way in.

The light catches his face again. His skin has the dull, waxy look of old candle wax. His eyes remain locked on whatever he's seeing. Or whatever he's seen. A muscle twitches in one hand.

Just once.

His fingers curl faintly against his lap, as though he's reaching for something in a dream.

"Professor?" I crouch slightly.

No reaction.

"It's Rachel." The words sound small.

"We met last week. You lent me a book, remember?"

Nothing. Not a blink. Not a flinch. Not even the slightest shift of focus. The silence presses harder. A familiar chill crawls up my spine. I've felt this before. In my apartment.In the hallway. Standing inside the circle. That same impossible wrongness. The feeling that something invisible is standing just beyond the edge of sight, watching and waiting.

My pulse stutters.

Looking at the professor, I can't shake the feeling that

whatever is sitting in that chair isn't entirely here.

"Riven," I murmur, glancing back. "What's happening to him?"

He shakes his head once, eyes fixed on the professor. "I don't know. Stay back."

But I can't. The stillness feels magnetic, something has hooked behind my ribs and is pulling hard.

"Professor?" I try again, louder this time. "Can you hear me?"

Nothing.

"Rachel," Riven warns, tone firmer now. "Don't—" he reaches out to stop me, I take a step forward out of his grasp.

The professor's hand immediately shoots out and clamps tightly around my wrist. I gasp. His grip is inhumanly strong, fingers digging deep enough to bruise. His eyes never move, still staring through me, like I'm not a person but a window. Riven lunges forward, but before he can reach us, the professor speaks.

His voice is thin and stretched, layered with something that isn't entirely his. It scrapes against the air like it doesn't fit in his throat.

"When the stars fall again, the door will open," he rasps. "The light will call for balance, and the void will answer."

My breath stutters as I try to pry his fingers from my wrist "What—what does that mean?" He doesn't blink. His hand tightens painfully. "It's already begun."

"Let her go," Riven snaps, fingers closing hard around the professor's wrist. For a split second, something flickers across Harland's face, a shadow under the skin, a faint shimmer rippling around his shoulders. Heat licks the air between us, sharp and wrong. Then his fingers slacken.

He releases me all at once, sagging back in his chair like a puppet whose strings were cut. He blinks once. Then again. His eyes focus slowly on my face.

"Oh," he says, voice suddenly normal, bewildered. "Rachel? When did you get here?"

I stagger back, clutching my wrist. "You—" My voice shakes. "You grabbed me."

He frowns, looking from me to Riven, then down at his own hand as if it doesn't belong to him. "Did I? I... I don't remember."

Riven steps slightly ahead of me, his stance protective, dark eyes locked on the professor. "What's the last thing you do remember?"

Harland looks around the room, dazed. "I was... reading," he says slowly. "Notes on the confluence sites." His gaze drifts toward the chalkboard, unfocused. "And then... I must have fallen asleep."

"I don't think you were asleep," I say quietly.

The professor blinks at me, confusion shading toward fear. "I—well, I certainly wasn't awake."

I glance at Riven. His expression has shifted not in surprise but in recognition.

"Riven?" I press, my voice dropping.

He doesn't look away from the professor. "We need to get him out of this room."

Harland tilts his head. "Out of the room? Why on earth would—" The overhead lights flicker. Once. Then again. The papers on the nearest table start to lift slightly, edges rippling as if caught in a draft that isn't there. Riven's jaw tightens. "Now."

The lights flicker a third time, then steady into a dim,

unnatural hum. The usual background noise of the building seems to fade until all I can hear is the low electrical buzz. The air thickens, heavy with static. The professor squints up at the bulbs. "What's happening to the lights?"

"Rachel," Riven says, his voice going low and urgent. "Stay close to me."

Something in his tone clamps around my ribs. I move toward him instinctively. "What is it?" He doesn't answer. His gaze is fixed on the far wall. The papers there begin to tremble, edges fluttering as though something is breathing against them. The red strings shiver.

The professor pushes himself upright, one hand braced on the desk. "It's... the frequency again," he mutters, more to himself than us. "The interference—"

"Professor," Riven cuts in sharply. "We need to go."

"I can't," Harland says, scanning his notes again. "You don't understand. It's happening again, the resonance—"

A sharp crack splits the air. The overhead bulb bursts, glass raining down in glittering shards. I yelp, ducking, arms over my head. The room plunges into semi-darkness, lit only by the wan silver glow of the desk lamp and the faint shimmer that now rims everything at the edges of my vision.

Riven grabs my arm, firmly. In an attempt to move me quicker out of the room. "Out. Now."

"What about him?" I shout back, nodding at the professor. Riven doesn't hesitate. He's already closing the distance, crossing the room in two long strides. "Professor, you're coming with us." The older man blinks up at him, dazed. "Go? Now? But I—" Whatever argument he's about to make dies when the temperature drops. Cold rushes through the room so fast I can see his breath bloom pale in the half-light.

And then I see it.

In the corner near the window, the shadows are moving. Twisting slowly, appearing to form a human shape. Just like the figure in my kitchen. "Riven," I whisper.

"I see it." His voice is steady, but there's iron underneath now. He steps in front of us, body angled between me and the shape. The shadow stretches along the wall, lengthening, until it looks nearly human.

Close enough for me. Time to run.

The professor stumbles backward, colliding with the desk. "No... no, that's not possible," he stammers. "It's—"

"Move," Riven barks, grabbing his arm. Harland flinches but doesn't fight.

I snatch the nearest flashlight off the table. It sputters weakly to life, beam thin and shaky, but it's something. I spin, heart racing, and follow as Riven hauls the professor toward the door. Behind us, the papers rip free of the walls in a sudden gust, swirling in a frantic storm. Some of them catch fire midair, bursting into orange for a second before curling into ash.

We burst into the hallway. The lights there are still on, steady and yellow, but I can feel it that same pressure, the watching. Whatever was in that room is the same thing that was in my bedroom and it's not finished.

"Keep moving," Riven says with no room for argument in his tone.

The professor's breath saws in and out. "What—what was that?!"

"Later," Riven snaps. "Outside first."

I run beside them, lungs burning, heart pounding so hard I can taste metal. Every few steps I risk a look back, expecting to see that shadow loping after us down the hall. Nothing is there. Just the echo of our footsteps and the complaint of old floorboards.

When we finally shove through the main doors, Riven slams his shoulder into the crash bar. They burst open in a rush of cold night air. We spill out onto the dark campus. The lamps along the walkway flicker as we pass, one by one, until we're moving through more shadow than light. Riven doesn't slow. He keeps a tight hold on the professor's arm, half-guiding, half-dragging him toward the parking lot.

His car waits at the far edge, black and sleek beneath a single, flickering streetlamp.

"Rachel, get the door," he says. I yank open the back door, and Riven practically pushes the professor inside. Harland collapses onto the seat, still trembling, muttering a jumble of words and prayers mashed together. Riven slams the door, his breath visible in thin bursts. "Stay inside," he tells the professor through the glass.

Then he turns to me, expression grim. "It followed us."

My skin goes cold. "How do you know?" He looks past me, back toward the building.

I turn.

In the top-floor window, the one we just left, the light flickers again. For a split second, a tall dark figure is there, framed by glass. Watching us.

The window suddenly shatters.

I flinch, gasping. Riven grabs my hand and hauls me toward the passenger side.

"Get in. Now."

"What about—"

"Now, Rachel."

The urgency in his voice leaves no room for anything else. I dive into the seat just as he starts the engine. Tires squeal, gravel sprays. The building shrinks in the rear view mirror, its remaining windows flashing like dying stars.

The only sounds are the wind, the engine, and the pounding of my heart. Whatever that thing was, whatever just happened back there, it definitely didn't want the professor talking.

Chapter 22

The professor sits slumped in the back seat, staring out the window, appearing in shock between what he saw and what he's willing to believe. His fingers twitch every so often in a tapping, counting motion or he's just losing his grip. I can't tell which.

Riven's jaw is clenched, knuckles pale on the steering wheel. Every few minutes his eyes flick up to the mirror, not really looking at me, but checking. Always checking. Confirming I'm still here. Still breathing. Still not collapsing into light, or shadow, or whatever the hell that thing wanted.

The car finally slows. I hadn't realized how tightly I'd been gripping the door handle until my fingers protest when I let go. Concrete walls rise around us. The headlights sweep across polished floors and rows of parked vehicles before Riven guides the car down a ramp and into an underground garage.

It's enormous. The sound of the engine echoes away into the distance. No oil stains. No puddles collecting in cracked concrete. Everything gleams. Fluorescent lights hum overhead, reflecting off brushed steel columns and floors polished enough to throw back warped reflections. The whole place smells faintly of concrete and ozone instead of gasoline.

For some reason, that bothers me more.

The engine dies. Silence rushes in behind it. I look around again. The garage feels less like a place people park and more like somewhere people aren't supposed to find.

"Where are we?"

Riven unbuckles his seatbelt.

"My place."

I blink.

"Your place?"

He reaches for the door handle. A small nod.

"As in your actual home?"

His mouth twitches. "Yes."

I stare through the windshield. This is not what I'd expected. Not even close. Somehow I'd assumed a tiny apartment filled with ancient books and questionable life choices.

Not... this.

"It's safer here."

The words pull my attention to the back seat. Professor Harland sits slumped against the window. His eyes are open. They don't seem to focus on anything. A chill crawls across my skin.

"Safer from what?"

For the first time since we left the university, Riven doesn't answer immediately. Riven just opens his door. "Come on."

Of course. God forbid he answer anything directly.

I climb out, boots echoing sharply in the cavernous quiet. The sound dies too fast, swallowed by concrete. He leads us to a nondescript elevator tucked behind a blank steel panel. No call buttons, no floor numbers. Just a black sensor. He presses his thumb to it.

The doors sighs open. Because of course he has a private

elevator. Inside, three walls are mirrored glass, floor to ceiling and it's bathed in warm, golden light. It's not flashy, but definitely expensive. The kind of understated luxury that says the money isn't new, and no one here has ever had to check the price tag on anything.

There's only one button. **PH.**

"Penthouse," I say flatly, giving him a look. Riven presses it without comment and without looking at me. The elevator rises smoothly, unnervingly fast. The professor leans weakly against the wall, muttering about resonance frequencies and echo sites and angles being wrong, so wrong, but all I can focus on is the pounding in my skull.

When the doors open, I actually gasp. Floor-to-ceiling windows wrap around a vast, open-concept loft, the city glittering below like spilled stars. The furniture is sleek and minimal, all clean lines and muted grays. Dark wood floors. Glass and steel every where I look. A few tall plants stand high, perfectly placed. The air smells like nothing. No cooking, no candles, no life. It's beautiful. And it feels... wrong.

I turn in a slow circle. "Okay... is this some kind of generational wealth situation you've been hiding?"

"Something like that," Riven says, flipping on more lights.

"That's vague."

He doesn't bother responding. He taps a control on the wall; automatic blinds glide down with a soft whirl, dimming the city into a warm, muted dusk.

The professor stumbles out of the elevator, dazed. Riven guides him to a long charcoal couch. "Sit. Breathe. Don't move."

"Yes—yes, of course," the professor murmurs. He sinks down into the plush cushions and sighs loudly. "What... what was that back there?" he asks, voice thin.

"Not here," Riven says, reassuringly.

I drift toward the window. From up here, the city looks unreal, like a model, or an interactive map. Tiny grids of light. Toy cars. People smaller than thoughts. The quiet presses at my ears until my shoulders finally sag and a shaky breath leaves me all at once.

Behind me,standing closer than I expected, Riven says, "We'll be safe here. For now."

"You said that about the library," I remind him. Turning to face him. Our chests nearly touching.

"This is different." I can feel his breath on my cheek when he says it.

"Why?" My eyes flutter close as I soak in the smell of him. Honey and sage.

A beat too long. "Because this time, I'm sure of it." Somehow that feels worse. I take a step back to put some space between us and my impossible thoughts. Just being near Riven makes me heart beat faster.

The professor hunches forward, both hands wrapped around the glass of water Riven gave him like it's a lifeline. His lips move soundlessly; his fingers twitch as if he's still counting waves of something only he can hear. The silence in here is the wrong kind. Not comfortable but curated.

I wander the space, absorbing details. The kitchen is all sleek black counters and stainless steel appliances that look unused. The books on the shelves are arranged like décor, spines evenly spaced, colors balanced. No dog-eared pages. No stacked paperbacks. No family photos. No ugly mug from a tourist trap. Nothing that says someone lives here. It doesn't feel like a home. It feels like a stage.

"You live here alone?" I ask.

"Yes."

"For how long?"

A pause I can't read. "Long enough."

That could mean a year. Or a hundred. Before I can push, the professor jerks upright, eyes wide. "It was watching me," he whispers. "All this time... watching. I thought the fluctuations were anomalies, but no... no, they were eyes."

My stomach drops. "Professor?" He blinks at me, pupils still too large. "Rachel. You saw it, didn't you? The shadow in the corner. It doesn't want the light to awaken again."

Riven's voice softens. "He needs rest."

"Rest?" I let out a disbelieving huff. "After that? He needs a sedative and maybe an exorcism."

Riven ignores me. He eases the professor back against the cushions, steady, unhurried. Harland's eyes flutter closed.

I wrap my arms around myself. "You really think it's safe here?"

"For now," he repeats, gently.

He moves to the window, scanning the skyline for something I'm not sure of. The city's reflection glows faintly across his face, halos of color flickering at the edges of my vision.

"You say that like you've had to hide before," I say quietly.

His gaze flicks my way. "Haven't you?" I don't answer.

He turns away first, crossing to the bar built into one wall. Cut crystal glints under recessed lighting. He pours something amber and sharp smelling into a glass. His movements are controlled and precise.

"What's that?" I ask.

"You wouldn't like it."

"That's rude." I step forward and pluck the glass from his

hand before I can talk myself out of it. "I can handle a drink."

"It tastes like fire and regret."

"I've had worse." I take a sip.

It sears my tongue, my throat and hell, it feels like it scorches straight through to my soul. Tears spring to my eyes. "Oh my God—what is that?!" I choke out between coughs.

"Told you," he says, reclaiming the glass, amused.

"You're not supposed to drink it. You survive it."

I wipe my mouth with the back of my hand, scowling. "You could have warned me properly."

"I tried."

Before I can retort, both our gazes drift back to the couch. The professor is fully out now, breathing slow and shallow. His hands have gone slack, but every now and then one finger twitches.

When the stars fall again, the door will open...

A shiver moves through me.

"Are you cold?" Riven asks.

"No, just a chill. He's freezing though," I whisper, as a way to deflect my own cold shiver.

Riven hesitates, then nods. "I'll get a blanket."

He disappears down a short hallway. The room shifts when he's gone. It some how feels bigger and much quieter. I study the professor's face. In sleep, he looks smaller and so fragile in a way that doesn't match the mind that wallpapered a room with constellations and warnings. Something about that hand clamping around my wrist, that voice hijacking his—*the light will call for balance and the void will answer*—lodges under my sternum and refuses to move.

Riven comes back with a soft gray blanket. He kneels, actually kneels and tucks it around the professor with careful hands. The gesture is simple, but there's something unexpectedly tender in it. Unguarded. When he stands, our eyes meet. I look away first.

"You have wine," I say, spotting a dark bottle half-hidden behind the stronger stuff. "Now that I can handle."

"Help yourself," he says.

I pour a glass. The red pools deep and dark, catching the light. It's smoother than I expect when I sip it, almost too soft for the night we've had. I sink into an armchair opposite him. The cushions swallow me whole. "So," I say quietly, "the shadow. The professor said it doesn't want the light to awaken. What do you think that means?"

Riven's gaze drifts back to the window. The city lies beneath us, and beyond that, clouds are gathering slowly, like heavy smudges on the horizon.

"If the stories are true," he says slowly, "light and void weren't enemies. They were balance. Two forces, not one 'good' and one 'bad'—just... necessary opposites. The Falling broke that."

"Broke it how?" I ask.

"Too much of one. Not enough of the other." He turns the glass in his hand, watching the liquid move. "Maybe what we saw tonight is that imbalance trying to fix itself."

"By killing us?" I say, sharper than I mean to.

"By reclaiming what it thinks was lost."

The wine suddenly feels heavy in my mouth. "And me?"

He looks at me then, really looks. "You touched the circle," he says softly. "You woke it. That makes you part of it— whether you meant to be or not."

The hum under my skin pulses in agreement.

"It feels like everything I touch turns into a warning," I

whisper.

"Or," he says, voice barely above the low city hush, "maybe it's showing you what was already waiting." The words land between us, soft and heavy and true. For a moment, the silence isn't frightening. Just... full of unanswered questions.

City lights flicker across the glass, shimmering faintly around our reflections. For a heartbeat, the colors at the edges of my vision flare brighter, outlining his shoulders, the curve of his jaw, the professor's sleeping form.

"He said it's already begun," I murmur. "If that's true... what happens next?"

Riven doesn't answer right away. His eyes stay on the skyline like he's waiting for it to shift, like he's checking for constellations only he can see.

"I don't know," he says quietly. "But whatever it is... it's not stopping here."

Somewhere beyond the glass, thunder rumbles faintly, still far away. The windowpane vibrates just slightly.

Chapter 23

The silk sheets are too soft. Too perfect. They slide cool against my skin, whispering every time I move, and somehow that makes it worse. I've been lying here for what feels like hours, staring at the ceiling, counting the faint city lights bleeding through the curtains. Sleep refuses to come. Every time I close my eyes, I see the professor's face, his pupils blown wide, the way his hand snapped out and clamped around my wrist. I hear the voice that wasn't quite his:

The void will call for balance, and the light will answer.

The words loop endlessly, quiet and wrong, a clock ticking just out of rhythm. Eventually, I give up. I push the sheets back and swing my legs over the edge of the bed. The floor is cool under my feet as I grab the sweater draped over the chair and pull it on. The guest room Riven put me in is beautiful in a minimalist, clean lines, no clutter kinda way. The kind of space designed to impress, not to rest. Nothing out of place. Nothing that says *someone lives here.*

I ease the door open and step into the hallway. The condo is quiet, except for the faint hum of the city beyond the glass. The air smells faintly of cedar and something darker. I move slowly, barefoot, soundless on wooden floors.

The lights are dimmed, pools of warm gold scattered

through the open space. The professor is still on the couch, curled beneath the blanket Riven tucked around him. He hasn't moved. His breathing is slow and steady, mouth slightly open in exhausted sleep. I watch his chest rise and fall for a moment, just to be sure.

Everything else looks exactly as we left it. The wine bottle still on the cart. Two half-empty glasses catching fractured reflections of the skyline. Curiosity tugs me toward the staircase I noticed earlier.

The steps are wide and shallow, leading up to a mezzanine that overlooks the main living area. The city spreads out below, vast and sleepless. Up here, the air feels different almost quieter and thicker, like sound doesn't quite reach. A wide doorway stands slightly ajar. I hesitate, then nudge it open.

It's a library.

Rows of tall shelves line the walls, filled with books in dark, uniform bindings, no colorful paperbacks, no jackets, just embossed titles in silver and gold. A massive desk dominates the center of the room, scattered with papers and a few open notebooks, a sleek lamp casting a pool of soft light over everything. Ink, leather, and the faintest trace of dust hang in the air.

It's beautiful in a cold, deliberate way. A place made for thinking, not relaxing. I step inside just far enough to look around, fingers brushing the edge of the desk. Everything is meticulously arranged: pens lined up in perfect parallel, stacks squared exactly, pages aligned. Even the open books are positioned with precise symmetry, as if whoever works here doesn't just read, they dissect. One wall is glass. Beyond it, I can see another closed door, dark wood, sleek handle, no markings.

His room, I would guess.

The thought hits harder than it should. I take half a step toward it, pulse kicking up for no good reason. God. What am I doing? Standing outside Riven's bedroom in the middle of the night like some kind of creep. I can hear Marin in my head: *"You? Breaking and entering into hot-guy territory? Bold move, sunshine."*

I retreat quickly, the hem of my sweater brushing my knees as I back away. The floorboard under my heel creaks and it's the first imperfection I've heard in this whole place and somehow that comforts me.

Back downstairs, the living room is unchanged. Professor Harland sleeps on, the lights dim and soft, the city humming beyond the glass. It all feels too still. Too fragile. My stomach growls, sudden and insistent. I realize I haven't eaten since before the cliff, before the vision took hold, before the shadow moved through the university. Food hadn't exactly been a priority between almost dying and being hunted by whatever that was.

I pad into the kitchen, scanning the sleek marble counters for anything that looks like it wasn't placed here by an interior designer. Nothing. The only light comes from the city through the huge windows casting the room in a soft glow that's gold and silver. I've already opened half the cabinets. So far I've found: protein bars, dried fruit, coffee beans that probably come with their own biography.

"You'd think a man who owns silk sheets would at least have snacks," I mutter, reaching for another cabinet. The wine has left my limbs warm and loose, my thoughts slightly out of focus, just enough for the edges of the night to blur. I can still taste it on my tongue, the after taste is sweet and sharp. I stretch onto my toes to grab a box from the top shelf when a voice cuts through the quiet.

"Can I help you?"

I scream. The box slips from my hands and thuds onto the counter. I spin so fast I nearly take out a stool.

"Jesus—Riven! What the hell?!"

He's leaning casually in the doorway, half in shadow, arms folded. The faintest curve of a smile tugs at his mouth.

"You have a real talent for breaking into other people's kitchens," he says dryly.

My heart is hammering so hard it hurts. my hand is on my chest trying to hold my heart inside it. "You can't just—appear like that. You almost killed me."

He tilts his head. "Pretty sure you've already used up your near-death quota for the week."

I glare, still breathless. "You're lucky I didn't throw something at you."

His gaze flicks to the counter. "You mean the box of... herbal tea?"

I look down. He's right. Not exactly lethal. "Still."

"Still," he echoes, and steps fully into the light. He's barefoot, hair slightly mussed, in a plain black T-shirt and joggers. Simple. Somehow that makes it worse. Or better. I don't know.

"I couldn't sleep," I mutter, pushing my hair back. "The bed's too soft, the silence is too loud, and apparently your pantry is all aesthetics and no substance."

"Sorry to disappoint," he says, passing me to open a lower cabinet. He pulls out a small container, sets it on the counter, and glances over. "Granola."

I blink. "You do have snacks."

He smirks. "I ration them carefully." I take the container, half-tempted to throw it at him anyway. "You could've mentioned that before scaring me into cardiac arrest." His expression softens, just a fraction. "Didn't mean to," he says. "You just looked…" He searches for a word. "…lost."

The comment takes me off guard. I pop the lid, focusing on the contents to avoid his eyes. "Well, your apartment's a maze," I say. "I was exploring."

He leans against the counter, watching me. "Find anything interesting?"

"Your library," I say around a mouthful of granola. "And a very closed door. I'm assuming that's your bedroom."

Something flickers in his eyes, amusement, maybe surprise. "You were upstairs."

I shrug, aiming for casual. "Briefly. Don't flatter yourself, I wasn't snooping."

His mouth curves. "You were curious."

"Curiosity is a survival skill," I shoot back. "Helps me not die, remember?"

"Fair point."

Silence settles. Not entirely comfortable, not entirely uncomfortable. The fridge hums softly. City light spills across the marble, gilding his profile. The wine buzz moves gently through me, softening edges. The quiet between us feels like something alive. I glance up and find him already looking at me, quietly.

"You're really not going to sleep, are you?" he asks at last.

"Probably not."

He nods once. "Then sit. I'll make coffee."

I blink. "You? Making coffee? I thought you survived on brooding and cryptic statements."

He gives me a sidelong look that's almost a smile. "Don't tell anyone. It'll ruin my reputation."

I laugh under my breath and hop up to sit on the counter. The marble is cold against my bare legs; goosebumps rise immediately. I fold one foot over the other to hide it, pretending it's the temperature and not the man standing ten feet away. I watch him move around the kitchen. He's calm again, all quiet precision and control, the same man who fought off shadows but somehow makes pouring water look practiced....and hot. What is the matter with me?

As the coffee brews, the smell spills into the room it's warm and familiar.

"Do you ever sleep?" I ask.

"Sometimes."

"That's not an answer."

He glances over his shoulder. "Sometimes is an answer."

Touché.

The machine clicks off. He pours two mugs and brings one over, setting it beside me.

"Here," he says.

"Thanks." My voice comes out a little rougher than I intend. He leans against the opposite counter with his own mug. The silence hangs between us again, suspended. I take a sip. The bitterness cuts through the remnants of wine and adrenaline. My fingers curl around the ceramic for something solid. Suddenly I feel bolder and curious all at once. I ask the question that's been lingering in the back of my mind all day.

"You never answered me earlier," I say quietly.

His gaze lifts. "About what?"

"What you said in the car," I murmur. "That you didn't know what you'd do if you lost me."

His eyes linger on mine for a long beat. Then he sets his cup down, slow and deliberate.

"You don't let things go, do you?" he says.

"Not when they sound like that," I reply.

He exhales, and it sounds like surrender. "I meant exactly what it sounded like."

I shift my weight, crossing my legs, more to give my hands something to do than because I need to. The marble seeps chill through the thin fabric of my shorts; another wave of goosebumps follows. Whether it's the counter or the way he's looking at me, I'm not sure.

"You barely know me, Riven," I say.

His mouth tilts. "I know enough."

He studies me, a faint half-smile ghosting over his lips. "You have this way of walking straight into the center of chaos like you belong there. You don't flinch from it, you meet it. Most people run."

I let out a small, disbelieving laugh. "You say that like it's a compliment."

"It is," he says simply. "You remind me what it feels like to be reckless. And free."

The words land deeper than they should. Something in my chest shifts. I look at him, suddenly unsure what to do with my hands, my face, my entire existence. The air tightens. He takes a slow step forward. Then another. The soft glow from the city paints his features in gold and shadow. My heartbeat skids and then races. I should say something, make a joke, tell him to back up, remind us both of the hell waiting outside these walls.

I don't.

I just sit there, pulse thudding, every nerve aware of him

closing the distance.

"I shouldn't say things like that," he murmurs.

"Then why do you?" I whisper.

He stops in front of me. His hand lifts, hesitates, then brushes a loose strand of hair away from my face.

"Because you make me forget what the right thing to do is."

The world narrows to the warmth of his fingertips against my cheek, the steady rhythm of his breathing. My gaze drops to his mouth before I can stop it, then drags back up to his eyes.

"This isn't a good idea," I manage.

"Probably not."

But he doesn't step back. His eyes search mine, and for a second I forget how to think.

"Riven..."

He's impossibly close now, my knees bracketing his hips as his hand slides to cup my jaw, thumb grazing the edge of my cheekbone.

"I keep telling myself to stay away," he says, voice low. "But every time I do, I end up here—closer than I should be, saying things I shouldn't say, wanting things I shouldn't want."

My breath stutters. "Then stop."

His mouth tilts in something like a sad smile. "I don't think I can."

And then he kisses me. It's soft at first, hesitant, like he's leaving room for me to pull away. I don't. The tension that's been coiled between us since the moment we met snaps, all at once. The kiss deepens, heat and ache and relief colliding. His hand slides to the back of my neck, the other resting warm and steady at my waist. My fingers find his shirt, curling into the fabric, anchoring myself. The air around us hums, faint and electric. Thoughts empty from my head.

When he finally pulls back, his forehead rests against mine. Our breaths tangle in the small space between us, too fast, too shallow.

"That," I whisper, "felt like a bad idea."

A quiet laugh ghosts against my lips. "Yeah," he murmurs. "But it didn't feel wrong."

Something in me breaks loose. Before I can talk myself out of it, I'm kissing him again, harder this time, fingers splayed in his hair, pulled by a gravity I'm too tired to resist. His hands tighten at my waist, drawing me closer to the edge of the counter. A surprised sound leaves me as my body slots more firmly against his. The world shrinks to heat and breath and the way he says my name against my mouth like a promise.

He lifts me with an ease that knocks the air from my lungs. Instinctively, my legs wrap around him, a gasp catching in my throat. The movement feels inevitable, like we've been moving toward this from the start. He carries me through the dim hall, our mouths finding each other again and again in stolen, breathless kisses. My hands clutch his shoulders, thread in his hair, trace the tense line of his neck. The warmth of him sinks through every layer between us.

When he pushes open the door to the room I saw from the library, the light inside is low and soft, washing everything in shadow. He sets me down on the bed gently, but the look in his eyes says he's not the only one trying not to break. For one suspended heartbeat, we just stare at each other. Then he pulls his shirt over his head.

The movement is unhurried. I forget how to breath. The faint city glow from the window traces the lines of him, lean and strong, skin catching gold at the edges. My breath catches again as I run my eyes up and down him. Suddenly, everything feels too real and that gravitational pull feels stronger.

He steps toward the bed slowly and leans over me again. One of his hands finds mine, fingers lacing together. The other braces beside my shoulder as he slowly lowers his body onto mine.

"This shouldn't happen," he murmurs.

"I know."

Neither of us stop. The kiss that follows is slower, deeper, the kind that empties out thought entirely. I can feel his heartbeat where his chest presses against mine, fast, unsteady, matching my own. His touch is warm and hungry all at once. For once, I make a choice not to analyze. Not to pick it apart or weigh the consequences. For once, I just feel.

The weight of him above me. The press of his lips. The way his hands map the shape of me like he's memorizing it. The way my body answers, every nerve alight, every breath catching like I've been waiting for this without knowing it. I want his bare skin on mine, I need more and as we kiss that longing becomes stronger. The world narrows to heat and the steady, impossible pull thrumming between us—

CRASH!

A sharp crash splits the air. Glass shatters somewhere in the apartment, the sound ricocheting through the quiet. We both freeze. For a heartbeat, we just stare at each other, breathing hard, the moment hanging between us, fractured.

Then it hits me. "The professor," I whisper.

Riven is already moving. He grabs his shirt, yanks it on in one swift motion, and bolts for the door. I scramble after him, heart pounding, the haze of what almost was dissolving into cold adrenaline. We take the stairs two at a time. The air feels wrong again, thick, charged, humming at the edge of my senses. When we reach the living room, the blanket that had been tucked around the professor is crumpled on the floor. One of the lamps lies shattered beside the couch. And the couch itself is empty.

Chapter 24

For a moment, neither of us move. The blanket Riven laid over the professor lies crumpled on the floor, one edge dark where the water glass spilled. The lamp beside the sofa is shattered, glittering fragments scattered across the hardwood.

"Professor?" I call, my voice small in the wide, quiet room. Nothing. Just the low hum of the city through the windows. Riven steps forward slowly, shoulders tight, scanning every corner. His body is all tension and calculation. He's ready to fight if something lunges at us from the darkness.

"Stay close," he murmurs. I nod, pulse already hammering, and follow him. "Do you think he's been taken?" I ask Riven, more concerned than afraid. Riven doesn't answer just keeps scanning the room. We move through the condo, past the dim hallway, past the kitchen with its flicker of light over stainless steel, the echo of our footsteps too loud in the stillness.

"Professor?" I try again. "It's Rachel. Are you—"

Something shifts. A sound, faint but unmistakable. A low muttering, someone talking through clenched teeth, coming from down the hall. Riven glances at me; I can see the same realization in his eyes. We follow the sound of low, rhythmic words, tumbling over each other. Too blurred to make out at first.

The noise leads us to a room at the far end of the corridor. The door is half open, darkness spilling out like ink. Inside, the professor stands with his back to us, shoulders rigid, head tilted at a wrong angle.

"Professor?" My voice trembles despite me. "Are you okay?"

He doesn't move. Riven's hand brushes mine, a brief squeeze before he steps past me. The closer we get, the clearer the words become. The professor is muttering under his breath, the same phrase over and over, each repetition a little more frayed:

"The light must answer, or the dark will consume it. The light must answer, or the dark will consume it..."

His finger drags across the wall in slow, deliberate strokes. When my eyes adjust, I see what he's doing. Symbols. Dozens of them. Carved directly into the wall with his own hand. The same circle with three lines I've been seeing everywhere. His fingertip is dark, and it's not ink, it's blood, smeared and drying, where he's clawed the pattern into the plaster with his nails.

"Professor," I whisper, stomach lurching. "Please stop. You're hurting yourself."

He doesn't. The scratching continues, steady and awful. His voice grows hoarse, but the words keep coming, more frantic with each breath.

"The light must answer, or the dark will consume it. The light must answer, or the dark will consume it—"

"Hey." Riven steps closer, voice low and careful. "Professor. You need to stop."

Nothing. The scrape-scrape-scrape of his nails against the wall feels like it's burrowing under my skin.

"Don't—" I start, but it's too late. Riven reaches out, slow and deliberate, his hand hovering just above the professor's shoulder. "Professor," he says again, firmer now. "Look at me."

The professor moves so fast it hardly looks human. He whips around, grabs Riven's arm, and shoves him back with a strength that doesn't make sense. Riven slams into the opposite wall, the breath leaving him in a harsh grunt. I barely have time to scream before the professor lunges at me.

His eyes, God. His eyes are wrong. That same white swallowed in black, pupils blown into bottomless pits look he had earlier. His face twists, and he's shouting, spit flying from his mouth, the same words tearing out of his throat:

"The light must answer, or the dark will consume it!"

I stumble backward, trying to run, but his hand clamps around my ankle. The force yanks me off my feet. I crash to the floor, pain shooting up my leg. I twist, kicking, clawing, trying to tear free.

"Let go!" I scream, voice cracking. "Let me go!" He doesn't. His fingers dig into my skin, nails biting hard enough to break the surface as he drags himself closer, still chanting that same phrase, over and over, like a curse:

"The light must answer, or the dark will consume it. The light must answer, or the dark will consume it—" His voice rises with each repetition, growing harsher, more frantic.

I kick at his face. My heel connects with his shoulder. He barely reacts. Instead, he surges forward. The professor's weight crashes into me, knocking the air from my lungs. My head slams against the floor hard enough to make white sparks burst across my vision.

I gasp.

Before I can roll away, his knees pin my legs. One hand still clamps around my ankle. The other shoots out and catches my wrist.

"Riven!" I scream.

The professor's head jerks toward me. Not toward my face. Toward my chest.

Toward the place where the hum always lives.

His expression twists in wonder and terror and then recognition. "The light," he whispers. Then his fingers close around my throat.

I freeze.

For one impossible second, I don't understand what's happening. Then he squeezes. Pain explodes through my neck. My breath cuts off. I claw at his wrist, nails scraping skin. Unable to scream. The professor keeps chanting, the words spilling from him between ragged breaths.

"The light must answer…"

His grip tightens.

"…or the dark will consume it."

The room begins to blur. The edges of my vision darken. My lungs burn. I buck beneath him, trying to throw him off, but he's impossibly strong. Stronger than anyone at his age should be.

His black-pit eyes lock onto mine. Not seeing me. Seeing something through me. Something inside me.

"The light must answer," he rasps.

My heartbeat pounds in my ears. The hum beneath my ribs surges violently. For a split second, I swear light flashes beneath my skin. And the professor smiles.

Then—another crash. Riven swings a heavy vase down. It shatters across the side of the professor's head with a sickening, dull sound. The older man crumples instantly, collapsing in a heap. Silence slams down. My breathing turns ragged. I gasp for breath as the oxygen returns to my lungs. My whole body shakes. The only sound left is the wild pounding in my ears. Riven drops to his knees beside me. His hand closes around my arm, steady, grounding. "Hey," he says quietly. "It's okay."

"He—he wasn't..." My throat won't cooperate. "He wasn't himself."

Riven looks down at the unconscious man, jaw clenched. "No. He wasn't."

"What was that?" The words rip out of me, thin and raw. "What the hell was that? It looked like he was possessed."

He exhales slowly, eyes flicking to the wall of symbols, still faintly glowing with a wrong sort of light. "I think..." He hesitates, then meets my gaze. "I think he was possessed. By what—or who—I don't know."

Tears sting the backs of my eyes. I look at the bloodied symbols carved into the plaster and feel my stomach turn. Riven reaches up, his thumb brushing gently along my cheek, wiping away a tear I didn't know had fallen. "You're safe now," he says softly. "I promise."

But even as he says it, I see doubt flash behind his eyes.

"Riven, I need answers. Why is this happening to me and the people around me?" My voice shakes as we haul the professor upright, his weight sagging between us. "No more vague warnings. No more riddles. Answers." He doesn't argue. Just nods once, jaw tight. "You'll get them," he says. "Help me get him to the car first."

The professor is heavier than he looks, unconscious weight,

limbs limp and uncooperative. I hook my hands under his arms while Riven takes most of the load, but still I stumble every few steps.

"God, he's heavy," I grunt. "How is it unconscious people always weigh more?"

"Gravity's cruel like that," Riven mutters, something between a sigh and a breath of dark humor. We maneuver him into the elevator, through the silent garage, and into the back seat of the car. I pull the seat belt across his chest out of habit and click it into place, then lean against the door for a moment, trying to catch my breath.

"Right," Riven says, dropping into the driver's seat. "Answers."

"Where are we supposed to get those?" I ask, sliding into the front.

He glances at me in the dim light. "Back to the library."

"The library? Now?" My brain short-circuits for a second. "We've already searched there. And also, tiny detail—we nearly got caught breaking in there."

"If the professor's right about what he's saying—about the light and the dark—we don't have time to wait until morning," he says.

He turns the key. The engine rumbles to life.

I sink back, mind spinning. "You're serious."

"Completely."

The city passes in smeared streaks of orange and white. Streetlights flash across the windshield like fragments of something broken. No one talks. The only sound is the low hum of the tires on wet pavement and the soft, uneven rhythm of the professor's breathing in the back. When we finally pull up outside the library, the building looms larger in the darkness than it ever did in daylight. The windows are blank, reflecting the streetlamps like blind eyes.

Inside, our footsteps echo in the empty foyer. It feels wrong to be here at this hour, with all the lights dimmed and every noise magnified. The air is too still. The silence feels loaded. Riven leads the way half carrying, half dragging the professor with us, his flashlight beam cutting thin slices of light through the dark. We pass aisle after aisle of sleeping books, the smell of paper and dust thick in the air, until we reach the far corner where the half-hidden door waits.

The same one from that first night.

He glances back at me. "You remember this door?"

"Hard to forget a secret passage," I say.

"Good," he murmurs, pulling it open. "Because we're going down."

The stairwell beyond is narrow and spirals into the earth, carved from old stone. The temperature drops almost instantly. The air smells damp and stale. Riven steps in first, his flashlight throwing long shadows down the steps.

"My family's kept books down here for centuries," he says, his voice carrying back to me. "Long before this library ever existed."

I blink. "Your family?"

He nods once, not turning. "Guardians. Historians. Hoarders, really, depending on who you ask. We protect what isn't meant to be lost. Or found."

I follow, one hand on the rough stone wall. "And you're just now mentioning this why exactly? This information would have been helpful earlier."

"I didn't know if I could trust you with this secret," he says, clipped. "And I don't come down here. Ever."

"Why not?"

He hesitates. The beam of light stutters for a second. "Because it remembers things I'd rather forget."

A shiver walks down my spine. We keep descending. The staircase turns and turns until my legs ache and I lose track of how far we've gone. The air grows heavier, colder, each breath filled with dust and the weight of too many years. Finally, the steps spill us out onto solid ground.

Riven flips a switch near the wall. A low hum fills the chamber. One by one, rows of dim overhead lights flicker on, stretching outward in both directions. I draw in a breath. Shelves. Endless shelves. Floor to ceiling, running into the shadowed distance. Books bound in cracked leather. Scrolls in glass tubes. Boxes with no labels. Everything coated in a fine layer of dust, as if the room itself has been sleeping.

"That's..." I let out a low, disbelieving whistle. "A lot of centuries."

Riven's mouth twitches, almost a smile. "Come on. We need answers."

He moves ahead, scanning the nearest shelves with a familiarity he probably wishes he didn't have. I follow, eyes wide, trying to take it all in. The air hums faintly around us, and the deeper we go, the more I swear the walls are listening. Every title we pass is strange, the languages unfamiliar. Symbols curl across spines like vines. Some books don't have titles at all, just etched marks in silver or gold.

For a moment, fear is edged aside by something else. The part of me that chased my dad's secrets through old archives and library stacks sparks awake. Somewhere in here, hidden under dust and ink, there's truth.

"Where do we even start?" I ask.

Riven exhales, his flashlight sweeping slowly across the shelves. "With the Falling," he says. "If there are answers, they'll be there."

So we start looking. Shelf by shelf. Row by row. The deeper we move into the stacks, the thicker the air feels, humming just below hearing.

Chapter 25

Time blurs in the depths of this place. Minutes smear into something shapeless, stretching long and indistinguishable. The air has grown denser, saturated with dust, as if every forgotten truth tucked between these shelves is leaning over our shoulders. I pull another book from the shelf and immediately cough as dust explodes off its cover. "Pretty sure I'm inhaling centuries," I mutter.

Riven, crouched a few feet away, glances up. "History doesn't come sanitized."

"Yeah, well," I say, brushing dust off my sleeve, "neither does black lung."

He doesn't smile, but I catch the ghost of one before he turns back to the shelves. I slide the heavy book back into place, but as the spine nudges the one beside it, a small puff of dust drifts off and hangs there, shimmering faintly in the air.

It's strange. Almost... deliberate. I frown and reach toward it. The book it came from is different, thicker, bound in dark, weathered leather. No title. No markings. Just a faint burnished symbol at the center: a circle with three intersecting lines.

My pulse skips.

"I think I found something," I whisper.

Riven straightens and crosses the narrow aisle to me. "What is it?"

"I don't know," I say, easing the book free. "But it feels... different." The cover is cold against my palms. Colder than it has any right to be. As I carry it back to a small table, my vision flickers with that faint rainbow shimmer that's been haunting me since this all started. It threads through the air, stronger now, until the whole room seems to hum with color.

"Riven," I say quietly. "It's happening again."

He's suddenly right behind me, close enough that I can feel his warmth at my back. "What do you mean?"

"The light," I whisper. "The aura. It's stronger when I touch it. It has to be this book."

I sit and lay it carefully on the table. The spine creaks like a sigh. Dust rises, catching the dim light and swirling into faint motes of color. Riven leans in, close enough that his breath stirs the hair near my temple. "Careful," he murmurs, voice low and steady.

A shiver skates down my spine.

"I'm fine," I say, except my pulse is doing acrobatics. He's too close. The space between us feels smaller with him this near. Focus, Rachel. Not the time.

I drag my attention back to the book and start flipping through brittle pages, the text written in elegant, looping script, half in a language I don't recognize. I skim line after line until one word jumps out at me, underlined twice:

The Falling.

My breath catches. "Wait."

Riven shifts closer, the desk groaning softly under his weight. "What is it?"

I trace the word with my fingertip. "It's here. Look—'The

Falling.' These are... records. Observations." I squint at the ink-smudged lines. "It says: 'Those struck by the light exhibited signs beyond mortal understanding. Healing, sight, strength. The marks upon their skin glowed with celestial residue.'" I flip to another page. The handwriting there is tighter, more clinical. "This one reads like a... medical log."

Riven scans beside me. "You're reading doctors' notes." I nod slowly, eyes racing down the page. "From people who were hit by the light during the Falling."

The words blur for a second, my pulse roaring in my ears. I can almost see it again, the rain of light, the screams, the way people didn't just burn, they changed.

"These are the first accounts," I whisper. "The ones who survived. And the ones who didn't... stay human."

Subject A exhibits unprecedented resonance. The Light answers before she calls. Observation suspended by order of the Court.

Overhead, the lights flicker once, softly but noticeable. We both look up. When they steady, the book beneath my hands feels different. Warmer and a faint vibration thrums through the parchment, humming against my fingertips. Riven notices. His breath catches. "Rachel," he says quietly. "It only did that when you touched it."

I blink. "What?"

He reaches out and presses the corner of the page. Nothing. Cold, dead paper. He nudges my hand back onto it. The hum returns instantly but stronger this time, resonating up my arm. Riven's gaze sharpens. Something clicks in his expression. "Look at the margins," he murmurs.

I glance down. Small notations crawl alongside the main text, scribbled symbols, half-faded diagrams, phrases. One line, smudged but still legible, makes my stomach dip: Only those who carry the mark can withstand what remains. The breath leaves my lungs.

Riven's voice drops to a whisper. "What if it's not just a record of what happened to them?"

I look up. "What do you mean?"

His eyes meet mine, steady but edged with something like unease. "What if the book was meant to respond," he says slowly. "Not to anyone who opened it but to someone marked by the Falling." He hesitates, as if choosing each word carefully. "What if it isn't preserving history at all?"

The silence between us tightens, heavy and expectant.

"What if it's a conduit?" he continues. "A way for what was buried to recognize what survived. Not a tool to unlock something—but a thing that listens."

My pulse stutters. A conduit. Something that doesn't open a door. Something that answers when the right presence stands before it. My fingers tremble as I turn the next brittle page.

The ink glints faintly. More notes. More sketches. The handwriting shifts between entries, different styles crammed together. The first page in this section is full of rough outlines of human figures, each marked with streaks of light drawn over their eyes, their chests, their hands. Beneath them, a single note, small and slanted:

They glow where the pulse first takes root.

My skin prickles.

I trace the ink, then turn the page. The next entry hits harder.

Subjects exposed to the Falling exhibited ocular distortion, like halos of refracted light visible only to them. They report colors beyond known spectrum.

The words swim for a second before snapping into focus.

"Riven…" My voice comes out small.

He leans closer, his shadow spilling across the page. "What is it?"

I swallow. "This—this is describing me. The colors. The shimmer I see. It's all here."

He doesn't answer right away. His eyes move over the text, jaw tightening. "Keep reading."

The next entries are worse, dense with details and invasive observations. They describe "subjects" losing control of their senses, seeing visions of the sky cracking open, hearing whispers in languages no one else can hear. My pulse drums harder with each line.

The resonance grows unstable. Light seeks balance. Those who endure will either burn away or awaken.

I shove the book back an inch, breathing too fast. "Awaken? What does that even mean?"

Riven's hand settles lightly on the back of my chair. "Rachel." His voice is low, steady. "Slow down."

"I can't slow down." My words tumble out, shaky. "You said it yourself—the light recognizes the dark. What if this is it? What if this book is literally showing what happens to people like me?"

He hesitates. "Maybe it's showing what used to happen."

But even as he says it, doubt flickers behind his eyes. I look back at the page. The next entry is short, the handwriting shaky, desperate.

The last of them cannot contain the light. It breaks the body. Only those who find balance survive.

My vision wavers, colors bleeding at the edges of the paper. I blink hard, willing it to sharpen, but the ink seems to ripple under the light. Then I see it. In the bottom corner, so faint I almost miss it, a symbol. The same circle, three intersecting lines, drawn tiny and repeating along the margin. Next to it, a single name.

Astrid.

The word hits like a spark.

Riven's hand tightens on the chair. "What is it?" he asks quietly.

I can't speak at first. The room feels distant, the hum of the lights, the smell of old paper, even Riven's warmth, all muted.

Finally, I whisper, "It says her name. The name from my dreams."

Riven crouches beside me, his expression shifting from curiosity to something softer and more serious. "Astrid?"

Several lines beneath the name had been violently scratched away. Not faded. Deliberately removed. Someone wanted Astrid forgotten.

I nod, eyes locked on the ink. "It's connected, Riven. I don't know how, but it is. The Falling, the symbol, my dad's death, the visions... her."

Beneath the name was a final notation, written in a different hand than the rest. The ink had faded almost to nothing. I lean in closer to read it.

Should she return, do not let her remember.

My stomach tightened. But the rest of the page had already begun to blur.

He stares at the open book, the shimmer reflecting in his eyes. "This isn't just a record," he murmurs. "It's a warning."

The silence thickens, heavy enough to feel. I don't realize I'm holding my breath until the book starts to hum again. A soft vibration, deep in the pages, faint but unmistakable. The ink shivers like water.

"Riven," I whisper.

He's already moving, reaching out to close it, but before his fingers touch the cover, the pages begin to turn on their own. The sound is slow and deliberate, parchment dragging against parchment, as though guided by an unseen hand. My pulse spikes. The air grows colder. The shimmer at the edge of my vision flares until every page glows faintly with color. Then the words start to change.

The ink writhes, smudging and reforming. Letters uncoil and settle into new shapes. Sentences appear where blank space was. The language twists, becomes something older. The handwriting shifts into sharper, more deliberate script.

"It's... rewriting itself," I breathe.

"No," Riven says, voice tight. "It's showing you what it wants you to see."

The pages still. The glow dims, but doesn't disappear. A new heading stands at the top of the spread, ink dark and fresh:

Year 612 After the First Fallen:

My mouth goes dry. "It jumped forward," I whisper. "Hundreds of years."

Below, the notes are different, cleaner, less frantic. Someone else picked up the work. Someone who didn't just witness, but studied.

"We have begun cataloging those touched by the starlight. Their bodies hum with resonance, their senses attuned to forces unknown. They mend faster, see further, burn brighter. Some claim they hear songs hidden within the stars themselves. They do not wield light. They wield Creation. We call them....."

The next line flickers. The ink ripples, then settles.

"We call them Celestials."

My chest tightens. The shimmer behind my eyes pulses

sharper, enough that I grip the table to steady myself.

Riven's hand finds my shoulder. "Rachel—"

"I'm fine," I lie. "Keep going."

I turn another page. The tone darkens.

"But for every Celestial born of light, there are those the light abandoned. Shadows took root in the hollows left behind. They move unseen, drawn to the pulse of what they are not. They call themselves the Voidborn."

Riven goes very still. I read on, the words burning themselves into me.

"Where Creation expands, the Void gathers. Where stars burn, gravity waits. The two forces oppose one another, yet neither can existed without the other."

My throat tightens. "This... this says Voidborn weren't made to balance the light," I say hoarsely. "They were born from what it left behind."

Riven doesn't move. His jaw is tight, eyes unreadable. I turn another page. The book trembles faintly under my hands, as if bracing itself.

"The light must answer, or the dark will consume it."

The same phrase. The professor's voice echoes in my head, ragged and wrong.

My stomach twists. "Riven," I whisper, "this is what he was saying. This is where it came from."

He nods once. "And someone or something wanted you to see it."

Before I can respond, the dark light bursting from the book flares white-hot, bright enough to erase the room. The shelves shake. Dust rains from above in soft gray clouds. I throw up an arm to shield my eyes. And then, just as suddenly, the glow dies. The book slams itself shut. Silence rushes in. I sit frozen, hands shaking, the sound of my heartbeat roaring in the vacuum it leaves.

"What was that?" I whisper.

Riven exhales slowly, his voice rough. "History," he says. "And a warning."

Chapter 26

The echo of Riven's words *history and a warning* follows me long after we leave the archives. I can still feel the book's light burned behind my eyes, bright and violent in a way normal light never is. My hands won't stop trembling. Something is wrong. I can feel it. The air feels heavier than before, like the silence itself is holding its breath. Even after Riven walks me to the door and tells me to get some rest, that prickling sense of being watched threads along my spine.

The light must answer, or the dark will consume it.

The professor said it. The book said it. The air seems to murmur it. By the time I reach my building, unease has settled into something sharp and cold. That's when I see it. My front door is unlocked.

My stomach drops. "Marin?"

No answer.

The living room light is on, but the glow is too bright, too sharp, humming loud enough to make my skin prickle. Marin sits on the couch, straight-backed, hands limp at her sides. Eyes wide open, unblinking.

"Marin!" I rush forward, pulse thundering. "Marin, hey!"

She doesn't look at me. Her lips are moving. Whispering.

"The light must answer, or the dark will consume it."

Over and over.

"Marin!" I grab her shoulders, shaking her. "Stop—please, stop!"

Her head tilts slightly, but her eyes stay unfocused. Her voice is flat, like she's sleep talking from inside a nightmare.

"Riven!" I shout, panic shredding my voice. He's suddenly there, the door slamming shut behind him, one arm looped around the professor, who's barely conscious. They stagger into the room, and the second they cross the threshold, the professor starts mumbling again, that same phrase, same rhythm, words twisting into something unbearable.

Riven lowers the professor carefully to the floor, his face grim. "Rachel, step back!"

"I can't!" I'm on my knees in front of Marin, gripping her wrists. Her skin hums under my palms, buzzing, charged. "She won't wake up! Riven, she won't wake up!"

Marin's head snaps back. Her eyes flare white. Not clouded. Not blind. Just pure, glowing white. Her hair lifts, strands floating like static caught in invisible wind. The air changes to something dense, electric, full of pressure that makes my ears ache. When she speaks again, her voice is layered and distorted, like more than one person talking through her.

"The light must answer, or the dark will consume it."

Behind me, the professor lets out a strangled noise and collapses forward, his hands clawing at the carpet. His voice joins hers, the two of them overlapping, echoing, repeating that same impossible phrase. Their voices are not identical. The words are. But beneath them I think I hear something else. A second phrase hidden underneath. Something about balance. Something I couldn't quite make out.

My vision fractures, color bleeding at the edges. "Riven—"

He's already moving, stepping between me and Marin, his voice low but edged. "Marin. Look at me. You need to stop."

She doesn't blink.

"Marin!" he shouts, gripping her shoulders. The glow in her eyes flares, flooding the room in blinding white. I stumble back, blinking spots out of my vision. The book in my hand jolts once, twice then explodes into light.

"Riven, it's doing something!"

Pages whip open and begin flipping on their own, too fast, the sound deafening, paper slapping paper in a blur. With every turn, the lights in the room flicker. My pulse feels synced to it, too fast, too loud.

"Make it stop!" I scream, dropping to the floor and clapping my hands over my ears. "Riven, make it stop!"

Marin and the professor are shouting now, their voices braided together until I can't tell which is which. The air tastes like ozone and metal. The book's glow climbs toward something blinding—

And then, all at once, it stops.

The light collapses back into the pages with a sound like thunder underwater. The book drops still and lies open on the floor, edges smoking faintly.

Silence.

The pressure in the air snaps. I gulp in a breath, my chest burning. Riven is crouched in front of Marin, hands still clamped on her shoulders. She blinks slowly. Her eyes are brown again. Her hair falls limp around her face.

"Uh," she croaks, looking between us, "why are you in my face like a disappointed dad and... who's the old guy?"

My body sags with relief so fast it hurts. I glance at the professor, he's slumped sideways on the couch now, breathing shallow but normal.

"She's back," Riven exhales, running a hand through his hair.

I barely hear him. The book is still open on the floor, faint wisps of light curling up from the page like smoke. My heart starts hammering again. I take one step forward. Then another.

"Rachel?" Riven's voice follows me, wary.

I don't answer. I crouch and look down at the page the book chose. The handwriting is different again it's smoother, the ink is darker than the writing in the rest of the book. Almost, like it's been written recently. At the top, one sentence glows faintly, written in ink that seems to shift color as I read it:

When the light awakens, the veil between worlds will thin.

My breath catches. Beneath it, smaller words appear, half-burned into the paper as though pressed there by heat rather than hand. My breath catches.

The resonance has been answered. That which was separated stirs.

Steam curls from the mugs on the table, the only movement in the quiet apartment. The adrenaline has finally started to drain, leaving behind that hollow, trembling sort of calm that feels like the world holding its breath. The professor is asleep on the couch, a blanket draped around him, courtesy of Marin, who declared him "a cute old man" before tucking him in like a burrito.

"If you'd seen him five hours ago," I say, fingers wrapped tight around my mug, "you wouldn't be calling him cute."

Marin grins, entirely unbothered. "What can I say? I'm a sucker for a good redemption arc."

Riven snorts softly into his tea, and for a moment the tension in the room eases just enough that I can breathe properly again. We've spent the last hour filling Marin in on everything at the library, the book, the pages that rewrote themselves, the voice that seemed to know me. She took it all with her usual blend of disbelief and sarcasm, but I didn't miss the flicker of unease in her eyes when I told her about her own eyes glowing.

"So," she says now, stirring her tea with the end of a spoon, "this whole resonance thing." She makes a vague circling motion. "Are we talking about some kind of object that does things, or is this more of a cosmic frequency, stars-aligning, metaphysical nonsense situation?"

Riven leans back in his chair, thoughtful. "It doesn't feel like an object," he says. "More like a response. As if something old recognized something it's been waiting for."

Marin groans. "Fantastic. So we're not solving a puzzle, we're triggering one."

I trace the rim of my mug, my fingers warm against the ceramic. "The book didn't say anything about opening doors," I say quietly. "It said the resonance was answered. Like something called out and something else replied."

"Which means," Riven says, his eyes lifting to mine, "you weren't meant to find it. It was meant to find you." His gaze lingers a second too long. I meet it without thinking, and for a heartbeat the room narrows until it's just the two of us and that quiet, magnetic pull humming beneath my skin.

Marin's voice cuts through the moment like a siren. "Okay, hold on."

We both blink and look at her. She's pointing between us now, her grin stretching wider by the second. "You two have absolutely kissed, haven't you?"

"What? No!" The word comes out far too fast. "Absolutely not. Why would you even think that?"

"Because," she says, propping her chin on her hand, "the air just went all intense in here, and you both forgot I existed for a solid ten seconds. Which is rude, by the way."

Riven clears his throat and suddenly finds the far wall fascinating. "You're imagining things."

Marin's eyes go wide. "Oh my god. You're blushing."

"I am not."

"You absolutely are."

I can't help it, I start laughing, the sound raw but real, shaking my head as the tension finally breaks. "Can we please focus on the ancient, reality-threatening mystery instead of whatever this is?"

"Fine," Marin says, still grinning. "But for the record, if you two start making out while the universe collapses, I'm getting popcorn."

Riven mutters something under his breath that sounds suspiciously like *unbelievable* and takes a long sip of tea. The laughter fades slowly, replaced by the low, familiar hum of the city beyond the windows. For a moment, everything feels almost normal, three people at a kitchen table, drinking tea, pretending they aren't standing on the edge of something vast and unnamed.

My gaze drifts to the book lying closed on the counter. It looks inert now, just leather and paper, but I can still feel it humming faintly in my chest, like an echo that hasn't finished answering. Whatever the resonance is, I know one thing with absolute certainty.

It isn't finished with me yet.

The apartment is quiet again. Marin's door closed hours ago, though I can still hear her voice in my head: "*I knew it!*" the moment Riven followed me into my room.

"Goodnight, Marin," I'd said, trying not to smile as I shut the door behind us. Now, silence drapes over us like a blanket, soft and steady in the dim light. The window is whole again, no broken glass, no cold draft, just the muted orange wash of streetlights on the walls. Riven lies beside me, one arm tucked behind his head, the other resting loosely around my shoulders. His skin is warm and steady. My head rises and falls with each slow breath he takes, the rhythm grounding me more than I want to admit.

I trace a small circle on his chest with my fingertip. "Do you really think that's what I am?" I ask quietly. "What they call a Celestial?"

His thumb brushes my arm, absent-minded and gentle. He hesitates. Only for a second. But I notice. "What?"

"Nothing."

His gaze drifts away.

"I just don't think Celestial is the whole story. I think the signs point that way," he says. "The aura, the visions, the way the book reacts to you. It's not coincidence."

I exhale, the sound catching on the edge of a laugh. "So I'm... what, a walking constellation?"

A faint smile tugs at his mouth. "Whatever you are, it's old and rare. Or at least... something no one understands anymore."

"That's comforting," I mumble into his chest.

He chuckles softly, the sound vibrating through me. "Didn't mean to make it sound ominous."

I lift my head just enough to look at him. "You kind of did."

His fingers trail up and down my arm, slow and steady. "You've seen what the book can do. How it reacts to you. It's not just history, it's a living record. It recognizes what it was made to remember." The words settle between us.

"I keep thinking about how it flipped to that page," I say. "How it just... stopped. Like it was waiting for me to see it. Like it wanted to show me something."

"It probably did," he murmurs.

I stare at him. "You say that like it's normal for books to have free will."

"With everything else you've seen this week," he says, "is that really the strangest part?"

I can't help smiling, even with the weight of everything pressing on my chest. For a while, neither of us speaks. His hand keeps tracing the same path along my arm, hypnotic. My leg drapes over his, our bodies tangled in a way that feels easy, unplanned, and somehow exactly right.

My voice comes out smaller than I'd like. "Riven?"

"Mm?"

"What if I can't handle this?" I whisper. "Being... whatever this is supposed to be?"

He tilts his head, just enough to meet my eyes. The streetlight softens his features, rounding out the sharpness usually carved there.

"You already are handling it," he says quietly. "You've survived worse than this."

The words hit a place I don't let many people touch. My throat tightens. "I just wanted to find out who killed my dad," I murmur. "And somehow I opened... all of this."

He brushes a strand of hair away from my face, his fingers lingering for a beat longer than they need to. "Whatever's coming," he says, "you won't face it alone."

Something in me finally loosens. I rest my head against his chest again, letting the sound of his heartbeat anchor me. "Promise?" I whisper.

His fingers tighten around my arm. "Promise."

For a while, the world outside the window could be anywhere, another time, another life. Just quiet breathing, and the steady rhythm of two people too tired to keep pretending they're not already tethered to each other.

Chapter 27

The smell of coffee reaches me before I'm fully awake. It smells rich and warm, like it's drifting in from the kitchen like a small kindness. For a few precious seconds I lie still, caught in the hazy space between sleep and morning, letting the scent coax me back to consciousness. The sheets are twisted around us, soft and warm from the night.

Riven's arm is slung over my waist, heavy and possessive even in sleep. His breath ghosts against the back of my neck, steady and slow. When I shift, he murmurs something low and rough, the sound vibrating through his chest and into my spine.

I roll over carefully. He's half-asleep, eyes closed, face unguarded in a way I rarely see. Without the shadowed tension he always carries, he looks younger. Softer. Almost breakable. My chest tightens unexpectedly. Before I think better of it, I lean in and press a light kiss to his lips. It's soft, quick, almost in a shy way.

He breathes in sharply. His eyes flutter open halfway through, catching me in the act. A slow smile curves his mouth, lazy and warm, and his arm tightens around my waist, drawing me in until our bodies align completely.

"Morning," he murmurs against my lips, his voice husky

with sleep.

Heat curls through me. "Morning. I didn't mean to wake you."

"Liar," he mumbles, and the word melts into a deeper, slower kiss that's more certain.

He shifts easily, rolling until he's above me, bracing himself on one arm while the other slides along my side, fingertips grazing bare skin. The sheets whisper around us. His body is warm and solid, caging me in a way that feels less like a trap and more like an anchor. His lips trail along my jaw, down to the curve of my throat, each brush sending a pulse of heat through me. He murmurs something soft, maybe my name and the sound of it nearly undoes me.

The world outside the room narrows, the chaos waiting for us slipping out of reach. There is only this: his weight, his warmth, the quiet between our breaths. He pulls back just enough for me to breathe, his forehead resting against mine. Our chests rise and fall together, the air thick with something heavy and tender.

"You know..." I whisper, still breathless, "you could sleep over more often. I wouldn't complain."

He gives me that slow, devastating smile. "Yeah?" His fingers brush the side of my thigh, light and deliberate. "I could get used to that."

Before I can respond, he kisses me again, this time it's unhurried, deep, like he's memorizing me. My thoughts scatter. Every fear, every half-formed worry dissolves beneath the warmth of his hands tracing down my back, the press of his chest against mine. I don't know when the careful distance between us became this. When danger and sarcasm and proximity turned into gravity.

His hand slides up my spine, fingers curling at the nape of my neck. The kiss deepens, heat sparking low in my stomach. I pull him closer, threading my fingers through his hair as the need between us sharpens, blurring into something terrifyingly real.

He whispers my name, barely a sound, more like a plea. It hits me like a spark to dry tinder. We both still at the same moment, foreheads pressed together, breathing hard. His thumb grazes my jaw, steadying us both.

"Tell me you want this," he murmurs, voice roughened by restraint.

I do. God, I do. Every part of me is screaming yes. But the words lodge in my throat. He searches my face, eyes dark and earnest, and he seems to understand anyway. He leans in again, slower now, giving me the chance to say no. I don't lean away.

Our lips barely brush when—

The door bursts open.

"Okay," Marin announces, balancing two mugs like a divine messenger of chaos, "either you're under attack or I just walked into the world's most committed slow-burn."

Riven recoils like he's been shot, rolling off me and stumbling to his feet. I yank the blanket up to my chest, cheeks burning so hot I could light the damn place on fire.

"Marin!"

She sets the mugs down, entirely unbothered. "What? I brought coffee."

She glances between us, a smirk forming. "Guess you two already found a way to... perk up."

"Out!" I groan.

Marin cackles. "Fine. Just don't ruin the sheets, celestial

lovebird."

The door clicks shut, leaving behind a heavy silence and the echo of my mortification. I bury my face in my hands.

"I'm never going to live that down."

Riven laughs softly beside me, low and warm. "Probably not." Then, leaning close, his voice drops to a whisper. "But I'm not sorry."

The scent of burnt toast eventually drifts in, Marin's signature culinary disaster. By the time I shuffle into the kitchen, she's perched at the counter, hair wild, pretending she's not waiting to pounce. Riven stands near her, calmly drinking coffee like he wasn't just half naked in my bed five minutes ago.

I grab a mug. "No comments."

Marin blinks innocently. "Who, me?" Riven snorts into his cup.

Marin takes a sip and says casually, "Sooo... how was your sleepover?"

I nearly choke. "Marin."

"Just asking! Though, based on the noises—"

"There were no noises!"

"So there could have been noises."

Riven tries and fails to hide his smirk.

I drop my head onto the counter. "This is my nightmare."

"Mine too," Riven murmurs, equal parts tease and truth.

Marin beams. "Look at you two. Mutual embarrassment. The foundation of all great romances."

"Oh my god," I mutter.

She waves me off. "Relax. I approve. He's broody, mysterious, probably writes sad poetry when no one's looking. Very on-brand for you."

Riven raises an eyebrow. "Sad poetry?"

"Don't ruin this for me," she says.

Despite myself, I laugh, a real one and something in the air loosens.

A groan from the living room cuts through the moment.

The professor shifts under his blanket, blinking up at the ceiling.

"Coffee," he croaks. "Please."

Marin practically skips over. "Coming right up, Professor Gandalf." He takes the mug, sips, sighs with reverence... and then looks at me with sudden, startling clarity. Like something inside him clicks into place.

"You should know," the professor says slowly, "that this wasn't random."

The room stills.

"None of what's happening to you feels like," he continues, "coincidence."

I frown, caught off guard. "You're going to have to be more specific than that."

Marin mutters, "Please tell me this is the caffeine talking."

But he doesn't smile. There's a steadiness to him now that wasn't there before, something sharpened and unsettlingly aware. "When whatever took hold of me earlier did so," he says, rubbing his temples, his voice lowering, "I wasn't fully gone. I was... pushed aside." He exhales carefully. "I saw fragments. Reflections. Like light breaking across shattered glass."

My pulse begins to thud in my ears.

"You were in them," he says, looking at me again. "Not clearly. Not as a face. But as a presence."

My stomach drops.

"It wasn't interested in your name," he continues, almost reluctantly. "It didn't care who you were. It cared what you carried. Your blood. Your resonance." He swallows. "It recognized you."

Riven goes rigid beside me, every line of his body pulling tight.

"The starlit bloodlines don't simply disappear," the professor says quietly. "They thin. They scatter. They hide. But every few centuries..." He hesitates.

"What?" I ask impatiently

His expression darkens.

"One returns."

His gaze doesn't leave mine. "Whatever is waking in you didn't come from nowhere."

Something twists painfully in my chest. My father's riddle. His disappearance. The dreams that never felt like dreams. The way the circle had hummed under my touch, as though it had been waiting.

"My dad must have known," I whisper. "He had to."

Riven nods once. "It would explain why he tried to keep you out of this."

"Out of *what*?" The question rips out of me before I can stop it. "The shadows? The Voidborn? What do they want from me?"

The professor's jaw tightens.

"In the vision or possession, or whatever name you want to give it, the entity repeated something," he says. "Over and over. Like a refrain it couldn't let go of."

His eyes lock with mine.

"Bring her home."

The words knock the air from my lungs. Marin shivers

openly. "I hate that. Deeply."

"It wasn't a threat," the professor says grimly. "Not in the way you're thinking. It was a claim."

Riven's voice is tight, barely controlled as he asks "And the Void doesn't make claims lightly?"

"No," the professor agrees. "The Void consumes what it cannot possess. It always has." His expression darkens. "And if they know what kind of resonance you carry, what you represent, then they won't stop."

Riven's hand curls into a fist. "Until they get what they want."

The professor nods once. "Or until the balance breaks again."

Silence folds over us, thick and heavy. I grip the table to steady myself. My blood. My past. The Falling. The Void. All of it feels like a storm tightening around me. "I need to know what they want," I say finally. "If they're coming me... I need to understand why."

Riven's steady, unflinching gaze meets mine. There's fear there, yes, but beneath it, something like a vow. When he speaks, his voice is low, certain, and meant for me alone.

"Then we'll find out."

My mind starts racing at his words, thoughts colliding too fast to separate. The vision. The bloodline. My father. The question forms before I can stop it, slipping out on a trembling breath.

"Do you think they killed my dad because of this?" I whisper. "Because of who I am?"

The professor looks away first. And somehow that frightens me more than any answer.

Chapter 28

Time seems to have stalled in the apartment, our mugs forgotten on the table as the weight of what was said settles in. The silence stretches thin between us, as if one wrong word might snap it. The professor is the one who finally cuts through it, clearing his throat while he gathers the loose papers scattered in front of him and smooths them out with the kind of practiced calm a man should not possess after upending my entire existence.

"Well," he says brightly, almost chipper, "I suppose it's time you saw my research properly."

Riven's gaze lifts from the counter where he has been leaning with his arms folded. "Research?"

"On the Celestials," the professor says. "On the Falling. On the fracture between realms that no one wants to admit ever existed." His tone sharpens into something focused and grave. "I have been compiling records for years, scraps of ancient texts, artifact schematics, eyewitness accounts, theoretical models. My office is where I keep the originals."

Marin squints at him. "You mean the office where you got possessed like a human USB port for cosmic evil?"

"Yes," he says pleasantly. "That one."

A headache needles behind my eyes, sharp and blooming.

"Why didn't you tell us earlier?" I ask. "Why keep all of this to yourself?"

He stops fussing with his papers and looks at me, really looks at me.

"Because none of it made sense," he says, his voice low. "Not until you resonated."

My pulse quickens. "Meaning what?"

"The vision," he says, tapping his temple. "Or the possession. Or the moment the Void tried to use my brain as a guesthouse." He exhales as if the joke costs him. "I saw pieces. Symbols. Movement. Fragments of language I could not translate. I dismissed it as hallucination until tonight."

Riven straightens subtly. "What changed?"

"You did," the professor replies, and he points toward me as if he is afraid the gesture will set something off. "When the book responded to you, everything I have been studying rearranged itself, as though someone finally handed me the missing page of a puzzle I have been trying to solve in the dark."

Marin lets out a slow whistle. "So you were not being cryptic. You were just genuinely lost."

"Precisely," he says, with a hint of pride. "Gloriously lost."

I sink back, trying to steady myself. "So you think you understand now why the Voidborn are resurfacing."

"I understand why the pattern is shifting," he says carefully. "I understand why the veil is reacting. I do not claim I understand the whole truth." He gathers his papers again, decisive now. "But the originals will help you. They will help all of us."

Riven's jaw tightens. "We need answers," he says. "And fast."

"Yes," the professor agrees, suddenly energized by purpose. "Which is why we are going to my office now."

Marin groans. "Fantastic. A field trip to the haunted academic funhouse."

Riven grabs his coat. "We're taking my car."

The drive to the university feels heavier than it should, as if the city itself has become aware of the direction we are heading and is quietly disapproving. No one speaks. Even Marin stays silent, watching raindrops trail down the window like they are trying to spell warnings. The professor dozes in the back seat, muttering fragmented nonsense in his sleep, while Riven grips the wheel too hard and keeps his jaw clenched like someone bracing for impact.

Celestial. Voidborn. Pulse energy. Fracture. Convergence.

If any of it is true, then what does that make me?

When we pull up to the professor's building, dusk has settled into a thin, gray-gold light that makes everything look like it is fading. Our footsteps echo down the corridor. The office door still bears scratches from that night, as if the building itself remembers.

The professor unlocks it. "Still standing," he murmurs. "Good."

Inside, the office is exactly as chaotic as before, with shelves overflowing and books stacked in precarious towers and pages littering the desk like archaeology in progress. He waves us in as if this is normal, as if this room is not a scar on the night.

"Most of what you have seen the symbols, the visions, appears in these accounts," he says. "Not as certainty. Not as proof. As attempts. People writing down what they could not name."

Riven crosses his arms. "Accounts from who?"

"Witnesses," the professor says simply. "And survivors."

He digs through the piles until he finds a thin, leather-bound journal with brittle edges, and when he opens it the pages are crowded with constellations, circles, runes, and streaks of light that look less like drawings and more like someone trying to capture something moving.

"This is what many scholars call the Falling," he says, tapping an illustration that shows the sky cracking into lines of light. "Historians later claimed it was a meteor storm, and in the human world that explanation survived because it was safer." He flips the page and the drawings darken, shadows stretching across landscapes. "But the oldest descriptions do not call it a storm. They call it a rupture."

Marin squints. "So," she says cautiously, "alien stardust superpowers."

He gives her a patient look. "In essence, yes." He gestures again to the journal. "The stars shed energy. Fragments of cosmic light rained down, and some of that light fused with the living, binding itself to blood, bone, and breath."

Riven's expression tightens. "And that created the Celestials."

"That is what the records suggest," the professor says, and the careful wording matters. "Some fragments burned and destroyed. Others embedded, and the people who survived those changes became conduits of what ancient scholars later called pulse energy."

My stomach twists as he names things I have only ever felt, never understood. He turns another page, and the sketches shift again into rougher, humanoid figures outlined in violent shadow. "But where there is creation," he says quietly, "there is also consequence. The light did not merely fall. It disturbed the boundary between worlds, and from that disturbance came its opposite."

"The Voidborn," I whisper.

He nods. "Not born of stars, but of absence. Of the silence creation leaves behind." His voice drops. "Some texts claim they were meant to balance what the light introduced. Others claim they were what rushed in when the boundary tore." He looks up at me. "Either way, the result is the same. Imbalance corrupts. The longer they lingered near light, the more they craved it."

"They learned to feed on it," I say, and I hate how certain the words sound in my mouth.

The professor's gaze holds mine. "They learned to draw it through resonance," he replies, "by weakening those who carry it." His expression tightens. "Some called it devouring. Others called it an intersection."

I glance instinctively at Riven, and he looks away too fast, too sharply, as if the professor has brushed a nerve he cannot afford to show.

"The Falling was not meant to repeat," the professor continues, "but remnants remained." He reads on, *"The stars were not the source. They were merely the first sign."*

He reaches for a separate page covered in the familiar circle marks. "Sites like the ones you found were described as anchors or scars, depending on the culture, and the accounts agree on one thing."

He meets my eyes.

"When resonance returns, both halves respond."

My throat tightens. "So the more I use it—"

"The more defined you become," he finishes. "Not louder.

Clearer."

Marin crosses her arms. "So she is not a beacon. She is a walking neon sign with emotional trauma."

"An unfortunate but accurate metaphor," the professor says grimly.

He pulls a battered folio tied with faded string from another stack and opens it carefully. Dust drifts from the pages like old secrets finally escaping.

"These accounts span centuries," he murmurs. "Before scholars had language for the Falling and before anyone dared to map pulse theory, people called the light-touched whatever their fear required." He gestures to a page depicting a woman surrounded by radiant markings, a halo of light drawn crudely around her head. "In the oldest records, those touched by the light were accused of witchcraft," he says. "Their resonance was mistaken for spellcraft, unnatural and dangerous, and many were hunted and burned."

My chest aches. "Because of something they didn't choose."

"Yes," he says quietly. "Fear always rushes in where knowledge fails." He flips to another page where Celestials are carved into stone. "In other regions, they were worshiped," he continues. "Called gods, star-born, fallen angels. Depending on where you lived, you were either sainted or slaughtered."

Marin huffs. "So basically holy or barbecue."

"Precisely," the professor says, and then he turns to darker drawings, charcoal figures cloaked in shadow, with light-touched people chained or bowed beneath them. "And some believed the light-touched were omens." His voice lowers. "They thought Celestials were living warnings that the breach between worlds was widening, and they were correct in a way they did not understand."

A chill ripples through me.

"But humans feared what they did not understand," he continues. "They tried to control the light-touched, use them, kill them, and over time survival became impossible." He closes the folio gently. "So they disappeared."

I blink. "Disappeared how?"

"Some vanished entirely," he says. "There are gaps in the records where bloodlines simply stop." His mouth tightens. "Some historians believe they fled beyond this world, and some believe that is only a romantic lie people tell themselves when they cannot bear an ending."

He pauses before he adds, "Either way, those who remained learned to hide in plain sight." He looks at me. "They buried their nature. They masked the light in their blood until the knowledge thinned and the abilities faded, and most descendants never knew what they carried."

My pulse thuds in my ears. "Until now."

He meets my gaze with something like awe. "Until you."

"You are awakening a resonance we have not seen coherently documented in generations," he says, and his careful wording makes the air in the room go thin. "Your light is not simply stronger. It is whole in a way the records insist should be impossible. And when that kind of wholeness returns, the Void responds."

Riven's jaw tightens.

"The Voidborn," I breathe.

"They feel you," the professor murmurs, "not as prey, but as a correction." His eyes flick down to the circles again. "Like a pulse rippling across the veil." He swallows. "Like the answer to something they have been waiting to hear."

Marin exhales. "Cool," she says flatly. "So she is a flare

with a name."

The professor reaches for a map so old the ink has bled into the parchment fibers, and he spreads it across the desk. "I do not believe we are searching for a fragment anymore," he says. "Fragments imply pieces of something lost." He taps the faded circle etched deep into the map. "What is waking in you suggests something else."

My stomach tightens. "What."

"A convergence," he says. "A scar left where the worlds pressed too close, and a place tied not to what was lost, but to what was sealed." He traces the ancient mark slowly, then taps the handwritten script beside it. "Where the stars were burned from the earth."

The room goes still.

"That is where the truth of the light-touched was buried," he says quietly. "That is where the wound between Light and Void was first made real." His eyes lift to mine. "If you want answers, that is where they will be waiting."

Back in the apartment later, thunder builds at the horizon with a low growl that rolls over the city like the sky is warning us too. Marin stares out the window with her brow creased, as if she is trying to replay every horrifying piece of lore we just learned. The professor collapses onto the couch and drifts quickly toward sleep. Riven checks the locks twice and begins pacing like a caged animal.

I cannot sit still either. My hand finds my bag before I fully understand what I am doing, and when I pull the book free the leather is warm, almost too warm, as if it has been holding heat for me.

Riven notices instantly. "You think there's more."

"Maybe," I say, although the truth feels heavier than that. I feel something in it now. Something awake.

Marin drops onto the couch beside me with her mug. "If it starts glowing again, I am fleeing the country and joining a goat farm in the Alps."

Before I can answer, the professor murmurs from his half-dreaming state, his voice distant and wrong.

"The light must answer," he whispers. "Or the dark will consume what remains."

A chill sweeps down my spine. Then the book glows. It does not flash violently, but shimmers softly, bending the air around it as if the room itself recognizes what it is. I barely manage to breathe.

"Riven," I whisper.

He is at my side immediately, crouched and protective. "Don't open it yet."

But something inside me leans toward it with a familiar tug, bone deep, like the pull I felt near the circles and beneath the stone. My fingertips graze the cover. The glow intensifies. The temperature drops. The air thins. A pressure builds low in my ears as if the room is exhaling around us.

Marin sits bolt upright, and her mug clinks against the table. "Absolutely not."

The light ripples outward, shifting from gold to violet to white, the same impossible shimmer the professor described, while the pages turn on their own with slow deliberation, guided by a hand that is not human.

"Riven," I breathe. "What's happening."

He grips the back of my chair and leans close. "I have you."

Letters twist. Ink bleeds and reshapes itself as if it is alive, and an image forms with terrifying clarity.

It looks like me.

And it doesn't.

The shape is familiar, but the features refuse to settle.

Every time I try to focus on the face, the ink shifts.

Marin's breath catches. "Rach," she whispers. "……that's you."

The professor shifts in his sleep and murmurs again.

"It recognizes its source," he breathes. "The bearer returns to the pulse."

My chest tightens. "What does that mean," I whisper. "Why me."

Riven kneels beside me, and the darkness that crosses his face is familiar now, the same expression he wore when the Voidborn shadow loomed in the professor's office.

"It's not reacting to the book," he says quietly.

A cold weight settles in my stomach. "Then what is it reacting to?"

He hesitates, and I know before he speaks.

"You," he says. "It's reacting to you."

The words land like impact. A pulse thuds beneath my skin, the same pulse that answered the circles and hummed beneath my fingertips, and the inked image flickers once, then twice, syncing with my heartbeat as if the page is echoing me.

Then the shimmer collapses. The book snaps shut. The room stops breathing. Riven holds my gaze. "Whatever that book is, it is not just a record," he says. "It is a conduit." He swallows. "A relic tied to the first fracture, and it is bound to you, not the other way around."

My hands shake. "But why," I whisper. "Why me."

His throat works. He looks away for half a second as if something sharp sits behind his eyes.

"I don't know," he says. But the lie hangs in the air like a pressure drop, unmistakable. Outside, the storm cracks with distant thunder. And in the silence that follows, one thought coils cold and certain in my chest. Something else felt the light answer. Something that has waited a very long time.

And now, it's awake.

Chapter 29

The silence that follows is suffocating, and even the air feels wrong, too still, as if the room itself is bracing for something and listening. The professor stirs on the couch, mumbling into his collar, his eyes flickering beneath his lids, before a sharp, ragged inhale tears him awake and he bolts upright.

"Professor?" I whisper, already on edge.

His gaze darts wildly around the room, skimming the walls and windows before landing on Riven, and then on the book in my hands. Whatever he sees there drains the color from his face as his shoulders sag with something like dread and recognition combined.

"Oh, God," he breathes. "It answered you again."

Riven steps forward at once, his posture shifting from watchful to ready. "Nothing was opened," he says firmly. "It responded."

The professor's fingers curl into the blanket, knuckles whitening.

"Then it's crossed another threshold."

Marin throws her hands into the air. "Okay, no. Cryptic escalation is not helping. What threshold?"

He exhales shakily and reaches for his coffee cup, as if the warmth might anchor him. "If the book is projecting her now," he says, his eyes never leaving me, "then her resonance is no longer dormant. It's coherent."

A cold knot tightens in my chest.

"Resonance of what?" I ask.

"The worlds," he replies softly. "Light and Void. Two forces that were never meant to exist in isolation, nor be sealed away indefinitely." He swallows. "Some texts suggest the Falling may not have been solely an emergence of light. A few imply it was also an attempt to contain something."

Riven's jaw tightens. "And when the Celestials vanished—"

"—the seal weakened," the professor finishes. "Not all at once, but gradually. Bloodlines thinning. Knowledge eroding. The balance holding by habit rather than design."

"If her resonance is stabilizing," Riven says carefully, "then the Void—"

"—will notice," the professor agrees. "She's becoming defined."

His gaze settles on me, heavy with something like fear.

"They already have."

Marin slams her mug onto the table. "You mean the shadow things that keep trying to kill her?"

"Not kill," he corrects gently. "Respond. The Voidborn can no longer sustain themselves on their own realm's absence alone. They are drawn to concentrated Light, not to destroy it, but to resolve the imbalance it represents."

My heart stutters. "They want my light?"

"You carry a resonance stronger than any documented in centuries," he says slowly. "Not because you are the only one left, but because what's waking in you is whole."

A tremor runs down my arms.

"So what does that make me?"

He hesitates, choosing his words with care. "Something the records struggle to classify." he says at last. "A resonance pattern we have no category for."

The word still lands hard.

"You are the kind of presence that could either reopen what was sealed," he continues, "or reinforce it in a way the records suggest hasn't occurred since the first fracture."

Marin lets out a low, strangled sound as she drags both hands down her face. Riven steps closer, positioning himself subtly between me and every shadow in the room.

"Then we protect her," he says. "Whatever it takes."

The professor shakes his head, not in disagreement, but in realism. "Protection may not be enough." He glances toward the window, the shadows beneath his eyes deepening. "The moment the book responded to her, the moment it projected her resonance outward, any Voidborn attuned to that frequency would have felt it."

"Felt it how?" Marin demands.

"Like clarity," he says quietly. "Like the answer to a question they've been circling for generations."

A chill curls up my spine. Riven's hand brushes my arm, grounding and steady.

"We'll figure this out," he says softly. "You're not alone."

But the professor's words echo louder than his reassurance. I turn toward the window. Beyond the city lights, the shadows feel deeper. Watching. Waiting.

Riven steps closer. "Hey. We'll find answers. That's what this is—answers."

"I don't even understand what I am," I whisper.

"That's what we'll find out," he murmurs.

Marin flops into a chair with theatrical despair. "Okay, so

apparently Rachel is cosmic royalty. Step one: figure out your starlight superpowers. Step two: don't die. Step three: therapy."

Riven huffs a quiet laugh despite himself. The professor clears his throat. "Then we begin with research. What the Celestials left behind. Early accounts. Manifestations. Pulse behavior." He hesitates. "Not to define what Rachel is... but to help her survive what she's becoming."

I exhale slowly. "So... back to the library?"

Riven meets my eyes. "The library."

I find myself back at the library again, but this time I'm more terrified of this power that keeps answering me. We settle at one of the long oak tables beneath the soft amber glow of reading lamps. The professor looks pale but focused, the kind of focus people get when pieces they've chased their whole lives finally start falling into place. Marin drops a stack of books onto the table so loudly the nearest lamp rattles.

"If even one of these starts whispering, I'm quitting this friendship."

I open the brittle leather tome in front of me. The pages smell like dust and cold stone. Symbols twist across the parchment. I can't read them, but something in me thrums, like the ink recognizes the way my attention settles on it.

"These," the professor whispers, brushing the page, "are manifestations. Early accounts of abilities following the Falling."

The drawings show luminous figures, halos of shifting light, hands wrapped in radiant tendrils.

Marin whistles. "Your ancestors walked around looking like rave lights."

Riven shoots her a look, but the professor ignores it, flipping to the next page. More sketches. More symbols. A diagram of two swirling planes, one bright, one dark, pulled apart by a jagged tear.

"Look," I say, tapping it. "This has to be the Falling."

The professor squints, adjusting his glasses. "Yes. This inscription... I can translate parts of it." He murmurs haltingly, "'When the light fractured... the wound yawned open... and the realms... drifted apart.'" He exhales. "So the Falling wasn't creation. It was separation."

"A wound," Riven says quietly.

"A rupture," the professor agrees. "And what followed was an attempt to patch it." He turns the page.

A new sketch appears: light pooling into a basin, shadow curling around its edges.

Marin frowns. "That looks like a glowing puddle."

"A Lightwell," the professor murmurs. "Or what some cultures believed served that function. Stabilization points. Attempts to contain the fracture."

Riven's jaw tightens. "Until they failed."

No one answers. He turns another page, and my heartbeat stutters. The title beneath the figure had been damaged. Most of the words are missing. Only the final portion remains:

...KEEPER

He turns to a darker page. Figures unraveling at the edges, forms sketched in shadow.

"Their manifestations evolved in opposition," he says. "Where the light anchors, the void destabilizes. They invert resonance."

"So they want to unmake her," Riven says quietly.

The professor shakes his head. "Not unmake." He hesitates.

"Exploit."

My throat tightens. "Pressure point."

"If the resonance grows uncontrolled," he says carefully, "it could reinforce the Veil." He pauses. "Or stress it beyond recovery."

Marin grimaces. "So, accidentally blow a cosmic fuse."

The professor winces. "Crude... but not inaccurate."

The room falls silent. "So Voidborn seek Celestials for sustenance," I whisper. "But they're drawn to me because—"

"Because if these accounts are right," the professor says softly, "figures like this haven't appeared in the historical record for centuries." He meets my eyes. "At least... not in any form we've been able to confirm."

Riven steps closer. "Then we help her. Train her. Keep her safe."

The professor nods. "Pulse responds to emotion. Intention. It can be guided."

Marin points at me. "Step one: cosmic anxiety powers. Step two: do not tear reality open."

"Preferably," the professor sighs.

Riven meets my eyes, steady and fierce. "We'll figure it out," he says quietly. "Not just what you can do... but who you are." And for the first time since the book answered me, the weight pressing on my chest eases just a little. Because I'm not running anymore. I'm learning. I read further down and see the scratched out text at the bottom of the page: *Bridgekeepers.* A second line: *Veilkeeper.* A third line: contradicts both and leaves me with even more question.

Chapter 30

By the time we cut through the path behind the apartment, the light's gone soft and honey-colored, stretching long over the grass. The field is mostly empty, just a worn bench, a leaning lamppost, and a strip of sky that feels wider than it should in the middle of the city. Marin immediately claims the bench as "official observation headquarters," thermos of tea in one hand, notebook in the other. Riven stands a few paces behind me in the grass, arms loosely crossed, eyes tracking every move I make. Always composed. Always still. Guard tower disguised as a man.

And me, I'm barefoot in the cool grass, staring at my palms like they're supposed to do something other than sweat.

"Okay," Marin calls, pen poised. "Let's see it. Beam of light, fireball, divine revelation—I'm open-minded." I glance at her over my shoulder. "What exactly am I supposed to do? Spontaneously combust?"

"Try a word," she says. "Books and movies always use words. 'Illuminate!' 'Shine!' You know. Drama."

Riven exhales through his nose. "It's not a spell."

Marin shrugs. "Says the guy who broods in moonlight like a gothic screensaver."

I roll my eyes and hold out my hand.

"Light," I say. Nothing.

"Okay," I mutter. "Maybe it likes enthusiasm." I take a breath. "Light!" Still nothing.

"Wow," Marin says, scribbling something down. "Mystical force of the universe: unimpressed."

"I think it needs instructions," I grumble.

Riven steps closer, his voice low and steady. "It's not about the word. It's about what you feel when you say it."

I turn slightly toward him. "Feel what? Confusion? Existential dread?"

"Anything real," he says quietly. "The pulse answers emotion, not logic."

He takes another step, close enough now that I can feel the warmth coming off him on my back. The air between us tightens, humming with something I'm trying very hard to pretend I don't notice.

"Close your eyes," he murmurs into my ear. "Don't think. Just feel." His voice slides under my skin like electricity. I swallow and do as he says. At first, there's nothing. Just wind in the trees, distant traffic, the rustle of Marin opening another snack she doesn't need.

Then Riven's fingers brush my forearm, warm and grounding. He guides my arm upward, his palm settling gently just below my wrist. The contact snaps the world into a different kind of quiet.

"Breathe," he says softly, near my ear. "Let it find you."

So I do.

I think of my dad, his laugh, the way he'd ruffle my hair, the warmth of his hand in mine that day in the park. I think of the way his fingers went slack. The hollow feeling in my chest as I screamed his name and no one listened. I think of the riddle he left me instead of answers. The grief. The anger. The wanting. Something inside me answers back.

It starts small, a tremor under my skin, then it builds, crawling down my arm, pooling in my fingers. The air thickens around my hand. The familiar faint smell of ozone curls through the evening breeze.

And then–light. Soft at first, like sunlight filtering through water. Then brighter. Threads of gold and white flicker beneath my skin, coiling through my veins like I've swallowed a star and it's finally remembered itself.

I gasp and my eyes fly open. The world sharpens. The edges glow. Color shimmers at the periphery of my vision, my aura flaring bright and alive.

Marin bolts upright on the bench. "Holy—Rachel, you are literally glowing."

Riven's hand drops from my arm like he's been shocked. For half a second, his face gives him away, a flinch, a wince, some small recoil he smooths over almost instantly. Before I can ask, his features are composed again, eyes steady, expression unreadable.

I look back down at my hand, too stunned to do anything but stare. "It's real," I whisper. "It's actually real."

Marin laughs, somewhere between awe and hysteria. "You're like a celestial nightlight. Do you know how much you could charge for custom ambiance?"

The light pulses once more, warm and sure, before fading back into my skin. The air feels emptier without it, like something important just stepped behind a curtain.

Riven exhales slowly, some of the tension bleeding from his posture. "That was the pulse answering you," he says. "The first time it's surfaced because you called it."

I blink up at him, still breathless. "So it's not all just... in my head?"

His expression gentles. "No. It's in you."

Marin points at me with her pen. "Observation one: Rachel glows under emotional distress. Observation two: I'm buying sunglasses."

A shaky laugh escapes me. "You're enjoying this way too much."

"Of course I am," she says. "My best friend just turned into a human solar battery. This is peak content."

Riven's mouth twitches into the tiniest almost-smile. "That wasn't random," he says. "You reached for something that mattered."

For a moment, I let myself believe him. The warmth echoing in my veins, the echo of light still ghosting my skin, it doesn't feel like a mistake. The sun dips lower, painting everything in gold. Marin raises her tea in mock toast.

"To discovering your inner flashlight," she announces.

I look down at my hands one more time, fingers still tingling, and I can't quite stop the smile. Because for the first time in a long time, I feel awake.

Sleep won't come. The flat is too still, the kind of silence that hums just beneath hearing, like the air is waiting for something to happen. Riven's beside me, already asleep. His breathing is slow and even. Marin's door is closed down the hall, faint music leaking from under it, tiny proof she's still there.

But every time I close my eyes, I see it again. The light in my hand. The way the world changed when it answered me. And the way Riven flinched, just for a second, like my touch burned him. The thought digs in and refuses to budge.

I slip quietly from the bed, tug on one of his shirts that's soft, over-sized, smelling like cedar and smoke and pad barefoot into the living room. The moonlight spills in through the window, turning the floor silver.

The book sits where we left it, dark leather catching the faint light. As I draw closer, I feel it, a low, familiar thrum in my chest. I sit cross-legged on the rug and hold my hand out in front of me.

"Okay," I whisper. "Let's see what you are."

Nothing happens.

A faint shimmer ripples under my skin, there and gone again like it's shy.

I sigh. "Great. Useless by daylight and moonlight."

But something in me isn't satisfied with that. Something old and restless and stubborn. I close my eyes and think of my dad. The park. The damp chill of the grass. The weight of his head in my lap. His voice, strained and breaking: *When the moon drowns in daylight, you'll find the door.* The way his hand slipped from mine. The sound of my own screaming. The way the world just... kept going. Cars driving by. People walking past. Like nothing had shattered.

The air thickens around me becoming charged.

"What did you know?" I whisper. "Why didn't you tell me more?" Light flickers under my skin again, faint, but steady this time. My pulse climbs to meet it. I think of the shadow in the flat. The mark burned into the floor. The thing at the university. The feeling of being watched every time the lights flicker.

"Was it them?" My throat feels tight. "Was it the Void? Were they the ones who—"

The thought snaps something clean in half. Light erupts from my hand, sudden and blinding, washing the room in white. And then—

Silence.

Not just quiet. The absence of sound. The air drops out of my lungs. Color drains from the edges of the room. The light collapses, leaving a gray half-world in its wake. I blink, heart pounding. The flat looks the same. Couch. Table. Window. But wrong. The edges blur slightly, like I'm looking through warped glass. Dust hangs in the air, suspended, moving in slow spirals along currents I can't feel.

"Marin?" My voice sounds wrong here, muffled and thin. No answer.

I walk down the hall to her room. The bed is perfectly made, covers smooth, lamp off. No music. No clutter. No Marin.

"Riven?" I call, louder now.

The silence presses in from all sides, heavy and unmoving. Even the air tastes different, thinner and metallic, like I've stepped into a place that forgot how to be lived in. I go back to the window. The city's still there but drained. Streetlights glow weakly, some flickering, others gone out completely. The sky is choked with a strange dust-like shimmer that glows faintly, like embers trapped in fog.

"I'm dreaming," I whisper. "I have to be dreaming."

But it doesn't feel like a dream. Dreams blur. This is sharp. Wrong, but vivid. The professor's words echo back: *Some accounts claimed certain Celestials could bridge, move between worlds unseen.* My mouth goes dry. I grab my jacket from the hook out of habit and open the door. Outside, the world is hollowed. The buildings are the same, but their colors are leached away. The cars are there, but still and dark, like props in an abandoned set. No engines. No voices. No sirens. Just that faint, endless wind that somehow never touches my skin. I know these streets. Every building stands where it should. Yet somehow everything feels borrowed. A copy made from memory.

"Marin!" I shout.

"Oh God," I whisper. "Where am I?" My voice echoes too far, bouncing off buildings like the street suddenly grew longer. "Riven!"

Nothing.

My footsteps ring out too loud on the pavement, each one swallowed by the empty space like I'm walking through a cavern instead of a city. A crumpled flyer lifts off the ground, floats in the air, then disintegrates into ash before it lands.

Panic crawls up my throat. How do I get back?

I stop and hold my hand out again.

"Come on," I whisper. "Please. Light. Just... *something*."

A small, fragile spark answers. It glows beneath my skin, a tiny anchor in the emptiness. The air around my fingers trembles, like the world itself took notice.

"Okay," I breathe. "That's something. That's—"

Then I see it. A figure at the far end of the street. It's tall and standing still and appears to be human-shaped. And somehow... darker than everything around it, as if the shadows decided to stand up and take a walk.

Relief hits first. "Hey!" I call, taking a few steps forward. "Hey—can you help me? I think I'm—"

The words die on my tongue. The figure doesn't move. Doesn't turn. Just stands there, its edges rippling slowly, like smoke trapped in a body trying to remember how to be solid. Something cold skates across my skin. I slow my pace.

"Excuse me?" No reply.

I get closer. Close enough to know that whatever I'm looking at is not a silhouette cast by anything. It *is* the shadow. "Please," I say, my voice cracking a little. "Can you help me? I think I'm lost." Nothing.

The air grows colder, seeping into my bones. The light in my hand flickers, dimming. I take another step. The shadow moves. Its head tilts, the motion wrong, jerky, like someone forgot how joints work. My pulse spikes.

"Who are you?" I ask.

No answer.

Then, in one horrible, smooth motion, the shadow turns around so quickly my mind doesn't process everything. Its hand shoots out and clamps around my wrist. The touch is a paradox like ice cold and burning at the same time, like frostbite and fire layered together. The light in my palm sputters.

"Let go!" I shout, trying to yank free. "Let—"

The rest of the words get strangled when its face starts to form. The darkness compacts, thickening where a head should be. Features bloom out of shadow, cheekbones carved from smoke, a jaw pulling taut under skin too smooth, too even, like wax molded by something that didn't quite understand human anatomy.

His lips form last, stretching into something that might have been a smile once and got stuck halfway to wrong. Then his eyes open. They're not eyes. Just pits of deep, endless black, swallowing what little light there is. Inside them, something flickers, faint, failing sparks, like dying stars sinking in slow motion.

My aura's faint glow reflects there for a heartbeat before

it's swallowed whole. He tilts his head, studying me. Bones creak under his skin, the sound soft but unmistakable. When he speaks, the sound doesn't belong to just one mouth. It reverberates through the dead air, layered and echoing, as if other voices are pressed up against the edges of this world, speaking through cracks.

"At last."

Every trace of warmth drains from my body. He smiles wider. Too wide. The sky above us fractures, hairline cracks of light spider-webbing across the darkness. The world tears open. Blinding white floods in. My scream shreds my throat as gravity drops out, and I'm falling backward through the rip, through light and noise and heat and cold all at once—

Hard floor.

Cold air.

Hands on me.

"Rachel!"

I jolt, eyes flying open. I'm back on the living room rug, chest heaving, lungs clawing for air that tastes like coffee and wax and something too familiar. Riven's in front of me, kneeling, hands braced on either side of my face. His touch is steady; his voice comes out shaky.

"Rachel, hey—look at me. You're here. You're okay."

I can't get the world to settle. The light from my aura is still flaring at the edges of my vision, pulsing. Sweat slicks my skin; my hands are shaking so hard I can barely keep them still.

"Breathe," Riven says softly, his thumb brushing under my eye. His jaw is tight, eyes dark. "Slow it down. You're safe. Breathe with me."

Behind him, Marin's voice is high and panicked. "What the

hell happened? One second you were gone, and then you're screaming like you're being murdered—Rachel, you scared the shit out of me!"

Her words barely reach me. The room is still... off. Colors feel too bright, shadows seem to linger a second too long before catching up with themselves.

Riven leans closer. "Rachel," he says, low and urgent. "Talk to me. What happened?"

I swallow, my throat raw. "I—" The word breaks. I try again. "I saw them."

His expression shifts, fear flashing there, then being buried fast under something colder and sharper.

"Them?" he repeats quietly.

I nod, dragging in another breath. "They're real, Riven. The shadows. The Voidborn. They—" My voice shakes. "They were waiting for me." The room goes very still.

Marin's breath catches behind me. "What do you mean, 'waiting'? Who was waiting for you?"

I look at Riven. All softness has dropped from his face. His eyes are fixed on me, too intent. His hands fall away from my face, curling slowly into fists against his thighs like he has to stop them from shaking. He looks at the wall for a second like he needs a target, then back at me. Whatever calm he usually wears is gone. What's left is something dangerous and old.

"Tell me exactly what you saw," he says. His voice was calm. Too calm. The kind of calm people use when they're trying very hard not to panic.

Chapter 31

The night is quieter now, just the distant whisper of traffic below and the soft tick of rain against the glass. The storm has moved on, but the air still hums with leftover energy. When we got to Riven's place, he said it was safer than our apartment. Marin had stepped into the penthouse and done a slow, stunned circle before muttering, "If this is your safe house, I don't ever want to see the dangerous one."

She'd eventually disappeared into the guest room after threatening to install a bell on my door "for safety," which everyone knew really meant, *so I don't accidentally walk in on you two again and have to bleach my eyeballs.*

Now, it's just me and Riven.

We're in his bed, the blinds half-drawn, the city smeared in soft gold and silver beyond the glass. I'm curled against his chest, his arm draped over me, thumb tracing the same slow pattern along my shoulder. My heartbeat has finally stopped trying to sprint out of my ribs, but my mind won't slow down. The image of the Voidborn won't let go. That wax-smooth face. That wrong smile. Those eyes.

We've been waiting for you, Astrid.

"It called me that," I murmur into the quiet, my words muffled by his shirt. "The shadow. It said, 'We've been waiting for you, Astrid.'" Riven's hand stills for half a second. Then it moves again, same soothing motion, but I can feel the slight tension in it now, the way his muscles pull tight beneath my cheek.

"Astrid," he repeats, like he's turning the name over in his mouth, testing its weight. "You're sure?"

"Yeah." My voice comes out thin. "At first I thought it… had me mixed up with someone else. But the way it said it—like it wasn't guessing. Like it was *remembering* me."

He's quiet for a beat. When he speaks, his voice is low, almost reverent. "Astrid shows up in the oldest Celestial records," he says quietly. "Most references don't survive intact," he says quietly.

"What do they say?"

He hesitates. "Different things."

His expression darkens.

"That's what bothers me." I stare at the faint shadows shifting on the ceiling. The city glow paints soft lines across it, but it feels a million miles away.

"I keep trying to remember," I say quietly. "If my dad ever said anything. About this. About me. But there's nothing. Just… flashes. Dreams that don't feel like dreams. Pieces that slip away when I reach for them."

Riven's fingers slow, his touch gentle. "I was reading some of the older records," he says. "From before the Falling, or whatever came with it, splintered what the texts call the starlit bloodlines. Some accounts claim they could alter memory," he says. "Even their own."

My breath catches. "You think my dad—"

He nods against my hair, his jaw brushing the top of my head. "If he knew what you were, and what you'd grow into… he might have taken some of your memories. Locked them away. To protect you. To keep your pulse from drawing attention before you were ready. To keep you hidden from the Void."

"Protect me from my own memories," I echo, the words sour in my mouth. "How does that even work?"

"There were rituals," he says quietly. "Bindings. The old texts talk about Celestials storing resonance in objects, in sigils, in places. Cutting threads in their own minds so that only certain triggers, people, words, events, could bring them back."

I think of the circle in the stone. The way my hand had fit into it like it had been waiting. The way my vision had cracked open and swallowed me whole.

"The sites," I whisper. "The circles. You're saying they could be... triggers. Anchors. The kind of place where what was buried comes back."

"Maybe not all of it," Riven says. "But enough. Enough for you to wake up again when the time came." The time has come, hasn't it? If my memories were taken, shouldn't something have cracked open the moment the Void touched me? Unless... it doesn't work like that. Unless it's waiting for something specific.

I swallow hard. "Why would remembering be dangerous?"

His hand stills, just for a moment. ."Because sometimes memory isn't just a story," he says. "It makes you clearer."

He doesn't argue. The truth hangs between us, heavy as the rain-damp air. I press closer to him, tracing a line along his chest through the fabric of his shirt, following the steady rise and fall of his breathing. He feels solid, like an Anchor in a tide I don't understand.

"Then what happens if they come for me again?" I ask, my

voice so small it barely feels like mine. His muscles go taut beneath my hand. When he answers, his voice is steady, but there's steel in it. "Then they'll have to go through me first."

I tilt my head to look up at him. The usual softness in his features is gone, replaced with something sharp and unyielding. As if the idea of them touching me flips a switch he doesn't try to hide. Part of me wanted to believe him. The other part knows I can't keep hiding behind him forever.

"Riven..."

He meets my gaze. His eyes are darker in the low light, but there's nothing uncertain in them. "I mean it, Rachel. Whatever they are, whatever they think they're owed, they don't get to lay a hand on you. Not while I'm still breathing."

Something in the way he says it is quiet, absolute, no room for bargaining, it hits somewhere deep inside me. The fear in my chest doesn't vanish, but it shifts. Softens around the edges. Makes room for something else, something warm. Dangerous in its own way.

I shift, rolling gently until I'm straddling him, my hair spilling over his chest in a loose, dark curtain. His hands find my waist automatically, fingers spreading across my hips like they belong there. For a heartbeat, we just look at each other. The faint shimmer of my aura clings to the edges of my vision, brushing faintly against the night-shadowed lines of his face. His darkness and whatever light I'm carrying collide in the small space between us, a strange, fragile balance.

"You're kind of impossible," I whisper, a smile tugging at my lips despite everything. "But I'm lucky to have you."

His mouth twitches, the smallest ghost of a smile. Something flickers in his eyes, something complicated and almost haunted, but his voice comes out soft.

"You have no idea," he says, barely above a whisper, "how lucky I am."

I don't know what to do with that. So I lean down and kiss him. It's slow at first, soft, testing. His lips are warm and familiar now, but it still knocks the air out of me, how easily everything else falls away. My fingers curl in his shirt, tugging him closer. His hands tighten on my waist, steadying me as I move against him, the blanket and sheets tangling around us.

The fear recedes, step by step, until all that's left is this: heat, breath, the quiet sound he makes when I shift closer. The feeling that, for once, I'm not being pulled apart by forces I don't understand. I'm choosing this. Choosing him.

My pulse hums under my skin, that faint Celestial spark answering something in him I can't name. Each time my mouth finds his, the air seems to thicken, buzzing just a little more, the room itself is caught between light and shadow and can't decide which way to go. His hands slide up my back, fingers splayed.

Every breath feels shared, the rhythm between us slipping into something wordless and instinctive. A small sound escapes me, a half-sigh, half-plea I don't mean to let out and the way his breath stutters against my mouth, the way his restraint frays at the edges, makes the room feel too small for how much feeling is suddenly crammed into it. He whispers my name against my throat, the sound rough, like it costs him something.

"Rachel."

The way he says it, warning and want tangled together, makes my chest ache. Then, all at once, he stills. The sudden lack of motion is jarring. One second, everything is heat and free-fall; the next, his hands are at my waist, holding me firmly in place.

"Rachel," he murmurs, voice raw. "Wait."

For a long, suspended moment, all I can hear is our breathing and the faint hiss of rain against the glass. The pulse in my ears, his heart hammering against my palm. The world feels narrowed to the space between our mouths, to the question hanging there.

"What's wrong?" I whisper.

His gaze searches my face, blue gone almost black in the half-light. Whatever he's feeling is right there, barely leashed.

"You've been through too much tonight," he says quietly. "You slipped between worlds. You met a Voidborn. It called you by a name you don't even remember having. I don't want this"—his fingers flex at my waist—"to become something you look back on and think I... took advantage of what you were feeling."

I shake my head, frustration and something softer tangling in my chest. "You're not. I know what I'm feeling."

His thumb traces an absent line along my jaw, slow and careful, like he's memorizing the edges. "I need you to be sure," he says. "Not just about me. About you. About this."

I swallow. My head is spinning, yeah, but not from panic this time. "I'm sure," I say softly. "About you, at least."

He exhales, the sound somewhere between a sigh and a laugh, pained at the edges. "You make it very difficult to remember what the right thing to do is," he admits, a faint, crooked smile ghosting over his mouth.

I lean in, brushing my lips over his in the lightest possible kiss, a promise instead of a demand. "Then remember me instead," I whisper. "Not all that's happened. Just... me."

His breath catches, but he doesn't pull me closer this

time. Instead, his arms wrap around me, firm and protective, dragging me down until my ear rests over his heart. The storm inside him doesn't fade, he still feels coiled, controlled, held together by force of will, but it shifts a little.

He presses a slow kiss into my hair. "I am," he murmurs. "I do."

The words settle in my chest like a weight and a comfort all at once. His heartbeat drums steady beneath my cheek as the rain softens against the glass. The city glows faintly beyond the blinds, distant and small. Somewhere out there, shadows are waiting. Names I don't remember are circling back to me. Old doors are stirring in their hinges. But here, in this narrow, fragile strip of night, I let my eyes close. For now, I just let myself be here with him.

That whatever comes next, whatever the Void wants, whatever the stars are still trying to finish, they'll have to get through him first. And for the first time since the world cracked open beneath my feet, the thought of tomorrow doesn't feel impossible. It just feels... uncertain. But not alone.

Chapter 32

Morning spills through the wide windows in lazy gold bands. The world looks peaceful, too peaceful for everything we've seen. Riven's still asleep when I wake. He's on his back, arm slung over my waist, hair tousled in a way that should be illegal. His chest rises and falls in a slow, steady rhythm that almost convinces me we're safe. Almost.

Carefully, I ease out from under his arm. He doesn't stir. For a second I just stand there, watching him, the softened edges of his face, the way the light catches the faint scar at his jaw. Something in my chest aches, sharp and unexpected. Then I shake it off and pad quietly into the kitchen. Marin's already there, humming off-key, her hair piled messily on top of her head. There's coffee brewing, toast in the toaster, and an alarming amount of crumbs.

She doesn't even look up before saying, "Morning, love-bird."

I groan. "Oh my God, don't start."

She smirks, eyebrows bouncing. "Can't help it. You've got that freshly kissed glow. If he starts cooking breakfast for you, I'm moving out."

I roll my eyes and grab a mug. "You're unbearable before caffeine."

"And yet," she says, passing me the sugar, "you keep me around."

For a few minutes, it almost feels normal, the two of us barefoot in Riven's too perfect kitchen, sipping coffee, pretending the world outside isn't unraveling.

It starts as a flicker, barely noticeable. A low hum at the edge of my senses, like static before a storm. Not a sound, exactly, more like my pulse catching on something outside me. The hairs on my arms lift. The mug in my hand trembles, faint ripples forming across the surface of the coffee.

"Rachel?" Marin frowns, setting her spoon down. "You okay?"

I can't answer. The world has shifted, just slightly, but enough I feel it in my teeth. The air presses in, heavy and charged, like the moment before lightning hits.

"Rachel," Marin says again, her tone edging hard toward worry now.

I barely hear her. My gaze is already drifting up the stairs, toward Riven's closed bedroom door. Where I can barely see into his room through the glass railing. There's something there. Not a noise, not a shadow I can see. Just a pull. A faint, invisible thread hooked through my ribs, tugging me forward.

"Stay here," I whisper.

"Wait, what? Rachel, what's going—"

But I'm already moving. Each step up the stairs makes the feeling stronger. The overhead lights flicker once, just for a heartbeat, but it's enough to twist my stomach. My pulse is a drumbeat in my ears. With every breath, the air gets colder, thinner, like it's being siphoned out of the walls.

Halfway up the stairs, I stop. There, a sound that's soft and steady. Too rhythmic to be nothing.

"Riven?" My voice cracks on his name. No answer. The metallic taste I've come to associate with the Void is on the tip of my tongue, Ozone, smoke, and something wrong. I take another step. Then another. The floor creaks, loud in the silence.

His door looms at the top of the stairs, closed but not all the way, a sliver of darkness shows through the gap. My hand shakes as I reach for the doorknob. It's cold. Too cold. The pull in my chest sharpens, almost painful now. My skin prickles like my own light is trying to drag me backward, away. I press my palm flat against the wood and push. The hinges groan, slow and reluctant, as the door swings open. The smell hits first: smoke and cold air, like the remnants of something burned out and wrong.

And then I see it.

For a heartbeat, my brain refuses to understand what I'm looking at. The room is dim, pale morning light bleeding weakly past half-drawn curtains. Riven's half-sitting up in bed, eyes wide and glassy with shock, breath caught between inhale and scream.

And above him—

A shadow.

Tall. Thin. Its edges ripple like smoke in water. The shape shifts as it moves, never fully solid, the air around it vibrating with a quiet, awful sound, like whispers layered over static. Something glints in its hand. Long. Sharp. Too fluid for metal, too solid for smoke. For one suspended second, I can't move. Can't breathe. Riven's gaze snaps toward me, and the fear in his eyes knocks my lungs empty.

"Rachel—run!"

I don't think. My body moves before my brain catches up. I

spin, crashing into the wall hard enough to rattle the frames. Behind me, something shrieks, a sound too distorted to be human, scraping clawed fingers down my spine. I take the stairs two at a time.

"Marin!" I shout, my voice cracking. "Marin!"

She's in the kitchen doorway, coffee mug halfway to her lips, eyes wide. "What the hell—"

"Run!"

The next thing I know, we're sprinting, bare feet slapping against the cold floor, my heart hammering so hard my chest hurts. I grab her wrist and yank, practically dragging her toward the elevator. The lights overhead flicker and buzz. The air pressure drops again, dense, crushing, like thunder about to break. Behind us: a scrape, then a rush, like wind being pulled through something too narrow to hold it. I don't look back.

"Rachel, what is that?" Marin gasps, stumbling beside me.

"I don't know—just move!"

The elevator glows ahead of us, gleaming silver, salvation. I mash the call button so hard my finger aches. The doors don't open fast enough. "Come on, come on, come on," I hiss, slamming the panel again.

Behind us, the lights explode with a harsh pop, showering sparks that fizzle in midair. The shadow barrels down the stairs, stretching across the walls like spilled ink, its form warping with every stride. The elevator dings. The doors slide open.

"Get in!" I shove Marin through the gap. She nearly trips inside. I jab the Close button with frantic force. The doors start to slide shut, agonizingly slow. The shadow rounds the corner. It moves wrong and too fast. Too smooth. Its body elongates, edges shearing and reforming, all hunger and intent. The temperature drops. My breath fogs in front of me.

The doors are halfway closed when it reaches us. A hand, or something pretending to be one, shoots forward. Long, thin fingers of dark smoke wrap around the door. Metal screams. I slam the Close button again and again. "No, no, no—" Marin's screaming beside me, her voice rising over the grinding metal.

The shadow forces the gap wider. Its arm stretches, reshaping, reaching—

Its fingers graze my wrist.

Pain lances through me like ice and fire at once. My skin burns and numbs at the same time. I cry out, jerking back. Instinct kicks in. Light flares from my skin on reflex. It bursts from the point of contact like a miniature sun. The shadow recoils with a hiss of rage that scrapes through my mind. The doors slam shut. The elevator lurches, then drops fast.

Marin and I crash against the wall, clutching the rails as the elevator begins to move beneath us. The car smells like hot metal. For a long, terrible second, all I can hear is the hum of the cables and the ragged pulling of my own breath.

Marin finally wheezes, "So... I'm guessing that wasn't your sexy morning wake-up call?"

A broken laugh escapes me, half-sob, half-hysteria. I press my shaking hand to my chest, feeling my pulse slam against my palm. The elevator dings cheerfully as we descend, as if we're just two people heading out for brunch. When the doors open into the lobby, we explode out of the car. We don't stop to explain. The concierge shouts something after us, but his voice fades behind the slam of the glass doors and the roar of the street.

The sky is clear, the sun too bright. Whatever is chasing

us doesn't read as 'real' to anyone not attuned; it bends perception the way heat bends air. People walk dogs, sip coffee, argue over phone calls. A bus hisses to a stop at the corner. Somewhere, someone laughs. It's all too normal after what we just experienced. We hurtle down the steps, nearly crashing into a man with a briefcase. "Watch it!" he snaps as hot coffee splashes onto the pavement. "Sorry!" I gasp, already moving past.

"Existential emergency!" Marin calls without slowing.

We weave through the crowd, messy hair, pajamas, bare feet slapping against unforgiving concrete. Heads turn. Someone mutters, "Drunk," under their breath. Another person pulls their kid closer.

"Rachel!" Marin pants. "Most people's morning workout is yoga, not... whatever this is!"

"Run faster," I choke out.

We nearly collide with a man carrying boxes; papers explode across the sidewalk. He swears, but his words vanish beneath the noise of the city and the roar in my ears. None of it matters. The world keeps moving like nothing's wrong. Like there isn't a monster in Riven's room upstairs. My chest burns. Every step sends a jolt of pain through my bare feet. My pulse feels like it's trying to claw its way out of my throat.

We cut down a side street, the noise dimming slightly. "Where are we going?" Marin gasps. "Because unless you've secretly booked us a flight to Mars—"

"The professor's office," I say, skidding around a corner. "He'll know what to do."

She stumbles after me, incredulous. "You mean the same guy who carved creepy symbols into your wall, got possessed, and tried to choke you out?"

"He came back from it," I say, breathless. "He's been studying this for years. If anyone knows how to stop them, it's him."

Marin exhales hard. "Fine. Lead the way, Celestial of questionable judgment."

We're only a few blocks away when my phone buzzes in my pocket. I almost ignore it, but something in my gut twists. I fumble it out, swipe to answer.

"Professor?"

Static crackles down the line. Then his voice bursts through it's high and frantic, shredded by interference. "Rachel— don't come here!"

I stumble mid-step. "What? What do you mean, don't—"

"They know you're moving," he gasps. "They know, Rachel! They're watching—"

The line crackles violently, shredding his words.

"Who's watching?" I shout, heart pounding. "Professor, what's happening?"

The static swallows most of his reply. Only one word punches through, distorted but unmistakable.

"Hide."

The call drops. The dial tone hums in my ear.

"Rachel?" Marin grabs my arm, eyes wide. "What is it? What's wrong?"

I lower the phone slowly, my hand shaking. "He said not to come. He said they know and they're watching."

"Watching how? Watching who?" she presses.

"I don't know." Frustration surges hot and useless. I shove the phone back into my pocket. "Damn it!" I kick a trash bin hard enough to send it clattering across the pavement. People stare. I don't care. Marin plants her hands on my shoulders, forcing me to look at her. "Okay. Then we don't go there. What's plan B?"

"Rivens in danger," I whisper. Saying it out loud hurts. "The professor too. If the Voidborn are after them because of me—"

"No," Marin cuts in sharply. "Don't do that. You didn't summon them. They've been circling you since before you even knew what you were."

"But they're in danger—"

"Then we move," she says, voice fierce. "We get to the car, we go to that circle. That's where this all started, right? Maybe that's where we get something we can actually use. Maybe that's where we can lure them away from Riven and the professor."

The circle. The first threshold. The place the light recognized me. It feels reckless and stupid, but running without a direction hasn't exactly been working either.

"Fine," I say hoarsely. "But if anything happens to them because of me..."

Marin squeezes my hand, hard. "Then we make sure it mattered."

We half-run, half-speed-walk the rest of the way to our building, trying to look like two normal, slightly unhinged people in pajamas, not Void-chased prey. On the stairwell, Marin bolts upward. "I'll grab shoes, clothes, emergency snacks. Get in the car and don't die."

I don't argue. I collapse into the passenger seat, lungs clawing for air, pulse thundering in my ears. The car smells like old leather and stale rain, normal, comforting and completely at odds with the metallic taste of fear coating my tongue. I grip the steering wheel even though I'm not the one driving, just needing something solid to anchor me. My hands won't stop shaking.

Come on, Marin. Hurry. Through the windshield, the street looks deceptively calm, people passing by with shopping bags, a couple arguing about parking, a kid chasing pigeons. Then, in the rear-view mirror, something moves.

Three figures at the far end of the street. At first, they're just shadows stretched long by the sunlight. But the longer I stare, the less human they look. Their outlines flicker at the edges, bending light around them instead of blocking it. Every step they take looks too smooth, like they're gliding. Recognition slams into me. No. No, no, no. They know I've seen them.

The shadows pause… and then they move, too fast for bodies, slipping through angles the eye refuses to hold.

"Marin!" I slam the horn, panic fracturing my voice. "Marin, now!"

She bursts out of the building, duffel bag over her shoulder, hair flying. "Okay, I've got shoes, clothes, snacks—why are you yelling—oh my God."

"Get in the car!"

She dives into the driver's side. The bag thuds into the backseat.

"Go, go, go!"

She doesn't need telling twice. The car jerks away from the curb, tires squealing. I twist in my seat to look behind us. The shadows are no longer running. They're climbing. Their forms rise above the street, stretching up and out, smearing across windows and brickwork like smoke glued to the air. They glide over parked cars and lampposts, gaining on us with terrifying ease.

"They're coming!" I shout.

Marin jerks the wheel to avoid a taxi. Horns explode around us. "I can see that!"

"Lose them!"

"Oh sure," she snaps. "Let me just outrun the laws of physics!"

She floors it anyway. We shoot through a red light. A bus slams on its brakes, horn blaring. My shoulder slams into the door. Someone on the crosswalk screams. In the side mirror, the shadows fold around the bus like ink around a rock. They don't slow.

I fumble for my phone, hands slick with sweat. "I'm calling Riven."

"Do that!" Marin mutters, white knuckled on the wheel.

I hit his contact. The line clicks.

"This is Riven. Leave a message."

"You have got to be kidding me." The voicemail beep sounds almost smug.

"Riven, it's me," I gasp. "We're being chased—Voidborn, three of them—we left your building, I don't know if you—just call me back, please—"

I hang up, shaking, and hit the professor's number. Straight to voicemail. "No answer," I whisper. The words feel like a stone in my mouth.

"So maybe they're already—" Marin starts, then clamps her jaw. "Never mind."

The city becomes a blur of glass and concrete, traffic and shouting. We weave through cars, horns screaming. A cyclist bangs on our trunk as we cut in front of him. The car shudders as something scrapes along the roof, metal on something that isn't metal. The sound is like claws across my nerves.

"Marin—"

"I *know*!" she yells, wrenching the wheel. We swerve onto a side street, narrowly missing a row of trash bins. Ahead, the bridge rises, sunlight flaring off its railings and the buildings beyond. For a heartbeat, I let myself think we might lose them in the confusion. Then I look up. They're there. Hovering above the bridge, three shapes suspended in the air like stains on the sky. Waiting.

My pulse spikes. "They're ahead of us."

Marin doesn't slow. "Then hang on." She guns it. We pass through where they were a second ago like empty air, heat, light but when I glance back, they're behind us again. They're not just following. They're herding. They're steering me toward something I already touched.

The city finally falls away behind us, shrinking to a jagged line on the horizon. The streets bleed into narrower roads, then into open country the rolling fields and wide sky in every direction. Out here, the air feels like it's cleaner, thinner, and too exposed without the skyscaper buildings and street traffic. The car hums steadily beneath us, a mechanical heartbeat. Every shadow that flickers across the windshield makes my stomach lurch. Every roadside tree looks like it could suddenly stand up and walk toward us. For the first time since we left, I let myself exhale.

It doesn't help much. The horizon stretches on and on, fields of gold and green bending under the wind. It's beautiful in an empty, lonely way. It doesn't feel safe. I press my palms against my knees to stop them shaking. The last few hours replay in jagged flashes: Riven's eyes when he saw the shadow. The professor's voice crackling through the phone. The Voidborn's cold, clawed grip on my wrist.

I hope Riven's okay. The thought lands hard and heavy. I can still see him, half-sitting up in bed, shadow hanging over him. Hear the ragged edge in his voice when he shouted my name. I've never heard fear in his voice before. And I left. He told me he'd protect me. But maybe I should've stayed. Protected him too. I push the thought away before it can spiral, but it doesn't go far. It just sits there, pulsing quietly under everything else. What do they want with me?

The question has been trailing me. The way the Voidborn move, track, turn when I so much as flare.

Celestial.

The word feels less like a title now and more like a target. If they're the dark half of what I am, the void to my light, then maybe this is what balance looks like now. One side hunting the other, trying to reclaim what fell away. The professor's voice echoes in my memory: *The light must answer, or the dark will consume it.*

Is that all I am to them?

An answer they're owed?

Or a meal they were promised?

My fingers curl into fists. The faint ache where the shadow touched my wrist throbs in time with my pulse.

"Hey," Marin says quietly, eyes still on the road. "You're doing that thing."

"What thing?" My voice is hoarse.

"Staring out the window like you're about to apologize to the sky for existing."

A broken laugh slips out of me. "I'm just... thinking."

"Dangerous hobby," she mutters. "Ten out of ten do not recommend right now."

I watch the fields blur past. "What if we're wrong?" I say. "About the circle. About everything. What if this is exactly where they want us to go?"

"Then we make it hurt," Marin says. "If they want you there, it's because they think you'll be weaker. Dumber. More scared." She glances at me. "They're wrong."

I don't feel particularly fierce. I feel like my bones are made of glass.

But I nod.

Because running forever isn't living. And waiting for the dark to find me hasn't exactly been working out. Somewhere ahead, beyond the fields and the road and the weight of everything I don't understand yet, the stone circle waits. The first place the light answered me. Maybe the place will finally show me why.

Chapter 33

By the time the road narrows into gravel, the world feels smaller. The sky has gone pale with cloud, sunlight dulled to a thin wash that makes the fields look almost colorless. The wind outside looks soft, but the car rocks slightly with each gust.

Marin pulls over onto the shoulder. The engine ticks as it cools. Neither of us moves. The silence doesn't feel peaceful or empty. It feels like something is listening. I unbuckle slowly, my fingers clumsy on the metal. When I open the door, a rush of damp air hits me, smelling of rain-soaked earth and crushed wildflowers, underneath that, something metallic, faint but cutting.

Marin climbs out, slamming her door a little harder than necessary. She slings the duffel over her shoulder and scans the horizon like she expects a monster to step out of the wheat.

"I hate this," she mutters.

"Yeah," I whisper, closing my door. "Me too."

Gravel crunches beneath our shoes, loud in the stillness. The birds are quiet. No insects buzz. The only sound is the faint tick of the engine cooling and our own breathing. The hill that hides the circle rises in the distance, a dark smudge of grass and stone against the washed-out sky. I can already feel it humming faintly beneath my ribs, that same pull that dragged me here the first time. It's weaker now, but steadier. Less like a siren, more like a heartbeat. Waiting. Something definitely feels off.

Last time, the air had felt alive up there, wrong, too bright, pulsing with invisible energy. Now it feels... hollow. Like whatever was here has gone deeper underground, drawing breath in, waiting to exhale. Marin adjusts the strap of the bag, jaw tight. "We stick together this time," she says. "I wasn't planning on letting you out of my sight."

We change quickly, trading pajamas for jeans and boots beside the car, shivering more from nerves than cold. Then we start walking, side by side, toward the hill. The grass snags at our pant legs, damp from an earlier rain. The climb is steeper than it looks from the road. My calves start to burn, breath fogging in front of me even though the air shouldn't be this cold. Halfway up, the wind shifts.

There's a faint and distant sound threaded through it. A murmur, too soft to make out, voices filtered through water. I stop dead, tilting my head, trying to catch it again. But I hear nothing but the wind.

"You heard that, right?" Marin asks quietly.

"Yeah." My chest tightens. "Keep moving."

The higher we climb, the thicker the air feels. My pulse syncs with our footsteps, each beat loud and insistent: up, up, up. When we crest the hill, the circle comes into view. It's worse than before.

The grass around it is flattened in a wide radius, singed in jagged patches, something burned here and refused to go out cleanly. The stone markings are clearer, carved deeper into the earth, their lines sharper and more deliberate than before. Faint light clings to them even in the flat, overcast day, a steady glow like coals banked under ash. A shiver rakes down my spine.

Marin exhales slowly. "Well. That's not ominous at all."

I swallow, hard. The hum under my skin sharpens into something like a vibration, making my hands tremble. The closer I get, the louder it becomes, like the circle is a speaker and my bones are the wire. We don't talk anymore. We just walk. Two small figures climbing toward an old scar in the world, toward a place that feels like it's been waiting not just for us, but for *me*. At the edge of the circle, I stop.

Up close, the symbols etched into the stone feel older than language. Some match the ones in the professor's books, stars, spirals, lines aligning with cardinal directions. Others are different. Newer. Jagged strokes carved over older marks, like someone added their own script on top of the original. My fingertips ache with the urge to touch them.

Marin shifts beside me. "You sure about this?"

"No," I admit. "But I don't think it cares."

She snorts softly. I draw a breath, step forward, and reach down. The instant my fingers brush the circle, the world rips apart. Light and sound fold inward, collapsing to a single, blinding point. For a fraction of a second there's nothing, no up, no down, no sky, no ground, just a pressure that feels like it's squeezing me through the eye of a needle.

Then the ground slams back under my feet. I gasp and open my eyes. My first instinct is to turn and grab Marin's hand, but the clearing behind me is empty. The circle is still beneath my boots, and yet she's gone, as if the world only carried one of us across.

The circle is still beneath me, but the world around it has...

shifted. The air is thick, heavy, tasting of ash and metal. Every breath feels like inhaling smoke that never quite clears. The trees along the perimeter are twisted silhouettes, their trunks warped, bark split and weeping some dark, viscous sap. Their leaves are black and shiver constantly, even though I can't feel any wind. The sky is wrong, hairline cracks of shadow vein through it, jagged lines that pulse faintly, as if something on the other side is pressing against the surface. My stomach lurches. This feels like the place I slipped into before, the hollow, echo-world, but denser. Closer to whatever lies on the Void's side of the wound. The in-between.

"Astrid." The voice comes from directly in front of me. My head snaps up. He stands at the edge of the circle. At first, he's just shape, a vertical streak of darkness, a man-sized absence where the world refuses to hold color. Then the shadows thin, bleeding away in slow, deliberate drips, and a face emerges from underneath. His skin is pale beneath streaks of soot and dried black residue that could be ash or blood. Or both.

His hair is black and disheveled, falling into eyes so dark they seem to drink in everything around them. There are faint movements in that darkness, tiny sparks sinking inward like dying stars being swallowed. A thin scar crosses his left cheek diagonally, silver at the center where the skin never fully healed. It glints when he moves, a mark that looks old and new at the same time, like it's been reopened more than once. He looks human. But not entirely.

In the thin skin at his throat and along his forearms, his veins pulse faintly with an inky shimmer, darkness moving beneath the surface like smoke trapped in glass. His clothes are worn and scorched at the edges, dark leathers, torn and singed, dusted with ash as if he walked out of a fire and never bothered to brush it off.

He looks older than he appears and tired. Like someone who has been fighting so long he forgot what it was like to stop. When he speaks, his voice slides through the silence, deep and rough-edged, threaded with an accent I can't place.

"Astrid."

He says it like a memory. The name curls through the air like smoke and lands in my chest with a weight I don't understand. Every instinct I have screams *no*. I stumble back a step, but the circle under my feet feels like glue, like it doesn't want to let me go.

He moves too fast for me to process. One moment he's at the edge of the stones, the next he's right in front of me, close enough that I can see the fine cracks in his skin where darkness seeps like ink. His arm lashes out, solid and inescapable. His hand closes around my throat.

The shock steals my inhale. His grip is ice-cold, cold that sinks deep fast, like it's trying to freeze the pulse in my veins. Pain flares bright and sharp, radiating down my chest. My fingers fly up to claw at his wrist. His skin is smooth and unyielding under my nails, but something thrums beneath it, a resonance that feels wrong and familiar at the same time.

His eyes lock onto mine. Up close, the black in them isn't flat at all. There's movement of tiny tides of shadow pulling inward, spiraling deeper. Starlight dies in there. I see my own faint shimmer reflected for half a second before it vanishes completely, swallowed.

Voidborn. Not the formless shadows in the street, not the half-formed thing that grabbed my wrist in the in-between. This is what they look like when they choose to wear a face. My lungs seize. I can't pull breath past his grip. Heat rushes to my skull, buzzing behind my eyes. "Let... go," I rasp, digging my nails deeper into his arm, leaving crescent moon shape marks in his skin.

His expression barely shifts. The scar on his cheek pulls as his mouth moves, a fraction.

"I have crossed worlds for you," he says, voice low and strangely calm. "You do not tell me when to release you."

The sky above us throbs, the fracture lines pulsing in time with my heartbeat. The circle under our feet hums harder, reacting to the collision of our defined energies. Light flares weakly from my skin, struggling against his touch. He leans in, his face close enough that I can feel the cold radiating off him.

"Do you know," he murmurs, "how long the dark has waited for you to wake? The one place where your name is threaded into the Veil?"

Spots bloom in my vision. My fingers weaken on his arm. He studies me with a strange, clinical intensity, "You do not remember." Something almost like relief flickers across his face. "Good. That will make this less painful."

My lungs are on fire. Every instinct screams at me to fight. Something inside me answers. Light surges in my chest, desperate and wild. It rushes down my arms toward his hand, flaring under his fingers. For a second, the darkness in his veins recoils, his grip loosening just enough that air scrapes into my lungs in a broken gasp. His eyes narrow.

"Still trying to burn," he says. "Even now." His hand tightens.

The world narrows to his fingers around my throat and the roar in my ears. The edges of everything bleach to white. The trees, the cracked sky, the circle, his face all washed out, fading. He leans in that last fraction of an inch, the scar on his cheek a bright line in the glare.

"Astrid," he whispers again. Not a greeting this time. A claim. The white swallows everything. And then there's nothing at all.

Chapter 34

I wake with a gasp that tears my throat raw. For a second, I don't know if my eyes are open or closed. Everything is just thick and dark. The air presses against my face like wet cloth. Then shapes slowly bleed into focus: the faint outline of a wall, rough and uneven; the curve of a metal door; a thin, ghostly line of light leaking in from somewhere behind me.

My throat burns. Swallowing feels like dragging sandpaper down an open wound. The air stinks of damp stone and rust, with something sour underneath. Each breath tastes faintly metallic and blood. I try to move. My body doesn't cooperate. My wrists are yanked back and bound behind the chair, rope biting into skin that's already raw. My ankles are tied to the chair legs so tightly the metal creaks when I test them. Every shift sends a jolt of pain through burning nerves.

Panic spikes in my chest, sharp and wild. I pull harder, twisting, ignoring the sting as the rope grinds deeper, skin tearing. "Hello?" My voice comes out rough, cracked, barely more than a croak. "Is someone there?"

I'm met with silence.

Just the slow drip of water somewhere behind me, each drop hitting stone in rhythm to a ticking clock. I force my lungs to slow down. In. Out. Shallow breaths. My heartbeat is too loud in the quiet, each thud echoing inside my skull like footsteps down a long, empty corridor.

Think.

I blink, letting my eyes adjust to the dim.

The room is small, square, its stone walls slick with moisture. The ceiling feels low, the air heavy enough that every breath has to push for space. A single bare bulb hangs from a wire in one corner, its light flickering in sickly yellow pulses that throw unsteady shadows across the floor.

No windows.

No movement.

No sound except dripping water and my own breathing. The chair beneath me is metal and cold enough that it seeps through my clothes. My shirt clings damply to my skin. I don't remember how I got here. One second, I was in the fractured clearing, the circle, the sky split with shadow, the man with the silver scar and eyes that swallowed light—

Astrid. The name hums through my head, low and poisonous. I swallow a curse that feels like broken glass. My vision blurs for a moment. I blink hard, forcing it to steady.

"Think," I whisper to myself, voice shaking. "Come on. Think." But my thoughts spin uselessly, catching only on flashes: his hand around my throat, the hum of the circle, the way the world went white. I twist again, harder this time. The chair rattles, metal legs scraping against concrete. The ropes cut deeper. I feel warm wetness at my wrists and know without looking that I've torn skin. Still no movement. Still just that slow, infuriating drip.

Then, faintly, from somewhere beyond the door—

Footsteps.

They echo down the hall: slow, heavy, deliberate. Someone

who knows exactly where they're going. My breath catches. The bulb above me flickers once, twice, then steadies into a trembling glow.

The footsteps stop just outside. There's a rattle of metal keys, the scrape of one being chosen, turned. The handle moves. The door groans open, and a blade of bright light slices across the floor, making me squint. Footsteps cross the concrete, the echo bouncing off the low ceiling.

He steps inside. The scarred man. He closes the door behind him with a slow, deliberate click. The lock snaps shut, final and heavy. Up close, in proper light, he's worse. The shadows no longer hide the details of his face, and something in my stomach twists. The thin scar that runs from the corner of his mouth to his cheekbone catches the bulb's glow, a line of Multan silver. His skin is pale but marred with faint smears of ash and something darker, sunk into the lines of his hands. His eyes are deep, endless black and seem to absorb what little light the bulb offers, rather than reflect it back.

His dark hair hangs loose, slightly damp at the ends, curling. His clothes look like they've survived too many battles: leather scorched and torn at the seams, hem charred, dusted with ash as if he walked through a burning city and simply kept going. He looks like something the world tried to bury and failed.

"Ah," he says, voice low and rough edged, rolling through the room like distant thunder. "You're awake."

My throat protests when I speak. "Who are you?"

He doesn't respond immediately. Instead, he moves. He circles me in a languid arc, each step measured, each shift of air chilling my skin. He studies me the way someone might examine a relic or prey they already consider theirs. When he comes to a stop behind me, the temperature drops so sharply that my breath catches. His mouth hovers near my ear, close enough that I feel the ghost of his breath.

"I," he murmurs, voice like a blade wrapped in velvet, "am what the dark made to correct the light's mistake."

"That's not a name"

The words slide along my nerves. He chuckles softly, in a cruel amused way. "I am Malvoryn," he says. "In your language, I would be called a High Keeper."

The name cracks through me. He watches the fear flicker across my face and seems delighted. Then he steps impossibly close, his presence bending the air as if gravity itself leans toward him. He studies me for a long, quiet moment. Then says, "You know," he murmurs, head tilting, "you were... inconvenient to find."

Then he smiles. He begins circling again, slower this time, almost thoughtful.

"You slipped between places before you knew places could be slipped between. A pulse here. A tear there. A threshold left trembling behind you." His fingers curl lazily in the air. "Every time we reached for you, you were already gone."

I force my voice steady. "I don't know what you're talking about."

"No." His smile sharpens. "That is what makes you dangerous."

He leans closer, the darkness in his eyes shifting like a tide.

"You were a ghost," he says. "A rumor in the Void. A name threaded through old wounds. The dark whispered *Astrid*, and every time we followed, we found only echoes."

A shiver races down my spine.

"And when your father hid you..." His expression changes. The amusement thins into something colder. "He nearly buried you well enough that even the Void lost your scent."

My chest clenches.

"My father protected me."

"He hid you," Malvoryn corrects softly. "There is a difference."

The words hit too close. I yank at the ropes, pain flashing up my arms.

"What do you want from me?"

His smile fades.

For the first time since he entered, his face goes still.

"We do not want to kill you, Astrid."

"That's supposed to make me feel better?"

"No." He steps closer. "It is supposed to make you listen."

Shadow trails from his fingertips like smoke pulled backward. It curls through the air, not touching me, but close enough that my skin prickles.

"You are not merely light-touched," he says. "Not a common remnant. Not some frightened descendant carrying a diluted spark in her blood." His gaze drops to my chest, as if he can see the pulse beneath my skin. "You are something older."

My throat tightens.

"What?"

"The records call your kind many things." His voice lowers. "Some names were lost. Some were burned. Some were forbidden to speak aloud." His eyes lift back to mine. "But my realm remembers one."

I don't breathe.

"Bridgekeeper."

The word lands hard.

I shake my head. "No."

"You do not even know what you are denying."

"I'm not opening anything for you."

His laugh is quiet. Almost pitying.

"You already have."

The bulb flickers overhead.

For one terrible second, the room seems to tilt, the shadows lengthening toward him like they are listening.

"You opened the book," he says. "You woke the circle. You stepped into the in-between and called it fear. You think these things happened to you." He bends close enough that the cold of him brushes my skin. "They happened because of you."

My breath stutters.

"No."

"Yes."

The certainty in his voice makes my skin crawl.

"You are the hinge. The place where sealed things remember how to move."

I swallow hard. "And you want to use me."

"At last," he says softly. "Something true."

The room seems smaller.

He turns away from me then, pacing toward the wall as though the story he is about to tell requires distance.

"For ages beyond your memory, Light and Void were not at war." His voice is quieter now. Not gentle. Never gentle. But weighted. "There was an Accord. The Wells were shared in cycles. Radiant season. Dark season. Creation and collapse. Expansion and return."

He looks back at me.

"Balance."

The word does not sound holy in his mouth. It sounds like a wound.

"The Celestials will tell you they guarded that balance. They will polish the story until it shines. They will speak of duty. Sacrifice. Order." His expression hardens. "They will not tell you about the Eclipsed Well."

A faint pulse moves through the shadows around him.

I remember the Court. The book. Riven's warnings. The phrase that keeps following me.

The light must answer, or the dark will consume it.

"What is the Eclipsed Well?" I whisper.

Malvoryn's jaw flexes.

"Ours," he says. One word. Filled with centuries.

"It was our cycle. Our lifeline. When we arrived, the Well was already faltering." His voice drops. "Dying."

The room feels colder.

"The collapse tore through our realm. Cities folded inward. Rivers became ash. Families unraveled before they could scream." His eyes fix on mine. "Do you know what it is to hear an entire world hollow itself out beneath your feet?"

I don't answer. I can't.

"We begged the Celestials for truth," he continues. "For explanation. For any acknowledgment that they had touched what was not theirs to take."

His mouth twists. "They gave us excuses."

The shadows behind him stir.

"Imbalance. Decay. A natural failing. Words clean enough to hide blood beneath them."

My hands go numb against the ropes.

"But they had drawn from it before our season," he says. "They had guarded it. They had sealed the records. And we were the ones left to starve."

I don't want to believe him. That's the worst part. I don't

want to. But something about his grief feels too old to be invented.

"So you drained them," I whisper. "The light-touched."

"We survived," he says.

"You fed on people."

His eyes flash. "We took what your kind hoarded while ours collapsed."

"My kind?" The words tear out of me. "I don't even know what I am."

"No." His voice softens in a way that makes my stomach twist. "But your father did."

The room goes silent. The drip of water behind me sounds suddenly too loud.

"My father didn't know anything about this."

Malvoryn only looks at me. The silence answers before he does. "He knew enough to run," he says. "Enough to hide you among mortals. Enough to bury your pulse under a human life and pray none of us ever heard it again."

My vision blurs. "You're lying."

"Am I?"

He steps closer.

"Ask yourself why he taught you riddles instead of truth. Why symbols followed you like ghosts. Why your memories fracture at the edges whenever the name Astrid is spoken."

My pulse hammers against my ribs. "I don't remember."

"I know." His expression changes then. For one breath, the cruelty fades into something stranger. Almost satisfaction. Almost sorrow. "You remember nothing," he murmurs. "But your pulse remembers everything."

He raises one hand. Darkness gathers around his fingers, thin as smoke, dense as gravity. I pull against the ropes hard enough to tear skin fresh. "Don't touch me."

He ignores me.

"Your father stole pieces of you," he says. "Perhaps to protect you. Perhaps to protect the worlds from what you might become." His hand hovers inches from my forehead. "Either way, he left us both with fragments of truth."

"No."

His eyes meet mine. "And I am tired of fragments."

The light under my skin flares, weak but furious. It crawls up my arms, threads of gold-white heat fighting the cold that presses in around him. Malvoryn watches it with fascination.

"There she is," he whispers.

Not Rachel. Not Astrid. Something in between. Terror and rage surge together, bright enough that the bulb overhead bursts. Glass rains down in a glittering spray. The room plunges into darkness except for the thin glow beneath my skin.

For one second, Malvoryn looks almost pleased.

"Let me show you," he says, "the memories he stole."

"No—"

My voice splinters. His palm presses against my skin. And the world breaks open.

Chapter 35

Cold. Then light.

It explodes behind my eyes, white-hot and blinding. The room rips away. The chair. The chains. The damp, stinking stone.

All of it falls.

There are only memories.

A woman lies in a narrow bed, candlelight trembling across her face.

She's beautiful and terrified. Sweat slicks her hair to her temples. Her breathing is ragged, desperate. A man kneels beside her, clutching her hand like it's the only thing keeping him anchored. My father. Younger, softer looking, but unmistakably him.

"Hold on, love," he whispers, voice breaking. "Just a little more."

"I can't," she gasps. "It's—burning—"

Light glows under her skin. It shines through her chest, through her ribs, pulsing like a trapped star trying to tear its way free. Her whole body arches with the force of it. The air hums with that same tone I've felt all my life but never heard out loud.

"It's not burning you," he says, tears in his eyes. "It's her. It's our child."

A final, strangled scream and then silence. A newborn cry pierces the room. The light vanishes. Every candle goes dark.

My father gathers the infant into his arms. His shoulders shake. He stares down at the tiny face. And for a long moment he looks as though he's witnessing a miracle. He sobs into the woman's damp hair, whispering a name like a prayer and an apology all at once.

"Astrid," he says. "You're... everything she couldn't hold."

The scene fractures into shards of color, sound, and heat, then shatters.

-

I'm asleep in a small wooden bed. Moonlight spills through dusty bedroom window. I'm young. Five, maybe. My father stands in the doorway, watching me. The room is quiet. Then something strange happens, my father's head snaps up and he scrambles to the window as quietly as he can.

The stars outside begin to brighten. One by one. As though responding to something. My father notices. His face drains of color. The stars continue brightening until they seem almost close enough to touch.

Then, slowly, they dim again. Returning to normal. My father closes his eyes and sighs loudly. Fear and exhaustion written all over his face.

"Please," he whispers to the darkness. "I need more time."

—

I'm older now. Eight or nine. I'm standing in the middle of a study and my father is pacing the room. A stranger looms nearby holding a book and scanning the pages quickly. The stranger bites his nails and then shuts the book hard. The sound makes me and my father jump.

"Leave the room." My father says to me. A command.

As I close the door slowly behind me my father and the stranger begin arguing. I press my ear to the door hoping to catch fragments of the argument.

The image flickers.

"What did she take?" the stranger demands.

My father says nothing.

The stranger slams both hands onto what sounds like the desk. "How much?"

Silence. Then:

"Enough." The word leaves my father's mouth like a confession.

The room falls silent. The stranger sounding defeated, "Oh God."

My father begins to cry.

—

I'm thirteen. We're in yet another small rental house, the kind with thin walls and a stained carpet that smells of the ghosts of other people's lives. Packed boxes and suitcases are stacked everywhere. He's packing a bag with shaking hands. He keeps glancing toward the window. Eyes searching the dark for something I can't see.

A knock rattles the front door. His entire body freezes. For a moment genuine panic flashes across his face. He glances to me quickly and then back toward the door. Another thundering knock echoes through the tiny house.

"Dad? What's wrong?" He startles, then rushes to me placing a hand on each shoulder.

"I'm so sorry honey, quickly, please close the curtains" He says urgently. He lets go of me and rushes to the hallway quickly locking every lock on the door.

As I close the curtains I catch a glimpse of my father sliding down the wall, his face buried in his hands. I have never seen him look so tired or so afraid.

"They're getting closer."

The words barely above a whisper leave his mouth.

—

My father sits beside my bed. He's older now with deep lines etched around his eyes, His face looks hollow from years of carrying something alone. I pretend to sleep, evening out my breathing to appear deep in dreams.

He doesn't notice. The stress of everything mounting and he's deep in thought staring straight ahead, looking at nothing but the blank wall in my room. With a sigh he reaches over to stroke the hair from my face. His hand rests there for a moment as he says,

"You deserve the truth."

His voice breaks.

"But if they know who you are..." He doesn't finish. His words cut off my silent tears streaming down his face.

"I'll lose you."

And for the first time, I realize something. My father wasn't hiding from the Void. He wasn't hiding from monsters. He was hiding me. The realization hits like a knife.

He lifts his trembling fingers. A soft golden light gathers around them.

"A little longer," he whispers. "Just a little longer."

His hand touches my forehead.

The world erupts.

—

The memories collapse inward, sucked back into darkness. The cell slams back into existence around me. The ropes dig into my wrists. My lungs drag in air like I've been underwater for too long. Sweat chills my skin. My head throbs with the weight of too many lives shoved into a single moment.

Malvoryn's hand drops away from my forehead.

He watches me, eyes dark and satisfied. "Now you remember."

The air hums faintly. My throat feels flayed. The chains seem tighter than before. My mother's scream. My father's shaking hands. The name Astrid ringing through all my senses. I force myself to meet his gaze.

"What did you do to me?" I rasp.

"I showed you memories," he says.

"No." I shake my head. "You showed me pieces." I shoot back, the words cutting my throat on their way out.

A faint smile touches his mouth.

"An improvement."

Anger flares hot enough to cut through the confusion.

"My father protected me."

The smile disappears.

"Did he?"

His laugh is short and harsh. "Protected?" he repeats. "He spent his life hiding you."

My chest tightens. "Why else would he—"

"Erase your memories?" Malvoryn interrupts. "Perhaps he believed he was saving you."

"Saving me from what?"

His gaze holds mine.

"Perhaps from yourself or perhaps from the truth."

For the first time, genuine irritation slips through my fear. "Stop speaking in riddles."

He rises and begins pacing. The shadows follow behind him as he moves. "We spent years searching for you," I stare at him. "Astrid"

The name feels wrong and familiar all at once. Like a scar I don't remember earning.

"You keep saying that."

"Because it is the name attached to every record we could find."

My pulse stutters.

"What records?"

"Fragments. Things erased from time," He gestures vaguely. "Stories. Warnings. Broken histories. Names scratched from stone. Pages removed from books." His expression darkens. "Evidence someone wanted forgotten."

A chill creeps through me. "And you think that I'm Astrid?"

"I think," he says carefully, "that every trail ended with the same name."

The room feels smaller. "You still haven't told me what you want."

His jaw tightens. For the first time, the answer comes immediately. "The truth."

I bark out a bitter laugh. "That's convenient."

"It is."

The honesty catches me off guard. Malvoryn stops pacing. "When our Well began dying, we searched for a reason." His voice lowers. "We found records-"

"The Eclipsed Well."

I interrupt. "What does that have to do with me?

He continues as if I never spoke. "The Celestials denied responsibility."

"You think they caused it."

"I think someone lied."

The distinction matters. I can hear it.

"So you started a war."

His expression hardens. "We started looking for answers."

The darkness around him stirs. "The war came later."

I don't know whether to believe him. That's the worst part. I don't know what to believe anymore. Who was my father? The Voidborn. The Celestials. Astrid. Every answer only creates more questions. Malvoryn crouches in front of me again.

"What did you feel?"

I blink.

"What?"

"When you saw those memories."

I hesitate. The answer slips out before I can stop it. "Like something was missing."

His eyes sharpen. "Exactly."

My breath catches. "You felt it too?"

"Every record ends the same way." His voice is almost a whisper now.

"Something removed." A knot forms in my stomach.

"By my father?"

"Maybe."

The answer surprises me. Not because of what he says. Because he doesn't know.

"Maybe not."

The silence that follows is somehow worse.

"You really don't know what happened, do you?"

A long pause.

"No."

The word settles between us uncomfortable and honest. He rises slowly from where he's crouched in front of me. "But I know this," His gaze locks onto mine. "The Celestials feared something."

My pulse quickens.

"What did they know?"

"I don't know." Again with the honesty. "But they erased records." He takes another step back, further into the room.

"They hid names, they buried histories."

He takes another slow step away from me. "And your father spent his entire life making sure you never remembered yours."

The room feels suddenly cold. Part of me is beginning to wonder if he's right. Not about everything. Just enough to terrify me about who or what I am.

"What am I?" The question escapes before I can stop it.

Malvoryn studies me for a long moment.

Then says, "I think," he says quietly, "that's the question everyone has been trying to answer."

Something ugly and sharp clicks into place.

"You killed him," I breathe.

Malvoryn tilts his head; the silver scar pulls as he smiles.

"He made it easy," he says. "All those years hiding you. Running. Erasing traces. Pretending you were ordinary." He shakes his head slowly. "One man against an entire realm."

My mind flashes back to the park, the world going eerily quiet, the burning brightness, the sense of something tearing open just beyond what my eyes could see.

"The second your pulse surged in that park," he continues, "you lit up like a beacon."

My stomach turns.

"You murdered him because of me," I whisper.

He crouches, settling so that we are eye-level, a wolf getting comfortable before it bites.

"We hunted him because he stood between us and answers. For years he hid the only person connected to the questions we've been asking since the Eclipsed Well began to die."

His dark eyes lock onto mine.

"He chose his side long before we found him."

The phrase lands strangely, but I don't have time to chase it. The temperature of the room drops.

Metal shrieks when the door slams open. Two Voidborn step inside. Their bodies look solid at first glance, but the edges of them fray into shadow, repelling light rather than reflecting it. One carries something limp. Someone limp. They drop the body onto the floor with a dull, sickening impact. My heart stops, then lurches violently back into motion.

Chapter 36

"Marin!"

Her name tears out of me, raw and broken. She lies there chained at her wrists and ankles, a band strapped across her chest like they're afraid she'll run even unconscious. Her head lolls to the side, hair tangled over her face, lips pale.

"What did you do to her?" The question rips from me soaked in panic and fury. I struggle to get free from my restraints but it's no use. "What did you do to her?"

Malvoryn steps out from behind them, his presence swallowing what little light remains.

"Nothing permanent," he says. "Yet."

I yank against the chains hard enough to make the chair skid. Pain sears through my arms. "Let her go!"

He chuckles, low and almost fond. "You have spirit. I'll give you that."

He moves behind me and settles a hand on my shoulder, heavy and possessive. "Stop fighting" he murmurs. "If you want her back, you'll answer my questions."

"Over my dead body," I hiss.

His grip tightens.

"We can arrange that."

The air thickens as a low sound rises in the room, something caught between thunder and breath a metallic taste spreads across my tongue. Marin's body rises. The chains clink as she's lifted from the floor, suspended by some invisible force, limbs dangling, head tipping back.

"Stop!" I scream, thrashing in the chair. "Please! Put her down!"

The cuffs bite into already shredded skin as I fight to get up and go to her. The light inside me flickers, frantic and useless.

Malvoryn leans down until his mouth hovers near my ear.

"Just tell me what you want."

His smile grows, satisfied. His hand drifts from my shoulder to the back of the chair, knuckles grazing the side of my neck.

"Ah," he murmurs. "Finally, the right question."

He crouches again, settling into that unnerving stillness. For a moment he says nothing. The shadows around him shift restlessly. His eyes lock onto mine. "Why did your father hide you?"

My chest heaves. "You felt it in the memories, I know you did." Malvoryn spits out.

I don't answer. I can still hear my mother screaming from the memory. The impossible light. that exploded out of her. The fear in my father's face. Then the next memory of the stranger asking how much I'd taken.

"Enough." My father had said. The memory flashes through me again. "What happened?" I whisper trying to remember even a scrap of what I might have taken.

Something flickers across his face. Not triumph. Frustration. Because he doesn't know either.

"That," he says quietly, "is the question that started all of this."

The room goes silent. Even Marin hangs motionless in the

air.

"What are you talking about?"

"The Eclipsed Well." His voice lowers. "The Celestials insist its collapse was natural."

"And you don't believe them?"

"No."

The answer comes instantly. "They buried records." His gaze sharpens. "They erased names." Another step closer. "They rewrote history." He crouches in front of me again. "And somehow every trail led back to this..Astrid."

My pulse hammers.

"You keep saying that name."

"Because every fragment says it." His voice softens. "Not always in the same way."

That catches my attention. "What does that mean?"

For the first time, Malvoryn hesitates. "The stories disagree."

I stare at him. "The stories of what?"

His expression darkens. "Some call Astrid a savior."

The shadows flicker. "Some call her a destroyer." A pause. "Some claim she never existed at all."

A chill races down my spine. "And what do you believe?"

His eyes meet mine. "I think somebody worked very hard to make sure nobody could answer that question."

The room feels suddenly smaller.

"The pulse in your blood is a map," he says. "Etched into you the moment the Well went dark and the sky split. Between light and Void. Between creation and unmaking. Between where you are chained and where we wait."

He glances at the chains, at the faint shimmer under my skin. He stands, satisfaction threading through his shadowed outline. He turns toward the door as if the matter is already decided.

"Wait!" I choke out, eyes locked on Marin's motionless form. "What about Riven? Where is he?" He stills.

For the first time since he entered, something in his composure shifts. His head turns a fraction, the name has hooked onto something inside him. His silence stretches. Then a slow, delighted smile spreads across his face.

"Oh," he says quietly. "I do love a surprise."

The way he says it makes my blood run colder than the stone beneath my feet.

Chapter 37

The door creaks open behind me. Footsteps, steady and measured cross the threshold.

"Let him in," Malvoryn commands.

My stomach knots. Riven walks through the doorway. He's not hurt. Not chained. Not dragged like a prisoner. His hands hang loose at his sides. Dust smudges his shirt; his black hair is mussed, his face pale but nothing is broken. Nothing visible, anyway.

"Riven?" My voice splinters on his name. Relief floods me so sharply it almost hurts. "Oh my God—thank God, you're—" But he won't meet my eyes. The relief stumbles. Falters. Something cold slips into its place. "Untie me," I plead, twisting toward him. The ropes burn my wrists. "Please. We have to get Marin, we have to—"

"Don't."

The word is quiet, but it cuts clean through the room. I go still. He finally looks up, and the expression on his face knocks the breath from my lungs. It isn't fear. It isn't confusion. It's something hollowed out, ashamed. My thoughts lurch, tripping over themselves.

Why isn't he helping me?

Why does he look like that?

Why won't he even look at me?

Something is wrong. Something I don't understand. Malvoryn steps smoothly into the space between us, the smallest satisfied curl at the corner of his mouth. "Oh," he murmurs, delighted, "he didn't tell you?"

My pulse stutters. "Tell me what?" My voice is barely there.

Malvoryn turns toward Riven, as though savoring every second of this. "Shall I?" he asks. "Or would you prefer the honor?"

Riven's jaw tightens. He says nothing. So Malvoryn does. "Riven," he says slowly, drawing out each syllable, "is one of us. Born of the Void. Voidborn."

The word hits like a blow. Riven flinches, not at Malvoryn, but at me, the shame on his face has nowhere else to go. The world heaves sideways. My pulse roars in my ears. I can't speak. Can't breathe. The only thing that leaves me is a whisper, thin and cracked, because anything louder would break me open:

"No."

"Afraid so." His grin widens, all teeth and cruelty. "The shadows you've been running from—the ones your father has been terrified of your entire life—you were sleeping next to one."

Images flash: the way Riven always knew when the shadows were near before anyone else did. The way my light flared when he touched me. The way he flinched from it like it burned.

"I don't believe you," I say, fighting the ropes, heart slamming against my ribs. "You're lying—"

"Am I?" Malvoryn tilts his head toward Riven, eyes gleaming. "Go on. Tell her what you are."

Riven's silence answers for him. The ground feels unsteady beneath the chair. A faint buzzing starts in my ears.

"Long before you were born," Malvoryn continues, voice smooth and poisonous. "the Eclipsed Well began to fail. Cities collapsed. Entire regions of our realm unraveled,"

His smile turns sharp.

" into nothing—the Celestials did nothing. They fled. They hid behind their Veil and left us to starve in the dark." He laughs once, softly, bitterly. "So we searched for answers. We found fragments. Missing records. Destroyed archives. Names scratched from stone." He steps slowly around me, every movement calculated. "And one name kept surviving."

Riven flinches.

"That's why you were looking for me?" I whisper, voice cracking.

Malvoryn doesn't even acknowledge me. "We were looking for answers and a way to restore our light well, restore our people."

"You happened to be attached to them." Tears threatening to burst from my eyes. I stare at him anyways.

"What does that even mean?"

"It means every trail eventually led back to Astrid." His voice lowers. "The Well." Another step. "The Falling." Another. "The missing histories." Another until he is inches from my face, "Your father." he spits out with more venom than I thought possible.

The knot in my stomach tightens. He continues, "We don't know exactly what Astrid was or why you were hidden."

The admission catches me off guard. A humorless smile touches his mouth.

"If we knew, we wouldn't still be searching."

"And Riven?" I ask.

My voice cracks on the name. Malvoryn glances toward him.

"Riven here," he continues, ignoring me, His tone turns almost conversational. "He was assigned to you," he says. "To slip beneath your guard. To get close to you. To understand your pulse—to make you trust him—to find out how you were connected to Astrid."

Assigned to you.

connected to Astrid.

My throat tightens. "No... He saved me. He—"

Malvoryn's smile sharpens. "He killed your father."

The air around me hollows out, the room exhales and leaves nothing behind. The walls pull away. My heartbeat drops into a cold, echoing void inside my chest. I hear Riven's breath catch, a sound so quiet it shouldn't mean anything. But it does. My lungs forget how to work. My fingers go numb around the ropes. A ringing starts in my ears, sharp and rising, drowning everything except the truth closing its fist around my ribs.

"You're lying," I whisper. The words don't sound like they belong to me. "You're lying." I say it again, as if repetition might make it untrue. Shock hits in a cold wave that steals everything warm, everything familiar, everything that ever felt safe about his voice, his hands, his presence beside me.

Malvoryn's voice drops, quiet and intimate, like he's sharing a secret. "He was the one who found your father first. Watched the light leave him. Your father begged him to spare you."

Riven's voice comes out raw. "Stop." He says it softer this time, like it hurts.

"Tell me he's lying, Riven." I force the words past a throat gone numb. "Tell me."

He looks at me. Not the way he used to, not with that guarded softness, not with reluctant warmth. His mouth opens. Nothing comes out. He doesn't deny it. The silence shatters something inside me.

"You knew," I whisper. My chest feels too tight, too small. "You knew. You were with me this whole time—"

"I didn't know it was you," he chokes out. The words tumble over each other. "Not until I met you. Not until—"

"Until what?" I spit. "Until you decided to finish the job?"

He flinches like I slapped him. "No," he says quickly. "I swear to you, I couldn't—Rachel, please—"

"Don't say my name!" The ropes bite into my skin, the shimmer in my vision flaring sharp and wild. "Don't say my name. Don't speak to me!"

Riven takes a step toward me before he seems to catch himself. Malvoryn's hand snaps out, wrapping around his arm with casual ownership. "Touching," the man murmurs. "Truly. Though I must say, Riven, you've gone soft. A Voidborn who falls for his prey? How poetic."

Riven's glare could burn holes through steel, but he doesn't speak. I'm shaking. My voice comes out small and broken. "You killed my father."

Riven's voice cracks. "I didn't know. I swear to you, I didn't know who he was until it was done. They didn't tell me. If I had known—"

"You still would have done it," I cut in. "You just would have felt a little worse about it afterward, right?"

Malvoryn chuckles, low and pleased.

Riven's shoulders sag like I've punched straight through his ribs. "That's not—Rachel, that's not fair. I was—"

"What?" My laugh comes out jagged, more like a sob

snapped in half. "Doing your job?"

He looks wrecked. "It was supposed to be another assignment. Names, faces, that's all they ever were. I didn't know I'd ever meet you. I didn't know you were his. That you were—" He cuts himself off, too late.

"You used me," I whisper. The words feel heavy enough to bruise. "All of it. Every moment, every word, every touch. It was all a lie."

"No," he says, too fast. "It wasn't. Not all of it. Not after I got to know you. Not being with you."

A bitter, broken sound escapes me, something between a laugh and a choke.

"You're pathetic."

He goes very still. I drag in a breath that hurts going down and force my voice flat, cold, the way I wish I actually felt. "You mean nothing to me," I say, to hurt him, to make him feel the same pain I feel right now.

He flinches like I've driven a knife in deep. He takes a half-step toward me anyway, his body hasn't caught up with the fact that I want him nowhere near me.

"And you never did," I add. The words come out calm, almost gentle. They land harder than any scream. For a moment, no one moves. Riven just stands there, shoulders slack, eyes hollow. I watch something inside him crack quietly, glass under too much weight, soundless. Malvoryn watches it all with bright interest, because he's just been handed front-row seats to his favorite tragedy.

"Well," he says at last, hands coming together in a slow, derisive clap, "what a tender little display." He glances toward Riven. "Enough of this. Come along, Riven. She's not ready yet."

Riven doesn't move. His gaze flicks back to me one last time. His mouth opens, closes again. Whatever he wants to say dies behind his teeth. Malvoryn's fingers tighten on his shoulder. "Leave her," he says lightly. "She'll come around. They always do."

They turn toward the door. I stare straight ahead, refusing to look at him. Refusing to give him that much. The door groans open, spilling a harsh strip of light into the dim cell. Riven doesn't look back. The lock clicks. Then they're gone.

The silence that follows feels endless. Only Marin's soft, ragged breathing breaks it, still unconscious, still chained, still suspended like some sacrifice waiting for the knife. My gaze drifts to the empty space where Riven stood. It feels louder than his voice, heavier than his touch, his absence.

The pain comes in a rush then, hot and overwhelming. Not the ropes. Not the bruises. The other thing. The thing in my chest. I let out a sound that doesn't sound human, a sob or maybe a snarl, and bow my head as the first tear hits the cold floor. They fall one by one, quiet and relentless. For the first time since this started, the anger, the fear, the betrayal all blur together into one clear, vicious thought: If I ever get out of here, I will make them both regret ever touching my light.

Chapter 38

I don't know how long I've been here. Hours, days maybe weeks. The dark eats time until it has no edges. The room never changes. Same damp air that sticks in my lungs. Same drip somewhere behind me that hits stone with maddening rhythm. Same metallic stink of rust, old water, and stone that's seen too much.

My clothes are damp from sitting in this cell. My wrists are bruised, skin split where the rope saws into it. My ankles ache from being tied to the chair for so long that my legs have forgotten what standing feels like. Sleep comes in brief, jagged bursts. Hunger comes in waves big enough to drown me. I've stopped shivering. Not because I'm warm, but because I don't have the strength left to shake.

Sometimes I close my eyes and try to remember what warmth felt like. Steam curling off coffee in the morning. Marin's laugh bouncing off kitchen tile. The low hum of the city at dawn. Riven's chest under my cheek, steady and solid.

NO!

I push the memory down. I refuse to think of him. The betrayal cutting deep. All the memories slip away a little faster each time. Good, I want to forget him.

Marin hasn't woken up. She lies a few feet away, still

chained, wrists, ankles, a band across her chest. Her normal white hair is a dark tangle. Her face is gray around the edges. Every few minutes I force myself to look for the rise and fall of her chest. I'm terrified one time it won't be there.

"Hang on," I whisper to her, my voice breaking on the rough syllables. "Please."

Malvoryn thinks he understands what he captured. The Voidborn think they've chained the answer to their questions. Maybe they're wrong. Maybe I don't know what I am. Maybe nobody does.

But if my father spent his entire life trying to protect me...

If the Void crossed worlds to find me...

If the Celestials buried records and erased names...

Then whatever they're all afraid of is still here.

The door opens without warning. Cold air knifes in, sharper than the chill in here, carrying a heavier tang of iron. A Voidborn guard steps inside, tall, grey-eyed, features half-lost in the shadows clinging to him. They all look like that here: not fully defined, as if the dark is still deciding what face they get to wear. He doesn't speak. He never does. A tin plate clatters onto the floor in front of me. The sound is so loud in the quiet that my whole body flinches.

A smear of thick stew, if that's what it is, slops across the cracked concrete. It's already cooling, congealing at the edges. I stare at it for a long time. My throat aches. My stomach knots so hard it feels like it's turning inside out.

The guard sneers faintly, I guess the fact that I'm still breathing is an inconvenient for him. He turns and leaves. The lock grinds home again, heavy and final. The smell of the food is almost unbearable. Meat or something pretending to be and salt and grease. I can almost taste it on my tongue if

I let myself imagine hard enough. My hands are still lashed behind the back of the chair.

I lean forward, trying to reach with my mouth, but the ropes pull tight across my chest. The edge of the chair bites into my ribs. Pain sparks down my spine. The plate stays just out of reach. My head drops forward, breath shuddering out of me.

A laugh escapes, a small, cracked sound that hurts my throat. "Guess we're past dignity, huh, Marin?" She doesn't answer. Of course she doesn't. The only reply is the faint rush of breath she lets out occasionally reminding me she's still alive. Time crawls again. I think about Riven. About his face when I said it.

You mean nothing to me.

The memory twists something in my chest so sharply I almost gasp, but I hold onto the anger anyway. It's the only thing keeping my spine from collapsing. He was one of them. He was always one of them. I stare at the cold stew until my vision blurs. My thoughts loop, the same three words circling. Just give in. It would be easier. Let them take it. Let it end.

My father fought for so long, and look where that got him. A mark in the dirt, a body that never stayed long enough to bury. A daughter who became a beacon in the dark anyway. Maybe he was right to hide me. Maybe I was never meant to survive this.

A drop of water hits my shoulder, cold and sudden. It rolls down my arm, catching the thin light from the bulb overhead. For a second, just a second, it glows faintly, remembering something. The light in me hasn't forgotten how to exist in this dark space. I close my eyes. The shimmer lingers behind my eyelids, soft, stubborn, refusing to go out. Even here. Even now. Some part of me refuses to die quietly.

The sound wakes me first. Boots on stone. The scrape of metal. The low moan of a lock turning. Then hands, rough, cold hands, clamp down on my shoulders and wrench me upright. Pain spikes down my neck and spine. My muscles protest, every fiber screaming as if it's the first time they've moved in years.

"Wait—" My voice comes out a rasp, dry and shredded. "Please—"

They don't listen. Two Voidborn guards haul me to my feet. My bare toes drag over the floor; my legs buckle uselessly. They keep moving anyway, dragging me like I weigh nothing. The room spins. Walls, ceiling, shadow smear together as we move. My skin feels thin and paper-dry. Sweat is cold on my back, my hair stuck to my face.

"Marin!" I twist in their grip, searching for her shape. No answer. Just the echo of our footsteps and the rattle of chains on my wrists.

"Wait, no! Marin!" I scream it this time, voice splintering. "Don't leave her there—"

One of the guards snarls and yanks harder. Fingers dig into my arms, sharp enough that bruises bloom on contact. The air changes. It grows colder, sharper. The damp, stale stink of my cell gives way to something else, metal and ozone and that thin, metallic tang of the this place. We're going up. Stone shifts to metal underfoot. Each dragged step echoes hollow and loud. A door slams open ahead, and a wash of dim light stabs my eyes, making them water. They pull me into a wide room.

It feels cavernous, the ceiling lost in shadow, the walls too far away. My first thought is how wrongly clean it is compared to my cell. No slime on the walls, no puddles. Just polished metal, the faint smell of oil, and something buzzing low in the air. A single enormous window dominates the far wall. Its glass is tinted a strange grey-blue, warping the light and whatever passes for a sky outside.

The guards shove me into a chair bolted to the floor. I hit hard, ribs flaring with pain, breath knocking out of me. Before I can suck in more air, the ropes are back, tight around my wrists, my chest, my ankles. Raw skin tears anew as rough fiber bites down.

When they step back, I force myself to look beyond them, toward the window. There's light out there. Not sunlight. Not moonlight. Something paler, flatter, metal polished too thin. The landscape beyond is barren, stretching into nothing, shifting slightly. The ground looks like ash pressed into shape, flaking at the edges. Far off, shadowy forms drift, slow and deliberate.

For half a heartbeat, I think about screaming. Maybe someone will hear. Maybe something. I think about running but have no idea where the exit door even is.

Then a door behind me opens with a soft, deliberate sigh.

"Don't even think about it," Malvoryn drawls.

I turn my head, heart hammering. He walks into the room, every step unhurried, absolutely certain the space belongs to him. That thin line of silver scar on his cheek catches the dull light. That same calm, almost pleasant expression sits on his face. This time he's in a perfectly tailored black suit that looks impressively expensive. His hair neatly in place, and clean......he could almost pass as handsome if he wasn't such a prick.

"No one will hear you," he says, circling toward my side. "Not here."

I swallow. My throat feels scraped raw. "Where is here?"

Malvoryn's fingers brush the back of my chair as he passes behind me, a casual touch that makes my skin crawl. He laughs quietly, no humor in it. He moves closer to the window, gesturing toward the warped grey-blue world beyond.

"This," he says, "is what we call The Hollow."

"The Hollow," I repeat, tasting the word. It settles heavy on my tongue. "What is it?"

He comes back into view, leaning one hand on the table bolted in front of me. "The place between," he says. "Where the dark lives when the light refuses to let it die."

I look out again. The sky is split with faint dark veins, hairline fractures spidering through whatever passes for the firmament. The ground shifts slow and restless. Far away, something tall and thin moves against the horizon, then vanishes.

The Hollow hums at the edge of my hearing a low, steady vibration, the heartbeat of something that has never lived yet refuses to die. The sound seeps through the stone, through the metal chair, through my bones, settling behind my teeth until they ache with the pressure.

For a long, suffocating moment, neither of us speaks. He paces in a slow, deliberate rhythm, occasionally rubbing the side of his face, each of his steps aligning disturbingly with the pulse of the Hollow itself, the two moving in tandem with each other.

My throat is dry and cracked when I wet my lips and force the question out.

"Why am I here?"

He stops mid-stride and turns fully to face me. His posture is composed, controlled; his eyes have gone dark and intent, the color flattened into something that feels bottomless.

"To see if you're ready," he says.

The motion of my brows pulling together tugs uncomfortably at the split skin along my cheek.

"Ready for what?" I say with a bored sigh. A faint twist interrupts his expression, something shaped like a smile but empty of anything resembling warmth.

"To submit"

The word drifts through the room like cold smoke, settling beneath my skin in a way that makes breathing harder. I push myself upright as far as the ropes allow, every bruise and cut screaming.

"Submit to what?" I snap. "Being your puppet?"

He steps closer, each footfall measured, echoing in the stillness.

"To finding my answers" he replies, voice low and unyielding.

"How am I suppose to do that?" I fire back, heat threading through my voice even as the chill in the room presses deeper into my bones.

Any lingering amusement drains from his expression. His eyes darken, hollow and fathomless. The faint curl of a smile disappears entirely. He looks at me with certainty. Cold certainty. As if he's already cataloged the ways I'll break.

After several minutes of his silent pacing, I come to my own conclusion, "You think I know something."

"I think your father made certain you wouldn't." His voice sharpens. "Your father hid you, why? Every piece of evidence connected to your name was scattered or destroyed." He stops pacing. "Why?" he demands.

I glare at him, "You tell me." I spit out with enough venom

in my words to kill.

His expression darkens. "If I knew, I wouldn't need you. I wouldn't need those memories buried in your mind."

For a moment neither of us speaks. The Hollow hums beyond the walls. I hold all the power here and he knows it, even if I don't rememeber anything.

"You want to know what happened to your precious well?" I say finally, defiantly.

"Yes."

"And you think I know."

"No." The answer comes immediately. "I think they do."

My stomach twists. The realization unfolds slowly. "The Celestials."

His smile widens in a satisfied way. "Yes."

Cold creeps down my spine.

"I want you to return where you belong."

I bark out a bitter laugh. "I don't belong there. I remember nothing about it."

"Perhaps not but they can help you remember."

His eyes gleam. The room suddenly feels much smaller. Much colder. "What are you talking about?"

" Go to Aetherion." The name sends an uncomfortable shiver through me. "Aetherion is sealed to us. Guarded. Protected. Every path we have found ends before its gates." He steps closer. "But not for you."

I hate how certain he sounds. "You don't know that."

"No," he agrees. "I don't." Another step closer. "But your father thought so."

My jaw tightens.

"And the fact that the Celestials spent decades searching for you too."

He crouches until we're eye level. "You can go where we cannot."

My pulse hammers. "And then what?"

His eyes lock onto mine. "Then you find the truth."

The words are almost gentle.

"Find what they erased." A pause. "Find what happened to the Eclipsed Well. Find out why they feared Astrid."

My throat tightens.

"And give those answers to you?" For the first time, something genuinely dangerous flashes across his face.

"Yes."

The single word lands heavy.

"No." The word drifts through the room, settling beneath my skin in a way that makes breathing harder. I push myself upright as far as the ropes allow, every bruise and cut screaming.

His smile fades. "No?"

"I won't be your puppet." I snap.

He steps closer, each footfall measured, echoing in the stillness. Any lingering amusement drains from his expression. His eyes darken, hollow and fathomless. The faint curl of a smile disappears entirely. He looks at me with certainty. Cold certainty. As if he's already cataloged the ways I'll break.

"You will do what I want," he counters, his voice sharpening with rising intensity. "or I will kill and torture everyone you love. Marin, Riven, the precious Celestials, I will wipe them out completely."

"I will never work for you," I say. Quiet, but certain.

He tilts his head, the scar across his face pulling tight with the motion.

"Never," he repeats, tasting the word. "That is a very long

time, Astrid."

"Then I guess I'll die saying it."

Something fractures across his face, something feral and furious. Without warning, his hand slams against the metal table in front of me. The impact reverberates like a gunshot, rattling through the floor. Dust drifts from the beams above. Despite myself, I flinch. He leans in until his scarred face fills my vision. Under his skin, flecks of living darkness swirl like ink suspended in water.

"You think this is bravery?" he asks, voice low and sharp enough to slice. "You believe defiance can change what I want from you? It cannot. You remember what happened and I want to finally hold those perfect Celestials accountable for stealing our light well." His gaze burns into mine, unblinking. "You will go," he says. "Whether by will or by the moment I break your light and torture you until you submit. The Veil does not care about your refusal. It answers your bloodline, not your words."

My heart slams against my ribs. I say nothing, just give him a cold unyielding, stubborn look.

"You'll rot in that cell," he continues softly, almost tenderly, "until you agree. Until resisting hurts more than obeying." His voice drops to a whisper. "You'll die in the dark with your own stubbornness choking you."

It takes everything I have left, every ounce of strength still clinging to me, but I hold his gaze. "Then that's how I'll die," I whisper.

For a suspended heartbeat, the room feels small enough to crush us both, it's just him, me, and the Hollow's relentless hum pressing into every corner. Then he straightens with abrupt finality, smoothing his suit jacket as he does. His shadow stretching long across the floor toward the window where the Hollow swirls.

"So be it," he says. He turns and strides toward the door, calling over his shoulder with the ease of someone giving an unimportant order,

"Take her back to the dark. Let her remember what hunger feels like."

Hands seize me immediately, rough and unyielding. Fingers clamp around my shoulders, my arms, my raw wrists. Every touch sends pain flaring along my nerves. As they drag me toward the exit, I twist once, needing just one more look. He stands before the window, perfectly still, hands clasped behind his back, a commander inspecting a battlefield. Beyond the glass, the Hollow shifts and coils like a living abyss, expanding and contracting in a slow, terrible rhythm.

He never turns to face me. He doesn't need to. His voice drifts across the room, steady and composed, delivered with the detachment of someone reciting a truth they consider inevitable.

"You will beg to go before the end, Astrid."

The door slams shut between us. The guards haul me down the corridor, their grips digging into bruises already screaming beneath my skin. The hallway stretches out before us like a throat carved from stone, swallowing the light with every step. The deeper we go, the colder it becomes.

My feet barely keep pace. My ankles drag with each step, toes catching against uneven stone. The guards don't slow; their boots thud in synchronized rhythm, marching me back into the dark as though returning something broken to storage. My wrists throb where the ropes have burned into raw skin. My breath shudders. My vision flickers at the edges. Not from tears, there are none left, but from exhaustion and the pulse beneath my sternum pushing against my skin.

At the bottom, the corridor widens into a single chamber carved from the stone. My cell sits at the end. A heavy chair waits in the center, built from rust-black metal, bolted directly into the stone floor. Shackles dangle from its arms and legs, each one humming faintly with a dull, pulsing light.

The guards drag me toward it without hesitation. One grips the back of my neck, forcing me down into the seat. The cold metal bites instantly through the fabric of my shirt. My body rebels, my muscles locking and my breath stuttering but I am too weak, too drained, too raw to fight.

The chains snap closed around my ankles first, metal sealing against bone. Then my wrists. Then a band across my chest tightens until I feel every beat of my heart thudding against it. Each shackle pulses once, synchronizing with something beneath my skin. The cell door groans shut behind me, sealing me in. The guards leave without a word. Their footsteps echo away, swallowed one by one by the Hollow's hum.

Silence folds over me. My breath trembles in the freezing air. The Hollow's vibration deepens, slipping into my bones, into my teeth, into the pulse behind my eyes. It feels like it's leaning closer, listening, waiting for me to break.

But I won't. Not for him. Not for the Void. Not for whatever fate they think was carved into me before I even took my first breath. I close my eyes, forcing my lungs to steady even as the cold creeps deeper into my skin.

I will not be their weapon. I will not be the hinge that shatters the balance between worlds. I don't know what the Celestials are, not really, not their laws, their history, or why the Void hates them so deeply. But I know one thing: they are not the ones torturing me, or dangling Marin's life like a noose. And if the Void needs me to avenge their well, then the one thing I can do, the only thing truly mine, is to refuse. Even if it kills me. Even if the darkness claws at the edges of my mind. Even if hope feels like a foolish, fragile thing... I hold it tighter. I will not be their spy.

Chapter 39

The cell door groans open, making my head jerk up. I didn't realize I had fallen asleep. Metal against metal grinding through my bones. The air shifts the moment he steps inside, that strange, electric pull that once steadied me and now feels like a bruise pressed too hard.

"Rachel," he says quietly.

I look away, keeping my gaze fixed on the wet stone floor. A trickle of water slides toward my foot, slow and cold. My throat feels like it's full of sand. My stomach is a hollow pit. But I refuse to let any of that show. Not to him. He crouches and lifts a cup to my lips.

"You need to drink."

"I don't need anything from you."

The words scrape out of me. I turn my head away from the cup, refusing to drink. His jaw tightens, but he keeps his voice steady. "If you don't, you'll die."

"Good." Silence hangs heavy between us, thick enough to suffocate. He exhales, exhausted. Worn in a way that looks permanent.

"Please," he murmurs. "You haven't eaten in days. Don't do this to yourself."

I finally drag my gaze up to his. He barely looks like himself, just the hollow outline of the man he used to be. His clothes are rumpled and unkempt. A dark bruise shadows his jaw. Dirt clings to his hair. The circles beneath his eyes are so deep it looks like he hasn't slept in weeks. Guilt hangs around him, heavy and unmistakable.

"You just want me alive long enough to open your damn veil," I say, voice cracking. "Is that it?" He opens his mouth, but the answer dies before it reaches the air. I look away.

"Go," I whisper. "Just go."

"Rachel—"

"I said go."

Something breaks in the space between us, thin and invisible but always there until now. He kneels still, frozen in place, then sets the cup down beside the cold plate of food. His voice trembles when he speaks again.

"I'm sorry," he whispers. "For everything."

A bitter laugh tears from my throat.

"Save it. He'll probably give you a medal." I spit with as much venom in my voice as I can muster. Riven flinches like the words physically strike him. For a long moment, he doesn't move. Doesn't breathe. And then, he cracks.

"When I met you," he says slowly, "I already knew what you were."

My breath stills.

"I was assigned to you," he continues, voice low and shaking. "To track you. To watch you. To guide you toward the Void and make you trust them, when the time came."

The air leaves my lungs in a single painful rush.

"Get out," I whisper between gritted teeth.

"No." His voice catches. "You deserve the truth."

I shut my eyes, but it doesn't stop the words from reaching

me.

"I knew exactly what you were," he admits. "But I didn't know who you were and what you'd become to me."

My pulse spikes, hot and furious.

"Don't," I warn.

"I never expected to fall for you," he says, softer. "It wasn't supposed to happen. It wasn't allowed to happen."

I open my eyes, and the hurt in his face nearly cleaves me in half.

"But then you started digging," he says, a shaky breath escaping.

"You went looking for answers. For your father. For the truth. And your curiosity... it almost got you killed. Again and again. Every time you pushed, every time you touched something you weren't ready for... the Void felt you," He swallows hard. "So I did the only thing I knew how to do," he says. "I tried to shield you. I blurred your resonance. Hid your pulse when I could. Lied to the Council. Lied to my own kind. I kept you close because distance was too dangerous."

His voice cracks.

"And because I couldn't stand the thought of losing you."

Anger and grief collide inside me, sparking something hot and painful.

"And my father?" I choke. "Did you shield him too?"

His eyes snap shut.

"No. Rachel, I swear it. I didn't even know he was your father until it was too late."

His voice trembles. "He was already marked. Already hunted. I tried to warn him, but he wouldn't listen. He only cared about protecting you."

My heart feels like it's being wrung out. Riven leans closer, desperation bleeding through every word.

"I'm trying to get you out," he whispers. "I have a plan. But you won't survive it if you don't eat. If you don't drink. If you don't stay strong enough to run when it's time."

I stare at him, at the broken creature kneeling in front of me, torn between what he was made to be and what he became. His voice softens to a fragile whisper.

"I'm begging you. Not for me. For you."

My stomach twists. My chains dig into my skin. The cup sits between us, trembling faintly with the Hollow's hum. Riven's voice breaks one last time.

"I'll come back," he says. "Even if you hate me now. Even if you always will."

He rises slowly, like every movement hurts. He pauses in the doorway, half-shadow, half-memory and looks back once, eyes burning with everything he can't fix. Then he slips out into the darkness and the door closes gently, quietly, as if the stone itself is mourning. The lock clicks into place. And I keep starving.

Time loses meaning here. The dark doesn't fade or shift the way normal darkness does, it settles, dense and patient, slipping into my lungs and threading through my bones. It waits with me. It watches the way prey does when it has all the time in the world. Every breath I take feels like it belongs to this place more than it belongs to me.

My back aches against the cold chair. The ropes bite into my wrists, grinding against skin already rubbed raw. Any sound drifting down the corridor jolts through my nerves in a violent ripple, my muscles tensing, my body bracing for hands that hurt, voices that lie, shadows that take.

When the lock finally grinds open, dread squeezes around my ribs. Two Voidborn guards fill the doorway. They're tall, their forms towering enough to make the ceiling seem lower. Their silhouettes ripple strangely, warping in the dim light as though their bodies can't quite maintain a single shape. The edges of them blur, then sharpen, then blur again. One of them catches my eye and lets out a thin, curling smirk.

"On your feet," he drawls. "Malvoryn wants another look at his prize."

One of the guards steps forward with a bored sort of efficiency. He doesn't hesitate; he simply unlocks the first shackle at my wrist, letting the metal fall away with a dull clatter. The release sends a spike of pain down my arm, blood rushing back into places starved of sensation.

Another guard removes the chain across my chest, then the ones at my ankles, each lock snapping open with a harsh metallic click that echoes too loudly in the small cell. The moment the last restraint falls, my body folds forward, barely supported by muscles that forgot how to hold me.

I don't even manage a full inhale before their hands clamp onto my arms, rough, brutal, unyielding and wrench me upright with enough force to drag a groan from somewhere deep in my ribs. My legs buckle instantly, refusing to hold my weight. The guards don't pause; they simply drag me, my feet scraping lifelessly along the stone. The grip is bruising, unkind. They yank me upward with such force that my knees buckle immediately. The guards don't pause; they simply drag me, my feet scraping lifelessly along the stone.

The words to protest, to ask, to beg, lodge somewhere deep in my throat and refuse to surface. My voice feels submerged beneath exhaustion and fear. One of the guards mutters to the other, voice unbothered and cruelly casual,

"He'll force compliance from her this time. Burn it straight from the bone."

Something cold coils inside me, sharp enough to make my breath falter.

Burn what?!

The question forms, but I'm too exhausted to give it breath. A heavy terrifying feeling sits heavy in my chest as they drag me deeper into the labyrinth of corridors. The walls feel narrower the farther we go. The air thickens until it's almost a substance, humming with a faint undercurrent of energy that pulses in time with our footsteps. As they pull me onward, that strange vibration I felt in the circles begins to stir beneath my skin again, unbidden, a thread pulling tight inside my ribs as if responding to a distant call.

The corridor widens suddenly. Light spills out from a large chamber ahead, bright enough to glow against the guards' shifting forms. The moment they shove the door open, the brilliance blinds me. I turn my head instinctively, but the guards force me forward.

The circle dominates the room. It spans nearly wall to wall, vast, carved with impossible precision straight into the stone floor. The lines radiate outward from the center in intricate arcs and curves, the design ancient and perfect, the kind of thing that feels like it wasn't created so much as uncovered.

The gold-white markings pulse in a steady rhythm. Each pulse syncs painfully with the pounding beneath my sternum, binding my heartbeat to the circle's hum. The air grows warm and electric, almost vibrating. My pulse responds before I consciously understand what's happening. The pull hits me with the force of déjà vu and fear tangled together. A small sound escapes me without permission.

"No..."

My voice fractures on the single word. I try to pull back, just enough to hesitate, to cling to the edge of the doorway but the guards shove me forward. They drag me straight across the glowing boundary and propel me into the center of the circle as though they are delivering something precious or something dangerous.

The moment my feet touch the heart of the design, the light brightens, answering something in me I don't understand and wish I could silence. The air here is... heavy and thick with a static charge that's waiting to be filled. The closer I get, the more the circle seems to reach for me, pulling at my lungs, my pulse, my skin.

Chains hit the floor. Cold metal clamps around my wrists. My ankles. My chest. I thrash with panic and survival but the metal doesn't budge.

"STOP!" I scream, breath tearing. "DON'T TOUCH ME!" They just laugh.

"Don't worry," one sneers as he tightens the last shackle. "You won't be the same when he's done." The door opens again. The air shifts. I know who it is without seeing him.

Malvoryn.

He steps into the circle's glow as if returning to a throne. The white-gold light bends toward him, washing over the silver scar carved across his cheek, making it gleam. His eyes brighten at the sight of me chained in the center, pulsing with the circle's faint rhythm.

"Awake," he murmurs, voice threaded with satisfaction. "Good. I wanted you conscious for this."

The chains rattle as I pull against them, metal scraping raw skin. Every inch of me aches, but I force the words out anyway.

"I won't be your spy."

His smile is slow and cruel.

"That," he says softly, "is where you're wrong."

A cold shiver races down my spine. He begins circling me, slowly, his footsteps steady against the humming floor. He moves examining me, a relic he already owns, admiring the craftsmanship.

"You think defiance will save you," he says. "That if you cling hard enough to that human name and that human skin, you can outrun what you are." His gaze flicks to the glowing lines beneath my feet. "But the pulse always finds its way back."

He stops in front of me, lowering himself until his face hovers inches from mine. I can smell cold metal and a faint smoky tang.

"I don't care what you dredge up," I say, breaths trembling. "You can hurt me, but I will not spy for you." He tilts his head, studying me with quiet amusement.

"You say that now."

He rises slowly, extending his hands toward the circle as though conducting a choir only he can hear. The gold-white light responds instantly, brightening, tightening, coiling upward, waking at his command.

"Your father hid you well," he says, voice calm. "He severed memories. Buried instincts. Broke you at the edges so the pulse would stay quiet." His expression hardens. "But even he couldn't silence your nature."

The circle pulses. Once, the air hums against my skin. Twice, something ancient stirs behind my ribs. Then the glow flares bright enough to burn the edges of my vision. A low vibration rises from the floor, deep, resonant, voices buried under stone. For a moment, I can't tell if the sound is outside me or inside me. Malvoryn watches with reverence.

"Do you feel it?" he asks quietly. "The your power waking? The threshold between the Void and Celestials world remembering its shape?"

My breath shudders. The light intensifies, surging up my legs and spine, threading itself through every nerve. My pulse latches to it like it's been waiting for its cue. Pain explodes through me, hot and cold and tearing all at once. A scream rips out of my chest, raw and instinctive. Through the agony, his voice reaches me with chilling clarity.

"Open the threshold and we won't need you as a spy. We will infiltrate Aetherion and get revenge on them."

The circle burns brighter.

"Let the Void return to its rightful state."

The light lashes upward, a tidal wave of heat and brilliance. The feeling of being pulled apart molecule by molecule has me loosening another scream. My vision fractures, white, gold, shadow, teeth, and something deep inside me begins to tilt, to shift, to awaken. His voice drops, soft and triumphant.

"Let the dark come home."

Chapter 40

The circle is alive. It writhes beneath me, breathing, light crawling up my skin in bright, tearing waves that feel too deliberate to be random. My body bows against the chains, every muscle dragged taut, threatening to snap. I don't even know how to open the threshold or what that even means. What is he evening doing?

"Stop—"

The word rips out of me, but the circle's roar devours it immediately, swallowing my voice as if it never existed. The air thickens with ozone and burning metal. Each heartbeat slams against my ribs hard enough to bruise, too fast, too violent, the light is trying to beat its way out through bone.

Another flare surges upward, hotter this time, sharper, hooking itself along my spine and dragging fire through every nerve. A raw scream tears out of my throat. Not a word. Not a plea. Just sound ragged, primal, forced from somewhere deeper than conscious thought. It scrapes my throat raw, but the pain barely registers over what's happening inside me.

My vision fractures into blinding shards of white and gold. The light isn't just around me, it's inside me, splitting me apart piece by piece. From skull to spine, it feels as if something ancient is trying to decide which parts of me should stay and which should be burned clean away.

Another scream claws free, louder this time, shaking my whole ribcage, tearing through the space between us. The world shatters in flashes of brilliance. Light. Heat. Pressure. A rising, unbearable crescendo that makes my bones feel hollow and stretched too thin. My body convulses against the chains. My head snaps back as another wave hits.

My lungs seize, then force out another scream, cracked and choking at the edges. Through the agony, through the blinding storm ripping through my veins, his voice cuts through, cold and sure, slicing straight into the center of me. "Open it, Astrid. Let it through."

No.

No. They can not enter all of Aetherion. I won't let an entire population of people die, even if I don't remember them.

But the light doesn't care what I want. It floods every vein, fills every breath until I'm choking on brightness. My scream rips out of me not from my throat, but from somewhere deeper, hidden, ancient. The walls tremble. The circle blazes so bright I can't see the edges anymore. And then beneath the agony something else. A pulse. Not the circle's.

Mine.

Slow. Steady. Older than the room. Older than my body. I reach for it. The light stutters, surprised. The world peels open. For a moment, I'm standing somewhere else entirely: between two halves of myself, one blazing, one shadowed. The space hums with that pulse, the heartbeat of something vast and star-strewn.

The scream inside me twists into effort, not pain. My fingers dig into the glowing sigil. The heat licks my palms but it doesn't burn. It recognizes. This isn't the light killing me.

It's remembering me. The brightness detonates outward. The chains snap like brittle thread.

Malvoryn shouts something guttural, but it's lost as the room cracks open, light leaking through the air itself. The light surges again, wild, devouring, too big for skin. Every breath is smoke and glass. My pulse detonates, a star trapped behind ribs. My body shakes so violently the chains rattle against the floor, some still connected, some already melted.

His voice cuts through the storm:

"Give in, Astrid!" He's wrong.

My head drops, breath burning my lungs. Sweat and tears blur everything into a smear of gold. But the pulse, the true pulse, is still there. Steady. Stubborn. I cling to it. My fingers curl against the inscription in the circle, the carved lines biting into my skin.

"No," I whisper. My voice is barely human. "You don't get to use me."

The light trembles. Not resisting. Listening.

"I'm not yours to command," I force out, the words scraping from the core of me. "That world isn't yours……It's mine." Something shifts.

The glow bends, toward me, not him. The hum deepens, sliding from agony into harmony. The circle aligns itself with my breath, my heartbeat. It's as if I finally stepped into the correct rhythm and the world snapped into place. I stagger to my knees. The remaining chains strain, glowing red-hot. Light curls along my arms, threading through my veins like molten gold. It gathers in my palms.

Alive.

Obedient.

Mine.

Malvoryn recoils, lifting his arm to shield his face as heat distorts the air between us. I can barely stay upright, but I raise one shaking hand and let the light answer for me. It lashes out, clean, bright, devastating. The blast throws him backward. His coat ignites at the edges. His snarl turns into something raw, astonishment sharpened into fury. He spits a command in the guttural, ancient Voidborn tongue. The circle buckles, fighting me. My vision blurs, the light flickering as exhaustion punches through my spine.

"Burn," I whisper, breathless. "I said burn."

The light answers. One last flare as bright as the sun. Then my strength collapses in on itself. My body crumples. The glow guttering in my palms dims, pulsing weakly. The hum fades to a distant throb. The world spins, gold bleeding into black. Malvoryn straightens slowly, brushing ash from his coat, laughter curling through the room.

"Look at you," he says, voice coated in disdain. "So much power—yet still so very human." Your power caged by your own father." My head hangs, everything swimming in fractured light.

Breathing hard, I lift my chin.

"My father…" My voice is little more than a rasp, each word scraping my throat raw. I hold Malvoryn's gaze anyway. "My father protected me." I collapse back to the floor, what little strength I had leaving me.

Before he can take a single step toward me, the atmosphere shifts in a way that is impossible to mistake. The air thickens, stretching outward as though something inside it is pushing against the boundaries of the room. A low vibration hums through the stone beneath my feet, rising in pitch until the very space around us begins to distort. The air doesn't simply ripple, it bends inward, gathering tension and then splits open with a sound that feels older than the room, older than language.

Light pours through a tear in the floor. Not the volatile Celestial flare ripping through my veins. Not the cold, predatory glow of the Voidborn. This is something different, ancient, precise, commanding without ever raising its voice. It floods the chamber in a wave that pushes the shadows back.

The opening widens until it becomes a doorway made of shimmering radiance, its edges rippling. Figures emerge from the brilliance, stepping through the light. It's not burning them like it does the voidborn.

Celestials.

Not illusions conjured by pain. Not echoes from the professor's research. Not flickers of old stories pulled from a dying book. Real beings. Their bodies shift between form and light, every movement weaving grace and power together. Armor gleams with threads of starlight, catching the glow in intricate patterns that make them look sculpted from constellations. Their hair shimmers, dusted with gold, their eyes reflecting a quiet brilliance that cuts through the darkness with ease. Light gathers in their palms, coiling in steady, controlled arcs that mirror the pulse within me.

Malvoryn's composure fractures. Color drains from his face, leaving his expression stark and unmasked. "No," he breathes, each syllable brittle. "This cannot be happening."

The Celestials advance. They move with speed that defies the eye, fluid, precise, almost silent despite the power radiating from them. The chamber reacts to their presence: stones tremble, shadows recoil, the temperature shifts from the cold bite of the Void to the warm, electrified air before a storm.

A streak of light arcs across the room as one Celestial reaches the nearest Voidborn guard. The impact is immediate. Darkness unravels on contact, dissolving the guard's body into a swirling haze that dissipates before it reaches the floor. Another Celestial follows, their light leaving trails across the air as they move, each gesture clean and exact, every strike final.

Malvoryn recovers enough to retaliate. He extends one hand and tears a blade from the shadows themselves, drawing the weapon out of the air. It materializes as a long, narrow edge of pure absence, a shape defined not by what it is, but by what it devours. When he swings it toward the nearest Celestial, the blow cuts through the light with the force of a collapsing star.

The Celestial blocks the strike, and the collision erupts in a resonant shock wave that splits across the room like thunder cracking open the sky. Light and Void collide. The chamber fills with radiance and shadow, everything shaking beneath the force of their clash. Stone fractures along the walls. Dust rains from above. Energy swirls in thick currents that whip at my hair and burn my skin.

My knees threaten to buckle.

The power holding them apart trembles inside me, fraying at the edges. I force more of it outward, gritting my teeth as pain lances through my chest. Light and Void surge through my veins like opposing tides, each pulling harder than the last. The room blurs. For a heartbeat, I think I might lose my grip completely.

Then the doors burst open.

Voidborn guards flood into the chamber, weapons drawn, shadows coiling around their limbs as they rush toward the Celestials.

"No!" The word tears out of me.

I throw what remains of my power between them.

A wave of silver light erupts from my hands, slamming into the advancing guards. The force staggers them backward, boots scraping across fractured stone. Some raise shields. Others brace against it. The barrier shudders violently, thinner than before, but it holds.

For now.

My vision swims. Blood trickles from my nose. Every breath feels like dragging glass into my lungs. I can feel the power slipping away, feel the cracks spreading through it, but I keep pushing.

Through the haze, one Celestial breaks away from the conflict and turns toward me. Their form stabilizes as they approach, shaping itself into something more familiar, more solid, though the glow still dances along the edges of their silhouette. They reach out a hand, steady, gentle, unwavering. Light gathers around their fingers in a way that feels protective rather than destructive.

And through the roar of battle, through the roar of power overwhelming every corner of the room, a voice threads its way to me, a voice soft enough to exist only between breaths, yet unmistakably clear.

"Astrid..."

The tone is warm, almost aching.

"...stay with me."

Something in me recognizes that voice before my mind can name it. The world begins to collapse inward, folding light over shadow, shadow over light, until everything narrows into a single point of radiance and then the power releases its hold on me entirely. Darkness rises, calm and consuming, and pulls me under.

Chapter 41

Warmth.

For the first time in what feels like lifetimes, warmth surrounds me. It seeps in slowly. A mattress cradles my spine instead of cold stone. Soft fabric brushes my skin where chains used to bite. The air smells faintly of honey drifting through sunlight, mixed with something bright and clean and beneath it all, a scent I've only ever felt in dreams. Starlight. It's too gentle. Too safe. Too much like everything I lost.

My eyes snap open. I wake with a start.

Pain detonates through my body so violently that I choke on my own breath. My throat burns, my limbs seize. Every inhale scrapes against memories of screaming until the sound tore out of me. But when I blink up at the ceiling, there is no stone above me, no damp, no crawling shadow. The ceiling glows softly, pale and smooth, light trapped beneath polished crystal ceiling fixtures. No cracks. No darkness. No Hollow.

I shove at the blankets tangling my legs, my trembling hands trying and failing to push myself upright. The room sways dangerously, tilting like a boat caught in a sudden wave. Black spots creep into the edges of my vision. Before I can collapse back into the bed, a voice cuts through the haze.

"Easy. Slow down."

I freeze.

Someone steps into view, emerging from the side of the bed where the light gathers brightest. A young man, no older than me, moves closer with careful, deliberate steps. His clothes are made of soft, silver-toned fabric that moves like water across his body, catching and bending light with every shift.

His hair is unmistakable. Pale gold, the exact shade that catches the sun in Marin's curls.

And his eyes, Storm-gray, threaded with blue, familiar enough to make my chest constrict.

"Marin?" Her name scrapes out of me before I know what I'm saying, fragile and raw.

He lets out a quiet huff of laughter, the corner of his mouth lifting in a lopsided, almost fond smile.

"Not quite," he says. "But I'm flattered you see the resemblance."

The words don't make sense. None of this makes sense.

My voice fractures as I cling to the part that matters most.

"Where is she? Marin—she was hurt—did she... did she make it?"

His expression softens immediately, the kind of softness that feels instinctive rather than performed. He lifts one hand in a calming gesture.

"She's safe," he says. "Resting in a room nearby. She refused to sleep until she knew you were breathing again."

Relief slams into me so hard it steals the strength from my arms. Tears sting before I can stop them. "I need to see her," I whisper.

"You will," he promises, and there's a steadiness in his voice that settles something trembling inside me. "But you need strength first. You've been unconscious for three days."

Three days. The words hit like a slap. I swallow, and my throat protests every second of it.

"The last thing I remember—"

My pulse trips over itself.

"The circle. Malvoryn. The light—"

His expression shifts to something gentle, steady, but not pitying, more anchored.

"You're safe now," he says. "None of them can touch you here."

"Here," I repeat, dazed.

Only then do I truly look at the room. The walls are smooth and pale, etched with fine, winding patterns, constellations caught in the moment before they shift into new shapes. The designs shimmer when I breathe, reacting to me, responding to something in my pulse I haven't learned to control. Light spills across everything with no visible source, a living presence.

And the window, it stretches from floor to ceiling, revealing a sky that looks painted in impossible dusk. A deep violet horizon, scattered with drifting stars that move as if alive, forming and unforming symbols my skin recognizes before my mind does.

Circles. Lines. The mark carved into my memories.

My chest tightens.

"This isn't the human world?"

"No," he answers softly. "It isn't."

The air tastes different. Not thin, not heavy, just… cleaner. Bright. The faint hum that has always lingered at the edge of my senses, the shimmer I kept trying to blink away, doesn't hide anymore. It fills everything. It recognizes me.

"Where am I?" My voice is barely a breath.

He steps closer, not crowding, but present, an anchor in the swirling unreality.

"You're in the Celestial realm," he says. "We call it Aetherion."

The word rolls through me, a chord struck deep inside my bones like it's familiar.

"Aetherion," I repeat, unsteady. "That's the name from the texts... from the professor's notes. The realm sealed shortly after the Falling."

His brows lift slightly, impressed.

"You've retained more than most. Yes, Aetherion. The realm that mirrors yours, untouched by the void."

I shake my head, trying to pull sense from all of this.

"I was in the Hollow. He... Malvoryn...he was trying to use me to open the threshold so the Void could come here, and I thought—" I swallow against the memory, the pain, the light splitting me apart. "I thought I didn't survive it."

"You barely did," he says quietly. "But the circle recognized you. It answered you instead of him."

I flinch as the memory flickers bright, my pulse tearing free, the world folding, the unbearable pull of two realms trying to claim me at once. "I lost control," I whisper. "I felt like I was tearing myself in half."

"You didn't tear," he says. "You bridged."

The word lands sharply. I look up, confused.

"Bridged?"

He gestures toward the window, toward the endless shimmering sky beyond it.

"You crossed between realms," he explains. "Between Aetherion and the Hollow. Between light and shadow. You didn't open the Threshold."

A note of awe threads through his voice.

"You tore yourself through it. It closed behind you. That's how we were able to find you and rescue you. It was......startling to say the least."

My breath stutters. "But Malvoryn said....he said....if I were to come here...I would be his spy.

The words feel thin, breakable, even as they leave my mouth.

He shakes his head slowly, eyes fixed on me like he's seeing something I can't yet understand. "Astrid, you will not be treated...."

I flinch like he struck me and interrupt before he can finish his sentence, "Don't call me that."

He tilts his head, studying me with frustrating gentleness.

"I'm sorry. What should I call you, then?"

"Rachel," I say quickly. "My name is Rachel."

A beat of stillness. Even the walls seem to listen. He nods once in a slow, deliberate, respectful manner.

"Rachel it is," he says. "No one will take that from you here."

Something inside me loosens, painfully and unexpectedly. For the first time, I truly look at him. Up close the resemblance to Marin is undeniable, same jawline, same smile tucked at the corner of his mouth, the same spark of mischief buried behind seriousness. But there's something older in him, something steadier, something that feels rooted in this place in a way that makes my pulse stutter.

He gives me a small, warm smile.

"My name is Emric," he says at last. "And whether you remember it or not, I've been waiting a very long time to welcome you home."

The room seems to breathe with the word *home*. Soft light

ripples across the constellations carved into the walls. I swallow hard.

"You keep saying that," I murmur. "That this is my home."

"That's because it is." His voice gentles even further. "It won't feel like it yet. But your pulse remembers."

"My pulse?" I echo.

He glances toward the faint shimmer drifting along my skin.

"It's already reconnecting to Aetherion," he says. "You'll feel it in waves. It's adjusting to being where it belongs."

I let out a strained laugh.

"Pretty sure I don't belong anywhere."

A flicker of sadness crosses his face, brief, but unmistakable.

"You do here," he says. "You always have."

I look down, struggling to steady my breathing.

"How long?" My voice dips. "How long was I... gone? From here?"

Emric steps closer to the bed, stopping just within reach. When he speaks again, his tone carries a depth that sends a shiver up my spine, something ceremonial, something ancient.

"A long time," he answers. "Longer than the mortal world has words for. Longer than history has recorded. Longer than your people have remembered your name."

The walls flare softly, a pulse of starlight responding to him and to me. His eyes remain fixed on mine, unwavering.

"You're finally home, Rachel," he says. "we've been searching for you for centuries."

Epilogue

RIVEN

The Hollow never sleeps. It breathes. The sky above the fortress twists in slow, silent storms of ash and shadow. Far below, where the jagged ramparts meet the barren plain, darkness churns, hungry and alive.

I kneel on the cold floor of the chamber, palms pressed to stone that vibrates faintly beneath my skin. The scars on my wrists, half-healed burns from void-forged chains, throb in time with the hum of this place. Every sound here reminds you who you belong to.

"Look at me."

His voice cuts through the air, quiet but absolute.

I force my head up.

He stands at the great window, the hem of his coat brushing against the floor. The Hollow's strange, metallic light glints off the silver scar that carves down his cheek, turning half his face into a razor-thin crescent of brightness.

"Do you know what I hate most about your kind of void-born?" Malvoryn asks, still watching the shifting horizon.

I say nothing. My throat is raw from earlier, from the questions, the accusations, the blow that sent me crashing into the wall. He turns slowly, shadows bending toward him like they're bowing.

"Softness," he says. "forgetting what they were shaped for. Mistaking attachment for purpose." His gaze pins me in place. "You forgot."

My jaw aches with how tightly I clench it. "I completed every assignment you gave me," I rasp. "Until her."

"Exactly." His smile doesn't reach his eyes. "Efficient. Precise. Controlled. You drained Celestials without hesitation. You went where the dark sent you and you did not falter."

He steps closer.

"Until you met her."

A cold twist cuts through my chest. I swallow it down. "She is not—"

"Spare me that nonsense." He waves a hand. "You had your little crisis of conscience. You betrayed your nature and your orders in one pathetic, predictable collapse. You ran. You hid her. You protected her."

"I tried to protect the balance," I say. The lie tastes like ash. "If the light dies, so does the dark. You taught me that."

His expression sharpens. "And now I am teaching you that it is the dark's right to choose when balance ends." He circles me once, slow, deliberate. My skin crawls with every pass.

"Tell me again," he says. "What you saw in the circle."

I inhale sharply, the memory slicing through me whether I want it or not, her body writhing in chains, light splitting through her, her scream turning into something fierce and defiant instead of surrendering.

"I saw the circle respond to her," I say slowly, the memory still sharp enough to sting. "Not to you. Not to the Hollow. The Veil recognized her."

Malvoryn's jaw tightens.

"And after that?"

Light flashes through my mind, blinding, ancient, impossible. Not Void light, not mortal light, but something purer, sharper, threaded with constellations that moved. Figures stepping through the fractures in the air, shaped from brilliance older than our histories.

"They pulled her out," I say quietly. "The Celestials came through the fracture the circle created. They took her into the light."

He is silent long enough that the quiet becomes dangerous.

"And the Veil?" he asks at last, voice low.

My stomach twists. "Not open," I say. "But… awakened."

The word settles between us like a weight. He steps closer until I can see the thin line of silver carved deep into his scar, pulsing faintly with Void light.

"Do you feel it?" he asks.

I close my eyes. And there it is, a faint, undeniable tug somewhere beneath my ribs. Not painful. Not overpowering. Just present and steady. A tether of light humming faintly against something hollow inside me, echoing its presence.

"Yes," I whisper. "I feel her. She's… farther than I expected. She's not anywhere in the mortal realm."

His mouth curves into a slow, cold smile.

"Good."

Anger spikes up my spine. My hands curl into fists.

"Good?" I snap. "You lost her. The Celestials took her. They know she's alive now."

His expression doesn't shift, not triumph, not fear, just calculation.

"That," he says quietly, "is why this is good for us."

My breath stutters at the implication.

"What are you talking about?"

"They always suspected she still lived," he says, voice sharpening. "Now they're certain. They'll shelter her, teach her what she is, help her understand the Veil's call." His gaze flicks to the faint tremor in the air between us, the one echoing her pulse. "And in doing so, they'll wake her resonance even further and return her memories for us to inevitably steal."

I stare at him, unable to form a response.

He continues, tone cool and clinical.

"We lost a battle, yes. But the Veil woke at her touch. That cannot be undone. The Hollow felt it. It will respond." His eyes gleam, hungry, not for her but for the shift she represents. "The awakening has begun. Everything else is inevitable."

A cold wave rolls through my chest.

"You think this is inevitable because she's alive?"

"No," he says. "Because she's aware. Awareness accelerates awakening. And you—"

His gaze spears through me.

"You are more tangled in this than you pretend."

My stomach tightens.

"What do you mean?"

"Don't insult us both," he says. "You touched her light. Lived beside it. Matched your breath to hers night after night. The Veil remembers bonds like that." He leans in a fraction. "You are tethered to her, whether you want it or not."

The truth of it hits hard enough to knock the air out of me.

"She'll never trust me again," I manage, the words scraping out. "You made sure of that."

His expression flickers into irritation, something darker beneath it.

"Trust is irrelevant," he says. "The bond isn't made of trust. It's made of resonance. And resonance does not care what you have broken."

He steps back, leaving the echo of her pulse thrumming in my chest like a wound I can't close. He leans toward me, voice dropping to a whisper.

"You will go after her. You will walk into the light and bring her back. And when you do, she will open the door to the veil whether she knows she's doing it or not."

My breath fractures. "The Celestials will kill me on sight," I say.

"Perhaps," he muses. "Or perhaps they'll see what she sees when she looks at you."

I stiffen. "And what's that?"

"A weapon," he says. "A weapon deciding which hand will wield it."

I don't respond. I don't have answers anymore. Not ones that matter. He turns away, hands clasped behind his back. "You leave when the Veil thins. The next surge. The Hollow will find a path."

"And if I refuse?"

The words leave my mouth before I can stop them, but the moment they're spoken, I know I've invited something I cannot take back. Malvoryn doesn't pause. He doesn't consider. He doesn't even blink.

"I will finish what you started with her father," he says, almost gently. "And I won't make it quick."

The breath leaves my chest in a violent, hollow rush. Her father's face flashes behind my eyes, the shock in his eyes before it dimmed, the way his body crumpled into the grass. Then Rachel's scream, raw, feral, ripping through the quiet park as she fell to her knees beside him, begging him to stay, begging the world to reverse itself for once. My stomach twists. I bow my head, because I cannot bear the weight of that memory and his threat at the same time.

"When the Veil thins," I whisper, "I'll go."

Malvoryn exhales like a man pleased with a tool finally accepting its use.

"Good."

He gestures for the guards to step back but then lifts a single hand, halting them.

"Wait," he murmurs. "Let him see."

The guards withdraw into the shadows, leaving me alone in the circle of Malvoryn's regard. Pain ripples through my body as I force myself upright, every muscle feels bruised, every breath edged with fire but I walk anyway, drawn toward the enormous window carved into the far wall.

The Hollow stretches beyond it in a vast, endless sweep. A world drained of warmth and color. A landscape gnawed hollow by centuries of hunger. But above it, grazing the highest reaches of the sky a thin, shimmering fracture trembles, a fault line made of pure light.

The Veil.

Or rather... the Veil beginning to stir. A possible path to her. Behind that frail seam of brightness, something pulses, faint at first, then rhythmic, steady, unmistakable. Not just light. Not just energy. A presence. Alive. Bright. Burning in a way that makes the Hollow recoil.

Her.

My breath catches painfully. I lift a hand, pressing my palm to the icy glass as though sheer will might collapse the distance between us.

"I'm coming," I whisper.

I don't know what the words mean, not yet. Not whether

I'm promising rescue or retribution, salvation or surrender or my inevitable death. Not whether I'm warning the Hollow or begging the light to accept me. But somewhere far above this broken realm, in a world built from starlight and breath and ancient memory, she shifts in her sleep. The air around her stirs. And the Veil between us shivers, a pulse echoing in two bodies at once.

About the Author

Kay Blake is a fantasy writer who loves building worlds where mystery, magic, and emotion intertwine. When she isn't writing, she can usually be found exploring hiking trails, getting lost in bookstores, or curled up with her beloved dog. *The Dark Between Stars* is her debut novel.

You can connect with me on:

- https://substack.com/@withlovefromkay
- https://kayblakebooks.com